Nichole Severn writes explosive romantic suspense with strong heroines, heroes who dare challenge them and a hell of a lot of guns. She resides with her very supportive and patient husband, as well as her demon spawn, in Utah. When she's not writing, she's constantly injuring herself running, rock climbing, practising yoga and snowboarding. She loves hearing from readers through her website, www.nicholesevern.com, and on Facebook, www.Facebook.com/nichole.severn

Julie Anne Lindsey is an obsessive reader who was once torn between the love of her two favourite genres: toe-curling romance and chew-your-nails suspense. Now she gets to write both for Mills & Boon Heroes. When she's not creating new worlds, Julie can be found carpooling her three kids around northeastern Ohio and plotting with her shamelessly enabling friends. Winner of the Daphne du Maurier Award for Excellence in Mystery/Suspense, Julie is a member of International Thriller Writers, Romance Writers of America and Sisters in Crime. Learn more about Julie and her books at julieannelindsey.com

Also by Nichole Severn

Also by Julie Anne Lindsey

Discover more at millsandboon.co.uk

THE LINE
OF DUTY

NICHOLE SEVERN

MARINE
PROTECTOR

JULIE ANNE LINDSEY

MILLS & BOON

First Published in Great Britain 2020
by Mills & Boon, an imprint of HarperCollins*Publishers*
1 London Bridge Street, London, SE1 9GF

The Line of Duty © 2020 Natascha Jaffa
Marine Protector © 2020 Julie Anne Lindsey

ISBN: 978-0-263-28050-0

1020

MIX
Paper from
responsible sources
FSC™ C007454

This book is produced from independently certified FSC™ paper to ensure responsible forest management.

For more information visit: www.harpercollins.co.uk/green

Printed and bound in Spain
by CPI, Barcelona

THE LINE
OF DUTY

NICHOLE SEVERN

This one's for you! You made this series possible, and while this might be the last book of the origin series, Blackhawk Security isn't finished yet!

Chapter One

He had a lead.

The partial fingerprint he'd lifted from the murder scene hadn't been a partial at all, but evidence of a severe burn on the owner's index finger that altered the print. He hadn't been able to get an ID with so few markers to compare before leaving New York City a year ago. But now, Blackhawk Security forensic expert Vincent Kalani finally had a chance to bring down a killer.

He hauled his duffel bag higher on his shoulder. He had to get back to New York, convince his former commanding officer to reopen the case. His muscles burned under the weight as he ducked beneath the small passenger plane's wing and climbed inside. Cold Alaskan air drove beneath his heavy coat, but catching sight of the second passenger already aboard chased back the chill.

"Shea Ramsey." Long, curly dark hair slid over her shoulder as jade-green eyes widened in surprise. His entire body nearly gave in to the increased sense of gravity pulling at him had it not been for the pa-

ralysis working through his muscles. Officer Shea
Ramsey had assisted Blackhawk Security with investigations in the past at the insistence of Anchorage's chief of police, but her formfitting pair of jeans,
T-shirt and zip-up hoodie announced she wasn't here
on business. Hell, she was a damn beautiful woman,
an even better investigator and apparently headed to
New York. Same as him. "Anchorage Police Department's finest, indeed."

"What the hell are you doing here?" Shea shuffled
her small backpack at her feet, crossing her arms over
her midsection. The tendons between her shoulders
and neck corded with tension as she stared out her
side of the plane. No mistaking the bitterness in her
voice. "Is Blackhawk following me now?"

"Should we be?" Blackhawk Security provided
top-of-the-line security measures for their exclusive clientele, including cameras, body-heat sensors,
motion detectors and more. Whatever their clients
needed, Sullivan Bishop and his team delivered. Personal protection, network security, private investigating, logistical support to the US government and
personal recovery. They even had their very own profiler on staff to aid the FBI with serial cases. The
firm did it all. Vincent mainly headed the forensics
division, but he'd take up any case with Shea's involvement in a heartbeat. His gut tightened. Hard to
ignore the quiet strength she'd kept close to the vest
when they partnered together on these past few cases.
It'd pulled him in, made him want to get to know her
more, but she'd only met him—and every member

of his team—with resentment. Not all Anchorage PD officers agreed with the partnership between the city and the most prestigious security firm in Alaska. Officer Ramsey led that charge.

He shoved his duffel into the cargo area as the pilot maneuvered into his seat. The small plane bounced with the movement. The cabin, he couldn't help but notice, filled with her scent. "I'm not here on Blackhawk business. I've got…personal business to take care of in New York. You?"

"I have a life outside of the department." She hadn't turned to look at him, her knuckles white through the taut skin of her hands as she gripped the seat's arms. The plane's engine growled at the push of a button, rotors sending vibrations through the sardine can meant to get them halfway to New York in one piece before they switched to another aircraft to make the rest of the trip.

"You guys ready?" the pilot asked. "Here are your headsets."

Hell, Shea was so tense as she took hers, she probably thought the wrong gust of wind could shoot them out of the sky. She closed her eyes, muscles working hard in her throat. The tarmac attendants removed the heavy rubber blocks from around the plane's wheels, and they slowly rolled forward. Every muscle down her spine seemed to further tighten.

Something inside him felt for her, forced him to reach out to offer assurance. Vincent positioned the headset over his ears, then slid his hand on top of hers. Smooth skin caught on the calluses in his palms, and suddenly those green eyes were on him. In an instant, her fingers tangled with his. Heat exploded through him, the breath rushing out of his lungs as she gripped on to him as though her life depended on it.

Pressure built behind his sternum as the small passenger plane raced down the runway, then climbed higher into the sky. His back pressed into the soft leather seats, but his attention focused 100 percent on the woman beside him. On the way her skin remained stretched along her forearm revealing the map of veins below, on the unsteady rising and falling of her shoulders when she breathed. Snow-capped mountains disappeared below the windows, only reappearing as the plane leveled out high above the peaks mere minutes later. The pilot directed them toward the mountains, but the pressure hadn't released from his rib cage. Not when Shea was still holding on to him so tightly. He raised his voice over the sound of the engine. "I'm going to need that hand back sooner or later."

"Right. Sorry." Shea released her grip, then wiped her palm down her thigh, running the same hand through her curly hair. Her voice barely registered above the noise around them. "You'd think five years on the job would give me a little more backbone when it came to planes."

"There's a difference between facing the bad guys and facing our fears." His hand was still warm from where their skin had made contact, and he curled his fingers into his palm to hold on to it for as long as he could. "At least there was for me."

She slid that beautiful gaze to his, the freckles dusted across the bridge of her nose and onto her cheeks more pronounced than a few minutes ago. "You were with NYPD's forensics unit for nine years before you came out here, right? Can't imagine there's much that scares you anymore."

She'd be surprised. Her words slowly sank in over the engine's mid-frequency drone, and Vincent narrowed his attention. She'd looked into him. There was no way she could've known how long he'd worked forensics by simply searching for him on the internet. NYPD records weren't public information. Which meant she'd used her access through federal databases. Out of curiosity? Or something else? His attention darted to his duffel bag. He'd booked a private passenger plane out of Merrill Field for a reason. The SIG SAUER P226 with twelve deadly rounds of ammo in the magazine was currently nestled in his bag. He'd worked with Officer Ramsey before. The background check the firm had run on her when Blackhawk had need of the department's assistance on past investigations hadn't connected her with anyone from his past. But what were the chances that she of all people had ended up on this flight? "Someone's been doing their homework."

"All of you Blackhawk Security types are the same. You take the law into your own hands and don't care if you jeopardize the department's cases. You run your own investigations, then expect officers like me to clean up your mess. You're vigilantes, and you endanger the people in this city every time you step out of your downtown high-rise office. So, yes, I've done my homework. I like to know who I'm being forced to work with." She pinned him to his seat with that green gaze, and the world disappeared around them. "And you...you were a cop. You used to have a conscience."

Vincent clenched his back teeth against the fire exploding through him. He leaned into her, ensuring she couldn't look away this time. "You have no idea—"

The plane jerked downward, throwing his heart into his throat. The engine choked, then started up again. He locked his attention out through the plane's windshield. His pulse beat loudly behind his ears. The rotors were slowing, grinding. He shouldn't have been able to track a single propeller if they were running at the right speed. Gripping one hand around his seat's arm, he pressed his shoulders into the leather and shouted into his mic. "What the hell is going on?"

"I don't know." The pilot shot his hand to the instrument panel. "We're losing altitude fast, but all of the gauges check out." Wrapping his hand around the plane's handheld CB radio, the pilot raised his voice over the protests of the engine. "Mayday, Mayday, Mayday. Merrill Field, this is Captain Reginald, a Robin DR400, Delta-Echo, Lima, Juliet, Golf, with total engine failure attempting forced landing. Last known position seven miles east of Anchorage; 1,500 feet heading ninety degrees." Static filled their headsets. "Can anybody read me?" The pilot looked back at his passengers. "The controls aren't responding! I'm going to have to try to put her down manually!"

Vincent pressed his hand to the window and searched the ridges and valleys below for a safe place they could land. Nothing but pure white snow and miles of mountains. Jagged peaks, trees. There was no way they'd survive a forced landing here. There were no safe places to land.

"No, no, no. No! This wasn't supposed to happen." The panic in Shea's voice flooded his veins with ice. She grabbed her backpack off the floor from between her feet and clutched it to her chest. Fear showed brightly in her eyes a split second before she was thrown back in her seat. She clutched the window. "This wasn't supposed to happen."

The engine smoked, and the plane jerked again. Vincent slammed into the side door. Pain ricocheted through the side of his head, but he forced it to the back of his mind. They were losing altitude fast, and dizziness gripped him hard. They had to get the engine back up and running, or they were all going to die. He couldn't breathe, couldn't think. Double-checking his seat belt, Vincent locked on Shea's terrified features. *This wasn't supposed to happen.* The mountain directly outside her window edged closer. "Watch out!"

Metal met rock in an ear-piercing screech. The mountain cut into the side of the plane, taking the right wing, then caught on the back stabilizer and ripped off the tail end. Cold Alaska air rushed into the cabin as luggage and supplies vanished into the wilderness. The plane rocked to one side, the ground coming up to meet them faster than Vincent expected.

He dug his fingers into the leather armrest, every muscle in his body tensed.

The pilot's voice echoed through the cabin. "Brace for impact!"

He reached out for Shea. "Hang on!"

THE SKY WAS on fire.

Red streaks bled into purple on one side and green on the other as she stared out the small window to her right, stars prickling through the auroras she'd fallen in love with the very first night she'd come to Anchorage. Rocky peaks and trees framed her vision, and every cell in her body flooded with pain in an instant. A groan caught in Shea Ramsey's throat, the weight on her chest blocking precious oxygen. Her feet were numb. How long had she been unconscious? Her hands shook as she tested the copilot seat weighing on her sternum. Closing her eyes against the agony, she put everything she had into getting out from under the hunk of metal and leather, but it wouldn't budge.

The plane had gone down, Vincent's shout so loud in her head. And then... Shea pushed at the debris again as panic clawed through her. They'd crashed in the mountains. The pilot hadn't been able to reach anyone on the radio. Did anyone even know they were out here? She couldn't breathe. Tears prickled at the corners of her eyes as the remains of the plane came into focus. Along with the unconscious man in the seat beside her. "Vincent, can you hear me?"

His long black hair covered the pattern of tattoos

inked into his arms and neck as well as his overly attractive face. His Hawaiian heritage and that body of a powerful demigod had tugged at something primal within her every time she was forced to work alongside him in the field, but she'd buried that feeling deep. He shouldn't have been here. The pilot had told her she'd be the only passenger on this flight. She hadn't meant for the Blackhawk Security operative to get involved—hadn't meant anyone to get involved— but she'd been so desperate to get to New York. That same determination tore through her now as the plane jerked a few more inches along the snowbank. Out Vincent's window it looked like they'd crashed at the base of a steep cliffside, with nothing but sky and snow in every direction. A scream escaped her throat as the cabin shook. One wrong move would send them down the short slope and over the edge.

"Shea." A groan reached her ears as Vincent stirred in his seat. Locking soothing brown eyes on her through the trail of blood snaking through his left eyebrow, he pushed his hair back with one hand. "That…did not go as I expected. But we're okay. It's going to be okay."

Was he trying to convince her or himself?

"I can't…breathe." Understanding lit his bearded features as he noted the seat pressing against her chest, and in that moment, her body heat spiked with the concern sliding into his expression. Memory of him holding her hand during takeoff rushed to the front of her mind. Vincent pushed out of his seat, and the plane slid another couple of inches toward the cliff. She closed her eyes as terror ricocheted through her. "No, don't!"

"Shea, look at me." His featherlight touch trailed down her jaw, and she forced herself to follow his command. He stilled, bending at the knees until her gaze settled on his. Her heart pounded hard at the base of her skull but slowed the longer he stared at her. "I'm going to get you out of here, okay? You have my word. I need you to trust me."

Trust him. The people he worked for—worked with—couldn't be trusted. None of them could. Blackhawk Security might help catch the bad guys, same as her, but at the cost of breaking the law she'd taken an oath to uphold. They didn't deserve her trust, but the pain in her chest wouldn't let up, was getting worse, and all she could do was nod.

He moved forward slowly, and Shea strengthened her grip on the metal crushing her. The only reason the seat hadn't killed her was because of the padded backpack she'd clutched before the crash, but how much more could her body take? The plane was shifting again, threatening to slide right toward another cliff edge. They'd survived a crash landing from 1,500 feet. What were the chances they'd survive another? Vincent crouched beside her, the plane barely large enough to contain his hulking size. Although the gaping hole at the tail end helped. "Hey, eyes on me, Officer. Nowhere else, you got that? I'm going to try to get this thing off of you, but I need you to focus on me."

Focus on him. She could do that. She'd spent so

long trying not to notice him while they worked their joint investigations, it was a nice change to have permission for once. Pins and needles spread through her feet and hands as cold worked deep into her bones. The back of the plane had been separated from the main fuselage, and the bloodied windshield had a large hole where she'd expected to see the pilot in his seat. They were in the middle of the Alaskan wilderness, and temperatures were dropping by the minute. "You're...bleeding."

"I've survived worse." He skimmed his fingers over hers, and her awareness of how close he'd gotten rocketed her heart into her throat.

"Worse than...a plane crash?" How was that possible? She'd read his service records, thanks to a former partner now working for the NYPD. Vincent Kalani had been assigned to the department's Detective Bureau's Forensic Investigations Division, collecting and analyzing evidence from crime scenes for close to ten years. Until suddenly he wasn't. There was nothing in those files about an injury in the line of duty. In fact, it was as though he'd simply disappeared before signing on with Sullivan Bishop's new security firm here in Anchorage.

"I think I've got this loose enough to move it. You ready? I need you to push the seat forward as hard as you can." Vincent handled the leather seat crushing her chest. "On my count. One, two, three." Together, they shoved the debris forward, and Shea gasped as much crisp, clean air as her lungs allowed.

"Thank you." The pain vanished as he maneuvered

the hunk of metal to the front of the plane, and a panicked laugh bubbled to the surface. Because if she
didn't have this small release, Shea feared she might
break down here in front of him. The ground rumbled beneath them, and she stilled. The plane hadn't
moved. At least, not as far as she could tell. So what—

Another shock wave rolled through the fuselage,
and she tightened her grip around the backpack in
her lap. "Vincent…"

Fear cut through the relief that'd spread over his
expression. "Avalanche."

Shea twisted in her seat, staring up at the rip-
ples creasing through the snowbanks high above,
her fingers plastered against the window. Strong
hands ripped her out of her seat and thrust her toward the back of the plane. Adrenaline flooded into
her veins, triggering her fight-or-flight response.
The plane tilted to one side as they raced toward the
back, threatening to roll with their escape. Cargo slid
into her path. Her boot caught on a black duffel bag,
and she hit freezing metal. The rumble was growing
louder outside, stronger.

"Go, go, go!" Vincent helped her to her feet, keeping close on her heels as the plane shifted beneath
them. With a final push, he forced her through the
hole where the tail end of the plane was supposed to
be, but they couldn't stop. Not with an entire mountain of snow cascading directly toward them.

Flakes worked into the tops of her boots and
soaked through her jeans. She pumped her legs as
hard as she could, but it wouldn't be enough. The ava-

lanche was moving too fast. She was going to die out here, and everything she'd worked for—everything she'd ever cared about—wouldn't matter anymore.

"There!" Vincent fisted her jacket and shoved her ahead of him. "Head for that opening!"

Trying to gain control of the panic eating her alive from the inside, Shea sprinted as fast as several feet of snow would let her toward what looked like the entrance to a cave a mere twenty feet ahead of them. Her fingers ached from the grip she kept on the backpack, but it was nothing compared to the burn in her lungs. A rush of cold air and flecks of snow blew her hair into her face and disrupted her vision, but she wouldn't stop. Couldn't stop. Ten feet. Five. She pumped her free arm to gain momentum. Sweat beaded at the base of her neck. They were going to make it. They *had* to make it. Glancing back over her shoulder, she ensured Vincent was still behind her, but the plane had already been consumed. Snow started to fall over the cave's entrance in a thundering rush, and she lunged for the opening before it disappeared completely.

And hit solid dirt.

She clutched the backpack close to her chest, as if it'd bring any kind of comfort.

Within seconds, darkness filled her vision, only the sound of her and Vincent's combined breathing registering over the rumble of them being buried alive. She reached for him, skimming her fingertips across what she assumed was one of his arms, but the padding of his jacket was too thick to be sure. Dust filled her nostrils as she fought to catch her breath. Silence descended, the wall of snow and ice settling over the cave. "You saved my life."

A soft hissing sound preceded a burst of orange flame. Shadows danced over Vincent's features, his battle-worn expression on full display in the dull flame of the lighter, and a hint of the awareness she'd felt when he'd held her hand during takeoff settled low in her stomach. Faster than she thought possible, he hauled her from the floor and pinned her against the wall of the cave and his body with one hand, her pack forgotten. "Tell me why you were on that plane."

His body pressed into hers. Shadowed, angry angles were carved into his features, unlike anything she'd seen before when they'd worked together. Shea pushed at him, but he was so much stronger, so much bigger. "Get off me."

"Before we crashed you said, 'This wasn't supposed to happen.'" He increased the pressure at the base of her throat, simulating the crushing debris he'd pulled off her chest mere minutes ago. "There was no reason that plane should've crashed unless it'd been sabotaged. You know something, and I'm not letting you go until you tell me who sent you after me—"

Turning one side of her body into him, she struck his forearm with the base of her palm and withdrew her service weapon with her free hand from the shoulder holster beneath her jacket. She aimed center mass, just as she'd been trained, but kept her finger alongside the trigger. "Touch me again and I won't hesitate to shoot you. Understand?"

He backed off, easing the blood pulsing in her face and neck.

"Nobody sent me after you, whatever the hell that means." In the dim light of the flame, Shea swallowed the discomfort in her throat as though that would make it easier to breathe, but she wouldn't lower her weapon. "I was on the plane because I need to get my son back."

Chapter Two

"What do you mean get him back?" Shea had a son. Of all the cases they'd worked together, neither of them had revealed more than they'd had to, but a son? Why hadn't that come up in her background check? How hadn't he known, and why did the thought of her creating life with another man tear at the edges of the hollowness inside him?

She lowered the barrel of her service weapon an inch, but kept the gun raised. Like the strong, stubborn, suspicious police officer he'd come to know. He shouldn't have pinned her against the wall, her sultry scent embedded now in his lungs. But more than that, he hadn't meant to intimidate her. Hadn't meant to drive a larger wedge between them than already existed. "My husband—my ex-husband—he…" Swiping her tongue across her bottom lip, Shea shifted her weight between both feet, but her gaze softened in the little bit of flame they had left. "He took Wells from me."

The muscles down Vincent's spine hardened with battle-ready tension. Rage, hot and fast, exploded through his veins. Her son had been taken. He could only imagine the hurt, the fear she'd had to live with this entire time, and she hadn't said a word. Every cell in his body urged him to find the bastard responsible and make him pay, to bring her son home, but there was nothing he could do for either of them right now. Sympathy flooded through him, and he raised his hands in surrender, the lighter clutched between his thumb and palm. "You can put the gun down."

One second. Two. She lowered the gun to her side but didn't holster it. Pressing her back against the cave wall, she slid to her haunches and collected the backpack she'd held on to so tightly during the flight. "Why do you think the plane was sabotaged? Flights go down all the time. It could've been an accident—"

"Because of the pilot," he said. "He reported the gauges were fine, but the engine had stalled. My guess is someone tampered with the fuel tank. Maybe replaced the fuel with some other kind of liquid. The gauge would've read full, but the engine can't run without gas."

"I didn't sabotage the plane." She nodded absently. "But I might know who did."

"Let me guess. Your ex." Hell. He'd been dispatched to enough domestic cases over the years to understand the lengths some guys went to keep their girlfriends or wives from escaping, but bringing down a plane? Kidnapping a child? Vincent forced himself to breathe evenly. Any evidence that someone had messed with the plane was gone, buried as deep as if not deeper than they were at the moment. No way to confirm Shea's ex-husband—or anyone else—was responsible, but he wouldn't discount the possibility that her being on that plane wasn't just a coincidence. "Tell me about your son."

"Wells?" Her lips tugged into a weak smile as she holstered her weapon under her jacket. Dark patches of water stained her jeans, and he realized she must be freezing right about now. The sun had already started going down when they'd woken up in the wreckage. So they'd have to make camp here tonight, get a fire going once he mapped out the rest of the cave. Maybe there was another entrance that hadn't been buried during the avalanche. "He's…a handful. Unlimited energy, great negotiation skills, even though he's not old enough to talk." A laugh escaped as she pushed her long dark hair over her head, but her smile disappeared as quickly as it come. "I found out I was pregnant a couple months after Logan and I got married. We were both so excited to be parents, but then… then everything changed." Shadows hid her expression as Shea wiped her palms down her jeans and stood. "My ex was able to convince a judge to give him temporary custody of our son after the divorce, but I have to fight for him. Logan has been doing everything he can to keep me from seeing Wells. Sending threatening messages, having me followed, but I never thought he'd bring down a plane to keep me from getting to the custody hearing. That he would try to kill me."

Whoever was behind this had almost succeeded, too.

"That's why you were headed to New York." Hell.

And they'd just crashed in the middle of the Alaskan wilderness. Vincent gripped the lighter in his hand; her gaze blazed in the dim light. They'd barely escaped with their lives and had been trapped in this cave under who knew how many feet of snow. As far as rescue coming, the tower had no idea they'd gone down, and their pilot had gone missing. Maybe had even been buried in the avalanche after getting thrown from the crash site. Vincent had taken leave from Blackhawk for the next week and a half. No one would know he hadn't made it to New York. As far as his team was concerned, he was going back home to Hawaii. So he and Shea...they weren't going anywhere. "Did you file a complaint with the police department?"

She hesitated, bottom lip parting slightly from the top, then shut down the slight hint of retreat as she leveled her chin with the cave floor. "I'm a cop. I can protect myself."

"If you can connect the messages and stalking back to him, you'll have a stronger case, but you already know that." Hell, she advised the same protocol when dealing with domestic violence victims on the job. Which meant she wasn't telling him the whole truth. Closing the small distance between them, he admired the way she held her ground, the way she locked her back teeth and flexed the muscles along her jawline as though to prove how strong she was, how capable and driven. And damn, if that wasn't one of the sexiest things he'd ever seen. "As of right now, we have to assume no one is coming to save us, but I'm going to do everything in my power to get you to that hearing."

"How? We're literally trapped inside a mountain under several feet of snow, our pilot is missing and the plane is gone." Shea ran her hands along the cave wall, shadows consuming her from head to toe. "Unless you have a couple shovels in that bag of yours and something to keep us from freezing to death, we're on our own."

"Then that'll have to be enough." Vincent knelt beside the duffel of supplies Blackhawk Security operatives were required to carry, no matter the situation. Couple bottles of water, a day's worth of emergency food, first aid kit, change of clothes, space blanket, lighter, small bundle of kindling, anything portable they—or their clients—might need to survive the harsh temperatures of Alaska. He unpacked his SIG SAUER from the side pocket and checked the magazine in the flame of the lighter.

"Why are you helping me?" Her voice wavered as chills rocked through her. Shea attempted to warm herself by folding her arms across her chest, but her clothing had already been soaked through. The only thing that'd keep their bodies from sinking into hypothermia was a fire—and each other. "We're not exactly friends. We work together occasionally. Nothing more."

"Either we survive together, or we die alone. I don't know about you, but I prefer the former." He dug a flashlight from the bottom of the bag and let the lighter's flame die. Sweeping the beam over her, he studied the glistening wall at her back. Alaska was known for its gold and silver mines, but a handful of precious metals weren't going to keep them warm. "Night's already falling, so we're not getting out of here until morning. We need to search the cave and find a spot to build a fire. Only problem is ventilation. If we don't find the right spot and we light a fire, we'll—"

"Suffocate." She turned away from him, following the flashlight's beam up along the cavernous openings above them. "My brother was an Eagle Scout. I helped him with a lot of his merit badges."

"So what you're saying is you're going to be the one to make sure we don't die." Hauling the duffel over his shoulder, he ignored the pain spreading up his leg and treaded deeper into the cave. Blood trailed down the inseam of his pants and into his boots. Freezing temperatures had already worked deep into his muscles, slowing him down, but the addition of the sliver of shrapnel from the crash threatened to bring him to the edge. They had to find a place to camp and get the fire going. Only then would he worry about his leg. "Now I feel safe."

Her laugh curled around him from ahead, echoing off the bare walls of the cave, a deep, rich laugh he'd never heard from her before. What he wouldn't give to witness the smile accompanying the sound, but she'd already moved a few paces ahead of him, weapon drawn once again. Caves like this were perfect for wildlife native to these mountains. Bears, wildcats. They couldn't be too careful. "Don't get your hopes up. I wasn't paying that close attention."

A smile tugged at one corner of his mouth. Of all the people who could've stepped foot on that plane, the second passenger had to be Shea Ramsey. Intelligent, driven, beautiful. She'd pulled at something inside him the moment she was assigned to assist one of Blackhawk's past investigations, a need he hadn't thought about since waking up in the middle of the crime scene he was supposed to die in.

Darkness intensified his other senses as they felt their way deeper into the cave, his awareness of her—of the way her jeans brushed together at the apex of her thighs, of how her hair fell across her back—at an all-time high. A rush of cold air hit him square in the face, and he dragged the flashlight beam along the ceiling. There. A small opening about thirty feet up that hadn't been covered in snow. Big enough to provide ventilation for a fire. Studying the ground around them, he kicked loose rocks and dirt away from the area. "We can build a fire here."

Shea rubbed her hands together in an attempt to warm herself, but it wouldn't be enough. Not out here. "Shouldn't we be looking for a way out?"

"We're not going anywhere tonight." Vincent dropped to one knee, unpacking the lighter and small bundle of kindling from his bag. Within a minute, a fire snapped, crackled and popped. They'd been exposed to the coldest temperatures Mother Nature had to offer, and the twigs wouldn't last all night. He straightened, tearing his jacket from his shoulders, then lifted his soaked T-shirt over his head. "Do you want to be the big spoon or the little spoon?"

HE COULDN'T BE SERIOUS. Of all the members of the Blackhawk Security team, Vincent Kalani ranked first on the people she fought to avoid in the field, with the firm's private investigator, Elliot Dunham, in a close second. Didn't matter that they'd crash-landed in the middle of the mountains and had to conserve body heat. She'd freeze to death before considering stripping out of her wet clothing in front of him. She attempted to control nervous energy in her gut, her chest still aching from where she'd been pinned against her seat in the plane. Vigilantes didn't follow the laws she'd sworn to uphold. And she didn't trust him. "I'd just as soon spoon a bear."

Heat drained from her neck and face as Vincent turned toward her. Intricate tattoos stretched across valleys and ridges of muscle all along his arms, up his sides and across his chest, and his question fled to the back of her mind. Her mouth dried as she studied him, studied the scars marring the designs along his shoulders when he laid his wet clothing on the ground to dry. So many of them. Curiosity urged her to close the distance between them, to run her fingers over the waves of puckered skin to see if they felt as soft as they looked. Did the scars stretch down his back, too?

"Considering where we are, that can probably be arranged. Although you might not live long enough to enjoy it. At least I don't bite. Unless you ask me nicely." His voice was gravelly. Vincent locked dark brown eyes on her, shadows dancing across his expression. Straightening to his full height, he suddenly seemed so much…bigger than he had before. He wiped his hands on his T-shirt as he approached with supple grace. "Got something you want to ask me, Officer Ramsey?"

She'd been staring. Taking a step back, she tried to gain control of her expression and the rush of emotions flooding through her. "I didn't realize you'd been injured."

"Yeah, well, there's a lot you don't know about me." He turned away from her, dark hair falling over powerful shoulder and back muscles. "Or my team."

She had to give him that.

"Can I…" She swiped her tongue between her lips. His heated gaze snapped to her mouth, and a rush of awareness chased back the tremors rocking through her. Her fingers tingled, but she wasn't sure if it was from the sensation returning to her hands or something more. Something that had nothing to do with hypothermia and everything to do with the man standing a few feet ahead of her. "Can I touch them?"

"What?" He lowered his hands to his sides, shock evident in the way he narrowed his eyes on her, in the way his voice dropped into dangerous territory.

Oh no.

"I'm sorry. I…" Shea blinked to clear her head, the spell broken. Her mouth parted. Had she really asked him if she could touch his scars? What the hell was wrong with her? "I didn't mean—"

"Nobody's ever asked me that before," he said. "Most people avoid them."

Most people? As in previous lovers? The fire crackled beside them. Her heart threatened to beat out of her chest as sympathy pushed through her. She'd understood the feeling of rejection all too well toward the end of her marriage, and the sudden urge to connect with Vincent reared its head. Or maybe she'd ignored her own needs for too long. She swallowed around the tightness in her throat. Nothing would happen between them. Not even if they were the last two people on earth. Swiping her suddenly damp palms on her jeans, she shook her head and stared into the fire. "I shouldn't have asked."

Vincent unzipped his duffel bag and dumped the contents onto the cave's floor. "We need to inventory our supplies and rest up."

Right. Because they were trapped inside a mountain with no tools to get them out, no rescue on the way and no communication to the outside world. She tugged her phone from her jacket pocket, chilled by the damp fabric. Still no bars, and the battery had already lost half its life with the dropping temperatures. Damn it. Her long curls slid over her shoulder as she settled on a large rock within the flames' glowing perimeter. Guessing from the size of the fire, it wouldn't last through the night, and she closed her eyes in defeat. Shea locked her back teeth against the truth. Without Vincent, she wasn't getting to New York. Hell, she wasn't even getting out of this cave. "We're going to have to cuddle, aren't we?"

"Only if you want to survive the night." He separated his supplies into piles, then handed her one of
the clear plastic containers with a red lid from his
pack. Food? "Look at it this way, at least I'm not a
bear."

Not the kind that would put her in immediate danger, anyway. The container emitted a slight warmth
through to her numb fingers. Out here, clean water
wouldn't be a problem with the dozens of feet of white
snow, but food? They'd be lucky to find an animal
who hadn't gone down for the winter. Even then,
the only weapons they had were their sidearms. Not
overly effective against larger prey, and too many
risks involved using them. They might miss, wasting their ammunition, or the sound could trigger another avalanche. But this… "You brought food with
you on the plane?"

"My mom makes sure I don't go anywhere without
a couple containers of her homemade meals. Makes
me lunch every day." A wistful smile tugged at his
mouth as he pried the lid from his own container.
Using his fingers, he scooped up a bite of rice and
tilted his head back as he dropped it into his mouth.
"Blackhawk requires all of its operatives to carry
supplies, but we don't know how long we're going
to be out here. We'll need to ration out our food and
collect some water in the morning."

Aromas of raw fish, mangoes, cucumber and soy
sauce tickled the back of her throat, and her stomach
growled in response. Poke. One of her favorites. Shea
couldn't remember the last time she'd eaten. As soon

as she'd gotten Wells's location from the same former partner at the NYPD whom she'd asked for Vincent's service record, she'd packed a couple days' worth of clothes and toiletries and jumped on the first flight out of Merrill Field. Vincent was right. They didn't know how long they were going to be stranded out here without help, and she wasn't stupid enough to turn away a filling meal when the opportunity presented itself.

She unsealed the container, crusted blood staining her knuckles from the crash, and shifted the fleshy muscles in the backs of her legs to get comfortable on the rock beneath her. Tears burned in her lower lash line at the offering, but she wouldn't let her weakness show. She'd survived the lowest point in her life by clawing her way out, fought to prove she could be the mother Wells deserved by seeing doctors, therapists, committing herself to the job. She wouldn't break in front of Blackhawk's operatives, least of all this one. But damn it, why wouldn't he fit inside the box she'd created for him at the back of her mind? Why couldn't he just be the lawbreaking investigator she'd made him out to be instead of a fellow survivor offering her half of his provisions? He had no reason to help her. "You don't have to share your supplies with me."

"Like I said, we survive together or we die alone." Dark eyes studied her as he withdrew a fresh long-sleeved shirt from his bag and threaded his arms through the sleeves, but Shea knew he wouldn't find anything in her expression. She'd mastered locking down her feelings months ago, learned from her mistakes. The minute she'd lost Wells to her ex-husband in the custody battle, she had nothing left inside, and old habits died hard. "I don't know about you, but I don't plan on dying out here."

Neither did she. Splitting the amount of food he'd given her in half, Shea ate as much as she dared and saved the rest for their next meal. There was nothing more for them to do tonight. Maybe in the morning, with the sun higher in the sky, they'd be able to navigate their way through the rest of the cave. Until then, they'd have to save their energy. Because this nightmare was far from over.

Vincent unpackaged a silver space blanket with his teeth, tearing through the plastic before smoothing out the fold lines. The material reflected the fire's brightest flames. "Put your jacket close to the fire so it can dry while we still have enough kindling. Do you have any other clothes in that bag?"

"A couple days' worth." But nothing that would hold up against temperatures hitting twenty below. Unlike him, she hadn't prepared for their plane to crash in the middle of nowhere. "Do you always carry around an entire arsenal of gear, or were you on your way to a survival expo?"

"No. It's part of my contract with Blackhawk." His laugh echoed through the cave, deep, rumbling, warming her in places she'd forgotten existed. Could be she'd ignored her own needs for too long, or the fear of dying alone without ever seeing her son again had hiked her body's systems into overdrive. Whatever the case, she'd hold on to it as long as she could.

To prove she could still feel something. Vincent maneuvered around the fire, space blanket in hand, before taking position on the ground with his back to the nearest wall. A defensive habit she recognized in soldiers and cops who'd been on the job for too long. "Every operator has to be prepared to protect and assist our clients, no matter the situation. Sometimes that includes plane crashes in the middle of the damn mountains."

"I guess that makes me lucky you were on that plane, too." He'd saved her life. And no matter how much it pained her to admit it, she'd never forget it. Shrugging out of her coat, she laid it flat at the base of the rock she'd taken up, her arms suddenly exposed to the frigid cold. She'd lived in Anchorage most of her life, her parents moving her and her twin brother to the last frontier when they were only toddlers after her father's career in engineering took a sharp dive. She knew how deadly the cold could be. Wrapping her arms around herself, she settled into the thin layer of dirt coating the cave floor in front of him, lying on her side to face the fire. Exhaustion, muscle soreness and his close proximity triggered tension down her back. Then increased as he shifted closer, but she couldn't ignore the heat he provided. "I still have my gun, Kalani. Don't think I won't use it if you get handsy."

Another deep laugh reverberated through him, fighting to break apart the knots down her back from behind. "Wouldn't dream of it, Officer Ramsey."

Chapter Three

She was asleep in his arms.

They'd survived the night despite losing their main source of heat, their bodies keeping each other warm. Her curls caught in his beard, and Vincent pulled his head back. His right arm had fallen asleep with the weight of her head on him, but he reveled in the feel of her body pressed against his. When had he wrapped his free arm around her waist? Sweat built at the base of his spine, but he didn't dare move. Not when the woman in his arms fit against him so perfectly, a woman who hadn't turned away from his scars in shock and disgust as so many others had.

They couldn't stay here. Someone out there had possibly brought their plane down, and there was a chance whoever had would scour these mountains to ensure they'd finished the job. Whether it was Shea's ex-husband as she believed or someone from his past, he had no idea. But he'd find out. The fact that his flight had taken a nosedive in the middle of the Chugach mountain range right after he'd had a break in the case couldn't be a coincidence. Maybe, after everything she'd already been through, Shea Ramsey had simply been in the wrong place at the wrong time. Maybe his past had finally caught up with him. No way to confirm unless they found the plane. And to do that, they had to get out of this damn cave.

"Please tell me it was all just a dream. I'm going to open my eyes, and none of this will be real." Her sleep-frogged voice caused the hairs on the back of his neck to stand on end, and it didn't take much to imagine waking to that voice anywhere else but on the floor of a snowed-in cave. Dangerous territory. He had a job to do—a case to solve—and no matter how driven, pragmatic and sexy as hell she was, he couldn't afford to lose his focus. There were too many lives at risk. She lifted her head, untangling herself from the circle of his arms, and pinned beautiful jade-green eyes on him. Swiping her hair out of her face, she sat up, clothing mostly dry, and shoved away from him. "Ugh. No such luck."

"Good morning to you, too, Freckles." Cool air rushed over his exposed skin without her added body heat. Vincent straightened, locking back the groan working up his throat at the pain in his leg, and reached for the jacket he'd laid out the night before. Dressing, he stood, stretching the soreness out of his back as Shea grabbed the single roll of toilet paper from their pile of supplies and wandered farther into the cave, out of sight. He grabbed one of the food containers they'd rationed last night, downed a handful of rice and fish, and started packing. This early in the year sunlight only lasted six hours at most. They had to get moving if they were going to prove the plane had been sabotaged and try to contact rescue. Footsteps registered off to his left, and he nodded toward the food he'd saved for her. "Eat up. We don't have much time to find the plane."

"10-4." Shea finished off the container, handed it back to him, and shrugged into her coat and pack. Ready in less time than it took most of his team to prep for tactical support. For a woman who'd woken up with a piece of debris crushing her chest in the middle of the wilderness, she'd taken their situation better than he'd expected. No questions. No complaints. Impressive. Then again, Shea had been trained in all kinds of high-level circumstances just as he had with the NYPD. Hostage negotiation, standoffs with gunmen, dangerous pursuits, interrogations and more. Everything about her was impressive. But last night, he'd seen a different version of her from the cop he'd gotten to know over the past few months, the cop he'd gotten to admire for her sheer professionalism. She'd given him a glimpse beyond the emotionless mask she'd secured during their joint investigations, and, with her guard seemingly back in place, Vincent found himself wanting more.

"Have you ever patched a pair of jeans before?" He shifted his injured leg toward her, barely enough light coming through the opening above them to make it visible. The pain had dulled overnight, but blood was still oozing into his pant leg. If he didn't get the wound taken care of before they trekked through the snow, it'd become infected.

"What?" Those mesmerizing eyes of hers caught sight of blood. In an instant, she closed the distance between them, crouching in front of him. Down on one knee, she framed the wound in the side of his thigh with both hands, and every cell in his body sang with a rush of electricity. "How long were you planning on keeping that to yourself?"

"I need you to remove the shrapnel and stitch the wound, if you wouldn't mind," he said. "I'd do it myself, but it's at an odd angle. There's a needle, thread and some rubbing alcohol inside the first aid kit in the bag."

She pulled the kit from his duffel and located the medical supplies. Washing her hands with the alcohol, she handed the bottle to him to do the same to his leg. Stinging pain raced down his leg a split second before Shea came back into focus. Hesitation flared in her expression as she turned back to him, the box of sewing thread and needles in her hand. "Any color preference?"

"Black is fine." The breath rushed out of him as she tore the hole in his pants wider, her fingers icy against his skin. Metal on rock resounded through the cave as she tugged the piece of shrapnel from his muscle. In minutes, Shea had cleaned and stitched the wound and secured a fresh piece of gauze over the injury. Couldn't say she wasn't efficient. "Thanks."

"Any time." Cleaning her hands once again, she packed the supplies and handed him a roll of duct tape to patch the hole in his jeans. Out here, exposure would kill them faster than anything else, especially if the wind had picked up overnight. "Now let's get the hell out of here."

They moved farther into the cave, systematically following piercing rays of sunlight to find an opening big enough for them to escape. So far, nothing. A combination of cold humidity and staleness dived into his lungs as they moved, but not enough to choke out Shea's familiar scent, and he couldn't help but breathe a bit deeper. Columns of stalactites and stalagmites were closing in on both sides of the path ahead. They'd already spent too long trying to find an opening, but if they couldn't venture any farther, there was no way they were getting out of here before they starved.

"I think there's an opening up ahead." Her words vibrated through him with the help of the bare rock walls narrowing in around them, pushing him harder. The stitches in his leg stretched as Shea half jogged toward the largest pool of sunlight they'd come across so far. Her bright smile flashed wide as she turned back toward him, and his heart jerked in his chest. From the sight of her happy or from their discovery, he didn't know—didn't care. They'd found an escape.

Melting ice dripped onto his shoulders from above as they passed into the outside world, exposed skin tightening at the sudden change in temperature. Vincent pulled his T-shirt over his mouth and nose as his lungs ached from dropping temperatures. The plane had gone down on the north side of the peak, and this entrance to the cave sat on the west. They'd have to navigate to the other side in several feet of snow and treacherous heights to get to the crash site. Climbing and hiking had been one of his passions over the years, but it'd been a long time since he'd been in the mountains, and he sure as hell hadn't climbed in this much snow. They'd have to take this one step at a time. A gust of wind blew snowflakes in front of them, whiting out his vision for a moment. Hell. Without getting to the plane, they couldn't contact his team or confirm his suspicions. They'd die out here. Which meant they didn't have a choice. Not if they wanted to survive. "I need you to take my hand. Follow in my footsteps, got it? It's the only way we're going to be able to do this."

"Okay." Nodding, she interlocked her fingers with his, gripping him tight as he took the first step. His boots disappeared into the sea of white, but he hit solid ground. Slowly he led them alongside the peak, his back to the mountain, Shea close on his heels. Each step brought them closer to the curve of the rock. The wind threatened to unbalance them, but right now, they had all the time in the world. Nothing existed outside of the small pocket of reality they'd created between the two of them. Nothing but the next step. She'd expressed her distrust with the Blackhawk Security team—more than once—but in this moment, she was relying on him to keep her alive, to get her back to her son. He wouldn't fail her.

"Almost there!" The howling wind whipped his words away. The sudden pain in his leg buckled his knee, and his foot slid beneath the snow. Her short-lived scream echoed in his head as she clenched his hand tighter. He righted himself before he slid down the mountain and pulled her in close. Sweat built between their palms. His heart threatened to beat out of his chest as he reevaluated their plan. They were in this—100 percent—and they couldn't give up now. They followed the curve around the northwest corner of the mountain, and the wind immediately died. Crystalized puffs of air formed in front of his mouth as he took in the sun glittering off the tumble of snow that'd buried them beneath the rock. Without thought, he brought her into the circle of his arms as relief coursed through him. Neither of them would've survived the night without the other. He might've helped save her life during the avalanche, but without her, he wouldn't have made it this far.

Her body stiffened beneath his touch, and he instantly backed off. Right. They didn't know each other, not really, but it was the way her eyes narrowed on a single point over his shoulder that triggered his internal warning system. She nodded, his name on her lips barely a whisper over the wall of wind howling through the trees. "Vincent."

He turned to see what she'd locked onto.

The plane's hull had been cleared, leaving it bare to the elements.

"Is that...?" Disbelief tinted her voice as she fought to catch her breath and stumbled into him. "How is that possible?"

Vincent released her and unholstered his weapon from beneath his coat. Thick trees impeded his view of the surrounding area, and his instincts prickled with awareness due to the fact that they were clearly out in the open. Vulnerable. "Because someone's already been here."

THEY WEREN'T ALONE.

"The pilot could've survived." Shea ducked deeper into her coat that wasn't nearly as thick as it should've been out here. She'd added a few more layers beneath, but the wind chill had dropped temperatures well below freezing. Her ears burned without anything to stop the cold from seeping in, the numbness in her toes and cheeks spreading. Her fingers tingled with pins and needles as Vincent released her hand, and she flexed them into the center of her palms inside her gloves. They'd made it back to the crash site, survived the night. Only they weren't the only ones. "He could still be out here. Maybe hurt."

There'd been so much blood on the windshield, she couldn't imagine their pilot would last long out here on his own, but there was a chance. If he was able to get to what was left of the plane's supplies, he could've staved off hypothermia for a little while longer. But then why not stay with the plane and wait for help?

Vincent shook his head as he circled around the plane's remains, attention on the ground. He kept a wide perimeter as though studying a scene and was trying to keep evidence contamination to a minimum. Out here, though, it wouldn't be long until the winds and the fresh snow buried it all over again. "I count at least four sets of footprints here."

"A rescue team then." Shea didn't dare let the hope blossoming in her chest settle. No one from the tower had answered their Mayday call, and they would've heard a chopper or another plane searching the area by now. Wouldn't they?

"No one brings down a passenger plane without good reason. Wouldn't get as much attention as a commercial flight, and there's no guarantee anyone would see the crash or find us out here." He reached through the shattered front window into the cockpit and tugged something free, and her stomach wrenched. The handheld radio wire had been cleanly severed from the device. Not a rescue team. Which meant… "Whoever unburied the plane was looking for something. Or someone." His massive shoulders rolled beneath his coat, snow sticking to his dark beard. "Which means one of us, including our missing pilot, could be a target for the people who did this."

No. No, no, no, no. Shea stumbled back a few feet, snow working into the tops of her boots. This was crazy. The adrenaline from the crash had worn off and now her wild theory about Logan didn't make sense. Her ex wouldn't hire a team of men to ensure she never made it to New York. They hadn't ended their marriage on the best of terms, but to outright want her dead because she hadn't signed her parental rights away crossed a line. There was no way he'd do that to Wells. Despite the bitterness she'd held on to for the past few months for Logan leaving her, for moving Wells across the country, she had no doubt he loved their son. Her ex wouldn't risk losing the one thing that mattered to them both. "Logan wouldn't do this. He doesn't have the funds to hire anyone to sabotage a plane or a motive to want me dead. I'm not trying to take Wells from him. I just want to see my son."

Vincent dropped his duffel into the snow and ducked into the side door of the plane, where one of the wings had been torn clean off by the rocks during their descent. "I've known people to kill for a lot less."

Unfortunately, so had she. More recently, while working a case with Blackhawk's private investigator, Elliot Dunham, and a woman Shea believed to be a murderer. In the end, the real killer had left a trail of bodies for fear he'd lose everything if news he carried the warrior gene found in his genetic makeup went public. She'd been the arresting officer on that case, forced to work beside Vincent Kalani at the chief's orders, to prove Elliot's client had been framed. So many lives taken for the sake of holding on to a reputation.

It hadn't been her and Vincent's first case together, but she'd done everything in her power since then to ensure it'd be their last. The way her breathing changed when he studied her, the way her heart rate picked up pace when he neared, even how every muscle down her spine seemed to relax when she caught his clean, masculine scent... Working cases with him had helped her break through the fog that'd cut her off from her family, friends and coworkers, made her feel things she hadn't felt since before giving birth to her son. But it wasn't enough to convince her he and his team were above the law.

A hunk of metal landed beside her boot, pulling her back into the present. Her ears rang. Terrifying memories seared across her brain as Vincent tossed more debris into the snow, and she focused on pushing one foot in front of the other to aid in whatever search he was navigating. Didn't matter they'd been stranded together or that they'd be partnered together on future cases between the department and Blackhawk. She wouldn't give in to the desirable impulses carving at the hollowness inside. Not with him. "What are you looking for?"

"The black box is gone." Vincent pulled free of the hull and dusted snow and dirt from his jacket before turning to her. Solid exhales formed in front of his mouth as he ran a hand down his beard. He slammed his fist into the side of the plane, and she flinched as the sound bounced off the peaks around them. "All the emergency supplies are missing, too. Probably sucked out the back with the rest of the cargo when the tail ripped off." His shoulders heaved with his overexaggerated breathing before he locked dark brown eyes on her. "What we have won't last more than a day, two at most."

"Then we need to try to get out of here on foot. West." Her gaze slid to the black duffel bag at his feet, and she threaded her arms through her pack, bringing it around to her front. Shea dropped to her knees and consolidated everything into the one bag. Easier to carry than the duffel but would leave one person without supplies if they were separated. In less than a minute, she slung it back into place, fingers gripped around the straps, and faced him. They could switch off carrying the supplies to conserve energy and camp for the night when it got dark. Leaving the plane was a risk. What if someone in the tower had heard their distress call? What if the footprints did actually belong to a rescue team? What if they were making a mistake? They were lost someone where in the middle of the Chugach Mountain range, with mountains surrounding them in every direction. Any attempt to head out of here on foot increased their chances of hypothermia, frostbite, starvation, getting lost, any number of possibilities that could end with their deaths. But Shea had to get to her son. And she wasn't going to let anything—anyone—else stand in her way. "The only way we're getting out of here is if we work together."

One step. Two. Vincent closed the distance between them, and she swallowed the urge to back away. To prove he didn't affect her. He brought his gloved hand up, setting his fingers at the back of her neck. Ice clung to where his gloves touched her exposed skin, but in that moment, she could only focus on the pressure building behind her sternum. "And here I thought you've been avoiding having to work with me."

She could still smell him on her. A mixture of something spicy and wild. Every time she moved, she resurrected the scent, but it was even more powerful now that he'd breached her personal space. An overwhelming sense of calm spread down her back and across her shoulders. Shea opened her mouth, not really sure how to respond—

A gunshot exploded from above.

The reaction was automatic. Her vision blurred as she slammed into him, and they fell into more than three feet of snow together. His hands wrapped around her arms to pull her off him as reality set in. They were out in the open. Vincent brought his head up, scanning the surrounding area a split second before he tugged her to her feet. Adrenaline surged through her as they headed for the closest patch of trees, his injury making him limp, her lungs on fire. The pack slowed her down, but she wouldn't ditch it with the possibility they'd have to keep running.

She skimmed her gloves over rough bark and doubled over to catch her breath. Searching up through the branches of the large pine, Shea watched for movement, listened for another shot—anything— that would give them an idea of what they were up against. She swiped her hand across her runny nose. "These mountains carry sound for miles."

"The shot sounded like it came from close by." His weapon was in his hand. His lighthearted expression she'd gotten used to since they'd crashed faded into a stone-cold wall of unreadability, as though he'd tear any threat apart with his bare hands. Vincent Kalani had served New York City as one of the best forensic investigators in the country, but in that moment, he'd become one of Blackhawk's vigilantes. Powerful. Dark. Dangerous. "But that doesn't make me feel any better, either."

"We need to go." They couldn't stay here. No telling if the team who'd unburied the plane had fired that shot or if they were here to help at all. Whatever the case, Shea wasn't interested in finding out.

A twig snapped from behind, and she spun, unholstering her weapon in the same move. She took aim as Vincent maneuvered in front of her, as though he intended to use himself as a shield to protect her. Her breath shuddered through her, the cold stiffening her trigger finger as they studied the shadows in the thick line of pines. Branches dipped and swayed, and the tension Vincent had chased back a moment ago climbed into her shoulders once again.

A man stumbled from the tree line, and she tightened her grip on her weapon. Black slacks, graying hair, white button-down shirt. Blood spread from the injury in the center of his chest and from a deep laceration on his head. Locking his gaze on Shea, the man collapsed to his knees and reached for her as he fell forward.

She lunged, catching their missing pilot before he hit the snow. Her gun fell from her hand as she laid his head back and studied the fresh bullet wound in his chest. She tugged her glove free with her teeth and set her fingers at the base of his neck. The breath rushed out of her. She looked up at Vincent, at a loss for words. It was too late. "He's dead."

Chapter Four

Their pilot was dead, they didn't have any way to contact the Blackhawk Security team, and there was at least one gunman closing in. He and Shea had to get the hell out of here.

They trudged through knee-deep snow as fast as they could between the trees, but the downward angle of the mountain threatened to trip them up with every step. His boot slid against hardened ice beneath the powder, but Shea kept him from rolling down the hill, one hand wrapped around his arm and the other around the tree closest to them. They'd had to leave the pilot where he fell. No time for a proper burial. Not with a killer possibly on their trail. He'd had basic medical training on the job, but it'd been too late. Someone out here had sabotaged their plane, cut their chances of communicating with the outside world, and already killed a man. Hell, he didn't even catch their pilot's name. The longer they stayed in one spot out here without moving, the higher the chance the cold would seep into them. Hypothermia was real. And it was deadly.

"Are we going to talk about what happened back there or pretend someone didn't just kill our pilot?" Her voice cut through the deafening silence around them. "At the crash site you said one of us might be the target of whoever took down the plane." The mountain blocked most of the wind, but an attractive red coloring spread over the freckles speckling her cheeks all the same. Her shallow breathing made her words breathy. "Why was that your first theory? Why not a terrorist attack or simple engine failure?"

"Our focus needs to be on surviving right now. Not theories." Vincent slowed his pace to give her a chance to catch her breath and take some weight off his injured leg. Scooping a handful of fresh snow into his mouth, he cleared the stickiness building under his tongue. A headache pulsed above his eyebrow where he'd swiped dried blood away. Must've gotten hit by something during the crash. Although he couldn't remember what it was. There were any number of reasons someone would've wanted to take down their plane. Any number of reasons they could be targets. In reality, too many to count. But none of them mattered out here. They'd left the safety of the cave out of necessity, but they wouldn't last long once night fell. They had to keep moving. He continued down the incline, but the lack of her familiar breathing said Shea hadn't followed.

"What aren't you telling me?" she asked.

Vincent turned back toward her, gravity pulling at one side. Pressure built from her intense questioning gaze, as though she were trying to read his mind to get the answers she deserved, and damn, he found himself powerless to the fire in her eyes in that moment. Powerless to her. "There's a chance this has to do something with the last case I was working for the NYPD."

She kicked up loose powder as she closed in, those mesmerizing green eyes still locked on him. "What case?"

Sense returned in small increments. He hadn't told anyone—not even his team—what'd happened that night. For good reason. The more people he got involved, the higher the risk to their lives. Then again, maybe he'd already sentenced Shea to death by getting on that plane.

"Doesn't matter." He stared out over the expanse of trees, rock and snow—miles of it—to escape the sickening clench in his gut every time those memories rushed to the surface. Vincent had fled to Anchorage and joined Blackhawk a year ago for one reason: to move on and to forget. Only now, with the discovery of a partial fingerprint from Internal Affairs Bureau Officer Ashton Walter's death scene, he couldn't hide from the truth any longer. Someone had killed two members of his forensic unit the day of the fire in an attempt to cover up the evidence left behind, but he'd survived. Now he was going to find out why. In any other circumstance, he would've had a lead on who'd tampered with the plane by now and possibly been able to connect the dots, but out here, with nothing but a day's worth of food, a first aid kit and a handgun, he was useless. "Unless we find shelter for the night, none of this is going to matter."

Shea moved into him, never breaking eye contact, so close he could count the freckles across the bridge of her nose. A bruise marred perfectly light olive skin across her left cheek, one he hadn't seen before now, as she drew her eyebrows inward. It was a small price compared to what could've happened when they'd crashed but still twisted his insides. If the people he'd suspected of killing that IAB officer had found him, Shea would be nothing but collateral damage to them. His fingers tingled with the urge to trace the dark outline of the bruise. Or was it frostbite finally settling in? She set her hand over his coat, directly over his heart, and his body temperature spiked. "Whatever you're hiding, it might've already tried to kill us." Her hand fell to her side, and he went cold as she pushed past him. "Just remember that in case we don't make it through the night."

He spun after her. "Shea, I—"

Bark splintered off the tree he was holding on to with a crack as loud as thunder, and Vincent fell forward. Her eyes widened a split second before he collided with her, then they were both falling. The gunman had caught up with them. Their surroundings blurred as they rolled down the incline, each clinging to the other. Momentum and gravity ripped her from his hands. Ice worked beneath his coat as he rolled, and all he could do was wait for the ride to end. Pain cracked down his spinal column what felt like hours later as he slammed into a large boulder. His head snapped back into rock, his ears ringing, but he forced himself to push to his feet. Couldn't stop. His vision wavered as Vincent stumbled forward. "Shea."

Where was she? Had she been hit?

The world righted itself, shouts echoing off the cliffs around them. He reached into his coat for his weapon but found only an empty shoulder holster. Damn it. He must've lost the gun when he'd rolled down the mountain. He'd tumbled at least one hundred feet. It could be anywhere. Snow clung to his hair and beard, and he shook his head to clear the haze holding tight. His heart threatened to beat out of his chest. "Shea!"

"I'm here. I'm okay." Movement caught his attention through the thick branches of a tree a few yards to his left seconds before her five-foot-three frame filled his vision. Relief swept through him at the sight of her, drawing him closer. Shooting her hands to his arms, Shea leaned on him, hiking his blood pressure higher, but he didn't have more than a few seconds to revel in the sensation. Her attention shot up the hill as shouts echoed down, and she sank a bit deeper on her back foot. She unholstered her weapon, fixing her index finger over the trigger through her gloves. Snow fell from the backpack of supplies and the ends of her hair as they took cover. "They're coming."

Determination and something he couldn't quite put his finger on pulled her shoulders back as she took aim. She was prepared to fight, but she couldn't hide the fear in her eyes.

"Listen to me. I need you to run. Don't look back.

Don't wait for me." He'd hold them off. At least until she found cover. Crouching, Vincent scanned the trees, senses on alert. They didn't have much time before the shooter or shooters caught up with them. "I'll distract them as long as I can."

"From the sound of those voices, we're outnumbered and outgunned." Shea widened her stance as the shouts grew closer. Brilliant emerald-green eyes narrowed on him, and his breathing slowed, as though his body had been specifically tuned to hers over the past twelve hours. "I'm not leaving you to face them by yourself. Survive together or die alone, remember? We're going to figure this out, but right now, we need to live until we can get that chance."

A bullet ripped past them, and Vincent automatically shielded himself behind the closest tree. They were pinned down. Any movement on their part would expose them to the next shot. They needed a distraction. These trees were thick, and the team on the other side of those guns had to be tactically trained. No way he and Shea could take them out with only the sixteen rounds from her weapon. "Toss me the pack."

She switched her weapon to her other hand before throwing their supplies at his feet. Another shot tore through the bark mere inches from his shoulder, and he dropped to the snow as Shea returned fire. Once. Twice. "I've got fourteen rounds left."

The shots reverberated through him and off the rocks surrounding them. He wrapped his grip around the flare gun he'd taken from the small case beneath one of the plane's seats. One shot. That was all he needed. Arching around the tree, he homed in on the dark clothing set against white snow about thirty feet above then took aim at the brush the bastard was using for cover and pulled the trigger.

The flare hit the dried tinder, catching it on fire within seconds. Black smoke billowed between them and the gunmen. The flame wasn't designed to last long. They had to move. "There's our chance, Freckles. Go!"

Shea took off, Vincent close on her heels, down the mountain. Muscles burned in his legs, the stitches in his thigh protesting every time he pulled his boot free from the powder, but he wouldn't slow down. Not until he got her the hell out of this mess. Another round of gunfire exploded from behind but never found its target. He pushed himself harder, careful to keep Shea in front of him as they sped down the incline in an effort to protect her from the next bullet.

The distraction had done its job, giving them enough time to put distance between them and the tactical team, but it wasn't permanent. Whoever'd sent those gunmen wanted something—or someone—and if they were anything like him and his team, they wouldn't stop until they got it.

SHE COULDN'T TAKE another step.

They'd been wandering through the wilderness, running off pure adrenaline, but Shea had nothing left to give. Her feet and hands had gone numb more than an hour ago, her lungs burning with every inhale.

Ice crusted to her hair and eyelashes. One more step. That was all she had to focus on, but she couldn't do it. She leveraged her arm against the nearest tree for support. They were still miles away from civilization, with no idea where they—

She saw the glimpse of dark blue in a land of white, brown and green. Straight ahead, topped with inches of snow, surrounded by a clearing of pines. But… She didn't dare breathe. Was it real, or had hypothermia already set in? Was this her body's final attempt to survive by giving her false hope? Her mouth barely moved to form his name, the muscles in her jaw aching from the cold. "Vincent?"

"I see it," he said, and everything inside her released. "Looks like a ranger station."

A sob built in her throat. She collapsed into the powder as relief coursed through her, but Vincent was there, pulling her upright. Before she had a chance to protest, he swept her over his shoulder in a firefighter's hold. She couldn't imagine the amount of pain he must've been in with her added weight, admired him for making it this far with his injury, but he held her tight. His steps were strong, evenly paced, as he hiked over uneven rocky terrain leading to the ranger station.

"I've got you." His words vibrated down his back and into her chest, and she believed him. Just as she'd believed he would do everything possible to give her a chance to get to safety when the bullets had started flying, even at the cost of his own life. But she hadn't been able to leave him. Not when she'd taken an oath to protect and serve. Not when… Not when he'd gone out of his way to save her life after the crash. To keep her warm when their fire had gone out. To share his supplies when they both knew there was only enough food for one of them.

She had no reason to trust him, other than neither of them would make it out of here on their own, but the bitterness she'd clung to on the plane seemed stupid now. The edges of her vision darkened as he lowered her feet to the ground, but she failed to keep her balance and fell back.

But still, he was there. Even with his dark Hawaiian complexion, color had drained from his face, a thin layer of snow and ice clinging to his beard and exposed skin, but he hadn't complained once. Hadn't let her give up. Vincent tore his glove from one hand, the other centered on her lower back as he helped her sit. When had he gotten her inside? "Hang on, Freckles. Stay here while I try to get the heat going."

He disappeared deeper into the station, her gun in his hand.

Shea gave in to gravity, falling back on a single twin mattress shoved into the corner of the main room in the station. The National Park Service had cabins like this all over the mountains. They were used as shelters for backcountry hikers who hadn't been able to escape bad weather or for support for rangers circulating through the area for their shifts. Which meant they'd hiked into a national park. They weren't lost anymore. Seconds slipped by in silence. Minutes? She had to get up. Had to find Vincent and make sure he hadn't succumbed to hypothermia. Because without him, she wasn't going to ever see her son again.

Stinging needles exploded through her hands, and Shea forced her eyes open. Haloed by a warm, orangish glow from behind, Vincent centered in her vision. He rubbed her hands between his big, calloused palms. He'd pulled her boots and jacket free, layering her in a thick quilt she hadn't realized kept the tremors in her body at bay until now. She must've fallen asleep. Or passed out. She wasn't sure which she preferred, but the truth was, she knew she was lucky to be alive. "You saved my life again, didn't you?"

"We saved each other." He massaged heat and pressure into her hands, then her wrists and arms, a known technique for combating hypothermia to get the circulation in her body going again, but it was more than that. There were no visible signs of frostbite on her fingertips and toes, yet he hadn't stopped touching her. Dark brown eyes studied her from head to toe, the sensation so raw it felt as real as physical touch. Or was that the lingering effects of the cold-induced delirium? "I'd have a bullet in my back if it weren't for you tackling me like an NFL linebacker."

A small laugh bubbled past her lips. The past few hours of memories played back as he continued rubbing small circles into her arms, and the warmth he'd generated drained. Them finding the plane unburied, the pilot stumbling from the trees with a fresh bullet wound in his chest, the destroyed radio. It all fit with Vincent's theory. Someone had sabotaged the plane, then hired a team to ensure no one had survived the crash. But who? Who would want either of them dead? "Why is someone trying to kill us, Vincent? What happened on your last case?"

His strokes slowed, then he pulled away altogether, and her stomach jerked in protest. Running one hand through his hair, he leaned back in his chair. "My forensic unit was called to the scene of an officer-involved shooting back when I worked for the NYPD. An Internal Affairs investigator named Ashton Walter. He'd been killed in the warehouse district, but the medical examinor couldn't give us anything solid to identify a suspect, even with small amount of evidence my team collected—or wouldn't. The victim had been looking into a handful of unsolved homicide cases I brought to his attention after my commanding officer shot down my suspicion the killer had to have been familiar with crime scene procedure and forensics. According to her, Walter wasn't supposed to have been in that area and had most likely gotten involved in something he shouldn't have, but nothing I recovered from the scene supported that theory."

"You think he was killed because he was looking into your unsolved cases?" Her heart jerked in her chest. That amount of guilt could crush a person from the inside, even someone as insightful, intelligent and innovative as Vincent.

"Officer Walter was a good guy, good investigator. He had a wife and a kid on the way at the time. Brass couldn't prove their corruption theory, and Homicide was instructed to close the case." A disbelieving laugh rumbled through him. Vincent crossed his arms over his heavily muscled chest, gaze distant as though he wasn't really seeing her in front of him. Shadows danced across his expression from the single lantern he must've lit while she'd been unconscious, hiding his expression, but she caught the soberness in his words. "So I convinced a couple techs from my team to take another look at the scene on our own. I just…" His thick brows furrowed over the bridge of his nose, those dark eyes centered on her, and the crash, the gunmen, everything disappeared for the briefest of moments. "I couldn't let it go. I was trained to follow the evidence, but the place had been wiped clean before we'd gotten there. There was no evidence to follow, and less than two minutes after we arrived on scene someone knocked me unconscious. Next thing I knew, the entire place and everything in it was on fire. Including me."

Her breath shuddered out of her, and Shea wanted nothing more than to reach out to him, but any kind of sympathy from her paled in comparison to what he'd already been through. "That's how you got your scars."

"I got out." He nodded, pressing his shoulders into the back of the chair. "But the other two members of my team didn't."

"I didn't realize…" What? That he wasn't the only one with a guilty past? That the Blackhawk Security operative she'd built in her mind over the past year wasn't the man sitting in front of her? Swallowing around the tightness in her throat, she pushed to sit up and swung her legs over the edge of the bed. In her next breath, she leaned into him, wrapping her arms around his neck, and held him. She didn't know what else to do, what else to say. The feel of him against her chased back the final tendrils of ice in her bones. Ducking her forehead into the tendon between his neck and shoulder, she breathed his earthy, masculine scent deeper. Until she couldn't take one more single sip of air. "I'm sorry."

The air around them shifted as Vincent threaded his arms to her lower back, holding her against him, and she gave in to him at that moment. Didn't matter she'd promised herself to keep her distance, not to get attached to the man she was so determined to hate. They'd survived a plane crash together, outrun an avalanche and fought off a team of gunmen after someone had killed their pilot in cold blood. She needed this. Right now, she needed to feel something.

Shea turned her head upward, planting a small kiss against his jawline, and pleasure unlike anything she'd ever felt before immediately shot through her. She and Logan had done what all married couples were supposed to do. They'd conceived Wells together, but this... This was different. She slid her mouth along the veins in Vincent's neck, smiled as his breathing shallowed, and a tremor shook his mountainous shoulders. *This* was unfiltered physical want. What *she* wanted. Something she hadn't let herself give in to for so long.

She'd traded her own path for the things others expected from her most of her life. She'd joined the Anchorage PD after her twin brother had been killed in the line of duty to carry on the family blue blood. She'd married the boy next door at her mother's insistence that she move on after the funeral. She'd gotten pregnant after Logan had convinced her a baby would fix their problems. She'd given everything to live up to her friends' and family's expectations and had been the only one left with the consequences afterward.

Vincent's beard bristled against her oversensitized skin as she framed his face with her opposite hand. Logic battled desire. They were practical strangers, believed in wholly different ideals. Not to mention someone had sent a team of gunmen to hunt them down, but, in this moment, none of that mattered. It was only the two of them here.

Now it was her turn to be happy.

Chapter Five

"Shea…" Damn, she felt good, her lips pressed against his throat. Vincent dug his fingers into lean muscle along her rib cage. He'd imagined this moment so many times before, to the point he hadn't been able to tell the difference between reality and his fantasies as he'd wrapped his arms around her back in the cave. The moment was real—she was real—but this couldn't happen between them. "We can't."

She swiped the tips of her fingers against his lips, a combination of salt and her sweetness flooding his system. An extra surge of desire exploded as she maneuvered off the bed and straddled powerful thighs on either side of him. Her frame fit against him perfectly as she explored the sensitive spot under his ear, and he couldn't hold back the quake of desire rocketing through him. "Don't say anything."

"This is just the stress of the situation." He'd said the words to convince himself more than anything else. They'd been through a lot over the past eighteen hours. The crash, nearly getting buried in the avalanche, surviving the night with only each other's body heat. Now the hit team tracking them through the wilderness. He couldn't blame her for giving in to the adrenaline. Hell, right now that seemed like the best damn idea to ignore reality, but he wouldn't take advantage of it. She'd made her feelings about him—about the way he worked—abundantly clear since they'd investigated their first case together. Even in the face of death, she didn't trust him. Gripping her arms, Vincent slowly settled her back onto the edge of the mattress. "We don't want to do anything we'll both regret."

When this happened between them—and it would—it wasn't going to be because of some chemical reaction brought on by fear or desperation. She'd want him as much as he'd wanted her these past few months, and there'd be no claiming it was a mistake in the morning.

Shea blinked at him, her lips parted, almost as though she didn't know what'd come over her. "You're right. I think I got caught up in the moment. That won't happen again." Brushing her curls back with one hand, she leveraged one hand against her knee, her attention on the lantern he'd lit. A quick laugh burst past the seam of her lips as she slid her gaze to him without turning to face him. "Are you going to be completely awkward around me now?"

He couldn't help but smile. The woman owned up to her impulse and tried to get him to laugh about it in the process. Damn that only made him want her more. If it weren't for the fact that their lives were at risk, Vincent wouldn't have stopped her. "Totally."

"Great. Glad we're in agreement on something."
Pushing off the bed, she crossed the main room
of the station. The same fingertips she'd brushed
against his mouth slid across the desk against one
wall, then the stone fireplace as she moved deeper
into the shadows the lantern's light couldn't reach.
All too easily, he imagined that fireplace alight, the
flames reflected in her gaze as she whispered his
name in pleasure. "These stations usually only have
a minimal food and water supply, no firearms or
ammunition, and too many sight lines for the two
of us to cover. With all these windows, we're easy
targets to whoever's tracking us, and we can't just
hunker down until we contact your team. So what's
our next move?"

His thoughts exactly, which only left them with
one option. "We wait." Vincent hauled himself to
his feet, his steps thundering across the old wooden
floor as he closed the distance between them. "Let
them come to us."

"You want to set a trap," she said.

It was the only way to keep her safe, to ensure
the coming fight didn't affect her chances of getting
her son back. "I recovered what I thought was a partial fingerprint before I escaped the fire that night.
It'd been melted into the handle of a gasoline can
nearby. I ran it in every database I could get access
to after I relocated to Anchorage with no matches,
but now I don't think it was a partial at all." Vincent
scrubbed his hand down his beard, tugging on the
hair toward the end. "I think whoever set that fire,

whoever wanted to destroy all the evidence of that IAB officer's murder, I think the killer burned him or herself in the process bad enough to erase half of their print. I want to know who."

"You think the person who killed your vic is the one who hired the team waiting out there." Shea parted the curtains he'd drawn over the windows to lower the shooter's visibility, just enough for her to scan the area. Apparently satisfied, she turned back toward him. "Why send them now? You said you recovered that print a year ago, that you've been running searches in the databases all that time."

He'd been wondering about that, too, but Vincent already knew the answer. He'd known it the minute the plane's engine had failed. Maybe even before that, but the work he and his team did for Blackhawk brought all kinds of threats. Being followed came with the territory. Their clients came to them for one reason: protection. Stood to reason the operatives hired to do the protecting would be put at risk in the process. Hell, he'd be surprised if he wasn't being followed on a daily basis. "Because I got on a plane to New York."

"Someone was watching you." Shea clasped her hands over the back of the desk chair, dropping her head down as she widened her stance. "They were waiting to see if you'd keep the investigation going on your own, and when you got on the plane, they wanted to make sure you wouldn't have the chance." She straightened, hands on her hips. "No matter who else was on board."

A sickening swirl of nausea churned in his gut. "Shea, I never meant for you to get involved. If I'd known—"

"I am on the brink of losing my son because of you. The custody hearing is in two days, and I'm not going to be there to fight for him. Everything I've done over the past year to prove I can be the mother he deserves was for nothing." Controlled rage raised the veins in her arms, the tendons between her neck and shoulders stark in the dim light. She pointed one long finger toward the floor. Disgust and fire contorted her expression before she turned away from him, shadows darkening the bruise on her face. Unshed tears reflected the small flame from the lantern. Facing him again, Shea stepped into him, every bit the officer he'd encountered during their investigations. "You could've gone to the police. You could've involved your former CO and gotten the case reopened, but instead of following the rules like everyone else, you put other people's lives in danger. Our pilot is dead out there with a gunshot in his chest because you and your team think you're above the law, that you're better than everyone else." She collected her gun and backpack from the desk where he'd set them earlier and headed toward the short hallway separating the front of the station from the rooms in the back. "I hope you can live with that when this is over."

Vincent only stared after her, curling his fingers into his palms. Because she was right. He could keep telling himself he'd pursued this investigation on his own to protect the people around him, but he knew the truth. Just as she did. It'd been his personal need for justice that'd kept him from reaching out to his old commanding officer, from trusting anyone else but himself with the evidence he'd recovered. He wanted to be the one to punish whoever'd killed his team-mates that night, who'd tried to kill him. Just like the vigilante she'd accused him of being. But no mat-ter how many times he'd convinced himself other-wise, he wasn't alone in this. Shea had been dragged into this nightmare the moment she'd stepped on that damn plane.

He traced her steps down the hall, following the sounds of rustling in one of the back rooms, then stilled as he studied her from the doorway of the com-munications-room-slash-pantry. Dark, curly hair fell in waves down her back as she riffled through the boxed food on the single shelf, and the blood drained from his upper body. No apology could possibly make up for what he'd done, especially if missing the cus-tody hearing kept her from her son permanently, but he'd sure as hell try. "Shea—"

"We should use the station's radio to try to put the call out to Anchorage PD." Lean muscle flexed along her arms as she scooped extra food and supplies into the backpack, the gun at the hollow in her back. She wouldn't look at him, wouldn't even turn in his di-rection, her anger a physical presence between them. "Assuming the tactical team out there is listening, they'll know exactly where to find us. Then we can put this whole thing behind us and go our separate ways. Move on with our lives."

Move on. She'd already gone out of her way to avoid working with him on joint investigations with Blackhawk Security these past few months. How much more distance did she intend to wedge between them? Vincent stepped into the room, gripped her arms and compelled her to look up at him. Her muscles stiffened beneath his hands in warning. Or was that her body's natural defense kicking in? Either way, Shea Ramsey obviously saw him as a threat, which was the last thing he wanted. He released his hold on her. Gave her the space she needed. "You were right. I could've involved the police or my team, but I wanted to be the one to bring down the bastard who tried to kill me that night." Hearing the words coming from his own mouth made them real, confirmed what he'd felt deep inside since escaping to Anchorage over a year ago. The NYPD didn't want him anymore, but that wouldn't stop him from getting justice the victims of those unsolved cases deserved. That he deserved. "Say what you want about Blackhawk and the work we do, but my team and me? We will do whatever it takes to get the job done, even when that means we have to break a few rules along the way. We fight for our clients. No matter the cost." Vincent swiped his knuckles alongside her jaw, smooth skin catching against the rough patches on the back of his hand, and her green eyes widened slightly. "Because when it comes to protecting the people we care about, there are no rules."

He crushed his mouth to hers.

SHE COULDN'T THINK. Couldn't breathe. Couldn't believe she was kissing him back.

His mouth on hers seared her skin, through muscle and into bone, and Shea couldn't force herself to turn away. She'd dreamed of this moment so many times. Late at night, alone in that empty house after she'd gotten home from working a long shift. Most of the calls she and her partner responded to on the job included robbery or violent crime, but the ones when she'd been paired with Blackhawk Security—with Vincent—brought her back from the darkness piece by piece.

The cases they'd worked together challenged her, tested her mental and physical endurance, gave her something new to focus on, even if she didn't agree with the firm's methods. Working investigations with him had given her a strength she'd forgotten she'd had, to the point she'd finally asked for professional help from her obstetrician then the department's counselor a few months ago. Vincent had unknowingly given her hope, a reason to keep going when the postpartum depression had convinced her she couldn't help anyone. Not even herself.

He maneuvered her backward until the back of her thighs hit the small desk with the radio equipment with a jolt, not breaking the kiss once. His tongue penetrated the seam of her mouth and the world exploded around her. He skimmed his hands around her lower back, wrapping her in the protective circle of his arms. That single touch awakened a sense of safety, of warmth, she'd forgotten existed since her ex had served her with custody papers, and she never wanted it to end. The small gasp of satisfaction at the back of her throat was followed by a laugh, and she set her hand against his chest to push away.

Her skin felt too tight, the thud of her heart too fast in her chest. Damn, the man could kiss, but he was right. This was nothing more than a pressure release in a stress-induced situation. A biological reaction her body needed to get back that sense of adrenaline. Hardened muscle formed ridges and valleys under her fingertips.

Because when it comes to protecting the people we care about, there are no rules.

Had he meant her? Shea traced a piece of loose thread in his shirt, a distraction from the wave of desire washing over her from the inside. "Why did you request me as your partner on the joint investigations between the department and Blackhawk?"

After seeing for herself how Vincent worked— how many laws he and his team ignored in their search for justice—she'd asked her captain to remove her as one of the investigators from the small partnership their respective organizations had formed. Only to learn the truth in the process: Vincent had specifically asked to work with her on the threat that he'd shut down the task force if her captain partnered him with anyone else.

Seconds ticked by. A minute? Shea forced herself to raise her gaze to his, the beat of his heart spiking under her palm, and she was immediately captivated by the inferno in his eyes. The walls closed in. There was a team of killers outside those walls, but right in that moment, he made her feel as though they were the only two people in the world.

"I've never been able to ignore a good puzzle. You're driven but adaptable. You stick to your core values and uphold the law, even at your own personal risk, but you'll pull your weapon on me for the chance to get your son back. I think you truly care about the people you serve and protect in this city, but you won't align yourself with Blackhawk because you don't agree with our methods when we're trying to do the same thing." His hands slid along her lower back, fighting back the cold creeping in as the sun went down. The battle invoked a shiver she couldn't repress across her shoulders, and she hated the fact that her body reacted to it, to him. "You're out to prove yourself, and that makes you a good cop, one I'm proud to have at my side. But to tell you the truth, none of that matters to me. Not really."

"It doesn't?" she asked.

"No." Vincent tangled his fingers through the hair at the nape of her neck; his large palm settled under her ear. "I requested you because not only are you a top-notch pro, but also one look from you makes me forget the nightmare I live with every day since waking up in the middle of that fire." He stared down at her, his eyes glittering in the dim light of the lantern she'd brought in here with her, and her breath caught. "The only thing I can't figure out is what you're hiding."

The hairs on the back of her neck stood on end, and Shea dropped her hands away from his chest. Impossible. There was no way he could see through her defenses that easily. Not with all the hard work she'd put into keeping up appearances. Her partner hadn't known she and Logan had divorced until she'd told him a few months ago. Had Vincent seen more? "What makes you think I'm hiding something?"

"I'm good at my job." Vincent stepped back, taking his body heat with him, and the cold started creeping in again. Physical or mental, she had no idea, didn't want to know. "I don't need to know your secrets, Shea. I need you to trust me. I'll do everything I can to get us out of this alive, and I'm not going to give up until I do. I'll get you to your son."

She'd spent the past year in a fog, unable to focus, so mad at everyone and everything around her because her mind hadn't been able to handle the transition to motherhood. She'd isolated herself from her friends, her family, from the things that'd once made her happy. She'd lost everything that mattered to her in the span of a few months. First, her husband when he couldn't understand what was happening, then Wells when Logan had moved in with and married a woman he'd met only a few months before. The job became her entire life, and soon her parents had stopped calling; her friends had stopped asking her out. Her partner stopped trying to talk to her on patrol. They'd all given up on her. The only one who hadn't turned away from her had been Wells, with his beautiful green eyes and chubby hands reaching for her as her ex had walked out the door with their son in his arms for the last time. And she'd just stood there. Frozen. Incapable. Weak.

But Vincent had just promised not to give up on her.

"I'm sorry for what I said. You've saved my life, I don't know how many times now, and you deserve better. I *know* the plane crash wasn't your fault, and it's not your fault I lost my son, either. I should never have put that burden on you." She nodded, lowering her gaze to the floor as she rubbed the goose pimples from her arms. Forcing herself to take a deep breath, she attempted to clear the last remnants of emotion from her system—in vain. It'd been so long since she'd been able to feel anything, she wasn't sure how to control her emotions anymore. If she could at all. "The truth is I'm the reason my ex started seeing another woman during our marriage, why he filed for divorce. And why he took Wells from me."

The weight of his attention settled on her chest, a physical presence she couldn't ignore. "He cheated on you?"

The anger in his voice rocketed her awareness into overdrive.

"Yes, but my point is… I wouldn't be here without you, and if trusting you gets me to my son, then that's what I'll do." Hell, did any of this make sense to him? She swiped her hand across her forehead. She shrugged despite the battle that'd been raging inside for so long. "Everything else…none of it matters."

"It matters to me." Vincent clasped his big hands

around hers, invigorating her senses with a fresh wave of his wild, masculine scent. "Your ex-husband has to be the stupidest man on the planet to push an incredible, strong, determined woman like you out of his life. It doesn't matter what reason he had. You are worthy of a man who will treat you with the care and respect you deserve. Someone who will stand by your side, no matter what. Who will protect you until his last breath and risk his life to be with you."

All too easily, she imagined Vincent as that man, the one who would wake her and Wells with breakfast in the mornings before he headed into the office for his next assignment, the one who'd spoil her to the ends of the earth with attention and love, the one who'd place a flower over her left ear to announce to his family he'd claimed her body, mind and spirit. She swayed at the intensity of the fantasy, at how incredibly real it was. At how much she wanted it to be true, but this, being stranded out here with him, it was about survival. Nothing more. Because there couldn't be anything more with her. Not anymore.

"I'm not the person you think I am, Vincent." Shea tugged her hands out of his. She'd already hit rock bottom over the past few months. What more could she have to lose by telling him the truth, by telling him that despite that gut-wrenching kiss and explaining the way he made her feel, nothing could happen between them? It was sweet the way he'd stood up for her, called her strong when she'd convinced herself otherwise the past nine months. But in reality, he was only able to see what she'd wanted him to see.

What she'd wanted everyone to see, including herself. That strength, the determination? None of it was real.

Vincent studied her with those incredibly dark, sexy eyes and her nerve endings fired in rapid succession, keeping her in the moment. Would he still look at her as though she were the only woman in the world after he learned the truth? That she was broken? That she wasn't worthy of all those things he'd described? "You have this picture of this immovable, dedicated public servant, mother and wife in your head, but it's all wrong. I'm not that woman." Shea dropped her gaze to the dimly lit floor, unable to stand another second of his worshipful attention. "You have no idea how much I wish I was her, but a woman like that doesn't cut herself off from everyone she loves. I'm not anything remotely close to that."

"You are to me." He tucked his knuckle under her chin, forcing her to look up at him, and every nerve ending she had responded. "Nothing you say is going to convince me otherwise."

Chapter Six

Cold worked its way under his heavy jacket as Vincent dropped the magazine out of their only weapon, checked the rounds and slammed it back into place. The sun had gone down, and his fingers numbed with temperatures dropping by the second. The trap was set, but he had yet to see any movement from the surrounding trees. Shea had drifted off to sleep in the only bed in the station about an hour ago, and he'd offered to take the first shift on patrol. He couldn't sleep. Not with their last conversation echoing through his head. He might've worked forensics for most of his career, but he'd read the truth easily enough: Shea didn't believe she was worthy of love. Not just from her ex-husband—the cheating bastard—but from her son, from her friends, family. Everyone in her life. She'd severed her connections to the people she was supposed to care about.

And he wanted to know why.

He'd gotten his hands on her case files before they'd started working together with permission of the Anchorage PD's chief of police, studied the way

Shea worked, if she stayed within the lines of the law as she claimed. There'd been a few close calls on the job, mostly domestic disputes that hadn't ended when she and her partner had arrived on the scene. One armed robbery in which she'd intercepted the getaway driver at gunpoint. Nothing to make him think something had drastically altered her life or would dictate how close she got to those she cared about the most. There was no doubt she loved her son. He'd seen her desperation to get Wells back from her ex-husband, how missing the custody hearing was tearing her apart from the inside. So what could've possibly happened for her to believe she didn't deserve to be happy, to be loved?

A branch shifted off to his right, and Vincent homed in on the movement. Waited.

A wall of muscle slammed into him from the opposite side of the clearing, knocking the air from his lungs, and he landed face-first in two feet of snow. Twisting, he grabbed a handful and tossed it into the face of the man who'd tackled him and took aim. His attacker grabbed the weapon and slammed it into Vincent's face. Once. Twice. Vincent blocked the third attempt, but, faster than he thought possible, the gun disappeared into the trees. White stars flashed in the corners of his eyes as he raised his fists. It'd take a lot more than a couple hits to the face to bring him down. His heart threatened to pound straight out of his chest as Vincent lunged, slamming his opponent into a nearby tree. Flakes fell around them, blocking his view of his attacker, as he clamped his grip around the bastard's throat. A knee to his kidney sent pain ricocheting through his entire right side, and his hold loosened. The station blurred in his vision as the SOB landed a solid hook to his jaw.

Movement registered as he straightened, closing in on either side of the cabin. Damn it. The bastard hadn't come alone. Sliding his index fingers between his lips, he whistled as loud as he could to give his partner warning. Shea. He had to get to Shea. He pushed his hair out of his vision, facing off with the first attacker once again. He couldn't let them breach the station. Pulling the small blade at his ankle, Vincent swiped high. His opponent threw himself backward, thrown off-balance, and Vincent rushed forward to strike again. Pain exploded through his right shoulder as a bullet tore through muscle and tissue from behind, and his scream filled the clearing. He clung to the wound as he spun toward the newest threat, switching the blade to his other hand. He threw it end over end as hard as he could.

The knife penetrated the gunman's coat and brought the shooter to his knees. One down, three to go. Blood trickled beneath his jacket down his hand as he turned back in time for the original attacker to close the space between them. Vincent hiked his injured shoulder back, ignoring the pain shooting through his nerve endings as a guttural growl worked up his throat. No time to check the wound.

Smoke tainted the air a split second before the flames registered. The two operatives had made it into the station. He only hoped the trap he'd set com-

bining gasoline and the lantern's flame when they'd
barged through the front door had distracted them
long enough to give Shea a way out. Vincent dodged
the swipe of a much larger blade, then another. He
blocked the third attempt and turned the knife back
around on his attacker before sinking it deep into
the man's side.

A gasp filled his ears as his opponent's legs failed
him, but Vincent kept the man upright. He wasn't
finished with him.

"You've got about twenty minutes before you bleed
to death, and believe me, you don't want that to happen out here." Vincent strengthened his hold on the
blade, both the wound in his thigh and the latest in
his shoulder screaming for relief. "Tell me who sent
you after me, and I'll make sure you aren't paralyzed
for the rest of your life when I'm finished with you
and your buddies."

"We're not only here for you, Kalani." The attacker sagged in Vincent's arms, his breath turning
into shallow hisses from between his teeth. He spit a
mouthful of blood into the snow, staring up at Vincent with agony contorting his expression. The man's
jacket slid to one side and exposed the brass shield
at his hip. "You should've left well enough alone."

"You're NYPD." Hell. The bastard confirmed his
theory. The murder of the officer from the Internal
Affairs Bureau had been connected to someone on
the inside. Whether that meant IAB Officer Walter
had been working for them was something Vincent
would have to prove another day. Right now, he only

had one priority: getting to Shea. He'd gotten her involved in this, and he'd get her out. Vincent pulled the knife from his attacker's side and pushed him off-balance. "You shouldn't have come after me."

His attacker hit the ground as flames inside the station broke through windows and consumed everything in its path. Two gunmen left. He swept the gun from the hole it'd made in the snow into his hand. Smoke billowed around him, and he covered his face in the crook of his elbow as he tracked a set of deep footprints around the north side of the ranger station. Heat seared his exposed skin, sweat building at the base of his spine as he maneuvered around the flames, but he'd push through the memories racing to the front of his mind. This wasn't New York City. He wasn't trapped by the fire here. Although the situations were more similar than he cared to admit.

The trap had done its job. First, to incapacitate the two remaining gunmen hunting them, and second, to signal fire and rescue. With their luck, emergency personnel was already on their way. Shea had been instructed to head west as soon as she escaped the station, to another ranger station they'd located on a map inside about three miles from here. Now he just had to find her and take down anyone still on her trail.

"Vincent." That voice. *Her* voice. "Don't come any closer."

He slowed, every muscle down his back tensing for battle as he took in the sight of her. Blood dripped down her nose and mouth, those impossibly green eyes even brighter in the flames. Gunmen flanked her on either side, weapons aimed at her midsection. Tendrils of her hair clung to her skin, the glow of the fire accentuating the freckles across her nose and cheeks. She hadn't gotten away. A soft buzzing filled his ears as he curled his hand around the gun. "She has nothing to do with this. You came for me. Let her go, and you can have me."

"What?" Shea tried to rip her arm from one man's grip, but he held on tight. "No."

"You brought her into this, Kalani. That makes her a loose end." The gunman at her right stepped forward, and a sense of recognition surfaced. Short brown hair, dark eyes, sharp features with a bristled jawline. Vincent had met this man before. But where? "You just couldn't stop yourself from looking into that IAB officer's death, even after we gave you a second chance." He jerked Shea into his chest and pressed a gun to her temple, and everything inside Vincent raged. "How many more people are you going to put in danger before you take a hint? First your teammates back in New York, now this one. She must not mean much if you were willing to risk her life to get what you wanted."

The opposite rang true. She was a motivating factor for him getting on that damn plane, the reason he didn't want to spend the rest of his life looking over his shoulder. She was…everything. His attention slid to Shea, to her almost imperceptible nod as the station burned behind him, and the pressure behind his sternum reached full capacity. "You have no idea who you're dealing with."

An evil smile stretched the gunman's mouth, and a flash of memory darted across his mind. His stomach dropped out as Vincent realized where he'd met this man before. The last homicide he'd worked... The gunman had been at the outer perimeter but inside the crime scene tape taking statements from witnesses. "I've done my research on you, Kalani. I think I'll take my chances."

The bastard was a cop, same as his attacker bleeding out on the other side of the station. Vincent studied the second gunman, caught the briefest hint of the SIG SAUER similar to his old service weapon. They were all cops. NYPD, if he had to guess. Alaska was far outside the lines of their jurisdiction, which meant the squad wasn't here in an official capacity. He locked his gaze on Shea. The tactical team that'd been hunting them these past two days was made up of corrupt NYPD officers.

"I wasn't talking about me." Vincent lunged forward, targeting the attacker on her right as Shea threw her elbow back into the man at her left. In an instant, he'd closed the distance between him and the first gunman. A bullet ripped past his ear as he collided with the cop, taking them both down. He hauled back his injured shoulder and launched his fist into the officer's face to finish the job.

Shea's sharp groan pulled at his attention from behind. The second gunman stood over her, and a predatory growl was torn from Vincent's throat. Nobody put their hands on her. No one. He shoved to his feet, but he'd made it only one step before something hard slammed against his head. He collapsed into the snow, pitched into darkness.

HER FACE THROBBED. Shea blinked against the sudden brightness around her as her body jerked to a stop. Hot. Why was it so hot? She'd spent the past two days chilled to the bone, but now sweat built beneath her heavy clothing. She tugged at the zip ties around her wrists and ankles. Ringing filled her ears as she twisted her head to one side, to the trees within arm's reach. Her last memories played across her mind in flashes and tensed the muscles down her spine. She'd been knocked unconscious. The tactical team had found them, and she'd barely escaped the station before the old wood floor had caught fire from Vincent's trap. She hiked her head back over her shoulder, snow crunching beneath the crown of her head. Now two members of that same team were hefting something heavy closer to the flames destroying the ranger station. The air rushed out of her lungs, but she bit back the scream caught in her throat. Not something. Vincent.

"Boss said destroy the evidence. Then we can get the hell out of here," one of them said.

No. Shea rolled onto one side, feeling for something—anything—she could use to break the zip ties. Her fingers sorted through loose rock, chunks of ice and broken twigs from the trees above. Eyes on both men, she slowly sat up and fisted a large piece of ice from beneath the powder. If the edge was sharp enough, it'd cut through the plastic. Unless the heat from her hands melted it first. She placed the icy blade's edge between her feet and started sawing at the ties around her ankles. Fire crackled and popped from less than ten feet away, her skin burning hot to the point she had to turn away to protect her face.

Pain pulsed across her cheek from where the second gunman had struck her, but she pushed it to the back of her mind as ice turned to water in her hands. Damn it. The ice was melting too fast. She wouldn't be able to get both her hands and her ankles free at this pace. Not before the gunmen dragged Vincent into the flames. She worked faster, harder. She strengthened her grip around the melting weapon as desperation clawed up her throat and clenched her back teeth against the numbness in her hand. "Come on."

The zip tie snapped from around her feet, but relief was short-lived. A shadow crossed over her, instantly cooling her exposed skin.

"Well, well, well. Looks like we've got ourselves a fighter here." The gunman, the one who'd knocked her unconscious, wrapped a strong grip around her arm and wrenched Shea to her feet. The sting of too much cologne burned her nostrils as he pulled her into his chest. Perfectly straight white teeth battled with the sneer stretching the man's cracked lips wide. His bruising hold on her arm increased as she maneuvered her bound wrists between their bodies. "I've always liked a challenge."

"Then you're going to love me." Shea brought up her hands, striking him right in the face as hard as she could. Her knuckles tingled with the hit, but she struck again. The gunman stumbled back, and she followed but didn't catch him drawing a blade in time before stinging pain exploded across her arm. She blocked the next swing and clamped both hands on to his forearm as she rammed her knee into his kidney. Once. Twice. He lost the knife, then she used his own fist to follow through with another punch to his face, knocking him unconscious. Shea dived for the blade as her attacker collapsed at her feet and cut through the ties at her wrists. She unholstered the gun at his hip, catching sight of the NYPD badge on the other side of his belt.

The men who'd attacked them, brought down the plane, they were…cops.

Breathing heavy, vision blurred, she reached out to the nearest tree to keep her balance. She took aim at the first gunman near Vincent as he unholstered his weapon. "Drop the gun and get your hands up where I can see them."

"Gotta say I'm impressed, Officer Ramsey." His voice sent an uncontrollable quake down through her as he raised both arms above his head, gun still in hand. One shot. That was all it would take to rip the man who'd helped bring her back to life away, but she'd pull this trigger just as quickly. "Although we've gotten close over the past hour, so I feel like I should call you Shea."

Her stomach lurched. Whether from the possible concussion or the fact that the man pointing a gun at Vincent had done his research, she didn't know. Her attention dipped to Vincent, to the slight rise and fall of his chest. He was alive. She still had a chance to get them out of here. She caught sight of their supply bag where their attackers had thrown it after intercepting her dash into the trees. She hadn't been fast enough, but she wouldn't make that mistake again. "Is the fact that you know my name supposed to scare me?"

"I could've gotten your name off the plane's passenger manifest or threatened to shoot your pilot unless he gave me the names of his passengers, but I didn't have to do either of those things." The gunman shook his head, dark eyes glittering with help from the fire. A humorless laugh burst from his Kevlar-covered chest. "We found out you've been partnering with Vincent here for a few months when we stopped in to check up on him. I got the feeling he wasn't going to heed our warning to back off his…independent investigation into a case from back home, maybe even trusted someone here with the intel he thought he had. Turns out, I was right. Then I find out you're on the same plane he is heading to New York, and that gets me thinking. Vincent could've been trying to use Anchorage PD resources to find out who killed his IAB friend. And, well, we can't have that." He waved the gun toward her, and she slipped her finger over the trigger of her own weapon. "I know what kind of cop you are, Shea. I know there's nothing I can say to get you to walk away now. So instead of coming in here and trying to convince you to forget you ever saw us, I had my guys in New York pay a visit to your ex."

The blood drained from her face. Logan? Her heart pounded hard in her chest, threatening to burst through her rib cage. She swiped her tongue across her lips to counter the sudden dryness in her throat. It was a manipulation, a desperate measure to get her to believe he had leverage over her. These dirty cops had come for Vincent, and she had no doubt in her mind they'd say anything to get what they wanted. But they couldn't have him. Her arms shook with the weight of the gun in her hand, but she held strong. "I said drop the gun."

"I get it. Exes are exes for a reason, right? You probably don't feel the same way about him as you would about, say, that little boy of yours." That smile was back, and her gut knotted tight. "What was his name?" The gunman lowered his hands slowly, and Shea stepped forward in warning. A slight pull at one corner of his mouth accentuated the sharp angles of his face. "Wells, right? Cute kid. It'd be a shame if he got caught in the middle of what we have going on here." The gunman nudged Vincent with his boot. "It's too late for your partner here, but you can still walk away. You can go to New York and get your son back. That's what you want, right? I can make that happen. All you have to do is stand down, Officer Ramsey."

He was threatening her son. Threatening Vincent. Seconds slipped by. A minute. She had a chance to get to Wells, to fight for him as she should've done in the first place. Sweat fell from her temples, her hands damp against the gun's grip. All she had to do was walk away. The fire had destroyed the ranger station in a matter of minutes and had started spreading to the nearby tree line. A groan reached her ears from behind. The attacker she'd taken down was coming around. She was out of time.

"I swore an oath to protect and serve." Shea lowered her weapon, shortened her shooting stance. Made herself a smaller target. Her gaze dropped to Vincent as his hand splayed across the white snow, leaving a print of red behind. He'd been injured trying to protect her, and every cell in her body screamed in retaliation. The man giving her the chance to run was a cop. His entire squad was made of cops, but they weren't playing by the rules. She wasn't an officer out here. She didn't have the manpower to arrest these men. So maybe Vincent had been right. Maybe the rules didn't always apply, and he and his team weren't the vigilantes she'd believed. She lifted her gaze to the gunman. "And that's exactly what I'm going to do."

Shea raised the gun and fired.

Vincent's attacker pulled the trigger at the same time his shoulder ripped back from the impact of her shot, but his bullet went wide. He fell with a pain-filled scream, the sound echoing off the rock around them.

"Vincent!" She dashed toward him, gun still in hand, and tugged him to his feet. Taking the majority of his weight, Shea half dragged him to their discarded supply bag and then into the tree line just as the second gunman got to his feet. Her attacker ran for his superior, taking up a nearby weapon as she hauled Vincent to her side. "Come on, we've got to get out of here."

Three shots exploded from behind, but she kept them moving. Blood trickled down onto her hand from his shoulder as she fought to keep Vincent upright. The faster they ran, the faster he'd bleed, but they couldn't stop. Couldn't look back. No matter what happened next, they were in this together.

Chapter Seven

Shea had chosen him.

His vision blurred as they stumbled through the trees, gunmen once again on their trail. Three miles of wilderness and bullets stood between them and the next ranger station, but Shea had taken her chances with him. Given up a shot at seeing her son again to save his life. Vincent pitched forward as another surge of pain crushed the air from his lungs. The bullet was still inside his shoulder, tearing through muscle and tissue. Every swing of his arm, every brush with the trees, was another lesson in pain tolerance, but he couldn't give away their position. Distraction. He needed a distraction. "You could've walked away."

"What kind of person do you think I am? I wasn't going to leave you with them to die." Her heavy breathing hitched as she checked back over her shoulder, the gun still in her free hand. The glow of the fire lit her eyes in an unnatural display of brightness, and Vincent couldn't look away. "I think you were right. The IAB officer's murder you were looking into in

New York goes a lot deeper than the investigating officers reported. The men trying to kill us are cops."

"They're corrupt cops. Part of an organization inside the NYPD I've only heard rumors about until now. Back in New York, I collected evidence from four different homicide scenes that'd been cleaned a bit too well, like the perp knew how to hide evidence. I even found proof a detective had broken into a witness's home in order to intimidate her to drop a complaint against his partner. They're not just cops. They're hit men, but these guys won't answer to just anyone." He locked his jaw against the shooting pain all along the right side of his body as deep snow jerked him down. The shrapnel in his thigh, a bullet in his shoulder and the hit to his head from behind. He was lucky he was still standing. Lucky to be alive. Vincent tried to keep most of his weight off of Shea, but any extraneous shifting on his part only increased the discomfort. Hell, he wouldn't be here if it wasn't for her. "They've got to have a superior officer giving orders. Someone in the NYPD who needed to cover up IAB Officer Walter's murder and put out the hit on me and my team that night. I'm going to find out who."

"The NYPD is made up of over fifty thousand officers and civilian employees," she said. "It could be anyone."

"I didn't say it would be easy." Numbness spread from his toes up his calves. The sun had gone down hours ago; every exhale froze instantaneously on the air. If they couldn't make it to the next station, there was a chance they'd die out here. Vincent slowed. "Why did you do it?"

He didn't have to elaborate. They both knew he wanted to know why she'd given up the promise of seeing her son again in order to save his life.

"They've already killed our pilot, an innocent man who, as far as we know, had nothing to do with your case in New York. I don't care what they were promising. They weren't going to let me walk away. Not after I'd seen their faces." She redirected her attention to the darkness growing behind them. Her voice hardened, the muscles along her jawline flexing in the dim light from their flashlight. "But I pulled the trigger because he threatened my son. I wanted him to realize he'd made a mistake bringing Wells into this."

"I think he got the message." Vincent put more pressure on his injured leg but kept his arm around her shoulders for support. How the hell had she dragged him at least half a mile through the wilderness without showing a hint of exhaustion in her features? She was strong, stronger than he'd originally estimated, but small cracks had begun to surface back at that station. She blamed herself for her divorce, for losing custody of her son to her ex, but when it'd come down to the wire, she'd stepped in to protect a man she'd resented from day one from a group of corrupt cops. She'd been right before. She wasn't the woman he'd built up in his mind. She was better. "Whatever the reason, thank you."

The growl of a distant engine reached through the trees.

"That sounds like an ATV," she said.

And it was closing in.

They didn't have much time before the cops who'd shot him headed them off. It'd be easy to track his and Shea's path through the snow, but ATVs couldn't navigate through these trees. Hell only knew how many of them were out there now, on foot. "That would explain how they found the plane so quickly. We wouldn't have been able to hear the engines from the amount of snow blocking the entrance of the cave."

"I thought it'd take them longer to regroup." Shea rubbed her hands together, then swiped her hand across her face. She tucked the gun into the back of her jeans and covered it with her coat, all the while never taking her arm from around his lower back. "These guys are persistent. I'll give them that."

"Which means we can't go to the next ranger station. They'll be waiting for us there." If they weren't already. He couldn't take the chance. Not after Shea had risked her life to save his. He'd promised to get her to New York to fight for her son, and he had no intention of failing her again. "We have to go deeper into the woods. North. They won't be looking for us there."

"Every minute we spend out here is another chance we don't make it out of these mountains." Wide eyes searched his face. "If we head north, we'll just be saving the guys with the guns the trouble when we die out here from exposure."

"I know what I'm asking of you, Shea." He'd never wanted any of this, but it was the only way. "We have to take the risk. Otherwise, they'll shoot us on sight. I need you to trust me." They still had their supply pack with the extra food she'd packaged and plenty of fresh snow to keep hydrated. The problem would be heat. They'd used all of the kindling he'd had and lighting a fire would only give away their position, and any they found out here would be too wet to catch fire. If they were going to make it through the night, they'd have to rely on each other. Trust each other. Completely. Vincent lowered his voice. This was it. This was the moment that would either drive them apart or bring them together. There was no going back. "We survive together."

"Or we die alone." With a small nod, Shea adjusted her hold around his back and brought him into her side. Her body heat seeped through his coat down into muscle. Her rich scent gathered at the back of his throat as they moved north through the trees as one in some kind of demented three-legged race. Only this race was for their lives. "I hope you're right about this."

"Me, too." Vincent couldn't let his past ruin her future. He'd never forgive himself for tearing apart her life. Not when she'd risked everything to save him back there at the ranger station. But even before then, he'd known he'd do whatever it took to ensure she made it out of this alive. She had to. For the innocents she protected, for her family. For him.

A grouping of flashlight beams bounced in the distance.

Vincent instantly killed theirs to stay hidden but

kept them moving. Damn it. How many of them were out there? A dozen? More? He spun them northeast and took a step forward. More flashlights. He turned back the way they'd come and froze. Shea's uneven breathing registered in the darkness as the lights danced around them.

"We're surrounded." She'd lowered her voice to avoid giving away their position, but it wouldn't do a damn bit of good. The corrupt officers he'd worked to expose back in New York had found them.

But he and Shea weren't dead. Not yet. He could still get her out of this mess. The flashlight beams steadied as the hit men carrying them slowed, closing the circle around them. His eyes had already adjusted to the darkness. He counted eleven hostiles, all heavily armed, and stepped away from Shea as every muscle along his spine contracted with battle-ready tension. A chance to escape. That was all he needed to give her. Vincent slipped his hand beneath the seam of her coat, over the gun at her back, but didn't draw. Any movement on their part could be his and Shea's last, but he wasn't finished with her yet. He studied the single officer stepping forward from the circle of cops, the one Shea had shot back at the station. The SOB's name had pierced through the haze as he'd watched her pull the trigger. Officer Charles Grillo.

"I gave you the chance to walk away, Officer Ramsey, and you shot me." Grillo raised his weapon, aimed directly at Shea. The flashlight beams highlighted the blood spreading across the officer's coat a split second before he pulled the trigger.

She wrenched back, her scream loud in his ears as Shea hit the ground.

"No!" Vincent crouched over her, applying pressure to the wound in her side. Her breathing shallow, her eyes shut tight as she fought against the pain of the bullet tearing through her. Rage—unlike anything he'd felt before—surfaced in a dark, overwhelming current. He focused on Grillo as he suffocated the agony from the shot to his shoulder. The cold had slowed the bleeding, numbed the area around the wound, but now he felt everything. "You're going to die for that, Officer Grillo."

"You got her involved in this. Not me. You could've walked away, started your life over, but instead you decided you wanted to play the hero." The officer swung the barrel of his weapon at Vincent. "We already know about Officer Ramsey here. Who else did you bring into your investigation?"

Containment. That was the only reason he and Shea were still alive. Whoever'd sent these bastards wanted to ensure nobody else had gotten hold of the evidence from Officer Ashton Walter's death scene. Otherwise, Vincent had the feeling Grillo and his team of corrupt cops would've already disposed of their bodies. Blood welled between his fingers as he increased the pressure on Shea's wound. She wasn't struggling anymore, her breathing slow. He'd run that print through the Integrated Automated Fingerprint Identification System—IAFIS—with the help of Blackhawk's network security analyst, which meant his entire Blackhawk team could be at risk now. Because of him. "Go to hell."

He wrapped his fingers around Shea's service weapon, drew and fired.

GUNSHOTS EXPLODED FROM all around.

Shea forced her eyes open, but the haze at the edges of her vision threatened to pull her into unconsciousness. More shots echoed through the night, shadows shifting around her. She couldn't make out anything distinctive. The ringing in her ears was too loud to discern the shouts, but the feel of her weapon at her back was gone. Vincent. He must've taken her gun. Curls slid into her vision as she turned on her side. Clamping her hand over the wound, she pushed upright. Lightning fired through her pain receptors, and she ducked her chin to her chest to keep the scream working up her throat at bay. Where was he?

Chaos pulled her attention to the broken ring of gunmen as another round of bullets pierced the night. Getting to her feet, Shea stumbled forward, free hand outstretched as her boot collided with something heavy and unmoving in the snow. Rocking back on her heels, she landed on her butt in the powder. She clawed for the flashlight discarded a few feet away and swept it over the body, her throat tight. Instant relief coursed through her. One of the gunmen. Not Vincent. She collected the officer's weapon and killed the flashlight beam. He was out there, taking on an entire ring of corrupt cops on his own. He needed help.

Shea straightened again, hugging her arm into her side, and took cover behind the nearest tree. There. Another gunshot exploded from nearby and a flashlight hit the ground. Several more closed in on the shooter's position, and she turned to approach the group from behind.

Stinging agony spread across her scalp as a fist clenched her hair, her back hitting solid muscle and a wall of Kevlar.

"Where do you think you're going?" The man Vincent had called Grillo shoved her forward, and she hit the ground face-first. "You're as much a part of this as your partner is now, and we're not done."

Ice worked beneath the collar of her coat and T-shirt, shocking her into action. Shea flipped over just as he lunged for her again and rolled out of his reach but lost her newly acquired gun in the snow. The wound in her side screamed in protest, but she forced herself to get back to her feet. He came at her, his fist aimed directly for her face. Dodging the first attempt to knock her out, she slammed her forearm into his as he tried again, but she wasn't fast enough to block his free hand. Bone met the flesh of her face. The momentum of his hit twisted her head to the side, her eyes watering from the hit, but she kept upright. Copper and salt filled her mouth. She spit the blood, the inside of her cheek stinging where her teeth had cut into the soft tissue.

"You shouldn't have sided with Kalani, Officer Ramsey," he said. "Because now I'm going to have to hurt you."

Dread curled at the base of her stomach. This man had access to her son. And no matter which way she looked at it, as a mother, as an officer, she couldn't let him leave this clearing. Not without risking him contacting the men he had watching Wells. Shea shot her fist forward, connecting with one temple, then landed a kick center mass to his chest before he could recover. "And you shouldn't have gone after my son."

Grillo stumbled back, but didn't go down, and she raised her fists for another attack. Unsheathing a knife in one hand, her attacker tried to circle around her position. He rushed forward, the knife leading the way, and the snow slowed her down. The tip of the knife cut through her thick coat and sliced across her upper arm. "You have no idea how much I'm going to enjoy this."

Another wave of pain helped her forget the bullet that had embedded in her midsection. She wrapped her numb fingers around his wrist as he lunged forward again, maneuvered behind him, and put as much pressure as she could manage against his injured arm. He let go of the knife as she forced him to double over, the weight on his elbow too much to do anything else. With enough pressure, she'd do irreparable damage. Her heart pounded hard in her chest. Blood pooled beneath her clothing, dripping into the waistband of her jeans. "Call off your men." Only his breathing registered, and she applied more pressure. His groan heightened the effects of the nausea swirling in her gut. She didn't like hurting people. She'd sworn to protect them, but she wouldn't let Vincent die out here while he fought to protect her. "Now."

A rumble of laughter vibrated through Grillo's chest and into her grip on his arm. "You going to kill me, Ramsey? Because that's the only way you're walking out of here. That's the only way you're going to save your son before my guys get to him."

She didn't get a chance to respond as Grillo swung his opposite hand up, grabbed on to her neck, and slammed her into the ground. The air crushed from her lungs, the darkness threatening to consume her all over again. Her head pounded in rhythm to her racing heartbeat as his shadow moved over her, but she wasn't going to die here. Shea kicked out, catching him in the stomach, and clawed for the gun she'd lost a few minutes ago. The metal chilled her hand as she brought it out in front of her and aimed. Her chest heaved as her lungs fought to catch up with the rest of her body. "Don't move."

"You already shot me once, Ramsey. You sure as hell better make sure you kill me this time." Grillo took a step forward, and she pulled the trigger.

Nothing happened.

She tried again, and again, but the gun wouldn't fire. Her lips parted. No. No, no, no, no. Silence descended. Ice worked through her veins, and it had nothing to do with the dropping temperatures. Raising her gaze to Grillo's, she caught the hint of a smile thinning his lips.

"Now it's my turn." He unholstered a hidden

weapon from his lower back, centering her in his crosshairs, and her insides clenched.

She'd been on the wrong end of a gun before in the line of duty, but nothing like this. No one had ever wanted to kill her, to kill one of her partners, to hurt her son. Whoever these people were working for—whoever'd sent them to kill Vincent—they were going to get away with it if she didn't get up. But she'd already lost too much blood. The ringing in her ears was back, weblike patterns at the corners of her eyes. She tried sitting up, tried blocking the path of Grillo's bullet with one hand, but the very idea didn't even make sense. There was nothing she could do. She couldn't save Vincent. She couldn't save her son. She couldn't even save herself. Just as she hadn't been able to after giving birth to Wells.

Vincent. His name echoed in her mind, and the fear holding her in place evaporated. The gunfire had died down. Was he injured? Would she survive long enough to make it to him in time? The man she'd kept at a distance due to her own private battle with the way he'd made her feel these past few months had saved her life out here. More times than she could count. Vincent and his team had skirted the law when it came to their investigations time and time again, but Shea couldn't deny the fact that they'd saved so many lives in the process. Including hers. The thought of this team of corrupt cops burying the forensic investigator she'd come to rely on churned her stomach. Shea put everything she had into getting to her feet, but it wasn't enough. Her knees buckled as a wave of dizziness washed over her. Now it was time to save his.

"You don't know when to give up, do you, Officer Ramsey?" he asked. "Maybe you and I aren't so different after all."

"I took the same oath as you to protect the innocent. The only difference between us is I actually try to hold up my end." Shea rushed her attacker. She'd trained in active shooter situations. The best chance she had of surviving—of Vincent surviving—was to get control of that gun. Dark eyes widened a split second before a wall of muscle slammed into Grillo from the right, knocking all three of them to the ground. The trees surrounding them blurred in streaks of black and white as she rolled down an incline. A scream escaped up her throat as she slammed into a boulder mere feet from where Grillo and another man struggled to their feet. "Vincent."

She scanned the area, counted the bodies around the clearing. Ten. Not including Grillo. He'd taken them all down. Who the hell had she partnered with these past few months? Shea smothered the fear climbing up her throat. He was injured, favoring his right leg and the gunshot wound in his shoulder. Grillo shook his head as though trying to clear it and attacked. Vincent blocked the first hit, then the next, but took the third and fourth directly to the kidneys. Pressing her hand to her own wound, Shea hauled herself to her feet. Adrenaline narrowed her focus on the weapon Grillo had dropped as they'd rolled down the hill. Wrapping her hand around the grip, she brought the gun up.

"I told you I enjoyed a challenge." A hand clamped over her mouth, wrenching her back. Icy metal pressed against her temple, the scent of stale cigarettes and cologne overwhelming, and everything inside her went cold. The cop, the one who'd knocked her unconscious back at the ranger station, lowered his mouth to her ear. "I'd prefer not to put a bullet in you before I've had my chance to pay you back for the new scar to my face. Get rid of the gun."

Hesitation coursed through her, but she'd lost the upper hand. The breath rushed out of her. Tossing the weapon a few feet away, she fought back the nausea and pain swirling through her as Vincent took another hit. He collapsed to the ground, those mesmerizing brown eyes settling on her as Grillo launched his knee into Vincent's face. Her protector slumped to the ground. Out cold. Grillo gathered the discarded gun and shot Vincent two times to the chest. Center mass. Exactly as she'd been trained.

"No!" she screamed from behind the hand braced over her mouth, the sound distorted and desperate. Her legs threatened to give out as the last of her adrenaline drained. Tears burned in her eyes, and she wrenched herself out of her attacker's grasp and launched forward. Only she couldn't reach Vincent in time.

Grillo pushed her toward his partner, his grip bruising.

The officer at her back spun her around and

pressed the gun's barrel to her temple once again. Those perfect white teeth flashed in a wide smile. Dried blood flaked from the laceration at his temple where she'd hit him as Grillo circled around to face her. "Let's talk about what's going to happen next, Officer Ramsey."

Chapter Eight

Vincent sat up, gasping for air. His lungs protested the sharp bite of cold as pain radiated outward from the two slugs Grillo had buried dead center in his chest. He locked his jaw against the groan in his throat as he battled to stay upright. Hell, it was hard to breathe with this damn thing on. Not to mention the impact of two bullets to the chest. Leveraging his back against the nearest tree, he closed his eyes against the soreness as he unzipped his heavy coat to examine the damage. A combination of pink and orange filtered across the sky, giving him enough light to pick one crumpled bullet from the Kevlar vest. The metal was still warm to the touch. Patterns in the snow a few feet away demanded his attention. Divots cut a path around him, south through the trees. And blood. His gut clenched as he crawled the few feet between him and the drops. Shea.

They couldn't have gotten far. If he hurried, he still might be able to save her. He'd gotten Shea into this mess. He'd fight to get her out of it, but more than that, he couldn't stand the thought of working with a new partner on the department's joint investigations with Blackhawk. Couldn't stand the thought of losing her. Not when he was beginning to break past those icy barriers and see the vulnerable, fiery, secretive woman beneath. They'd survived this long as a team. He wasn't about to give that up.

Struggling to his feet, he ignored the slight drag of his right leg and the throbbing in his shoulder as he patted down one of the men he'd taken down. He unholstered an extra weapon, checked the magazine, and loaded a round into the chamber. Numbness had worked through his fingers and toes, but oddly, the rest of his body was slick with sweat. These bastards had taken her, and he was going to get her back. Then he'd hunt down the SOB who'd ordered Grillo and his team to take him out. "Hold on for me, Shea."

He followed the droplets of blood until the trees thinned, every cell in his body screaming in protest. The faster his heart pumped, the more blood he'd lose, but he wouldn't stop because his body was tired. Only when the job was done. The trail ended at the bank of a frozen lake nestled between two mountains, but there was nothing but open views and thick ice out here. Pops and cracks echoed in his ears. Grillo wouldn't have crossed the lake with a hostage in tow. Not with these open sight lines and the chance of falling through the ice. Too risky. Realization hit as strong as another shot to the chest as he turned to study the trail. "The bastard must've doubled back."

He'd been following a dummy trail, made to look as though the corrupt SOBs who'd taken Shea had come this way. Puffs of air crystalized in front of his mouth. Damn it. He had to stay dry. Any hint of moisture led to hypothermia, and Shea was already running out of time.

Movement caught his attention from behind, and Vincent swung around, gun at the ready. Grillo's partner—the one who'd taken Shea at gunpoint—latched onto his wrist and slammed Vincent into the nearest tree. The bastard went for the weapon, and Vincent let him as he swung a hard left directly into his attacker's face, followed by a kick to the gut. The partner stumbled back with a groan, but recovered fast, trying to deliver the same kick. Only he missed. One hit to the kidneys knocked the guy off-balance, but the next to the cop's collarbone resulted in a sickening crack of bone. The attacker's scream pierced the silence as snow fell from the sky. Threading his fingers between Grillo's partner's, he twisted the bastard's hand backward and brought the cop to his knees. "Where is she?"

Laughter mixed with a pain-filled moan. The dirty cop spit blood into the snow a few feet away. "Interrogate me all you want, Kalani. I'm not giving you a damn thing."

Light from the auroras above glinted off a hint of steel a moment before pain seared across Vincent's leg. He released his hold on the SOB but closed the space between them fast. Dodging the next swipe, he pushed the man's arm away with one hand and slammed his palm into the bastard's broken clavicle with the other. Grillo's partner dropped to one knee.

Swiping the gun from the snow, Vincent crouched, pressing the barrel to the cop's temple. Just as he'd done to Shea before Vincent had been knocked unconscious. He ripped the badge off the man's waistband, the nickel silver heavy in his hand. City of New York Police. Detective. A humorless laugh escaped Vincent's bruised chest, resurrecting the ache from the two rounds Grillo had shot into the vest. He'd had a shield almost exactly like this. Before he'd lost everything.

Vincent tossed the detective's badge into the snow. "You know, back in New York, my forensic team and I were called out on a handful of homicides that made us believe the perps had to have knowledge of crime scenes. Everything had been wiped down. The bodies had been moved from one location to the other, which made it nearly impossible to identify the original crime scene, or we couldn't even identify the victims because there was barely anything left to identify. Evidence connected to the cases even started going missing from lockup, which led me to believe the killer had to be law enforcement."

Vincent studied the deep laceration on the side of the cop's head, right where Shea had knocked the jerk out cold, and a rush of satisfaction washed over him. "Of course, I couldn't prove it. You and your buddies back there in that clearing had done too good a job, and nobody up the chain of command wanted to hear that their own officers were involved in the very homicides we were trying to solve." He crouched beside Grillo's partner. "So I took my theory to Internal Affairs. I'm guessing when Officer Walter got too close to identifying the cops involved, your boss had him killed, right? But not before someone tortured him to the point he gave up the source of his intel. Me. That's why you tried to have me killed, isn't it? Only there's something you and your buddies here are forgetting, Detective."

He lowered his voice as the rage he'd caged all these months started to break through the cracks. "I was one of the best forensic investigators in the country, and I know exactly how to dispose of your body without leaving any evidence behind. Your family won't ever know what happened to you when I'm done." A flash of fear contorted the detective's face as Vincent released the safety on the weapon. "So I'm only going to ask you one more time before I pull this trigger. Where is Shea Ramsey?"

"Grillo didn't tell me where he was taking her." Panic outlined the tendons between the cop's neck and shoulders as though he expected the bullet to come next. "He left me here to take care of you in case you came after us again, but I swear I don't know where she is now. Said the less I know, the less could be tied back to us in case Blackhawk Security or Anchorage PD started looking for her. We had orders...that's all. None of this was personal, Kalani. I swear." The guy closed his eyes as Vincent increased the pressure of the gun against his head, hands raised in surrender. The bastard had to know something—anything— that could get him to Shea. "Go on, do it. If you don't kill me, if they think I gave you anything, they'll go after my kid."

The inferno burning through him cooled in an instant, and the gun's barrel slipped down a few centimeters as he processed each word out of his attacker's mouth. "What'd you say?"

His expression smoothed as he opened one eye, then the other, to stare up at Vincent. "The people I work for, they'll go after my kid if you don't kill me."

The same way they'd go after Shea's son if she didn't walk away. Grillo had been in touch with the men watching Wells back in New York. Which meant his team had to have a satellite phone or radio that worked out here between the mountains. If he could get his hands on it, he and Shea had a chance to call in backup and send one of Blackhawk's operatives to intercept the men sitting on the boy. The scent of smoke clung to his coat and hair as he forced himself to breathe evenly. Vincent adjusted his grip around the gun, finger positioned alongside the trigger. "Which direction did Grillo take her?"

"Out there." He motioned with his chin out across the lake.

The pops and cracks he'd heard before… They hadn't been the lake naturally settling. They'd been initiated by the extra weight of two adults moving across the surface of the ice. Vincent lowered the weapon to his side. What exactly had been Grillo's plan? Kill her, then drop her body beneath the ice? Despite popular belief that water washed away evidence, the freezing temperatures would only preserve it out here. Only no one would know where to look for her. Not even the most aggressive district attorney would be able to charge Grillo with first-degree murder without a body. No. He couldn't think like that. Because if he lost her... If he didn't get the chance to tell her what he'd been afraid to admit over the past few months—how she'd been the source of his need to finally solve this case—he feared he'd never stop hunting the SOBs who'd started this war in the first place. He refocused on the detective at his feet. "You're going to want to take some pain medication when you wake up."

Confusion contorted the cop's expression. "What—"

Vincent slammed the butt of the gun into the base of his attacker's neck and let him collapse forward. The bastard would wake up with a hell of a headache, but he'd live long enough to get his kid to safety. He trusted the guy could find his way back to the city. Right now, he had to get to Shea. Holstering the weapon at the small of his back, he put his weight back into his heels as he descended toward the lake's shoreline and stepped onto the ice.

ONE MORE STEP

The ice groaned and snapped under her weight, dendritic patterns spreading out from where her boots landed. An ache flared as Grillo pressed the gun into her back. They must've walked at least half a mile by now. How much farther did he expect her to go with a gunshot in her side? If he didn't kill her soon, the blood loss from her wound or hypothermia settling in would do the job for him. Maybe that was his plan. Other than the bullet lodged inside her, not even the best forensic investigator in the world would be able to tie her death back to him or his ring of dirty cops, but he could remove the slug easily enough. When she wasn't able to fight back. Shea blinked to clear the haze clouding her vision. One more step. She only had to make it one more step.

"How much farther?" She dared a glance over her shoulder, back toward her attacker as her boot skidded across the surface of the lake. Throwing her blood-ied hands out for balance, she held her breath until the world righted. Her body ached, her head hurt, and her heart…she'd just watched it take two bullets to the chest in her defense. Vincent. She cleared the tears—the memories of blood and gunpowder and pain—and forced herself to keep moving forward. The hole she'd struggled to patch over the last nine months after losing her son had ripped wider and more violently than she'd expected when Grillo had pulled that trigger. And now… Now she was being led across a frozen lake threatening to engulf her at any moment with a gunman at her back.

"Until I say stop." Grillo knocked her forward, and her palms hit the ice hard.

She skidded to a stop, exhales ricocheting back into her face. Cold burned the exposed skin of her palms, but she didn't have the energy to move. In the past two days her plane had gone down, she'd barely survived an avalanche and she'd been knocked unconscious and shot. How much more was she expected to endure before her body shut down completely?

"Get up." His boot nudged at her injured side.

Shea bit her tongue against the agony tearing through her, fingertips melting through the thin layer of snow that'd built between her and mere inches of ice. If Grillo pulled that trigger again, would the bullet break through? Could she force him beneath the hardened layer in a last-ditch effort to make it out of here alive? The thought penetrated through the cloudiness clinging to her brain. The effects of hypothermia had already started settling in. Confusion, slurred speech, lethargy, but the idea she could survive the organization that'd killed Vincent long enough to bring them down on her own brought clarity. In a sea of family and friends whose faces had drained of color in her fight against the postpartum depression, his had stood out in full hues. Working cases with Vincent had been a lifeline when she'd needed it the most, his challenging yet easygoing nature the only thing she'd been able to hold on to during her fight for mental health. Bringing her in on the joint investigations had saved her life in more ways than one. Physically. Mentally. Emotionally. She owed him this.

A gust of wind kicked up snow and dead foliage around her, and the hint of something clean, masculine even. She breathed it in a bit deeper, reminded of the way Vincent had so easily closed the distance between them back at the ranger station. How he'd grazed her jawline with his knuckles, resurrecting pulses of desire she'd never thought she'd feel again after her divorce. The memory of his kiss chased back the tremors racking her body now. Vincent had given his life to ensure she survived. She couldn't let it be for nothing.

"I said get up, Ramsey." Grillo fisted her hair, pulling her upper body off the ice, and her hands shot to relieve the pressure—to no avail. He was stronger than her, faster than her, but Shea wasn't going to give up. "Unless you're perfectly happy dying here. I was planning on burying you in a nice spot up here a ways, but—"

Launching her heel into his shin, she braced for impact as Grillo lost his balance and slammed down on top of her. The air crushed from her lungs, but she forced herself to her feet as his gun slid across the ice. She clawed for it, Grillo catching her ankle before she was able to reach the weapon and hit the ice again. Pain receded to the back of her mind as her fight-or-flight response focused her attention on getting free. She rocketed her heel into his nose, heard the sickening crunch, and he released his hold on her.

The ice underneath her dipped with a loud, echoing crack. Her heart rate spiked into dangerous territory as water flooded up through the crevices around her. Shea scrambled back, kicking at the ice for purchase, but it only broke apart faster.

"Shea!" Recognition flared.

In an instant, she locked on the figure running across the ice toward her. Vincent. He was alive. Fear and relief battled for supremacy as she flipped onto her stomach and dug her fingernails into the ice. A sob built in her throat, but she couldn't let the emotions tearing through her free. Not until she confirmed he was real and not some construct her mind had created in an effort for survival.

But with one more gut-wrenching crack, the surface of the lake broke. Both she and Grillo fell through, their screams cut off by ice-cold water. Every nerve ending in her body shrieked in shock as the subzero temperature paralyzed her limbs. She couldn't think. Couldn't move. Strands of her hair blocked the view of the dim light of the auroras filtering down through the hole above, and of her attacker.

Grillo tugged her into his body, squeezing what precious oxygen she'd held on to from her chest. The bubbles tickled her overexposed skin as they raced to the surface. She targeted the gunshot in his shoulder, digging her finger into the wound, and twisted as hard as she could. His muffled scream barely reached her ears, blood spreading around them fast. She wrestled for freedom, but he only held her tighter.

The brilliant dance of lights above the surface diminished. Without air, they were sinking in a violent battle for dominance to the bottom of the lake. There were no guarantees the hole they'd fallen through would still be there when she came back up. Grillo maneuvered behind her, locking her neck in the crease of his elbow. She jerked her knee toward his head as hard as she could, but the water only slowed her momentum. Her body was growing heavier by the second, her movements rigid. This man was a corrupt cop, following someone else's orders. Was he really willing to risk his life to ensure she lost hers? Blackness clouded the corners of her vision, the cold and lack of air leaching her strength faster now, but she wouldn't give up. Couldn't. Not when she'd just started to explore the possibility of getting her son back, of moving on with her life. Of seeing if the connection between her and Vincent was real.

A shadow passed above them.

Grillo jerked behind her. His grip loosened from her neck as the water in front of her face turned red with blood.

She was still sinking, limbs refusing to respond to her brain's commands. Muscled, tattooed arms surrounded her, and her head sank back into a wall of familiar ridges and valleys. Gravity warred with the lightness overtaking her as they shot toward the opening in the ice. Below, the dark outline of her attacker faded into the deep. Her head broke through the surface, lungs automatically gasping for oxygen.

"I've got you." His voice penetrated through the erratic pounding of her heartbeat in her ears, but she couldn't win the fight against the sinking sensation taking over. Her head fell back against one muscled shoulder as he struggled to get them onto solid ice. "You're safe now."

"Where…is your…coat?" Her words slurred, her tongue too heavy in her mouth. Shouldn't he be wearing more clothes out here in the open? He was going to freeze to death. A low thumping filled her ears. Shea fought the exhaustion, the pain, the heaviness, but it was all too much.

"Don't worry about me. Help is coming. Focus on staying awake, you hear me?" Vincent increased the pressure around her middle. Sounds of dripping water overwhelmed the thumping in the distance as he slid her onto the ice, but she didn't have the energy to do anything more than close her eyes. Her body was shutting down, she knew that, but at least she wasn't alone this time. A hint of warmth bled into her face as Vincent framed her chin with one hand. "Shea, look at me. Open your eyes."

She wanted to. With every fiber of her being, she wanted to commit his face to memory. Wanted to thank him for saving her life. Wanted to tell him how working with him had given her a reason to keep going when she had nothing left to lose over these last few months. Putting the remnants of her strength into following orders, Shea narrowed on dark brown eyes tinted with a hint of green in the middle. She'd never noticed that before, the green. She'd spent so long trying to tamp down the way he made her feel when they were in the field together, she hadn't taken the time to really appreciate the man above her. But right now, her body was making the choice for her. She had all the time in the world. Water clung to his beard and hair, the tips already crusted with ice. His normally smooth, tanned skin had lost a bit of color, but the fire in his gaze pierced straight through her.

The pounding grew louder, vibrating up through her legs and into her chest. They'd taken down Grillo and his team—together—but the job wasn't done. Her attacker had contacts back in New York, people he'd ordered to surveil her ex-husband and her son. The organization that'd sent him, it was bigger than she and Vincent could've imagined, but she couldn't protect them anymore. "Find... Wells."

Vincent engulfed her hand in his, pressing the backs of her fingers to his mouth. "We're going to find him, Shea. Together. Just hang on."

The steady thumping pulsed at the base of her neck as rotors and a chopper's frame moved into her vision, but she couldn't win this war anymore.

"Shea," he said. "Shea!"

Chapter Nine

"You look like hell," a familiar voice said.

Vincent breathed through the relentless pain around two cracked ribs, a gunshot wound and the beginning of infection in his thigh, then focused on the woman beside the hospital bed. His stomach dropped. Not Shea. Although he wasn't disappointed to see Kate Monroe—the team's resident psychologist— hers wasn't the face he needed right now. Fluorescent lighting reflected off her blond-streaked hair pulled back in a low knot. She looked good, considering she and her thought-to-be-dead husband had barely survived a serial killer's hunt less than two months ago. Now here she was, her skin almost glowing, but maybe that was a side effect of the pregnancy. Vincent leveraged his weight into the mattress with his uninjured hand, careful of the new sling around his arm, and positioned himself higher in the bed. His head throbbed at the base of his skull, the lights too bright. "You say the nicest things, Doc." He couldn't stop the groan rumbling through his chest as he moved to throw off one of the hospital's heavy blankets. "Where's Shea?"

"Officer Ramsey is resting comfortably down the hall. The surgeon was able to retrieve the bullet in one piece without any complications. She'll make a full recovery as long as she gets the rest she needs. But knowing what I do about her, I don't see that happening anytime soon. That being the case, I'm having Braxton keep an eye on her." Kate crossed one leg over the other and sat back in the chair, that all-too-knowing gaze weighing on him. "You want to talk about what happened out there? About why you used Blackhawk resources to investigate a case, but didn't feel the need to involve the rest of your team?"

"Elizabeth." The network security analyst's name was torn from his mouth. He'd asked her to run the fingerprint he'd recovered from the warehouse fire that night through IAFIS. He should've known she'd push it up the ladder, but he couldn't blame her, either. Blackhawk's founder, Sullivan Bishop, required honesty from all his operatives. It wasn't fair of him to put that kind of pressure on one of his teammates. Or one of his closest friends.

"Give her credit." Kate crossed her arms and sat forward. "She didn't brief Sullivan about the fingerprint until after Search and Rescue recovered you and Shea on that lake. I think she was honestly more worried she'd missed something than anything else." Bright green eyes assessed him, as though she were trying to see inside his head. "We were all worried, Vincent. You've helped save every single one of your teammates' lives in the field. Did you really think we weren't going to do the same for you?"

Nausea replaced the focus of pain. "Everyone I've involved has paid the price, Kate. I've already lost two of my best investigators in New York, and I almost lost Shea out there." The thought spiked his blood pressure as acid climbed up his throat. This was on him. Everything—the plane crash, the bullet in her side, the fact that her son had been put in danger—it was all because of him. Her death would've been on his shoulders for the rest of his life. Just as IAB Officer Walter's would be. "I'm not going to risk the team."

"It's not over, is it? The people who shot you, whoever brought down your plane... They're still out there," Kate said. "They're not done with you or Officer Ramsey."

She was right. Shea had become as much a part of this as he had the moment he'd requested her as his partner on the joint investigations between Blackhawk and Anchorage PD. Had those bastards been watching her all this time? Watching her son and ex-husband in New York? If he'd known whoever'd killed IAB Officer Ashton Walter would come for her, Vincent would've stayed the hell away, kept her out of danger. "I can't tell you anything, Kate. Not without putting you and the baby, even Declan, at risk."

"We're a team, Vincent. You were there for me when the Hunter started closing in on Declan and me. You've been there for every single one of us. No matter the personal cost. Now it's time for us to be there for you." Her shoulders sank away from her ears with a hard exhale. Kate produced a pale manila folder, those inquisitive green eyes centered on the name written on the tab. Even from this distance, he read the label easily: Shea Ramsey. "When Blackhawk and Anchorage PD partnered on investigations a few months ago, I was asked to vet the officers who'd be working with us and get permission for the department to share their psych evals with me. Including Shea Ramsey."

Vincent sat a bit higher in the bed, the pain in his shoulder and thigh forgotten. "Don't do this, Kate."

"I can hear the difference in your voice when you talk about her, Vincent. I've seen the way you study her when you're working together." Kate ran her fingers over the edge of the folder. "I was there when the EMTs pushed you two through the emergency room doors. You were asking for her, even when your body was shutting down from diving into that lake. You're already falling for her, but she owes you the truth—"

"No, she doesn't." He bit back the anger in his voice as her head snapped up, shock evident in her expression. His pulse pounded hard behind his ears in perfect rhythm to the machines tracking his vitals, creating a tingling sensation beneath the skin of his face and neck. He understood the firm's need to vet the officers involved in their joint cases, but nothing—not a damn thing—would change his feelings for Shea. Anything important enough he needed to know about, she had the right to tell him herself. Not some department shrink who'd spent less than sixty

minutes with her and come to some half-baked con-
clusion. Tugging the IV from the inner crease of his
elbow, Vincent swung his legs over the bed. Over
two hundred stitches, a mild concussion from being
knocked unconscious, beginning stages of hypothermia…none of it mattered. He needed to see her. "I
understand you're trying to look out for me, but this
isn't the way to do it, Kate. Not only would I be be-
traying her privacy, but you're also putting yourself
at risk by even thinking about telling me what's in
that eval. I know who Shea Ramsey is, and nothing
in that file is going to convince me otherwise."

The profiler stood. Giving him room to maneuver to the end of the bed, she lowered her gaze to
the floor, the file still clutched in her hand. "Even
if it means she's not in a position to love you back?"

Vincent slowed. Cold worked up through his bare
feet and deep into muscle. From the white tile floor
or Kate's question, he had no idea and didn't care.
Shea had stood by him when Grillo and his men had
given her the chance to walk away. She'd prevented
those bastards from throwing his body into the ranger
station fire and given him something he'd lost a long
time ago: hope. He wouldn't have made it this far
without her, would've never discovered the truth
about that night in the warehouse. She'd given him
that, and so much more. Whether she realized it or
not, he owed her his life. In more ways than one. Kate
wasn't wrong. He'd started falling for Shea Ramsey
a long time ago, and if she didn't feel the same way
because of some deep-seated secret spelled out in

that file… The pain in his ribs flared on a slow inhale. He wanted to hear it from her. "That's not your call to make."

"I don't want to see you get hurt," Kate said.

"You've seen the scars on my back, the stitches in my shoulder and the bruises on my ribs, Doc. Seems all I've known lately is hurt." Stillness enveloped him as he thought back to that moment between him and Shea in the ranger station, before Grillo's men had burned the place to the ground. To the moment she'd blamed herself for her ex-husband cheating on her, for him filing for divorce and for the bastard taking her son from her. There were only a handful of reasons he could think of for a strong, determined woman like Shea not to fight back every step of the way, but for her to sever ties with her family and friends, for her to throw herself into her work more over the past few months than ever before, narrowed it considerably. Only one reason stood out from the rest, explained why she'd been able to show up for her city day after day as though nothing could break through that hardened exterior she was determined to hide behind despite the hardships going on in her personal life. And it'd all started after she'd given birth to Wells. Vincent met his teammate's gaze as understanding hit. He hadn't seen it until now, how much Shea had been suffering all this time. Afraid. Alone. How could he have been so blind? "Better than feeling nothing at all, right?"

"Right." Kate picked up a duffel from beside her

chair he hadn't noticed until now and handed it to him. "Just be careful. With yourself, and with her."

He nodded. Vincent took the bag, waiting for the profiler to leave before he dressed in the fresh set of clothes she'd brought, but he'd have to leave his boot laces untied on account of the bullet wound in his shoulder. He couldn't wait any longer. Wrenching open the door with his free hand, he headed down the hall, to the door where Braxton Levitt—Elizabeth Dawson's chosen partner and father of her child— stood armed and ready to protect Shea. Vincent acknowledged the former intelligence analyst, then knocked as Braxton stepped away from the door before pushing his way inside.

The breath rushed out of him as he caught sight of her at the end of the hospital bed. Long damp hair rested across her shoulders, revealing smooth hills of lean muscle along her back. He studied her wound beneath the bandage in nothing but a black lace bra and an unbuttoned pair of dirty jeans. Muscle and bruising. So much bruising his gut tightened. In an instant, fierce green eyes locked on him, and every cell in his body forgot the haziness of morphine he'd been under for the past few hours. She'd just gotten out of surgery. They both had. Now it looked like she was ready to run. "Where the hell do you think you're going?"

"I'm going to New York." Dropping her hands from the gauze taped at her side, she notched her chin level with the floor. "I'm going to get my son back."

Tension drained from him. Vincent tried crossing

his arms over his chest, only to be reminded one of them was in a damn sling. She wanted to go to New York? Fine. He couldn't stop her, but he wasn't letting her get away that easily. Not after everything they'd survived together. "All right. When do we leave?"

"ANTHONY AND BENNETT have already made contact." Vincent maneuvered into his seat beside her, his clean, masculine scent overriding stale circulated air and body odor. He was trying to distract her. They'd taken off from Ted Stevens International Airport a few minutes ago, along with a hundred other passengers, and right now, she didn't want to focus on anything else other than him. Not the plane crash. Not the fact an organization of corrupt cops had gone after her son and nearly killed her in the process. And not about what her ex-husband would have to say the minute she showed her face at the safe house after he'd told her she'd never see Wells again unless she got herself help. "We'll be meeting your ex-husband, his wife and Wells in a secure location in two days to avoid tipping off Grillo's men. Until then, we'll hole up at one of Blackhawk's safe houses in Brooklyn."

"Two days." Anthony Harris, Blackhawk's weapons expert, and Bennett Spencer, the firm's newest investigator Shea had never met, had both volunteered for the job to protect her son. If Vincent trusted them to protect Wells until she could reach him, then so did she, but her nerves still hadn't settled. Had nothing to do with the chance the plane would go down, or that she'd nearly died in the exact same mountains they were flying over right now. It was Vincent. No matter how many times she'd tried, she couldn't reconcile the vigilante operative she'd known with the man who'd risked his own life to dive into that lake and save her. The man who'd fought off almost a dozen armed corrupt cops to keep her safe. It'd been in those last few moments, with Grillo's arm around her throat as freezing lake water had seeped past her lips, that'd she'd realized the truth. Vincent wasn't who she'd believed. Not the secretive, infuriating know-it-all keen on breaking the rules whenever he got the chance, but more. He'd detached himself from everyone around him in order to protect them, kept them all in the dark about his personal investigation, including his team, but he'd trusted her. Why?

The plane jerked downward, and she couldn't stop the flood of memories crashing through the barrier she'd built as a distraction. The uncertainty, the fear, the terrifying thought she'd never see her son again. She closed her eyes against the incessant shriek of the plane's engines, forced herself to breathe evenly as her heart threatened to beat out of her chest. It was just turbulence. She knew that, but—

Warmth enveloped her hand clutched around the shared armrest, and everything inside her stilled. The thudding at the back of her skull faded, nothing but her own breathing filling her ears as she opened her eyes. Her wet hair had dampened the back of her T-shirt after she'd showered back at the hospital, but that had nothing to with the sensations running down her spine now.

It was Vincent.

He'd pulled his hair back, exposing the fresh bruises along his jaw where Grillo had left his mark— bruises similar to hers—but none of it took away from the gut-wrenching intensity in his expression. Sensations simmered low in her abdominals the longer he studied her, and she suddenly found herself incapable of pretending he hadn't gotten to her these past few months. That he hadn't broken through the haze she'd been hiding behind for so long. The edges of where his tattoos met the scars on his back peeked out from beneath his T-shirt, and in that moment, she wanted nothing more than to trace the flesh with her fingertips. Just as she'd wanted to do back in that cave, buried under all that snow. His exhale tickled the oversensitized skin of her neck, and she couldn't fight back the shiver spreading across her shoulders.

"Careful, Freckles." His words practically vibrated through her, he was so close. "You keep looking at me like that and I might start to get ideas of finishing what we started back at the ranger station."

Heat surged through her. That kiss...it'd been everything she'd imagined and more between them. The desire, the rush of adrenaline, the familiarity despite the fact that they'd practically been strangers before getting on that plane. The backs of her knees tingled at the memory of his mountainous body pressed against hers, the feel of his heart beating hard beneath her palm. She'd done that to him. She'd spiked his pulse higher with desire, but with one kiss, he'd ripped her apart. Helped her remember who'd she'd been, and she never wanted to go back. Never wanted to be trapped in that lonely shell again. If anything, she wanted more. Because of him. What that meant for the future—if they had one—she didn't know, but the idea didn't seem impossible anymore. Not after everything they'd been through. His eyes glittered with brightness as though he could see the battle wreaking havoc inside her. "Thank you for what you did. For…getting me out of the plane, for sharing the food your mom packed, even when it meant you'd starve if I didn't make it."

"Oh, don't worry, she packed more." Vincent released her hand and hauled his bag from between his feet, showing her the row of food containers inside.

"I'll be sure to thank her." A laugh burst from her chest, resurrecting the agony in her side. She couldn't remember the last time she'd let go like this, but the hollowness in her chest still hurt, and her laugh died in a renewed drone from the plane's engines. She set the crown of her head back against the headrest. Flittering her fingers over his forearm, Shea noted the rise of goose bumps across his skin where she touched him.

"I haven't felt like myself for a long time now, but you…" She forced a smile, the pressure of unshed tears building. The swirl of brown in his eyes warmed her straight to her core, drowning the uncertainty clawing through her. He deserved to know the truth after what he'd done for her, deserved to know that her path to healing wasn't over, that anything that happened between them might not end the way they imagined. Not right now. But she would always be grateful for him demanding to be her partner, even if he and his team believed they were above the law. She breathed in his light hint of soap, held on to it as long as she could. Would he still view her as that strong, determined, independent woman he'd described back at the ranger station when he learned the truth? Would he still want to partner with her when all of this was over? Dread pooled in her stomach. Would he still trust her?

"Shea?" he asked.

Shea removed her hand from his arm. Her ex-husband hadn't understood why there were days when she hadn't been able to get out of bed, hadn't been able to make love to him or to take care of Wells. Why she'd thrown herself into her work to the point she couldn't keep the details of her cases straight from working double and triple shifts straight through. Tears prickled at her lower lash line, but she held on to them. The answer was clear. Nobody could understand the mental war she fought to stay present every day. Not even Vincent. "Working with you these past few months saved me. Thank you."

"You would've saved yourself sooner or later." He maneuvered the duffel back onto the floor between his feet, the pain in his ribs evident as his expression contorted. He'd taken two bullets to the chest for her. If it weren't for the Kevlar vest he'd retrieved from one of Grillo's men, she wouldn't have made it back to the surface of the lake. She owed him her life, and she'd do whatever it took to pay him back. "I was just there to get the crap kicked out of me."

"Oh, *that's* why you were following me down the mountain. It all makes sense now." Stinging shot through her mouth as she forced another smile, and she set her hand against her lips. They'd fought off the men sent to kill them two days ago, but the pain of her injuries hadn't lessened. "For what it's worth, I wouldn't be here if it weren't for you."

"Guess that makes us even." He leaned back in his seat, closing his eyes. Couldn't blame him. He hadn't gotten a whole lot of rest before she'd checked herself out of the hospital to get on the next flight to New York. Neither of them had, but she wasn't going to sit around and wait for whoever'd sent Grillo and his men to take another run at her son. She'd already failed Wells once. She wouldn't fail him again. "Blackhawk would be looking for my toasty remains if you hadn't shot that bastard."

"Right." A minute passed, maybe two. The flight attendant's voice from the front of the plane fought to keep her in the present, but Shea only had attention for him. The way his dark lashes rested on his cheeks, how a set of stitches from his fight with Grillo slashed down through one naturally arched eyebrow. She couldn't help but memorize every detail, every imperfection, every ridge and valley of muscle exposed in the light of the plane's dim lighting. All too easily, she envisioned the woman lucky enough to have him all to herself. He was a warrior and a hell of an investigator. He'd protect his life partner until his last breath, just as he'd protected her after the crash, and a knot of jealousy formed behind her sternum. What would it be like to be his? She followed the curve of his neck to the point where his tattoos climbed to the base of his skull.

"You still want to touch them, don't you?" he asked.

How had he known? The pressure of his attention gave her pause, and a prickling sensation spread into her face. She didn't know what to say, didn't know how to explain the compulsion to touch him. Not the Blackhawk Security investigator he presented to the world but the man he'd been before that, the one he kept hidden under sarcastic remarks, secrets and banter. She wanted to touch the cop who'd almost died in a fire in the middle of a crime scene so he could find the truth.

His seat protested over the high-pitched drone of the engines as he shifted forward, close, so close. Dark brown eyes steadied on her, and the hairs on the back of her neck stood on end. "All right, Freckles, as soon as we're safe, I'm all yours."

Chapter Ten

He'd meant every word on the plane.

Shouldering his duffel up the eight stairs off Herkimer Street, Vincent hit the four-digit code into the keypad beside the large black double doors leading into the safe house and motioned Shea inside. Instincts on alert, he scanned down both ends of the street. Her fresh scent chased back the smell of recycled air, diesel and humidity as she maneuvered past him, but he couldn't pay it much attention now that they'd finally made it to New York. Grillo was dead, but that didn't mean he and Shea hadn't been flagged by the rest of his organization when they'd landed. The brownstone Blackhawk's founder and CEO had secured them for the next two days had to have cost the firm well over Vincent's yearly salary, but in this situation, no amount of money was too much to keep his partner safe.

Windows positioned only at the front and the back of the property, military-grade security system installed by Blackhawk specialists, closed-circuit surveillance at the front and back doors recording every car that passed, every face that came within ten feet of the door. The place was located less than ten blocks from the safe house Anthony Harris and Bennett Spencer had secured for Shea's son. He'd made her a promise, and Vincent didn't intend to back down. He'd get her to Wells.

She slid her backpack—the same one that'd saved their lives in the wilderness—from her shoulder, but still clutched the worn strap as she studied the house. The front entryway led into a massive living room with pale hardwood floors and an extravagant old fireplace repainted white, with the entire upper half of the wall made of worn red brick. Gold-and-white art had been hung on either side of the fireplace, attempting to bring the hundred-year-old building into this decade, but there was a physical history to these houses. Vincent heard it in the way the floor creaked as Shea moved toward the turquoise couch positioned at one end of the living room, saw the dust that'd built up on the higher rows of bricks along the wall. Sunlight pierced the floor-to-ceiling glass doors at the back of the house, just beyond the modern white kitchen, making the green of her eyes somehow brighter. In that moment, the bruises faded, the color in her cheeks returned, and shadows under her eyes disappeared. She made broken look beautiful, and he couldn't look away. "This is a safe house?"

He nodded toward the alarm panel set behind him off one side of the entry doors. "We did the security work for the owner a few months ago. When I briefed the team about the case, Sullivan reached out to see if he'd be willing to let us rent the house for a couple days. Guess they came to an arrangement."

"It's beautiful." She skimmed long fingers over the railing of the banister leading up to the second floor. Notching her chin over one shoulder, she refused to meet his gaze. "And the security system—"

"We'll be safe here." He'd make sure of it. Vincent closed the small space between them, his boots echoing from the combination of hardwood flooring and the open concept architecture of the home. He dropped the duffel at his feet. Sliding his hand to her hips, he tugged her into his chest. Stress corded the tendons between her neck and shoulder as he traced his mouth along the outside of her ear, and she relaxed back into him. Ebbing pain spread from the bruises where he'd taken two to the chest, but he'd choose the discomfort over ending up six feet under. Pain had become his friend after the fire, his ally. It told him he wasn't dead yet. "I gave you my word, Shea. I'm not going to let anything happen to you or your son. I'm going to end this."

"No." She turned in his arms, her tired gaze locked on his. Dark hair fell in curls around her face, and he ached to run his hands through the strands to confirm they were as soft as he remembered. "We're in this together, remember? A team. Survive together or die alone."

"This isn't your fight." Grillo and his men had nearly killed her. He couldn't stand the thought of putting her life—her son's life—at risk again because he hadn't been careful enough, but letting her walk away, move on with her life… Vincent breathed in her sultry scent, held on to it, made it part of him, then let it go. He'd walk away to keep her safe, to help her get her life back. No matter what'd happened in the past or what that damn psych evaluation said, she deserved to be happy. With or without him. He spread his free hand over her arm, locking down the flood of desire rushing through him. "Elizabeth can get you and your son new identities. You could go anywhere you wanted, get as far away from this nightmare as possible. You'd be safe. They'd never be able to find you."

For her protection, neither would he.

Shea lowered her chin, and his heart jerked in his chest. Would she take him up on his offer? Would she disappear from his life? Reaching out, she intertwined her fingers with his, then looked up at him through long dark lashes. She pulled him toward the stairs leading to the second floor, her hair falling in waves over her back. Nervous energy pulsed down his spine as they climbed each stair, then exploded as she led them into the first bedroom on the second floor. The same pale hardwood ran along the length of the room with another wall of deep red brick wrapping one wall. The fireplace, similarly painted as the one downstairs, demanded attention near the queen-size bed, but Vincent only had awareness for her, for the hesitation in her expression as she faced him in the center of the big room. Her lips parted, her tongue swiping between them, and his insides jumped. "I'm safe with you."

Angling her head up, she stepped into him, fingers fisted into his T-shirt as she rose on her toes to reach him. Her soft mouth smoothed over his slowly, unsure, but after a few moments worked to claim every part of him. Faster, deeper, desperate. Her fingernails bit into the back of his neck, searing his skin, as though she intended to make them one, but he didn't pull away. Hints of mint toothpaste teased his senses, and goose bumps rose on the back of his neck. Hell, he couldn't get enough of her. She tasted of strength, stubbornness and vulnerability, and she was hiking his blood pressure higher with each stroke of her tongue against his. The bullet wound in his shoulder protested as he leveraged his free hand under her rib cage and lifted her against him.

She wrapped those powerful legs around his waist, easing the pressure in his arms, but he didn't give a damn about the pain. There was only her. Threading her fingers through his hair, she broke the kiss as he pressed her back against the brick wall surrounding the ornate fireplace. Her unsteady exhale skidded across his neck as she framed his jaw with one hand. Desire swirled in the jade-green depths of her eyes. "I'm glad you're here."

"Me, too." He toed off his boots, still holding on to her as best he could. Because there was no way in hell he was letting her go. Not now. Not ever. Stitches pulled tight in his right thigh, but there wasn't a damn thing that was going to stop him from memorizing every inch of her body. "Otherwise I might not be able to get this sling off myself."

"I can help with that." The sensual promise in her voice hit him square in the gut. With a brilliant smile, she straightened her legs, sliding along the length of him until she hit the floor.

She worked her fingers under the straps of his sling, and within seconds, he was hauling the material and his T-shirt over his head. Her eyes widened as she took in the damage from the two bullets he'd caught in the vest, the bloodied gauze taped to his shoulder. But before he had the chance to tell her it was okay, that they didn't have to do this, her hands were on him. Heat tunneled down through his skin, into muscle, as she traced the patterns across his chest. "I don't want to hurt you."

Even if it means she's not in a position to love you back? Kate's words echoed through his mind. The truth was, Shea could hurt him. Worse than any fire, any bullet and any piece of shrapnel, but for the first time since Sullivan Bishop had found him in that warehouse with second-and third-degree burns over 30 percent of his back, Vincent was willing to take the risk. He didn't give a damn what some department shrink had written in her psych eval. They didn't know Shea like he did. He caught her hand in his, brought the tips of her fingers to his mouth. The lie came easily enough. "You couldn't ever hurt me, Freckles."

"What makes you so sure?" she asked.

He slid his hand into the waterfall of hair above her ear. Hell, it was just as soft as before, maybe even more so, but he saw past that beauty to the steel underneath, to the woman who'd risked her life for a chance to save his, the woman who'd suffered so much, yet kept putting others' needs ahead of her own. "Because you protect people. I know you'd never hurt anyone if you could help it. Not even me."

He offered her his hand, as she had downstairs, and maneuvered her through the bathroom door to their left. He hit the light, out of patience to notice anything other than the wall of glass housing a large open shower. In seconds, he twisted the rain shower head on and stripped them both bare as steam filled the space, being careful of her wound. Leading her beneath the spray, Vincent reveled in the feel of her skin against his. Hot water seared his skull and seeped into his wounds, but it was nothing compared to the sensations her hands generated as she traced the pattern of scars on his back. He claimed her mouth again, sweeping his tongue past the seam of her lips, memorizing her, making her part of him. Making them one.

SHE HADN'T BEEN intimate with anyone since her divorce. Not until Vincent.

She could still smell him on her, the hint of soap and man that somehow had been driven deep into her pores. Shea shifted in the passenger seat of the rental SUV as the memories of those delirium-inducing hours played across her mind. After their shower, they'd managed to make it to the bed, and she'd lost herself in him, in pleasure, in escape, to the point she hadn't been able to tell her fantasies from reality. There'd only been him. He'd been all male, full of power he barely contained as he'd pushed her entire body into overdrive. His touch had awakened feelings and sensations she'd lost to the darkness of her depression. Within just a few hours, everything had returned to full color.

They'd talked, laughed, learned about each other. She'd listened as he recounted the night of the fire, how Blackhawk's founder had found him barely breathing and gotten him the help he'd needed. How Sullivan Bishop had recruited him to the firm and promised to help Vincent find the people who'd lit the match. She'd opened up about her brother's death, how she'd become a cop to keep the blood running blue in her family. How she'd crossed oceans for people her entire life who hadn't ever considered crossing a bridge for her, people like her ex. She'd drifted off to sleep sometime in the afternoon, wrapped in his arms. Wrapped in safety. Shea cut her gaze to him in the driver's seat, her breathing steady despite the pain in her side. She hadn't felt that kind of peace in a long time.

Now they were parked outside the warehouse where it'd all begun. The murder scene of IAB Officer Ashton Walter and the two technicians Vincent had lost the night of the fire remained eerily quiet, nothing but her rhythmic pulse soft at the base of her throat. Dim street lighting revealed graffiti painted across boarded windows and doors. A strip of yellow crime scene tape lifted from the pavement in front of one of the rolltop doors with the breeze. Burn patterns darkened the perimeter of the second-floor windows at one end of the warehouse, and her insides clenched. All too easily, she imagined Vincent at the center of an entire building threatening to come down on him at any moment, the flames closing in, the pain. All because he'd been doing his job. If it hadn't been for the man who'd become his boss, would Vincent have made it out alive? She didn't want to think about the answer.

"No movement." Nothing to suggest they were walking into an ambush, but they weren't going to move into position until they were absolutely sure Grillo's organization hadn't been doing their own surveillance. Sliding her hand over his, she studied his hardened expression. "Are you sure you want to do this?"

"I have to. It's the only way to uncover the truth." In her next breath, he reached into the back seat for the pair of bolt cutters and a borrowed forensic case and shouldered out of the SUV. He hit the pavement, and she followed close on his heels.

Shea scanned both ends of the street lined with warehouses, parked cars and strobing fluorescent lighting from worn signage. The district played host to a variety of industries, mostly industrial with lots stretching as far back as the East River like this one. Easier access for deliveries from the docks. Jogging across the street, she followed him to the east side of the building and pressed her back against the cinder blocks while he cut through a padlock located beneath the warning sticker NYPD had sealed against the door. Her instincts told her they should've looped in local authorities, but then again, the men who'd attacked her and Vincent in the mountains had been local authorities. They couldn't trust the police. And if she couldn't trust the very people who were supposed to protect innocent lives, she didn't know who to trust anymore. Except Vincent.

"Got it." The door hinged inward, nothing but darkness and the scent of burnt toast and gasoline on the other side. With a glance toward her, he nodded once before his mountainous outline disappeared inside.

Shea retrieved the flashlight from her jacket and brought the beam to life before unholstering the weapon Vincent had given her back at the safe house. The hairs on the back of her neck stood on end as she shuffled through debris, broken glass and puddles of rain water that'd come through the leaking roof. The small amount of research she'd done on that night reported it'd taken NYFD close to six hours to extinguish the fire. An accelerant had been used, officials narrowing it down to gasoline, which explained the slight burn in her nostrils. She tried breathing through her mouth, focusing on Vincent's outline, and pushed ahead to a cleared section of ashes. Dread collected in the pit of her stomach. Every inch of the floor had been covered in debris, except for the two body-sized areas here. Was this where EMTs had found Vincent's team?

"Over here." His voice echoed off what was left of the aluminum roofing, intense, isolated, and warning slid up her spine.

She found him crouched over a similar cleared section of ash, her beam highlighting the tension in the muscles down his back. Winter in New York City wasn't quite as frigid as Anchorage, but the cold still worked through her clothing and into her bones. Her breath solidified into crystalized puffs in front of her mouth as she redirected the flashlight beam to the floor—and froze. "That's a bullet casing." Warped from the looks of it. At least old enough to blend into the landscape of ash, dried blood and dirt. She wouldn't have recognized the casing for what it was unless she'd been looking in that exact spot for evidence. She scanned the area around the casing but couldn't see more than a few feet in circumference. "Hard to believe the techs or the fire department managed to miss something like that after the fire. They would've had investigators all over this place."

"Without having access to my lab, my guess is the casing is about the same age as the fire. This one is nearly melted into the floor." The sound of plastic over gravel shot her heart into her throat as he slid his forensic case closer and popped the lock. He snapped latex gloves over his hands and peeled an evidence bag from the roll in his kit. Carefully, he collected the casing from the floor and dropped it into the bag, and she couldn't help but watch every move he made. This was what he'd been trained for. He was in his element here, intense, focused, alert, and she couldn't help but admire his attention to detail. "But the casing over there is newer." Vincent redirected his flashlight a few feet from where he crouched, highlighting the metallic shell. "Both were shot from a .38 Smith & Wesson. Same caliber the medical examiner recovered from Ashton Walter's body."

Two casings. Two different time lines. "You think the people who killed that IAB officer might've kept using this location to carry out their executions?" On one hand, that theory made sense. FDNY and NYPD had condemned the building after the fire, making it impossible for another business to occupy the space, which gave an organization of corrupt cops the exact opportunity they needed to carry on with business as usual. On the other hand, using the same location where they'd committed their previous crimes could be considered careless. "I don't see a man like Grillo leaving evidence behind for us to find."

"No." He studied the first casing in the glow of his flashlight. "In my experience, cops make the best criminals." Shifting his gaze to her, he straightened and pocketed the evidence bag. He directed his flashlight to the second piece of evidence. "They know how to clean up after themselves, which means someone could've left this beauty behind on purpose, or the shooter has gotten too comfortable with their overloaded sense of power and figured no one would be able to connect the evidence to them if it was recovered."

Warning screamed through her.

"But Grillo knew you hadn't dropped the case. He knew you'd come back to this scene if he didn't stop you." Shea spun on her heel and swung her weapon high as movement registered from the door they'd broken through. She backed up a few steps, instinctively maneuvering herself in front of Vincent. Her shoulder brushed against his arm, and she lowered her voice. "The casing could be a distraction to keep us here."

"It's a trap." Vincent wrapped his uninjured hand around her arm and tugged her back. Her foot collided with a metal bracket, the scrape of steel and concrete loud in her ears. Exactly what the people who'd followed them would need to locate them. Staticed voices echoed through the shadows. "Follow me. Stay low and use me as a shield if you have to."

"We can't leave the other casing here. It's evidence." She reached for the shell.

Vincent pulled her into his chest and shoved her forward before she had a chance to collect the evidence. "We don't have time."

She switched off her flashlight to conceal their position, gripping the gun in her hand tighter. Before her eyes had a chance to adjust, Vincent was pulling her deeper into the warehouse, her hand enveloped in his. Shouts pierced the sound of her shallow breathing, then a gunshot overhead. She ducked low while trying to keep pace with Vincent, heart in her throat as they ran through the maze of debris and structural damage. How could've Grillo's organization known they were here?

Glass shattered to her right a split second before a bright burst of light and an ear-piercing boom threw her off her balance, but Vincent fought to keep her upright and moving. "I've got you. Just keep going."

Smoke filled her lungs as they raced to the back of the property. There were more flashes, more explosions from behind. The muscles in her legs burned. They couldn't go back to the SUV. If the same people who'd sent Grillo had been surveilling the building all this time, there was a chance they'd already flagged the plates and were waiting to follow her and Vincent back to the safe house. They couldn't risk it. They'd have to escape on foot.

Vincent released her hand, then lowered his uninjured shoulder as he rammed into the only door at the back of the warehouse. But it wouldn't budge. He tried again. Nothing.

The door had to have been padlocked, like the one they'd come through at the front. The voices were getting closer, the smoke from the stun grenades thinning. Shea raised her weapon, bracing one leg slightly behind her as she'd been trained, her weight on the balls of her feet. The windows back here were boarded, nothing but burnt cinder blocks surrounding them. There was nowhere else to go, and she wasn't sure she had enough rounds to take on another team of corrupt cops. Her breath rushed out of her. "Vincent…"

The door swung open, and Shea twisted around to follow him out. Only someone was blocking the door. Two shots. Three. The bullets ripped past her left arm almost in slow motion before embedding into two gunmen who'd broken through the layer of smoke. They both went down, and Shea turned to confront the woman with the gun.

"Hello, Vincent." Long blonde hair draped over the woman's shoulder as she lowered her weapon to reveal a stark face and bright blue eyes. "I told you this case would get you killed."

Chapter Eleven

"Officer Shea Ramsey, Anchorage PD, meet Lieutenant Lara Richards, my former commanding officer." The last person he'd ever expected to see. Vincent pressed his back against the cold countertop in the kitchen of their safe house. They'd barely made it out of the warehouse alive. Wouldn't have if it weren't for Lara, but he didn't believe in coincidence. Grillo's people hadn't been the only ones watching that location.

"Nice to meet you." Shea stretched out her hand with a nod, shook Lara's hand and stepped back. "Not sure we would've gotten out of the building if it weren't for you."

Lara's bright blue gaze studied Shea. At well over five foot ten, with lengthy, model-like features, perfectly straight teeth and lithe movements, Lara Richards had done their forensics unit proud for the nine years she'd been his commanding officer. With her help, his team had an 85 percent closure rate. They'd closed so many cases—new and cold—she was being considered for a captain's position at the Eleventh at the time he'd left the squad. Vincent had even considered taking her job once she made the move. Until she'd shut down his theory IAB Officer Ashton Walter's murderer had come from law enforcement. She'd warned him to drop the case, said his personal investigation into who shot Officer Walter would get him killed. She hadn't been wrong. After the fire, Sullivan Bishop had gotten him out of town so fast, he didn't have the chance to prove his theory to her. Now here she stood. "Can't say I was there by coincidence. I've been watching one of the officers who was at the warehouse tonight for the past few months. Ever since I heard about what happened to Vincent here the night of the fire." Lara turned her attention back to him. "You're lucky to be alive."

Wasn't the first time someone had said those words to him. "What are you doing here, Lara?"

"For starters, I wanted to apologize. I should've listened when you originally came to me about the four unsolved homicides over a year ago. If I had, maybe I wouldn't have lost three of my best investigators that night." She pulled her shoulders back, the lighting from overhead shifting across her leather jacket. She lowered her chin toward her chest, eyes down cast to the purse she'd set on the counter. Pulling a tablet from within, she swiped her fingers across the screen, then handed it to him. "But maybe I can make up for that now."

"What's this?" He scanned the documents on the screen. Case files. The four files he'd been assigned to investigate. Shea stepped into his side, her light scent in his lungs, and just like that, he fell into the memories of her body wrapped around his between the sheets. She'd trusted him for those short few hours, given him a part of herself she hadn't given to anyone since her divorce. He'd never forget that, never forget the glimpse of unfiltered happiness he'd witnessed as they memorized every inch of each other's bodies. He'd never seen anything more beautiful than when she'd smiled at him afterward. His back tingled in remembrance, the feel of her nails tracing patterns across his scars fresh. Unlike the other women he'd been with, she hadn't turned away from him in disgust or refused to look at the damage. If anything, she'd been drawn to it, as though she understood the physical and mental pain he carried.

"After you disappeared, I went back through your files and dug these out of cold cases. In your notes, you'd reported all four scenes had been cleaned by a professional, maybe someone in law enforcement or with forensic training." Lara crossed her arms over her chest, sinking in on herself as she leaned against the countertop. "You couldn't find any connection between the victims other than the first two, an investigative reporter for a local paper and her assistant." Her heels clicked on the tile as she rounded the island, and she swiped her finger across the tablet's screen in his hand. "The third victim was a public defender, and the last a rookie barely out of the academy more than two months. All four victims were shot with a .38 caliber, matching most of the NYPD's service weapons, and I think they were all killed for trying to uncover the truth."

"That's the same caliber of the casing we recovered from the warehouse," Shea said. "So you know there's a group of corrupt cops growing within the NYPD?"

"Yes." The weight of Lara's gaze pinned him in place, and she swiped her finger across the screen once more. "And I have proof. Like I said, I've been following one of the men from the warehouse for a few months now. I was able to clone his phone to see who he's been contacting, surveil his email, access his photos, everything. It seems the NYPD is aware of the group's existence and what they've been doing, but it's impossible to identify members of the organization or bring charges against them without raising suspicion. Any threat to the organization, like these four victims, is dealt with in-house. And they're good at what they do."

Vincent understood that better than most. "Brass has to be involved then. There's no way an entity like this could cover their asses so thoroughly unless they had upper management running the show."

"You might be right," Lara said.

"What have you been able to recover from the officer you're following?" Shea took the tablet, long fingers scrolling through the evidence his former commanding officer had gathered. "Anything we can use to expose the organization and what they've been doing?"

Lara straightened. "As far as I can tell, he's low on the totem pole, more like an errand boy. He and a partner hit up small-business owners for protection money, deliver and collect shipments, surveil and photograph targets. Guys like this follow orders, even the ones that involve executions like your four victims here." She stopped Shea from swiping to the next screen. "And those orders? They're all coming from one source. Officer Charlie Grillo."

Shea's soft exhale filled his ears, and it took everything in him not to bring her into his arms. Looking at the face of the man who'd threatened to kill her son, who'd almost killed her, was bound to cause a reaction, but now wasn't the time to forget why they'd come to New York in the first place. "Grillo came after us in Alaska. He brought down our plane, tried to kill us because Vincent ran the fingerprint he recovered from the death scene of that IAB officer through IAFIS. Ashton Walter."

"You think Walter was another victim who got too close?" Lara asked.

"I went to IAB after you refused to run my theory up the chain of command, and Grillo's people killed him for it. Then the bastards tried to kill me." Dread pooled at the bottom of his stomach as he studied the SOB's service record. Vincent had seen the original homicide crime scene photos before, but now, knowing who might be behind the killings, his blood pressure spiked higher. He could've stopped this, could've done something to keep these dirty cops from endangering innocent lives sooner. Like their pilot, like Shea and her family, his team. Vincent tried to keep the emotion out of his voice. It'd be easy to pin everything that'd happened up until now on Officer Charlie Grillo. There was just one problem. "Grillo was a beat cop. Hard to believe he had the power to keep an entire organization in line on his own, let alone convince his superiors to look the other way. Someone else—someone with a lot more authority—has to be pulling the strings now that Grillo's dead."

"If there is, I haven't been able to prove it." Lara shifted her weight between both feet, her expression never changing. "The two men who came after you tonight have been sitting on that building for a while. My guess is they were waiting for you. There's a chance they don't know their boss is dead yet. Could've just been following orders."

Or the real head of the organization was waiting to finish the job Grillo had started.

"You said you recovered a casing from the warehouse where I found you?" Lara asked.

"Haven't gotten the chance to run testing on it yet, but it could be exactly what we need to bring these bastards down." Vincent wrapped his hand around the warped bullet casing recovered from the warehouse inside his jacket pocket. He'd left his forensic kit back at the scene once the bullets started flying, along with the second piece of evidence, but his instincts said this casing was more important than being simply used as a distraction. He needed to get it analyzed. "But without access to the NYPD's labs, I'll need my team to run the tests, and that's only going to put the rest of them in danger."

"I can get you access," Lara said.

Shea's sharp gasp hiked his pulse higher, and she closed the distance between herself and the counter, shoving the tablet at Lara, and every cell in his body woke with battle-ready tension. "This photo... Where did you get this photo?"

"I don't..." His former commanding officer's mouth parted slightly, obviously taken aback by Shea's panic. "I don't know. Maybe from the officer's phone I've been surveilling. I didn't see how it was relevant to the case, so I... I buried it in the back of the file until I had more time to identify the subjects."

Vincent spun the tablet toward him. The photo had been taken with a phone, nothing fancy, but clear enough for him to recognize Anthony Harris, Bennett Spencer, Logan Ramsey, Logan's new wife and Shea's son. Wells. "We can identify them." He shifted his attention to Shea, watched the color drain from her face. She stumbled back a few steps, but he caught her in time before she hit the opposite counter. Bringing her into his side for stability, he leveled his attention on Lara. "The location, too."

Damn it. The second safe house had been compromised. Shea's family was still in danger. He tapped the information button on the screen to check the time the surveillance photo had been taken, but it didn't look like the image had originated from the officer's phone. It'd been sent to him. Three hours ago. Right as he and Shea had arrived on scene at the warehouse. Gravity pulled at him. Shea had been right. Grillo's people had been counting on him to return to the warehouse, left the fresh bullet casing as a distraction to keep them occupied. So the bastards could follow through with their threat.

"Call them." Shea's voice shook as she stared up at him. "Now."

"What's going on?" Lara studied the photo, confusion evident in her expression. "Who are these people?"

Vincent didn't answer, punching in Anthony's cell number, and brought the phone to his ear. One ring. Two. Before voice mail. Desperation climbed across his chest, into his wound. He dialed Bennett's phone next.

No answer.

THE FOG WAS BACK.

Her pulse thudded loud behind her ears, the floor pulling at every muscle she owned. Everything seemed to move in slow motion. Three hours. Three hours since they'd gotten confirmation the safe house where Wells had been secured had been raided. Three hours her son had been out there, alone, in the hands of killers.

Blackhawk operatives moved around the house, relaying orders, taking both Logan's and his new wife's statements as they patched head lacerations and checked their cognitive reflexes, more men and women trying to get a location for her son. Light from a laptop screen illuminated Elizabeth Dawson's face as she reviewed hours upon hours of traffic camera footage. Elliot Dunham, Blackhawk's private investigator, had never looked more serious than he did right then huddled over Elizabeth's shoulder. Sullivan Bishop checked and inventoried weapons as he barked orders at the rest of his team. Even Kate Monroe, the psychologist, had caught the next plane to New York, her green gaze steady on Shea, but she wasn't in the mood to talk about her feelings, about what was going through her head. She wanted her son back. Anthony Harris, the operative assigned to protect Wells, was still missing, along with Bennett Spencer. The entire Blackhawk Security team had rallied with a single call from Vincent.

Shea didn't recognize the other agents. Didn't care. The safe house had been secure. How had Grillo's organization found her son? Her ears rang, and she pressed the tips of her fingers to her temples in an attempt to drown out the horde of bees buzzing in her head. Wells was supposed to be safe.

"Shea." Vincent crouched in front of her. His warm hands slid up her thighs for balance, but she couldn't focus on him. Not even with him this close. "I need to know what's going through your head right now."

"I should've been there." The words left her mouth without any inflection, a mere ghost of the numbness clawing through her insides, and she winced against the effect. Sliding her gaze to his, she felt as though she were standing on the edge of the cliff. All it would take was one tug, one slip, and she'd lose everything all over again. "I should've protected him."

He shook his head as though to tell her there was nothing she could've done. "We had two of our best operatives assigned to protect him—"

"Then how the hell did this happen?" Anger exploded through her, sharp, hot and unfiltered. Shea pushed to her feet, forcing him to back up a few steps, and slammed her hands against his chest. Then again. Heat seared from her scalp down to her toes, and she gave in to it because it was better than feeling nothing at all. "How did they get to my son, Vincent? I want to know!"

He didn't answer. Only took everything she had to give and more, absorbing each hit as tears burned in her eyes. Wrapping his arms around her, he fought to contain her, to comfort her, but it wasn't any use. She'd failed her son. Again. Vincent tugged her into his chest as the sobs tore through her until she stilled, her ear pressed against his heart. He tangled his hands down through her hair, his cheek pressing against the crown of her head. "Whoever's behind this—whoever sent Grillo—they're trained just as well as we are, they're armed, and they've already proven the law doesn't apply to them." Silence descended in the house, but she didn't dare open her eyes, didn't want to see how many people were watching them. "But I told you Blackhawk protects their own, no matter what it takes, and we're going to get your son back."

She forced her eyes open, nails biting into his chest.

Every single operative in the room stood around them, frozen. Then the ice she'd felt for the team she'd resented for so long started to melt. Elizabeth stood up from her laptop and nodded. Elliot Dunham half saluted with that sarcastic grin she'd come to hate over the course of the past two years. Vincent's former commanding officer took position beside Elizabeth, and Kate Monroe smiled as Sullivan Bishop approached with a gun in his hand. Sea-blue eyes steadied on her. "When someone attacks one of us, they attack all of us, Officer Ramsey. And we're not going to let them get away with it. You're not alone in this fight." He studied the team behind him, then turned back to her. "You never will be again."

A fresh wave of tears threatened to fall, but Shea forced herself to straighten, to wipe the back of her hand across her face. To do what it'd taken her so long to do the first time: accept help. With the entire Blackhawk Security team on her side, the last people she ever would've asked for help, her confidence grew. They were going to get her son back. "Thank you."

"I want a location on Anthony and Bennett in the next minute, Liz, or I'm going to partner you with Elliot to hunt them down on foot." Another nod from Sullivan ended the conversation, and his agents got back to work. He shifted his attention to Vincent. "Get this woman a gun."

The buzz in her head died as Vincent pulled a weapon from his lower back and offered it to her, but she didn't dare meet his gaze when her fingers brushed his. He'd always viewed her as a strong, driven, independent woman, but her weakness had just rushed front and center for everyone to see. She cleared her throat as she checked the weapon. "Did Logan and his wife say anything that will give us a lead on who took Wells? Or how Grillo's organization found him in the first place?"

"Last thing Anthony reported back was his intention to move your family to another location because he'd spotted the same man walking past the safe house three times within a couple hours. From what Logan and his wife stated, Anthony left the safe house after telling them to lock the doors behind him, and that's when the explosion happened. A car bomb right outside the building. It happened so fast, Bennett hadn't been able to enable the security system before they breached the safe house." His hand remained on her lower back, steadying, comforting, but nothing could chase back the fear boiling under her skin. "With Anthony out of the way, he wasn't able to hold off the four-man team as they went for Wells. They were outnumbered and outgunned."

She couldn't breathe. Couldn't think. Shea closed her eyes against the images in her head, her fingernails biting into the center of her palms. Setting her forehead against his chest, she listened to the beat of his heart in an attempt to escape the desperation spreading through her. Fire and police were on scene at the safe house, but without the location of her son, there was nothing they could do. "And there hasn't been any contact from the team that took him."

"No, but..." Vincent's hesitation took on physical form when he didn't elaborate.

The tension only increased as she looked up at him. Living through the numbness over the past year had been the worst experience of her life. She didn't want to fall back into that cloud of darkness. She wanted to be there for her son, to be the mother he deserved, to feel like the woman Vincent believed her to be. But if she lost Wells... "But what?"

"I need you to understand something, Shea. Anthony and Bennett are two of the best-trained operatives we have. Both served in the military and never would've given up Wells easily, even under torture. Anthony's got a kid of his own and one on the way, and Bennett risked everything to find his sister when she went missing." Pressure built in her chest the longer he stared down at her. "The only way they would've backed down was if the gunmen threatened to hurt your son."

She pulled back as the truth hit. "They're using Wells to draw me out."

"You're not just a loose end anymore, Shea." His uninjured hand slid along her forearms, eliciting goose bumps along the way. "Whoever's behind this is targeting you because they know how I feel about you, and they will use any means necessary to take me out."

The breath rushed out of her, heat flaring in her face. "How you feel about me?"

He closed the small distance between them.

"I lost everything that night. After I recovered from the burns, I couldn't trust anyone with what I knew for fear it'd put their lives in danger, which only isolated me more from the people around me, including my team. I was at the point of giving up on this investigation, of living with this guilt for the rest of my life because there was nothing else I could do. Not without risking more innocent lives." Vincent wrapped her hand in his. "Until I met you. You're the reason I want to solve this case, Shea. Working with you these past few months, getting to know the woman who wouldn't back down from any challenge in her way, gave me the push I needed to see this through. Because if I don't solve this case, I don't have a future. And I want a future, Shea. With you."

He did? Her mouth parted, her response on the tip of her tongue. "I—"

"Vincent." Elizabeth's voice penetrated above the buzz of voices and chaos around them. "I've got something."

The world sped up, throwing her back into the present, back into the safe house filled with Blackhawk operatives and Vincent's former commanding officer doing everything in their power to recover her son. Had Elizabeth found a location? Shea pulled out of his grip, heading straight for the network analyst, but couldn't ignore the rush of pleasure rolling through her. He wanted a future with her. "What do you have?"

"Since Lieutenant Richards has been tracking these guys for a few months, she's helped me narrow down a list of possible locations the organization might be using as stash houses." Elizabeth spun the laptop toward Shea as Vincent stepped in beside her. The picture zoomed out to show a map of the city with five circles pinned across the screen.

"Each of these locations has been used as a drop

point for the cash and drugs Grillo's runners collect off the streets. Runners go in with the goods, come out empty-handed." Lara tapped each one on the screen. "There's a chance your son is being held in one of these sites."

They had a lead. Her heart threatened to beat out of her chest, pent-up energy telling her she had to go after him now.

"Then we split up." Vincent took the weapon his former commanding officer offered over the table. "And we don't stop searching until we find him."

Chapter Twelve

Shea's strength didn't come from how much she could handle. It came from how she'd survived after she'd already been broken.

Hell, he'd watched her crumble right in front of his eyes, and there hadn't been a damn thing he could do about it but hold her, but she'd held her head high. Only now the cracks had started to show through. She stared out the back passenger-side window as he studied her from the SUV's rearview mirror, a line of tears in her eyes. She hadn't spoken a word since they'd left the safe house, her expression neutral. She'd thrown those invisible walls he'd worked so hard to tear down back into place the minute they'd gotten into the vehicle.

"This is it." Lara Richards pointed to the dominating shadow of the abandoned power plant on the shore of the Hudson River as the sun rose to the east. Two massive smokestacks demanded attention as his former CO shouldered out of the vehicle. Abandoned since 1963, the Glenwood power plant would make the perfect location for Grillo's organization to operate from, but every window from this vantage point remained dark. No sign of fresh tire tracks as he hit the dirt. Nothing to suggest they had the right location, but Vincent wasn't about to give up. Not with Wells's life at stake. Graffiti covered the original red bricks of the building and boards nailed against the windows. "I followed one of Grillo's men here about two weeks ago. He went inside with a fresh stack of cash for a few minutes then came back out empty-handed."

"He didn't notice you were tailing him?" Hard to believe, seeing as how there was nothing but open water, hills of dirt and rock, and few places she could take cover, but it was possible her suspect had only been focused on making the drop. Shipping containers cut off sight lines to one side of the structure. They'd have to go around to access the main entrance. The odor of river algae and something toxic burned his nostrils as he rounded the front of the SUV. His pulse hiked higher as Shea did the same, and he slowed. She hadn't given him an answer—hadn't said anything—since he'd laid it all on the line back at the safe house. They'd risked their lives for each other out there in the wilderness, trusted each other. In a matter of days, she'd become the single most important connection he had to the world, and she'd deserved to know. If she didn't feel the same—if she couldn't because of her past… His stomach jerked. No. He couldn't think about that right now. Getting to Wells. That was all that mattered.

"Must've been in a hurry." Lara hiked her hands to

her hips, showing off the Smith & Wesson holstered under her jacket. "Guy never even looked my way before he fishtailed out of here like a bat out of hell."

Dirt kicked up around Shea as she bolted around the sand hill straight ahead of them and disappeared behind a grass-green shipping container.

"Shea, wait!" Vincent ran after her, the wound in his thigh protesting with every step. Dust dived deep into his lungs as he raced to catch up with her, but it was too late. She'd already gained a substantial distance on him, not even looking back toward him as she ripped open the door to the plant. Footsteps pounded behind him as he pumped his legs harder. Lara. They hadn't had time to do a proper perimeter search, to evaluate the risk, to clear the area. Shea could be walking into the middle of a—

The explosion knocked him back with the force of a brick wall headed straight for him at seventy miles an hour. Air crushed from his lungs as the fire and debris engulfed the door where she'd gone inside in an instant. He slammed into the dirt, rolling head over heels, as the all-too-familiar feeling of fire lanced across his exposed skin. A high-pitch ringing filled his ears. He fought to cough up the dirt stuck in his throat and locked his jaw against the pain as he rolled onto his back. Black smoke filled his vision, and the ringing grew louder. Twisting his head back over his shoulder, he searched for her. No. Not her. Vincent put every last bit of strength he had left into getting to his feet. He stumbled forward and hit the dirt again. "Shea!"

Her name growled from his mouth.

The bastards must've known they were coming, must've rigged the explosion to trigger once the door was opened. "Shea!"

"Vincent!" His name barely made it through the ringing in his ears. Lara Richards covered her mouth with one hand as she stumbled toward him coughing. Caked with dirt, her normally blonde hair had darkened considerably, the blood from the laceration across her forehead staining the strands red. She clutched him, nearly tugging him to the ground. He had to get her back to the car. His former CO was alive because she'd been far enough back from the epicenter of the explosion. But Shea... He searched the massive hole blown into the side of the building. Had she been lucky enough?

He fisted Lara's leather jacket, dragging her to safety. The bullet hole in his shoulder screamed for relief, but he couldn't focus on that right now. Shea. He had to get to Shea. He deposited Lara near their vehicle. Turning back toward the plant, he forced one foot in front of the other. Fire climbed the boarded windows, scarring the bricks of the plant. He raised his uninjured hand to block the heat of the flames from his face. Images of that night—memories— lanced across his brain. The pain, the smell of gasoline, the screams of his team echoing around him. He physically shook his head to shove them into the box he'd kept stored at the back of his mind for so long, but there were too many similarities. The people responsible, the abandoned building. Only this time it wasn't his team in danger. It was his partner, and he wasn't going to lose her. He couldn't. Her son couldn't. "Shea!"

Still no answer.

The high-pitched keening in his ears subsided with every step gained. Ornate brick fell in chunks at the edges of the hole the device had ripped into the side of the building where the door used to be. Humidity hit him in a wave as he hiked through the opening, loose rubble threatening to trip him up. Pools of water and garbage lined the vast atrium that used to hold the plant's turbines. Windows above created a cathedral-like feeling, trapping smoke against the glass. A steel girder fell from the second floor, and Vincent flinched as the combination of metal on cement vibrated through him. She had to be here. There were no other options. Not for him. "Answer me, Freckles."

Another sound broke over the crackling of fire, and he spun around to narrow it to the source. Had it been her? Brick and remnants of the large wooden door she'd gone through piled against the southern wall after the blast, and he vaulted over the mass in order to sift through the rubble. His heart launched into his throat as he spotted a single ash-covered hand among the debris. There. "Shea." Tearing his sling from his injured shoulder, Vincent groaned against the pain as he worked to clear the debris from on top of her. He didn't care how much damage he caused to the muscles and tissues in his arm. He'd take a hundred more bullets if it meant getting to her in time. "Almost there, baby. Hang on."

"Vincent." Her voice came from behind, and every cell in his body awoke with awareness. He twisted around to find her standing at the opposite side of the atrium. Ash clung to her pale skin, eyes shadowed, but there she stood. Unharmed. Alive. But if she'd gotten enough distance between her and the explosion, who had he been trying to unbury from beneath the rubble? She stepped forward, reaching for him as he maneuvered around the piles of rock and steel to get to her. Relief coursed through him as she buried her head against his chest, his fingers threaded into her hair. She shook her head. "He's not here."

"It's going to be okay. We're going to find him. I promise." He'd already deduced that fact after the effects of the explosion had cleared from his head. Whoever'd taken Wells wouldn't risk harming him until they got what they wanted. Her. In order to hurt him. Pushing her back, he searched her for fresh blood, injuries, anything that contradicted the fact she was standing here, unharmed, after the blast. "How did you get clear from the explosion so fast?"

"It doesn't matter." Her watery green gaze, brighter when surrounded by dark ash and dirt, shifted to the body beneath the rubble. In an instant, she slid her attention back to him, her hand pressed flat over his heart. "Wells is still out there somewhere, and I need to find him." She leaned her cheek into his palm, closing her eyes. "But after what just happened, after everything that's happened over the past few days, you should know I..." His beard bristled as she opened her eyes and trailed a path down toward his chin with one hand, his nerve endings burning. "I want a future with you, too."

His heart skipped a beat. "Really?"

"Yeah." Her nod was all the confirmation he needed. Shea pushed her hair from her face, that brilliant smile tunneling through the nightmare of the last four days and straight into his core. His wounds, the organization they were up against, the case he hadn't been able to solve for over a year, none of it mattered. This, right here. She mattered. There wasn't anything he wouldn't give for her. "I was lost, for a really long time, but working with you on the joint cases these past few months has been the most frustrating and exciting time in my life." Nervous energy played across her expression. "There's something I need to tell you before we decide to give whatever this is between us a chance."

"Shea." He smoothed the pad of his thumb beneath her eyes, ash and dirt smearing across her soft skin. "I don't care what's in your psych eval. I told you before. There's nothing you can do or say to convince me you're not the woman I've gotten to know over these last few months."

Surprise contorted her expression, and she stepped out of his hold. Her mouth parted, eyes narrowing at the edges, and Vincent realized his mistake. Too late. "What did you just say?"

VINCENT HAD ACCESS to her department psych eval? No. Not possible. That information was privileged. In order for him to get his hands on it...

"Blackhawk Security got a copy of my eval." The words left her mouth no louder than a whisper, her voice hollow. "They wanted insurance the officers you'd be working with during the joint investigations were trustworthy or mentally stable, right? Even though all that information falls under doctor-patient confidentiality." The blood drained from her face, gravity pulling her body toward the ash-covered floor. She'd managed to avoid getting blown up after charging through the front door. She'd spotted the explosives around the doorframe and pulled Grillo's man in front of her as a shield before the blast, but right now she felt as though the organization that'd kidnapped her son—that'd tried to kill her—had succeeded. Her stomach soured, bile working up her throat. She shook her head to dislodge the truth. "But this is the kind of thing Blackhawk does, isn't it? You and your team skirt the law when it suits you. Anything to solve the case. Everyone else be damned."

Including her. What had Sullivan Bishop said back at the safe house? That she was one of them, that they protected one another? Rage burned hot and fast in her veins. They protected one another, all right, but she'd never been part of their team. She'd been a resource, an access point in which to collaborate with Anchorage PD and evaluate sensitive information for investigations. Nothing more. But what hurt more? Vincent had been an integral part the entire time.

"Everything you said is true. Our psychologist vetted the officers we recruited for the task force with the department's permission in case one of our investigations went sideways." He tried to close the distance between them, but she countered his every step. A combination of hurt and surprise contorted his expression, but she didn't have the energy or the motivation to let it affect her. Not anymore. He dropped his shoulders away from his ears, almost as though in defeat. "Yours was one of the evaluations, but Shea, I swear I never read your file."

"I don't believe you. I know exactly the kind of lengths you and your team will go to to get what you want, Vincent. Why should this be any different?" If he hadn't read that file, he wouldn't have known about the one thing that'd kept her from giving herself over to him fully, that'd resurrected her fear of him walking away every time she'd wanted to tell him the truth. Smoke burned her nostrils, sweat building at the base of her spine as the embers continued to consume the plant. Everything inside her ached, head pounding in rhythm to her pulse. She'd trusted him, had started to imagine a future with him, believed him when he'd said he'd never turn his back on her. He'd taken that trust and used it against her. Same as her ex-husband had when she'd found him in bed with his assistant, just before he'd walked away with her son. Same as her family and friends had before deciding she wasn't worthy of their help or love. "Was that why you requested me as your partner all those months ago? Because you thought you could use my mental health in order to leverage me to cooperate?"

He took another step toward her, but this time she held her ground. "What? No. I would never—"

"Don't lie to me." She wouldn't let him see how much it hurt. Instead, Shea gave in to the familiar explosion of rage she'd tried to keep locked away. Anything to help her sever the connection they'd forged over the last few days, to keep herself from admitting how hard she'd fallen for him. The muscles in her jaw ached as she steadied her gaze on his. "How long have you known?"

"I had an idea of what you'd been struggling with that night in the ranger station. You kept trying to convince me you weren't the woman I thought you were, and I didn't want to believe you. Nothing you said lined up with what I saw during our joint investigations." Vincent's voice deepened, his throat working to swallow. "But Kate confirmed it in the hospital when she confronted me about how I feel about you. She said you might not ever be in a position to love me back."

Shock of his admission rolled through her, but she did everything she could to make sure her expression didn't change. He loved her. But that wouldn't alter the fact that she couldn't trust him—or his team—ever again. Her fingernails bit into her palms as loss tore her apart from the inside, a distraction to keep the tears at bay. She'd wasted enough time. Wells was still out there. Alone. Afraid. Clearing her throat, Shea kept her head high when all she wanted to do was sink onto the floor as the power plant collapsed around her. She stepped into him, ignoring the rush of heat his body elicited inside, and drove her hand into his jacket pocket to extract the SUV's keys. She clutched them harder than necessary, forcing herself to stay in the moment, then looked up at him. "Kate was right. I won't ever be in a position to love you, Vincent. Not as long as I can't trust you."

"Shea, don't do this." He locked his hand around her arm. "If you go after Wells alone, they're going to kill you, and I won't be there to stop them. Please. Let us help you find him."

"I've always been alone." That'd been a truth she'd accepted until she'd crash-landed in the middle of the Alaskan wilderness with a forensic technician who'd given her a glimpse of real happiness. But as she'd come to realize too late, it'd been a fantasy all along. She ripped her arm out of his grip, her skin burning where he'd touched her. "Grillo gave me the chance to walk away, and as soon as I recover my son, I'm taking it. I'm sure your team can give you a ride back and help you bring down his organization without me."

Shea maneuvered around him and headed for the hole blasted into the side of the power plant. Tendrils of fire climbed around the edges but not hot enough or dangerous enough to stop her from escaping. The weight of his attention on her back crushed the air from her lungs. The tears fell then, but she wouldn't turn back. There was nothing to go back to. Wrenching the SUV's door open, she caught sight of him positioned where the door she'd gone through used to stand. Heat waves distorted his features, his intensity burning hotter than the flames around him. It must've been difficult for him to charge into that fiery building for her after what'd he'd already been through, but right now, she couldn't let herself care. She climbed inside the vehicle and hit the button to start the engine. Dirt kicked up behind the SUV as she sped from the scene, entirely focused on the road. Elizabeth had messaged them a list of all of the stash houses the network analyst and Lieutenant Lara Richards had narrowed in on as part of Grillo's operation. She'd hit every single location until she found her son.

Lieutenant Richards… Shea hadn't seen Vincent's former CO since she'd breached the power plant. Lifting her foot from the accelerator, she let the SUV slow to a crawl before turning onto the main road that'd take her to the next location. Had there been another operative stationed at the power plant, one who could've gotten to Lara while Vincent had torn Shea's heart from her chest? She hesitated at the thought of turning back around, of facing the man who'd betrayed her after what'd just happened, but Lara deserved better. The lieutenant had helped them every step of the way with the investigation, handed them leads Blackhawk Security wouldn't have been able to find, offered to run testing on the casing she and Vincent had recovered from the warehouse…

Shea stepped on the brakes, her weight shifting forward as the SUV skidded to a stop. Leather protested under her hands as she tightened her grip on the steering wheel. Lara Richards had been at the warehouse last night, arriving within moments of Grillo's men closing in, and shot two corrupt officers with a .38 Smith & Wesson without hesitation. So why hadn't NYPD dispatched homicide detectives or

IAB investigators to get her and Vincent's statements about what'd happened? Why hadn't Lara called it in?

Lara's weapon was standard issue for the NYPD, and the lieutenant had admitted to taking a keen interest in the organization's movements over the last few months. To the point she seemed to know more about Grillo's crew than the NYPD did. What if her involvement in the case was more than an attempt to make up for turning her back on Vincent before the fire? He'd theorized the killer who'd shot the four original victims and the IAB officer must've had forensic experience. As a lieutenant, Lara Richards would have authority over Grillo. She could've ordered him and his team to bring down her and Vincent's plane, to take care of loose ends.

Shea swallowed around the tightness in her throat. Only problem was everything running through her head right now would be viewed as circumstantial evidence, but if she was right, Lara Richards had means, opportunity and motive to take out both her and Vincent.

She had to go back. She had to at least explain the possibility to Vincent. Slamming the SUV into Reverse, Shea hooked her arm around the passenger-side headrest. And gasped.

"Hello, Officer Ramsey." Cold metal pressed against her temple as Lieutenant Lara Richards straightened from the second row of seats. Dirt was caked to her leather jacket and jeans, the collar of her white T-shirt underneath crusted with blood from the wound across her forehead. Blonde hair slid over her shoulder as she leaned in closer, close enough for Shea to catch hints of smoke and perfume. "Hand over your sidearm, please."

Her breath sawed in and out of her chest. She shifted her attention to the weapon Vincent had given her back at the safe house, fingers tingling. Could she get to it fast enough? "I should've seen it sooner. You're not investigating Grillo's organization. You *are* Grillo's organization."

"This isn't how or when I wanted to reveal myself, but you and Vincent just wouldn't leave well enough alone. Not even after I tried to have you killed." Lara reached over Shea's shoulder, unholstering the weapon herself, before setting it on the back seat beside her. "No one has gotten as close as you and Vincent. I'd normally take care of the problem myself, as I did with all the others, including IAB Officer Walter, but you have something I want."

The casing. Lara was trying to clean up her own mess. "And you have my son."

"I'll make you a deal." Lieutenant Richards pushed the barrel into Shea's temple, breaking skin. "You tell me where Vincent is keeping the casing he recovered from the warehouse last night, and I'll let you see your son again."

Chapter Thirteen

He didn't know how he was going to win her back, but he sure as hell was wasn't going to lose her. Vincent stepped away from the nearest explosive device, gun in his uninjured hand. Blocks of C-4 had been wired to detonate when triggered above every door and window of the plant. But as far as he could tell, this location had never been used as a stash house or a place Grillo's organization would use to hold a nine-month-old boy hostage. Warning settled between his shoulder blades. One signal. That was all it would take to make it so the best medical examiner in the state couldn't identify his remains, but rigging one of their own places to blow didn't make sense.

Unless it'd been a setup from the beginning.

He bit back the curse on the tip of his tongue. Shea was out there on her own trying to track down her son. He'd screwed up. Even if he hadn't read her department psych eval directly, he'd given her mistrust weight by not telling her his employer had access to it in the first place. She'd trusted him, and all he'd done was prove she was right about him, about his team.

Sullivan Bishop had founded Blackhawk to take cases the police couldn't or wouldn't prioritize, asking his operatives to do whatever it took to protect the client. Including skirting the law as Shea had accused. Vincent had solved dozens of cases over the past year by living up to that standard. He'd made a difference he hadn't been able to as an NYPD officer, but in the end, the same principle that'd given him purpose— that had saved so many lives—had driven her away.

She deserved better. Better than him.

She'd survived the worst kind of mental torture he could imagine for a new mother to suffer through, but now, looking back, he understood it wasn't the fact that Blackhawk had access to her psych eval at all. Her desperation to fight for custody of her son, her determination to lose herself in her work, the walls she'd built to keep everyone out. It was all part of the fear that everyone would know—that he would know—how weak, worthless, she'd convinced herself she'd become. But Vincent knew the truth.

Underneath that fear of failure, past her invisible defenses and the guarded expressions, there was a woman who'd never backed down from a challenge, even when she'd lost everything that mattered to her. She was charming, intelligent, authentic and gracious and had more ambition than anyone he'd come across. She wasn't weak. She wasn't worthless. She was everything he'd ever wanted, everything he'd needed to keep him going these past few months. She was... the woman he needed in his life.

She'd brought out the best in him, kept him from

isolating himself even further, from losing all contact with the people he cared about in the name of protection. By working at his side, she'd kept him in reality when all he'd focused on the past year was the case that'd almost gotten him killed. He loved her. And it didn't matter if she couldn't love him back. He owed her his life. That would be enough for him.

Vincent moved farther along the atrium floor, kicking rubble and garbage out of his way. Scaffolding lined the walls, an impressive collection of cogs courtesy of the Philadelphia Alfred Box & Co. The crane demanded attention from above, rust and buildup clear from thirty feet below. Grillo's organization might not be holding Wells here, but the officers involved had been here. They'd rigged every entrance and exit with explosives and left a man behind to detonate. It was Locard's principle. Everyone left a piece of themselves behind and took something with them from a crime scene. Fingerprints, fibers, DNA evidence. Which meant there had to be something here.

This was what he'd been trained to do. Search for the evidence, analyze the scene, find the suspect. He cleared a set of stairs leading up to the second level but slowed. "Evidence."

Holstering his weapon, he pulled the warped casing he'd collected from the warehouse from his jacket pocket. Sunlight reflected off the bronze, even through the plastic evidence bag. He'd left his forensic kit back at the warehouse, but there were other ways to lift prints from evidence in the field. Vincent wound his way back into the atrium and out through a side door facing the Hudson. Collecting a handful of fine dirt, he settled on the edge of an old set of stairs that protested under his weight. A light breeze pushed his hair into his face, his throat burning from the instant drop in temperature. Perfect conditions.

He ripped the adhesive section from the evidence bag, keeping it close, but froze. The second he touched the casing without gloves, it'd be inadmissible in court. Whatever defense attorney would go to bat for these bastards could argue the evidence had been tampered with, and in a case like this, where a large part of the NYPD could possibly be linked to Grillo's organization and charged with a slew of felonies, he'd land behind bars right beside them.

Then again, he wasn't part of the NYPD anymore, and there was nothing he wouldn't do to protect Shea and her son.

He extracted the casing with his index finger and thumb, keeping contact with the metal to a minimum. His shoulder protested as he tried to grip the evidence, but this was the only way to prove what his instincts had been telling him since he and Shea had barely escaped with their lives from the warehouse last night. He picked up the dirt with his free hand and held it above the casing. Then let it go. The wind did exactly as he'd hoped, redirecting most of the sand away from the casing, but the few grains that'd made contact with the bronze clung tight to the oils that whoever'd handled the evidence had left behind. Fingerprint ridges formed in arcs, whorls and loops, but abruptly stopped at one edge as though the print was only a partial.

Just like the fingerprint he'd recovered from the gas can the night of the fire.

Whoever'd loaded this casing into their weapon's magazine and been at that scene the night he'd lost two teammates to the fire. Maybe had even lit the match. The smooth surface of the print on that side meant one thing: whoever'd started the fire that night in the warehouse had burned themselves badly enough they'd lost half of their fingerprint.

His own scars tingled as though remembering what that kind of pain had felt like, which was impossible. He'd lost feeling in almost all the nerve endings in over 30 percent of his injury site. Except when Shea had run her hands over his skin. Hell, he'd never meant to betray her trust. He had to get her back, had to prove he was the one person in this world she'd be able to count on.

But first, he had to bring down the organization Grillo worked for. Dropping the casing inside the evidence bag, he shoved it back into his pocket and retrieved his phone. Every rotation he forced his shoulder to make shot pins and needles down to his fingers, but nothing—not even a gunshot wound—would stop him from getting to Shea. He brought the phone to his ear, and the line connected. "Elizabeth, I need you to send me the location of my SUV and a replacement vehicle to the Glenwood power plant."

Making his way around the side of the building, toward where he'd parked their rental SUV, Vincent scanned the landscape. Where was Lara? He'd left her right here. He dropped the phone away from his ear and spun full circle. No movement. No body.

"Vincent?" Elizabeth's voice barely reached his ears over the rush of wind coming across the river, and he brought the phone back to his ear.

"Yeah, I'm here." Two sets of footprints led away from the plant, but he only recognized one of them belonging to Shea. Dark drops of blood peppered the second set. Had to be Lara. She'd suffered a laceration across her forehead after the explosion. From where the SUV's treads indented the ground, he traced her to the back passenger seat of the vehicle. Confusion rushed through him. Lara wouldn't climb into the back seat in order to catch a ride with Shea. She'd take the front. He gripped the bullet casing in his pocket, the muscles in his jaw ticking with his heartbeat. Something wasn't right. Shea had every reason to get the hell away from him, but Lara? She wouldn't have left him out here without a good reason. "Have you heard anything from Lieutenant Richards or Shea Ramsey?"

"Let me get this straight. You need a replacement SUV because yours suddenly went missing, and you lost both of the officers you took with you?" Keyboard strikes filtered through the line. "I think this is going to put a strain on the relationship Blackhawk has with law enforcement."

He searched the area again to make sure he hadn't missed anything, but there was no sign of either of them. "It's a long story."

"Only Sullivan has checked in. He recovered Bennett at one of the addresses Lieutenant Richards gave us for possible stash house locations," Elizabeth said. "They did a number on him before leaving him to die, but he'll pull through. Autumn is flying in from Anchorage as we speak. Still waiting for Kate and Elliot to call with what they've found at the other two addresses I gave them."

Damn it. Which meant Anthony Harris was still out there. Without him, they might not be able to ID the bastards who'd taken Shea's son. He unclenched his hold from around the evidence bag. Unless... Vincent had already come into contact with the suspect. "I'm going to have to call you back."

He ended the call, studying the footprints in the dirt. Lara's wound hadn't been bad enough that she should've climbed into the back seat of the SUV. Pocketing his phone, he dropped to one knee, his shrapnel wound screaming in protest. He'd recovered the same print from both the gasoline can the night of the fire and the evidence from the warehouse. The suspect had been at both locations, but unless Grillo's organization had been surveilling the murder scene of that IAB officer, which was possible, no one in the NYPD had known Vincent and his teammates were investigating the case on their own. No one except their commanding officer. He scanned the property again. The lack of tire tracks, the explosives... They'd been lured to this location.

His stomach shot into his throat, and he unholstered his weapon with as little contact with the metal as possible. He'd gone to Lara with his theories over a year ago, but she'd shut him down despite the evidence he'd handed over. Solid evidence. Was it possible she hadn't been at the warehouse last night by chance? That'd she'd been waiting for him and Shea all along? That she'd been the one to send Grillo and his team to sabotage their plane? Vincent ran the same test on the barrel of his weapon as he had with the casing, the gun Lara had handed him back at the safe house. Once the dust had settled, the pieces of this murderous puzzle slammed into place. The second print, her middle finger. It was an exact visual match to the others he'd lifted.

Lieutenant Lara Richards was part of the organization bent on killing him.

"Damn it." She'd inserted herself in the investigation to stay a step ahead of them. Now she had Shea in the vehicle with her. He extracted his phone once again and hit redial. The line connected instantly. He didn't bother with small talk. He was running out of time to save the woman he loved and her son. "I know who kidnapped Shea's son, and I know where she's headed."

A GROAN SLIPPED past her lips, waking her from a dreamless unconsciousness. How many times were people going to hit her over the head before her brain decided it'd had enough? Rolling onto her hands at the small of her back, Shea blinked up at the pattern of lights dancing over a white ceiling as the crevices in the floor rubbed against the newest addition to cuts on the back of her head. She'd been restrained in cuffs. Lara... The lieutenant had knocked her unconscious with the butt of her weapon. The floor jerked beneath her, and her entire body slid across the slick surface. Not a floor. The cargo space of a van. The pattern of lights on the ceiling was headlights from oncoming cars.

She struggled against gravity in order to sit up. Keeping out of sight of the rearview mirror in case the driver spotted her through the thick metal mesh separating the driver's cab from the cargo area, she leveraged her boots against one side of the van. She pressed her back against the other and positioned herself behind the driver's seat. She'd always kept a spare handcuff key in her back pocket. If she could reach it, she—

"I know you're awake, Officer Ramsey. I can hear the change in your breathing." That voice. No. It wasn't possible. She'd watched him sink to the bottom of that lake. "Looking for something?" Officer Charlie Grillo held up a set of handcuff keys for her to see. "As long as you're in those cuffs, I have the chance to pay you back for the damage you and your partner inflicted to my men."

"You couldn't kill me back in Alaska." Every instinct she owned screamed warning for her to get out of the van right then, but when she drove her hands into her back pockets, she only met denim. Shea searched for something—anything—she could use to pry her hands out of the cuffs or as a weapon, but the van had been emptied, presumably to keep her right where Grillo wanted her. She bit back the panic rising, forced herself to keep her voice even. "What makes you think this time will be any different?"

"Because no one is coming to save you this time, Shea." His use of her name—almost intimate—raised the hairs on the back of her neck. "I gave you the chance to walk away back in those woods. You should've taken it."

Those same words echoed in her mind as she thought back to her last moments with Vincent. He'd hurt her far more than Logan had when he'd left, almost as much as it'd hurt when she'd been served with custody papers for Wells. Blackhawk Security had knowingly gotten her psych eval without her knowledge and proven her assumptions about the way Vincent and his team worked. But the worst part? If she was being honest with herself, it wasn't the fact that they'd skirted the law. Vincent alone brought down almost a dozen corrupt cops in those woods to save her life without hesitation and promised to do whatever it took to bring her son home. She hadn't questioned the lengths he'd go to protect her for a single moment.

No. The worst part was he no longer saw her as the woman he'd convinced himself existed, the one she'd desperately wanted to be for him. Strong, full of passion, valuable to their joint investigations, determined, worthy of a man like him. Happy. He'd made her feel as though she had become the center of his entire world, but now that he knew the truth, that she couldn't measure up to the woman he may have built her up to be in his head, it'd be impossible to get that feeling back. No matter how many times he tried to convince himself otherwise, he couldn't love her. He didn't even know her. Not the real her.

The van slowed before taking the next turn, bringing her back into the moment. No windows. Nothing that could tell her where they were without exposing herself to the driver. She closed her eyes against the sudden nausea churning in her stomach. Grillo was supposed to be dead. She had to get out of here. She had to get to Wells. Setting the crown of her head back against the side of the van, she caught sight of wiring framed along the back doors leading into a junction box a few feet away. She forced herself to take a deep breath, then slowly pressed her hands into the floor behind her to scoot toward it. The wires most likely led to the van's brake lights and blinkers. If she could signal the drivers behind them, she might have a chance. She twisted her head toward the driver's cabin as she moved. "Where is my son?"

The moment she got free of these cuffs and escaped, she was going after him.

"Don't worry, Shea. Lieutenant Richards will take good care of your boy." Grillo took a sharp right, pressing her into the frame. "Little guys like that sell for a lot of money nowadays. Plenty of needy couples willing to pay top dollar for a chance at being parents. Think of it this way. We're doing you a favor. He'll have a good life, never knowing you weren't strong enough to take care of him yourself."

"What?" The floor felt as though it'd disappeared out from under her, and even after a few seconds, she couldn't regain her footing. They were going to put her son up for illegal adoption, and she'd never see him again. Blinking against the fog threatening to consume her, Shea pulled at the cuffs around her wrists until she drew blood. It trailed down the back of her hands, dripping from her fingertips. The pain forced her to focus. No. They weren't going to sell her son to the highest bidder. She'd fight for him until she couldn't stand. She'd sacrifice everything to get him back. Because she was strong enough, damn it.

Shea worked her palms beneath her glutes, ignoring the strain in her wrists until she was able to maneuver them to the backs of her thighs. In seconds, she threaded her feet through the hole her arms made and brought her hands to the front of her body. She slid to the breaker box beside the doors and pried it open. "You read my department psych eval."

She had to keep him talking, distracted.

"Part of the job. I've seen what depression has done to a few guys on the force. Most of them ate their guns at the end, leaving their families with nothing but debt and anger, but you didn't. That says something," he said. "You're a good cop, Ramsey. I think you would've done the NYPD proud given the chance. Unfortunately, we'll never find out if that's true."

The van slowed. Grillo was going to finish the job he'd started back in those woods. Tie up the loose end. Her.

Adrenaline dumped into her veins. Diving her hand into the mechanical box, she gripped a white metal lever that would cut power to the vehicle and pressed her feet against the doors as she pulled it back as hard as she could. The metal groaned loud in her ears, then snapped, and she fell back. She didn't have time to pick the lock on the cuffs. The best chance she had in getting to Wells in time was survival. And she'd do whatever it took. Her breathing shallowed as her nerves hiked into overdrive with awareness.

"What the hell?" Grillo hit the brakes.

Momentum threw her deeper into the van, and she slammed against the mesh separating the cargo area from the driver's cabin. He shouldered out of the driver's-side door. The handle. Where had she dropped the handle? She felt along the cold surface of the van's floor but couldn't find it anywhere. The back door was wrenched open, Grillo's dark outline taking up her only escape.

She didn't have time to think—only act.

Shea lunged, tackling her abductor head-on. She hit the dirt and forced him to roll with her but ended on her back with him hovering above. Thrusting her palms into the base of his throat, she knocked him off-balance, then swept the bastard off his feet with both legs, but he recovered faster than she thought possible as she struggled to her feet, still in cuffs. He aimed a fist directly at her face. She dodged the attempt to knock her out, and he launched forward. Hurtling her elbow into his spinal column, she shoved him with her entire body, and Grillo went down. She stood over him, ready to end this once and for all. "You're not taking my son from me."

"We already have, Officer Ramsey," a familiar voice said from behind.

Something hard struck the tendon between her neck and shoulder. She hit the ground, the sound of footsteps loud in her ears as she struggled to get her bearings. A pair of black heels moved into her vision.

"You weren't supposed to be part of this, Shea. So I'm going to give you one last chance before I have Grillo get rid of your body where not even the best forensic investigator in the country could find it." Lieutenant Lara Richards crouched beside her, her rich perfume surrounding her. Clean blonde hair skimmed Shea's face, no sign of blood from the cut on the lieutenant's head. No sign of the cut at all. Had it really been there or had Shea imagined it? Had anything been real? "Where is the casing Vincent recovered from the warehouse?"

Shea twisted her wrists inside the cuffs, halfway sitting up, but the wound in her side wouldn't let her do much more than that. "Go to hell."

A light laugh rolled off Lara's lips, her forearms crossing in front of her body as Grillo got to his feet behind her. "I can see why he likes you so much. You must've been one hell of an investigator to get Vincent's attention. I know how little he lets get to him when he's focused on solving a case." The lieutenant gripped Shea's chin between long fingers, and it took everything inside Shea not to pull away. "Pity for all that talent to go to waste. I could've used someone like you on my side." Lara straightened. "Get her inside. It's time to put an end to this."

Chapter Fourteen

There was only one place this could end.

Vincent pressed his foot down on the accelerator, the momentum pinning him back into the seat. If he was right, Lieutenant Lara Richards wasn't just part of Grillo's organization. She *was* the organization. She'd turned cops into criminals, all while taking a cut along the way, and he hadn't seen it until it was too late. Now she had both Shea and Wells. If his former CO hurt either one of them... Vincent tightened his grip around the steering wheel until his knuckles turned white.

He redialed Shea's number for the tenth—or was it the eleventh?—time. She wasn't going to answer. Not if Lara had gotten to her, but he couldn't stop himself from trying again and again. The SUV's interior filled with her voice as the ringing cut to voice mail, and the tension in his hands drained. Streetlights blurred out the side windows as he sped through the city. "I'm not giving up on you, Freckles. Ever. If you don't believe anything I've said this far, I need you to believe that. I'll be seeing you soon."

He ended the call from the steering wheel and took the next left toward the waterfront. Rain peppered the windshield, the hint of humidity clarifying.

"Five minutes out. Everyone check comms." Sullivan Bishop's orders came through loud and clear from the device in Vincent's ear. The founder and CEO of Blackhawk Security hadn't spent much time in on assignment since proposing to his army prosecutor, Captain Jane Reise, but when it came to the safety of his own people, the former SEAL preferred the field over his massive oak desk.

"Monroe and… Monroe checking in," Kate said over the line, her husband's laugh reaching through the comms.

"Dunham's got your back." An engine growled in the background of Elliot Dunham's earpiece. As much as Vincent hated to admit it, he needed the private investigator's help to recover Shea. He needed all their help. He'd tried solving this case on his own for so long and gotten nowhere. Now he needed his team. "But I'd like to point out, Waylynn is making a bigger sacrifice than all of us by babysitting your demon spawn for this event."

"And there you go ruining the moment." Elizabeth laughed, parent to one of those demon spawn. "Dawson and Levitt checking in."

"Chase in position. I've got eyes on at least two dozen hostile NYPD officers positioned at the west and south sides of the warehouse." The echo of a rifle loading crackled over the channel. Former Criminal Investigation Command special agent Glennon

Chase, Anthony Harris's pregnant wife, had jumped at the opportunity to bring down the organization responsible for taking her husband. And if there was one thing Vincent could be certain of tonight when it came to Glennon, she wouldn't fail. Her former partner, newest Blackhawk Security investigator Bennett Spencer, had already been left for dead. She wasn't going to lose anyone else. The woman had fought too long and too hard to keep her small family together.

They all had.

Vincent tapped the earpiece. "Kalani on location." One breath. Two. The weight of the situation settled under his rib cage. He pulled up beside another Blackhawk SUV on the north side of the warehouse and got out, gun in hand. Streetlights highlighted the dozens of officers and squad cars positioned between him and the woman he wanted to spend the rest of his life with. "I owe you guys one."

"I might just be speaking for myself, but we wouldn't mind some of your mom's cooking in exchange for our services," Elliot said.

"Elliot, one more word out of your mouth, and I'll revoke your firearms permit." Sullivan's warning ended the conversation as he climbed from his SUV and stepped to Vincent's side. The former SEAL had seen battle plenty of times and fought a war with his own brother to save his woman. Vincent wouldn't do any less. "You ready for this?"

Within thirty seconds, the rest of his team pulled into the parking lot and took position, each armed and ready for the coming fight on either side of him. Eight

Blackhawk operatives up against an entire organization of corrupt NYPD officers. At least two dozen cops studied them from across the street, in addition to the snipers Vincent had no doubt had centered his team in their crosshairs. No one was going to get out of this fight unharmed, but he wouldn't back down. Not this time, and not when it came to Shea and her son. Squaring his shoulders, he strengthened the hold on his weapon. "I am now."

"This is the NYPD," a staticky voice said over a megaphone from one of the patrol vehicles nearby. "Drop your weapons, get on your knees and put your hands behind your heads or we will be forced to take lethal action."

"I don't have a clear visual inside the warehouse. The windows have been boarded," Glennon said from one of the buildings east of their location into their earpieces. "No confirmation on the target's location or if the hostages are inside, but I do have a great view of the two snipers aiming their rifles directly at your heads."

Vincent tapped his earpiece. "No matter what happens, Glennon, I need you to get me inside that building."

"You got it," she said.

Stepping forward, he holstered his weapon. There still might be a way out of this that didn't include bloodshed. He shouted loud enough for his voice to carry across the street and dug the evidence bag from his pocket to put it on display. "I know you're in there, Lara, and I know what you want. Send out Shea and her son, and we can both walk away from this. No-body else has to die."

"You expect me to believe you're willing to walk away from your little investigation once I hand them over?" The grouping of officers under her control cleared a path as Lieutenant Lara Richards stepped into view. Her laugh hiked his warning instincts into overdrive. She'd been a good cop once, a good com-manding officer. What the hell had gone wrong? Or had he even really known her at all? Her wide smile vanished, that cold gaze steadying on his as she un-holstered her service weapon and brought it to her side. "I know you, Vincent. I know what you're ca-pable of, and that even if I let Officer Ramsey and her son go free, you'll never stop coming for me." She brought the gun up and aimed. "You're too good a cop."

"You set the fire that night." He tightened his grip on the evidence bag. "You killed two of your own men to try to cover up your operation."

"I warned you before you went to the warehouse that night this case was going to get you killed." She cocked her head to one side. "You should've listened to your CO."

"And the others? The journalist and her assis-tant, the rookie, the defense attorney and IAB Offi-cer Walter. They were getting too close, right? They suspected your organization was turning the NYPD into nothing more than a hit squad for hire, and you couldn't let them find out the truth." Everything was starting to make sense. "You were willing to risk everything to keep yourself in power, but you made a mistake." He held up the casing discarded after Lara shooting Officer Walters center mass, and lines deepened around the edges of her eyes. He'd questioned the motive behind the shooter leaving evidence at the warehouse scene, but now it made perfect sense. It hadn't been used to keep him and Shea in that building longer after all. "You did the dirty work yourself, but you handed off the cleanup to someone else. And now it's going to cost you."

Lara lowered her weapon, closed her stance as she straightened. "Kill them and pry that casing from his cold, dead hand if you have to."

Gunfire exploded from inside the warehouse, the crack of thunder loud in his ears. Blood pooled in his lower body, cementing him in place. "Shea."

The first bullet sliced across the skin of Vincent's injured arm as Lara's men closed ranks around her. He took cover behind the driver's-side door of his SUV and pulled the trigger. The officer who'd shot at him hit the ground as the rest of the Blackhawk Security team took position and returned fire. Adrenaline coursed through him and sharpened his senses. He tapped his earpiece. "Glennon, get me inside that warehouse. Now."

"Snipers neutralized." The former CID special agent fired again. "I'll clear you a path between the first and second cruisers straight ahead of your position." The sound of rifle shots ricocheted off the surrounding buildings, and Glennon's targets collapsed. Lieutenant Richards's men shouted, crouching behind their vehicles as they searched the rooftops. One called into the radio strapped to his shoulder, but Vincent doubted the bastards would get an answer. "That's your cue, Kalani. I'll cover you until you're in the building. After that, you're on your own."

"Give 'em hell," Sullivan said. "We've got it handled out here."

"Copy that." Vincent pumped his legs as fast as he could as Glennon kept the path through the two head squad cars positioned in front of the main warehouse door clear. He jumped over an officer who'd collapsed to the pavement, then ducked to avoid the fist of another keen on keeping him from breaching the line. Swinging his elbow back, he slugged the SOB and kept running. Pain in his shoulder and thigh clawed for his attention, but the sound of those gunshots from inside pushed him harder. Fifteen feet. Ten. Another officer closing in hit the ground as Glennon kept her word to get him inside the warehouse. He slammed into the door, the rusted hinges detaching as the wood hit the wall behind it. Every nerve ending in his body caught fire as the scent of charred wood and ash filled his senses.

Gun raised, he hugged the east wall as he heel-toed it toward the area where he and Shea had recovered the bullet casing the night before. Muted gunfire from outside punched through the sound of his own breathing. His heart pounded hard at the base of his skull as he took cover behind a blackened stack of pallets. Craning his head around, he spotted his former CO. "Give it up, Lara. There's nowhere to run."

"Run?" Lara fired at him, splinters of wood exploding over his right shoulder. The growl of an engine filled the warehouse, and he chanced another look around the pallets. Brake lights darkened Lara's outline behind her. "I built this organization from the ground up, Vincent. I'm not going anywhere, but I can't say the same for Shea and her son."

"It's okay, baby. I've got you." Shea leaned against Wells as much as she could as she tugged at the cuffs around her wrists. His soft hair tickled the underside of her throat. She set her cheek against his head as his screams filled the back of the van. She couldn't hold him. Not with her hands cuffed to the anchor above her head, and everything inside her screamed that if she could get him into her arms, he'd be okay. They'd both be okay. The sound of gunfire was giving him anxiety, and the fact that he'd been ripped away from her ex-husband wasn't helping. Who Lara's men were fighting off, she had no idea. The police who hadn't bought into the lieutenant's ideals? Blackhawk Security? Vincent?

The cuffs cut deeper into her skin as she used her feet to reach for the diaper bag Grillo had thrown into the back of the van before slamming the door in her face, but she had to push the pain to the back of her mind. The canvas slid across the van's floor easily but fell to one side and spilled its contents. His pacifier tumbled from the bag. She pinched it between both boots and brought her knees into her chest to drop it beside him. He clutched it in his tiny hand and brought it to his mouth, but his tears hadn't dried. "I'm going to get us out of here. I promise."

The driver's-side door slammed shut, and Grillo started the van's engine.

No. Sitting up, she tried twisting around to see out the windshield, but the angle only made the cuffs cut into her deeper. The gunfire outside had thinned. No more than a few shots here and there. Had Lara's organization succeeded? Shea kissed the top of Wells's head as the van lurched forward. She caught sight of the white metal handle she'd pried loose before Grillo had brought her to the warehouse. He hadn't seen it when he'd thrown the diaper bag in, and she straightened. "Where are we going?"

No answer.

A bullet dented a section of the van's back door. Wells's cries pierced the ringing in her ears again, and she tried to bring him in closer but couldn't reach him. She had to get out of these cuffs. Someone was still out there, and she found herself wishing it was Vincent. He'd risked his own life for hers. He'd given her a glimpse of real happiness, their cases taking so many layers of hurt and fear away that'd built over the last year. He'd shown her what real strength looked like, and that she could be the woman he'd imagined her being if she only believed it was possible. She wasn't ready to give that up. She wasn't ready to give him up. "Grillo, where are we going?"

"I've got my orders, Ramsey." Darkness fell over the inside of the van as they passed through the warehouse's rolltop door at the north side of the property.

The side that faced the water. "And no one is coming to save you or the boy this time."

"What do you mean?" Panic rose in a hot rush. She kicked at the van floor, but her heels only slipped along the surface. "You said you were going to have him adopted. That he'd get to live out the rest of his life with a new family."

"Change of plans," he said, the weight of his responsibility in his words. "Boss doesn't want any evidence left to come back to haunt her."

"No." She pulled at the cuffs as hard as she could, biting back her scream as the metal ripped across her skin. She turned around toward him. "Please, don't do this. Please. You can have me but let him go. He doesn't deserve any of this. He's just a baby—"

The driver's-side door flew open, a rush of salt-tinted air filling the van. Her hair flew in chaos around her face a split second before a hand reached in and pulled Grillo from the driver's seat. His scream was silenced as the van's back tires rolled over something solid. The officer's body? Vincent climbed behind the wheel and slammed his foot on the brakes. Her heart was full enough to burst.

"Vincent!" His tangled mass of hair penetrated through the mesh as he tried the brakes again, but the van didn't slow. Something was wrong, and her stomach sank. Realization hit. Oh, no. "Vincent..."

"Bastard cut the brake lines and disabled the button to take the van out of cruise control. Looks like he was going to ditch the vehicle on the way to the water." He hit the brakes again, a sea of blackness growing closer over his shoulder out through the windshield. They couldn't swerve surrounded by rows and rows of steel girders, couldn't stop without putting everyone in the van at risk. Vincent half spun toward her. "Shea, I'm going to need you and Wells to brace for impact."

"No! I can't protect him with my hands in the cuffs." Her heart launched into her throat as reality set in. Closing her eyes, she accepted the truth of the situation. He wouldn't have enough time to save them both. Shea set her head back against the metal mesh, then turned her attention to her son. She committed everything about him to memory in the matter of seconds, the way his hair smelled, his big green eyes that matched hers, how his thumbs never properly straightened. Logan would have to make sure the doctor took a look at them when he was older. "I love you. No matter what your dad tells you or what you find out on your own when you get older, please remember that. You're everything, and I will always watch over you."

Calm settled over her then, not the numbness she'd become accustomed to, but something lighter, warmer. These past few days with Vincent had done that. Because of him and the word they'd done together, she knew her son would grow up happy and healthy. The man she loved would keep Wells safe.

Leaning down, she kissed Wells one last time and raised her voice loud enough for Vincent to hear. "When we started working those cases together, it was like I'd been pulled out from beneath a crushing wave. Our investigations were the only thing that got me out of bed most days, but if I'm being honest with myself, part of it was you, too. I wanted to see you, to be around you. When you requested me to work on the task force, you helped get me through the worst year of my life, Vincent. I don't know how, but I know I'll never be able to thank you for that. And it seems unfair for me to ask anything more of you, but, please. You have to get him out of here. Save my son."

Wells's cries filled the inside of the van once again, and she couldn't fight back the tears as the weight of what she was asking drilled straight through her. She was asking him to make the choice to save Wells's life over hers.

"I'm not leaving you. We're all going to walk away from this." Shadowed brown eyes lifted to the rear-view mirror. "I give you my word."

"You're good at keeping your word. That's why I know you'll do this for me." The tears fell then, and the pressure that'd been building for so long released. She'd fought like hell to gain some semblance of the woman she'd been before giving birth to her son, but because of Vincent, because of the work they did, she realized she wasn't that woman anymore. She was more self-assured and stronger than ever. And she'd give anything to have her son grow up knowing his mother loved him as much as she did. "I know you'll protect him."

Vincent's voice overwhelmed the drone of the van's engine. They were running out of time. The dock was coming up so fast. "Shea, what are you—"

She braced herself against the oncoming pain before breaking her right thumb. Her scream filled the cabin, scaring Wells into another round of tears, but she pushed past her urge to comfort him to do the same to her other hand. This time, she bit back the groan and slipped her hands free of the cuffs. Sweeping the metal handle she'd detached from the van's breaker box in to her hand, she wedged it down into the small space between the mesh and the driver's seat and pushed as much of her weight into it as she could. The metal gave way, but not enough to get her son to Vincent. She inserted her uninjured fingers into the slots and pulled with everything she had left. The bolts around the edges of the mesh held tightly to the van's frame, but she'd created a hole big enough to get Wells through. Scooping her son into her arms, she kissed him one last time then handed him off, his small fingers sliding against her palm. "Get him out of here."

The van jerked up over the beginning of the dock. "Shea—"

"Go," she said. "Now!"

"I'm coming back for you." Vincent wedged the driver's-side door open with his foot, those brown eyes she'd loved so much steady on her. In her next breath, he jumped from the vehicle with her son in his arms.

She clutched the metal mesh as she watched her partner and Wells disappear beneath the surface of the water in the van's side mirror. Then she was flying. A sea of black consumed the windshield as the vehicle launched itself over the end of the dock. The impact slammed her against the divider, her fingers automatically tightening in the slots as the cabin slowly filled with water. Her head ached where her face had met metal, slowing her reaction time. She'd saved her son and told Vincent the truth. He'd changed her life, helped her heal in more ways than she could imagine. Wells would know she fought for him and become the mother he'd deserved from the beginning. That was all that mattered.

Murky water seeped through the mesh, and Shea forced herself to stand. She had maybe another two— three—minutes before her remaining oxygen escaped the cargo area, but she wasn't ready to die. Not yet. The van hadn't sunk entirely yet. There was still a chance she could escape. She stared straight up at the back doors of the van. The slick surface and her broken thumbs would make it hard to climb, but as Vincent had made abundantly clear, she'd never backed down from a challenge. Least of all given up. "You can do this."

Wiping her wet hands down her jeans, she used the wheel wells of the back tires for leverage. The water soaked her ankles now and was only filling the van faster. Her boot slipped off the wheel well, threatening to pull her back into the water, but she held on to a bracket that made up the frame of the vehicle with everything she had. Her feet dangled below her, the water climbing higher now. She just had to get to the back doors.

A hard thud reverberated down through the frame,

and she forced her head up as one back door of the van swung open. Strong, familiar hands wrapped around her wrists, and she couldn't help but trust he'd carry her weight. Just as he always had. "I told you. We survive together."

Chapter Fifteen

Vincent pulled her from the water after their short swim to shore, careful of her broken thumbs, and into his chest. Red and blue patrol lights swept across her features as she steadied herself on the end of the dock. Long hair trailed over her shoulders as she studied the scene behind him. Sullivan, Kate, Elizabeth, Elliot and Glennon watched her and Vincent's backs as a fresh wave of NYPD officers closed in on the scene, Wells safely held in Elizabeth's arms. In an instant, she stepped out of his hold and reached for her son. The boy was all too eager to see his mother again, a giant four-toothed smile crinkling the edges of his eyes as he reached right back for her. Vincent had protected him as best he could when they'd hit the water, determined to keep his promise to Shea, but that was when his team had arrived. With their help, he'd gotten to her before the van submerged. He could've lost her forever if it hadn't been for the support of the men and women around them.

"Thank you," she said to the team.

Sullivan nodded. "Like I said, we protect our own,

Officer Ramsey, and Vincent has made it clear that list includes you."

"Damn right it does." Wrapping one arm around her waist, he reveled in the feel of her body pressed against his, in the strong beat of her heart in her chest. Wells tugged on his beard with another gut-wrenching smile—his mother's smile—and laughed. Not even fazed from their short dive into the river. Vincent couldn't resist the wrap of the little guy's fingers around his thumb. "It's over, Shea. We don't have to run anymore."

"I wouldn't be here without you, without any of you." She turned toward Glennon with Wells wiggling in her arms. Smoothing her hand over his nearly bald head, she readjusted her hold on him with a wince, and Vincent couldn't help but smile at the idea of her being so affectionate with their own babies. If that was what she wanted. After everything she'd been through the past year, hell, even the past five days, he'd understand her hesitation to have another kid…or six. But there were more ways to have children than getting pregnant, and he couldn't wait to see her in action. "But what about Anthony? Were you able to find him?"

Glennon's smile broke through the tension of possibly losing one of the best, most-trusted members of the Blackhawk Security team. "Why don't you see for yourself?"

They piled into Vincent's SUV, Shea and Wells beside him in the back seat. Because there was no way he was going to let either of them go. Not now.

Not ever. She'd admitted she'd loved him seconds before the worst moment of his life—watching the van
launch off the end of the dock into the river. And he
loved her. If Shea gave them the chance, he'd spend
the rest of his life ensuring they were happy, and that
no one would take them from him again. He slipped
his arm around her, bringing both her and Wells into
his protective hold. Jade-green eyes raised to his as
she relaxed her head back against him, and everything inside him heated.

"Did Grillo...survive?" She stared up at him, the
slightest quake in her voice.

"Paramedics didn't get to him in time." But Vincent couldn't gather any sympathy for the bastard.
Officer Charlie Grillo had tried to kill the woman he
wanted to spend the rest of his life with, along with
her son and his team. The NYPD would be better off
without a man like him in their ranks. "He'll never
touch you again. No one will."

Sullivan maneuvered the SUV back toward the
warehouse where spotlights and a perimeter had been
set up by NYPD. The low vibration of the engine
through his body urged him to give in to the exhaustion of the past few days, to fall asleep with Shea in
his arms, but he knew she'd spend the rest of her life
looking over her shoulder if she couldn't confirm the
nightmare had really ended. That was just the kind
of woman and cop she was. The vehicle stopped beyond the officer rolling out crime-scene tape across
the rolltop door where he'd watched Grillo escape
with Shea and Wells in the van, and Vincent inter-

twined his fingers in hers. Tugging her from the vehicle, with Wells on her hip, he held the tape up for
her to pass beneath, and they stepped back inside the
warehouse where his entire life had changed course.

Orders echoed off the cinder block walls as Shea
slowed, her attention focused on the woman in the
middle of the room. Cuffed and on her knees, Lieutenant Lara Richards and a dozen surviving officers she'd recruited into her organization waited to
be hauled back to the precinct. With Anthony Harris, aviator sunglasses and all, standing watch. "You
found him."

"Lara had me pinned down behind those pallets
over there while Grillo took off with you and Wells
in the van." Vincent motioned to the stack, the memories of those few agonizing seconds where he'd given
in to the fear of never seeing her again still so clear.
He turned to her, fingers tracing a path over her wet
clothing. Hell, he still couldn't believe she was here,
standing in front of him as though he hadn't almost
lost everything that'd mattered to him. "I didn't think
I was going to make it to you in time. I was willing
to do anything—and kill anyone—to get you back,
but before I pulled the trigger, Anthony caught her
by surprise. Without him…" Vincent steeled himself against the emotions rushing through him. "I
don't know what I would've done if I'd lost you again,
Freckles. I love you. I want to be with you, make babies with you, wake up beside you every morning,
even if I have to compete with this guy. I will do anything it takes to keep you two safe." He framed her

jaw with one hand. "I should've told you I had access to your department psych eval, but I promise you, I will never keep anything from you again. If you'll just give us a chance. Please."

They were in the middle of a damn crime scene, officers collecting evidence and making arrests around them, but seeing as how that was exactly how he and Shea had met, the location for this conversation couldn't be more perfect.

"Vincent, I don't care about you or your team having access to that damn report. I was surprised, angry, and yeah, I felt betrayed you'd kept the truth from me, but..." Shea closed her eyes, spotlights deepened the shadows under her eyes, and his gut clenched. She shook her head, then lifted that beautiful green gaze to his. "I just... I wanted you to keep believing that I was the woman you admired back in that ranger station, the one you'd requested as your partner all those months ago, and I was worried once you discovered the truth, you wouldn't feel that way about me anymore. So many people have walked out of my life because they didn't understand what was wrong with me. I didn't want to lose you, too."

His heart pounded loud behind his ears. He tried to process her words, over and over in the span of a few short seconds, but shock still coursed through him. The pain in his leg and shoulder, the controlled chaos going on around them, it all disappeared. Until there was only her. Vincent threaded his fingers through her hair. "You're never going to lose me, Shea. I might not understand what you're going through, but I'll do whatever it takes to find out. I'm going to be there for you. I'll go to doctors' appointments, I'll watch Wells when you need a break, I'll cook for you and talk you through your cases. However you need me, I'll be there." He trailed a path down her forearm and slipped his hand into hers. "And if that means Kate was right, that you're not in a position to love me back, I'll respect that. I just want you to be happy."

"Really?" Tears welled in her lower lash line as he nodded. She swiped her tongue across her lips, and she dropped her attention to his T-shirt. A distraction. "You said you wanted to make babies with me, but I don't know if I can do that, Vincent. I don't think I can go through what happened to me after I had Wells again."

"I know," he said. "So we'll adopt if we decide we want those babies. We'll babysit Katrina and Hunter and Kate and Glennon's babies when they get here. We'll have Wells when he's not with Logan, and I will still be the happiest man on this planet because I'll be doing it all with you."

The shadows in her eyes dissipated, and his heart jerked in his chest. "Partners?"

"For the rest of our lives." He pushed wet hair behind her ear.

"That would make me happy." Stepping into him, she set her ear over his heart. Right where she belonged.

"Wells?" Logan Ramsey's voice penetrated through the bubble he and Shea had created in the middle of the crime scene, bringing them back to reality. Shea's ex-husband and his new wife pushed past the perimeter, but Anthony Harris cut them off before they got anywhere close. "Wells!"

"The court date." Her eyes widened, and she fisted his shirt with her unbroken fingers with one hand as she clutched her son with the other. "Vincent, I missed the custody hearing. Logan is going to make sure I never see Wells after this. He's going to take my son away. Maybe for good." Closing her eyes, she smoothed her lips against Wells's forehead, and a sudden calmness unlike anything he'd experienced came over her. She opened her eyes. "But I can't keep him from his father, either. I've lived through that, and I wouldn't wish it on anyone. Not even Logan." Shea maneuvered around him, but Vincent wasn't far behind. "It's okay, Anthony. I've got this."

Vincent nodded at the weapons expert in appreciation as arresting officers hauled Lieutenant Lara Richards to her feet. Blazing blue eyes locked on him before his former commanding officer—and what was left of her crew—was forced into the back of NYPD squad cars. Corruption of justice, murder, attempted murder. The district attorney was going to make himself a hell of a career out of this one. Reaching into his pocket, Vincent pulled the bullet casing he'd recovered and handed it off to one of the officers searching the scene. They were going to need it, and in a few months, Vincent would have to come back to New York City to testify. She'd gone after Shea, after her son, and nearly killed him. He'd make sure the lieutenant got everything coming her way. With Shea, his partner, at his side.

VINCENT SMOOTHED HIS hand across her lower back, but nothing would help her process her ex-husband's words any better. Not even him.

"What do you mean? I came all the way to New York for the hearing." The hollowness she'd fought back for so long threatened to consume her, and she could only hold on to Wells tighter. If this was another way for her ex-husband to get back at her, to punish her even more... "Now you're telling me you've already talked to the judge? Logan, please, I know things haven't been easy between us. I wasn't there when you both needed me, but we can work this out—"

"A team of armed men showed up at the house claiming they worked for some security company, told us we were in danger and whisked us away to a safe house, Shea. Then a bomb exploded in front of us, and a bunch of cops took our son out of my arms. They kidnapped him because of something you got him involved in." Logan Ramsey reached for Wells, and it took everything in her power to hold back. She'd meant what she'd said to Vincent. She wouldn't keep Wells from his father. Her son deserved better than that. He deserved to be happy, and if that meant she couldn't be involved in his life, she'd have to live with that. Logan's new wife slid her hand across his shoulders, and the tension seemed to drain out of the man she'd once planned on spending the rest of her life with. "But the men you sent to protect us, Bennett and Anthony, they told us what you did. They told us you were taking on an entire organization of corrupt police officers to make sure we would be safe. So yes, I talked to the judge about custody. Since I'm his legal guardian, I had him approve a new custody agreement while you were searching for our son." Logan pulled a white envelope from his inner jacket pocket and handed it to her. "It goes into effect immediately."

Her hand shook as she took the thick envelope. Vincent pulled her into his side, the only thing keeping her on her feet. She unfolded the documents, tried to read the small print, but it took a few tries before everything became clear. A flood of surprise rocketed through her, her knees threatening to collapse right out from under her. "You..." She looked up at her ex-husband for confirmation. "You're giving me equal custody?"

"After everything you've done for Wells, after hearing how far you went to protect him, I realized you're not the same woman you were when we left Anchorage. You've changed. You seem...better. Stronger than before." With a glance toward Vincent, Logan switched their son to his other arm and pulled his wife to his side. "I want Wells to grow up knowing both his parents love him. Even if they're not together. We want you to see him as much as you can. Here in New York or in Anchorage. We can work out the details later. I just needed you to know."

She couldn't think, couldn't breathe. Vincent's hand at her back warmed her straight to the core, and for the first time in so long she was…happy. She'd found love with the man who'd saved her life and had a strong future in line for her son. "Thank you."

With a final nod, Logan Ramsey, Wells and his wife were escorted toward a police cruiser that would most likely take them straight home. After living through the chaos of the last few days, she couldn't blame them for not sticking around. Every cell in her entire body wanted to collapse into bed and try to forget the feeling of almost losing her son, the panic. Of almost losing her partner.

"Let's get those thumbs looked at." Vincent led her toward one of the many ambulances parked outside the perimeter of the scene as police worked to clean up Lieutenant Richards's mess. Dozens of bodies littered the ground from an apparent shoot-out, but the Blackhawk Security team—Sullivan, Elizabeth, Kate, Elliot, Glennon, Anthony—looked as though they'd pulled through. Leaning against their vehicles, they watched as NYPD processed the scene.

Whatever they'd done, however many laws they'd broken in the process, she owed them her gratitude. She let EMTs examine her thumbs and the back of her head where Lara had struck her, all the while trying to keep Vincent from lunging when she groaned from them resetting the bones. As the investigating officers took their statements, Shea couldn't keep herself from touching him as he settled beside her on the back of the ambulance. Just as she'd done in that cave after their plane had gone down. She'd known then she'd fall for him, this intense, protective and thoughtful man. It was inevitable, but she had the feeling it wouldn't end here. It'd be the forever kind of fall. The investigating officer returned to processing his scene, and Shea rested her head against Vincent's shoulder.

"Well, we managed to bring down an entire organization of corrupt cops and solve five cold cases, Officer Ramsey. I'd say we make a pretty great team when we get along." His mouth pressed against the top of her head, his warm breath fighting to chase back the bone-deep cold of the river. He slid his hand up her throat and tipped her head back. He closed the distance between them and pressed his mouth to hers, and everything around them disappeared. The red and blue patrol lights, the fact that his team stood nearby, the crime scene techs. None of it mattered right then. He pulled back enough to speak against her lips. "So does this mean we get to keep working joint investigations together when we get back to Anchorage?"

She couldn't help but smile at the idea. He was right. They did make a great team, and she couldn't wait to see what kinds of investigations they'd be partnered on next. Over the course of the last few days he'd become more than her partner. He'd become her protector, her everything. "Not if it means spending nights in caves, outrunning avalanches or nearly drowning in the back of a van."

"I think we'll survive." Vincent's laugh rumbled through her before he kissed her again. "Somehow we always do."

* * * * *

MARINE
PROTECTOR

JULIE ANNE LINDSEY

To Lyndy.

Chapter One

Rivulets of sweat ran down Lyndy Wells's temples and
between her shoulder blades as she trekked back in the
direction of her car, having completed another hefty evening walk. Toting thirty extra pounds was enough to
make anyone sweat, but coupled with the uncomfortable weight of winter boots and her wool maternity coat,
the act was exhausting. Not only did she have fifteen
pounds of baby weight left to lose, she had the baby himself strapped to her chest in a snowsuit and carrier she'd
initially suspected might require three engineers and a
rocket scientist just to put on.

Gus was already five months old, and the pressure was
on to lose those unwanted pounds. It was late in the season, and before long, the snow would come to her northern Kentucky town. Then her evening walks would go
from tolerably chilly to downright impossible. Until then,
she'd keep doing her best to take eight thousand steps a
day, or as many as possible while carrying her son. At
the moment she just wanted to get to her car, collapse
behind the wheel and gulp the spare bottle of water she
kept in the console.

She paused near the lake to bend and lift each rubbery
leg, hoping to alleviate the growing burn in her ham-

strings and catch her breath. A smattering of dried leaves skated across the still water where ducks and moms with bread-bag-wielding toddlers had gathered regularly on summer evenings. The ducks still made an appearance, but the families rarely did. The days were too short now, and Lyndy imagined most folks had fallen into a new evening routine. Unlike her. Gus was sound asleep against her chest now, as he normally was by this portion of the workout, but he was sure to be wide-awake when they got home. Just in time to make it impossible for her to shower right away.

The sun was low on the horizon as Lyndy settled into a slower, cool-down pace, the apricot and amber sky quickly giving way to twilight. Unfortunately, the same mountain shade she'd savored in the late summer afternoons resembled an ominous cover by dinnertime these days. She frequently imagined coyotes or bobcats creeping out from behind her car as she strapped Gus into his rear-facing car seat with complicated five-point safety harness. Another baby item probably designed by NASA.

She rubbed Gus's back as she pushed on, only to stop a few steps further when the tiny hairs along her neck rose with the breeze. Her intuition spiked a silent warning, but there was nothing and no one in sight to be wary of. She picked up her pace anyway, filled with renewed motivation to reach the safety of her car. The strange, nearly indescribable sensation plucked her already tightened skin, insisting something was simply *wrong,* and her gut pinched and flipped with every step.

She crossed the little wooden bridge from the park's walking path to the parking lot at a clip, already unearthing her keys and beeping the doors unlocked. Her headlights flashed on in response, adding a mixture of light and new shadows to her world.

"Almost there," she whispered, as much an encouragement to Gus as to herself. "A few more steps and we'll be locked in tight." The muscles along her neck and shoulders bunched, and her heart climbed as she came within steps of the car.

The wind blew again, and a strange scent caught Lyndy's nose. Not floral. Not natural. She couldn't name it. Couldn't place it, and it only alarmed her further. Not cologne. Not perfume. She broke into a jog, fear running its icy fingers along her spine and into her sweaty hair.

Her heavy breaths and footfalls stirred the baby on her chest. "Shh," she cooed. "Shh. Shh. Shh. It's okay. Mama's got you."

Finally, Lyndy wrapped panicked and trembling fingers around the handle of her car door, and for one brief heartbeat, they were safe.

Then her head jerked back with the force of a bull. Long, angry fingers clamped over her mouth and curled deep into the hair at the base of her neck. A scream locked in her throat, strangled silent by terror. The car keys clattered at her feet.

Confusion crushed every thought in Lyndy's head. Her fight-or-flight response was set to *flight*, and she cradled her baby with both arms, attempting to change their backward momentum and break free.

Gus struggled in his coat and carrier, a tiny whimper of complaint breaking free.

Lyndy dug her heels into the ground, but the hand only yanked her back again, harder, dragging her away from the lot. Her feet twisted and faltered beneath her. She flailed one arm for balance, while the other attempted to hold Gus tight.

The soul-crushing realization that this was how she would die, alone in a park where children fed ducks and moms pushed strollers, forced the confusion from her mind. She knew with pinpoint clarity that her son would be orphaned, become a foster child, a ward of the state, *if he was spared.*

If she didn't fight.

Adrenaline ignited in her veins like electricity on a power-plant fence.

This would *not* be her end, and it damn sure wouldn't be her son's. She let herself go limp, dropping the full weight of her new, heavier body onto the ground.

Lyndy was no longer tired. She was no longer weak or fat or out of shape, or any of the other things she'd cursed herself for on the nightly two-mile walk. She was a mother bear with a cub to defend, and she'd do it or die trying.

Her assailant stumbled beneath the sudden change, and when he loosened his grip on her head to clutch her beneath the arms, Lyndy began to fight. He lifted her off the ground with some effort, pressing her back to his chest once more, this time tightening one forearm across her throat.

She slammed her boot against his shin, then his knee, then his instep. She aimed the point of her bent elbow into the meat below his ribs, and when his grip loosened again, Lyndy screamed. She gave another hearty thrust of her foot, and a flurry of curses flew from the assailant's lips.

Lyndy bounded forward, holding tight to her screaming baby and sliding over the wet grass along the lake's edge. A feral growl erupted behind her, but she wouldn't look back. She couldn't process, couldn't think. Her body had switched its goal from flight to fight, and back again. Now all she could do was run. She fumbled up the little grassy hill, sliding in goose mess and turning her ankles over rocks and sticks. Down to her knees, then up again, away from the danger, away from death, into the street beyond the parking lot where she'd dropped her keys.

Gus's cries rang in her ears. She had to get him as far away from the man as possible.

The sudden blinding force of headlights trapped her in their glow, and Lyndy threw up her arms to protect her baby from an impact that didn't come.

Instead, the vehicle stopped. Two front doors cracked open and dark figures climbed out. "Ma'am?" the slow, steady drawl of an unknown man asked, his figure manifesting gradually through bright headlight beams. A savior? Or another assailant? "Are you hurt?" He drew closer, and Lyndy stepped back. The man lifted his palms, and Lyndy recognized the familiar navy blue uniform of an EMT.

A woman in matching gear appeared opposite him in the light. "Are you okay, ma'am?"

"No," Lyndy cried, overcome by the rush of assurance, safety and salvation, even as her baby screamed in hysterics. "We're not all right." Hot tears poured over her stinging cheeks as her knees buckled and her limbs began to shake.

THE HOSPITAL WAS bright and loud. Everything smelled of bleach, burnt coffee and bandages. People rushed in every direction, not appearing to see anything but what was directly before them. Maybe that was how they survived a career submerged in horrific and abounding tragedies.

Lyndy paced the overpolished floor beside the bed where her baby was poked and prodded by a nurse, doctor and what seemed like a half-dozen medical trainees. She'd been given a cursory evaluation and released from further care, allowed to oversee what was happening to Gus. Lyndy had a few scrapes and bruises on her knees and shins from falling, some light bruising across her mouth and neck from being manhandled, but nothing serious. Nothing lasting. It was Gus she was worried about. What if he had brain damage or shaken baby syndrome from all the jostling and jolting? What if she'd broken his tiny fingers, hands or arms during one of her falls, or damaged his hearing with her screams?

It was lucky she hadn't escaped a madman only to get her baby mowed down by a giant truck when she ran stupidly into the street outside the park.

Ambulance, she reminded herself. The vehicle had been an ambulance, and it had probably saved both their lives.

"Mrs. Wells?" A middle-aged man with a lab coat and stethoscope approached, hand extended.

Lyndy wrapped her arms more tightly around her middle. "Ms.," she corrected. She wasn't married. She thought everyone in their little community knew that by now. Half had probably attended Sam's funeral, or maybe it had only seemed that way. "How is he?" she asked, forcing the tougher thoughts away.

The man cleared his throat and dropped his hand back to his side. "I'm Dr. Mustav, and your little man is going to be just fine. I've given him a very thorough evaluation, and he appears to be completely unscathed. Thanks, no doubt, to his mother's quick thinking. Whatever you did out there, you saved his life. Both of your lives, really. I'm sure you're eager to get home, so I'll leave you to it." He raised his hand again slightly before letting it drop once more, and exited with a small nod.

Lyndy blinked back the tears. Gus was fine. *He was fine.* A deep rush of breath coursed through her, strong enough to knock her off balance.

"Ma'am?" A smiling nurse in teddy bear scrubs bopped cheerfully into view. "Gus is fast asleep now, but he's good to go whenever you're ready. I just need you to read over these discharge papers and sign before you leave." She handed Lyndy a clipboard with a stack of white pages and a pen. "Take as long as you need."

Lyndy dropped the clipboard onto the table and went to stroke her son's soft brown hair. His round cheeks were pink with color and his little button mouth worked in tiny circles, probably enjoying an imaginary bottle. A tear fell onto his forehead and he winced. Lyndy dried her eyes and his head quickly, then stroked his back gently until his mouth began to work on the bottle once more.

Suddenly, the weight of the night settled over her and pressed heavily on her soul. She backed into the uncomfortable bedside recliner, pulled her knees to her chest, wrapped her trembling arms around them and sobbed as quietly as possible against the dirty fabric of her pant legs.

She woke to the sound of her name. Her sore and tired eyes peeled open with considerable effort. Her feet had returned to the floor and her arms hung east and west across the arms of the chair.

"Ms. Wells?" An older gentleman in a suit and trench coat stood before her. His white hair and round glasses made him look like he belonged behind a library table or in a boardroom. The detective's shield on his coat said otherwise. "I'm Detective Harry Owens. How are you feeling?"

Her gaze jumped to the sleeping baby in the crib at her side. His chest rose and fell with strong, steady breaths.

"Okay," she said on instinct. "Better," she corrected.

"Good." He handed her a business card. "I've been assigned to your case, and I'd like to talk to you sometime. Are you feeling up to it?"

"No," she blurted. In fact, she doubted she'd ever feel up to reliving the horrors of her night. "Gus and I are free to go," she said, recalling the doctor and nurse's promise, "and it's been a terrible night, so we're going to go." The stack of papers caught her eye. She couldn't take Gus without at least signing the release papers. Could she? What would they do? Chase her down?

A noose tightened on her throat as the memory of being chased returned like a battering ram. She touched careful fingers to the tender skin where she could still feel the man's arm pressing down on her windpipe. Her cheeks flushed hot, and she concentrated on not passing out. Maybe she could stay long enough to sign the papers. Something else came to mind. "My car," she said. If she did run, where would she go? To a bus stop? Not without any money. She'd locked her purse in her glove box. "The ambulance brought us here."

"I can take you to your car," Detective Owens suggested. "We can talk on the way, or I can drive you home, if you'd prefer. You can give me your keys, and I'll bring the car to you later."

Her teeth began to chatter. "I dropped my keys in the lot."

"Look, Ms. Wells," Detective Owens began, dragging another chair next to hers. He sat forward, resting his elbows on his knees, and he looked at her as if he truly cared. "I'm going to be honest with you about something that I don't think you're ready to hear right now, but truthfully, I don't know when a great time to tell you would be. So here it is. You fit the profile that federal officials have associated with a serial killer circling our community. Police departments in three neighboring counties are working with the FBI on similar cases, and they think your attack tonight is one that needs looking into. Unfortunately, they can't be sure, so I can't offer you much in the way of police protection other than some additional patrols of your street." He shifted his feet beneath the chair and locked his ankles, then folded his hands on his lap. "If you asked me for my advice, or if you were my daughter, I'd suggest you buy a gun and get to the range, but you don't look like my daughter, and you didn't ask for my advice, so I'll tell you this instead. There's a private protection firm in Lexington made up of former military men, good ones, honorable and smart ones. You could hire one of them to look after you until this thing gets sorted out, if you're interested. I understand their fees are fair, and they've been known to work pro bono where the need requires it. I'd say this situation fits the bill. They can probably get someone out here tonight. I've heard nothing but good things about them, and I don't make recommendations lightly. Ms. Wells? Can you hear me?"

Lyndy tried to nod her head, but it didn't move. "Serial killer?" she choked the words through a suddenly dry mouth, the syllables falling like stones from a sticky, swollen tongue.

Detective Owens didn't answer. He pulled a cell phone from the inside pocket of his coat and dialed before pressing it to his cheek.

She felt her attacker's hands on her. Felt his breath on her skin. The heat of him against her back. *A serial killer?* Bile rose in her throat, and her grip on the chair arms turned white.

"Ms. Wells?" The detective was on his feet. His phone was gone, and his coat was buttoned. "Come on, now." He outstretched a hand. "My wife's on her way. I think you might feel better with a woman along for the ride tonight. She's an angel, my Gracie. While we wait for her, you can finish those papers and we'll take you to get your car."

LYNDY PULLED INTO her driveway an hour later, and Detective Owens walked her inside. Her keys had been under her car, kicked slightly behind her wheel, her car still unlocked. Detective Owens made a loop through her home and waited on the porch before leaving while she locked up again. He'd assured her a member of the Fortress Defense team he'd told her about was on the way. Cade Lance, a former marine and honorably discharged vet. She triple-checked the locks and put on some coffee, then sat on the couch, watching through the front window for signs of trouble or her hired protector. She didn't even know what it cost to have a bodyguard, only that she couldn't afford not to have him, and Mr. Owens had set it all up while she'd been emotionally catatonic. Hopefully he'd been right about the sliding pay scale.

A flash of headlights opened her eyes. She hadn't realized that she'd closed them. A silhouette climbed down from the driver's side of a very tall, very black pickup truck outside her front window. A flutter of concern rocked through her as doubt over his identity crossed her mind: she hoped this was the man from Fortress Defense and not the man from the park. How did Detective Owens say he knew these guys? Were they buddies of his? All retired military? The beast of a truck looked nothing like Detective Owens's sensible sedan, and the lean silhouette moving forward with strong, confident swagger certainly didn't resemble the stout father figure who'd watched over her and Gus tonight.

The man took another step, and the motion sensor for her porch light switched on.

"Whoa," she whispered, rising to her knees on the couch for a better look through her front window. She drank in the broad shoulders and narrow hips of the unexpected cowboy with sincere appreciation. A large black Stetson cast long shadows over eyes that sent a chill skittering down her spine. Not a turn-and-run chill like the others she'd had tonight. This was the kind of tingle that made her insides flush hot, especially after she caught a glimpse of his square jaw and tight blue jeans.

The cowboy walked the length of her porch in both directions before returning to her front door and knocking.

Lyndy approached the door on unsteady legs and peeked through the small window before grabbing the knob.

His cool blue eyes met hers instantly, pale and fathomless in the thin porch light. "Ms. Wells. I'm Cade Lance, Fortress Defense. Detective Harry Owens called me."

Lyndy turned the knob, enjoying the veil of heat sliding across her skin at the sound of his slow Southern drawl, and then opened the door to meet her new personal protector.

Chapter Two

Cade waited outside the open door for the little blonde to look less shell-shocked before stepping inside. "I'm sorry if you've been waiting long. I know it's been an awful night. I got here as quickly as I could."

She scanned him with wide blue eyes, her lightly freckled cheeks flushing with color. "Come in." She locked the door behind him and tugged it twice before seeming to accept it as secure. "I'm Lyndy Wells. Thank you for coming on such short notice."

Cade offered her a hand to shake. "Cade Lance. Short notice comes with the job. I don't mind."

Her small, soft hand fitted easily into his larger, rougher one, and he felt the tremor she'd been hiding. This woman put up a good front, but she was terrified.

"Coffee?" she asked.

"All right." Cade nodded, and Lyndy hurried away. Her short blond hair didn't quite reach her narrow shoulders, and the cotton T-shirt and pants she wore seemed oddly large on her petite frame.

Cade followed her through the tidy house splattered in baby gear, blankets and toys. "Where should I put this?" he asked, swinging the black duffel bag off his shoulder. He had more in the truck, but the rest could wait for morning. The go-bag he kept at the ready had everything he'd need for now.

"Oh." She stopped abruptly and changed directions, heading down a long narrow hall. "Here." She swung the first door open and motioned him inside. Her cheeks darkened again as she approached the tall bed with at least fifty pillows in every shape and size. "I forgot to make it up. That bedding's probably been on there since I moved in last year. No one's ever needed the guest room."

Cade dropped his bag on the bed and gave the place a slow look. "This is just fine."

Stacks of boxes lined one wall, four high and two rows deep, as if she still needed to unpack. Most of them had the letters SAM scribbled across one side. The rest of the room looked as if his grandmother had decorated it. Pink-and-white floral everything, complete with a big round shag carpet beneath a pillow-filled rocking chair. The whole place smelled like vanilla. It was a far cry from his utilitarian apartment, and even farther from his living quarters overseas.

Lyndy headed back down the hall to the kitchen, and Cade followed again. He gave the rattle on the highchair beside the table a gentle shake. "Detective Owens said you have a baby?" She certainly didn't look like someone who'd recently had a baby. She barely looked old enough to own a home, but she was twenty-seven, according to the social media profiles he'd checked while packing for the assignment.

He was twenty-seven. Did he look like a kid to other people?

"I have a five-month-old son, Gus. Do you take cream or sugar?" she asked, offering him a cup of coffee.

"No. Thank you." He accepted the cup and gave the

homey country kitchen a cursory look. Too many windows. French doors. Too many points of entry. "You live alone with your son?" he asked. It was a large home for one woman and a baby. At least three thousand square feet. A sprawling one-floor ranch.

"Yes," she answered softly.

Cade moved to the glass doors overlooking the rear patio and dark expanse of land. "How many acres are here?"

"Eight acres," she said. "We don't own as much as it seems. There just aren't any neighbors for a good quarter mile or more."

Cade turned back to her. "We? You and your boy?"

Lyndy frowned. "Yes."

Cade stepped in her direction, attempting to gauge her strange response. *Was there an ex-boyfriend? Ex-husband?*

She sighed. "I bought the property with my former fiancé early last year, and we moved in a couple weeks before the wedding was scheduled."

Cade folded his arms, balancing his steaming mug just below his lips. There was heartbreak in her eyes. The agonizing, life-altering kind. He'd seen it before. Lived through it himself. *Grief.* "I'm sorry about your loss."

Her shining blue eyes snapped in his direction, full of unshed tears. "How did you…" She let the question hang. "Thank you." She wet her lips and took a seat at the table. "He was on his way home from a weekend of fishing with friends. A long-haul trucker fell asleep at the wheel, crossed into oncoming traffic. That was that."

Cade adjusted his hat, unsure what to say from there. He tightened his stance and gave her time to continue or change the subject if she wanted. Surprisingly, he hoped she'd continue. There was something about her that made him curious in a number of ways, most of them unprofessional, but all of them genuine.

"Sam was older," she said. "Thirty-six. Some folks thought the age difference was weird, but it wasn't to us. He was a good man." She took her time sipping the coffee she'd poured for herself. "I guess you've lost plenty of good men, too. I hear you're just home from overseas."

"I am."

Lyndy ran a fingertip along the rim of her steaming mug. "Detective Owens said you were a marine."

"That's right." Cade shifted, uncomfortable with the questions directed at him. A wry smile caught his lips. Hadn't he done the same to her? It was necessary, he supposed, to get to know one another if he was going to live there temporarily and protect her. They needed a level of comfort and trust. "I was enlisted eight years. I did three tours overseas."

She tipped her head over one shoulder, maybe evaluating the answer. "Do you miss it?"

That was a good question, and no one had asked him before. Did he miss combat? The blazing hot, relentless heat? Being a stranger in a foreign land? Facing off with faceless assassins? No. But did he miss being part of something that big, fighting for the people who couldn't fight for themselves, wearing the uniform, earning the title of US marine? Hell yes. The answer was far too complicated for him to sort quickly, so he decided on the simplest truth. "I'm glad to be home."

"What was it like?" she asked.

He shrugged. Another question too complicated to answer thoroughly. "What's it like to be a single mom with a baby living alone out here?"

"Lonely," she said almost immediately, "and some-times scary." She looked away, but the truth of the words was there in her soft voice.

Cade understood both answers quite well. "Same," he said.

Lyndy returned her gaze to him. "What about you? Any kids back in Lexington?"

"No." Cade took the seat beside hers. "I don't think having a family is in the cards for me. My father left a lot to be desired." He let a small smile form on his lips at the horrendous understatement and kicked himself mentally for oversharing. Normally he was notorious for one-word answers. Choosing to become Susie Chatterbox now, when he was supposed to be making a good first impression on a new client, was a huge error in judgment.

"He ruined the idea of family for you?" she guessed, tilting slightly forward, as if the answer mattered.

Cade considered the question. His father had ruined a lot of things for him, but not the desire to have a family. A real one. One that loved and supported one another. "I just think it's probably best I pass on the opportunity to share what I learned about parenting, which isn't much and none of which is good."

Lyndy's small mouth pulled down at the sides. "I'm sorry."

Cade's muscles stiffened. He took a deep drink of coffee and made solid plans to shut the hell up.

Lyndy sat straighter and rubbed the freckled skin beneath a wisp of pale blond bangs. "I should let you get settled. It's late and Gus is an early riser."

"Of course." Cade stood when she did and waited while she passed. "I'll be here if you need me."

He tried and failed to keep his eyes off her as she

walked away. He imagined he wasn't the only man to feel that way, and a protective instinct tugged at his core.

She vanished a few steps later, and he released a heavy breath.

Maybe it was the fact she looked so small and vulnerable, or maybe it was the fact she was a new mother, but Cade's jaw locked at the memory of why he was there. Someone had tried to hurt her tonight.

He'd make darn sure that didn't happen again.

LYNDY DIDN'T SLEEP well despite her new home-security cowboy. She'd set up Gus's travel crib in her room, then shoved her tallest dresser in front of her window and her heaviest one in front of the locked bedroom door. Still, she'd remained awake most of the night.

Gus woke at two, then again at seven sharp.

She was waiting. Already dressed in her best-fitting jeans and a faded old T-shirt, she'd combed her hair and driven a lip gloss wand over her lips before she heard his first cry. A little mascara, and she was ready to face the day.

She changed Gus into his blue onesie covered in lassos, stretched a pair of faux jeans over his dimpled legs and diapered bottom, then brown socks, designed to look like little cowboy boots, over each chubby foot. Perfect. Adorable. *Safe*. She released a steadying breath with the final thought, then scooped him into her arms and crept down the hall to her kitchen, careful not to wake the man sleeping in her guest room.

The first rays of sunlight drifted through her French doors, warming the cool linoleum beneath her bare feet. Cheery red and green decor met her at every turn, an effort to make Gus's first holiday season magical. Thanksgiving had been a bust, but what could be expected with a single mom watching her figure and a baby on formula and pureed peas?

She strapped Gus into his highchair and gave the clear plastic snowman on his tray a playful shake. The toy wobbled without falling, stuck to the tray by a suction cup. Gus followed suit, giving the snowman a whack that rattled the tiny blue and white balls inside him.

Lyndy smiled. "I'll be right back with your bottle."

The patio door swung open as she pressed the brew button on her coffee maker, and Cade strode inside. She suspected the shock on his face rivaled the expression on her own. "I hope I didn't wake you," he said, stripping out of the wool-lined denim coat. He hung the jacket on the rack beside her French door and turned his Stetson upside down on the counter. The material of his pale gray T-shirt clung to the planes and angles of his chest and torso.

She hadn't dreamed it, as she'd suspected, or blown his attractiveness out of proportion as she'd tossed and turned through the night. Cade Lance was smoking hot. Which, in her experience, probably meant he knew it and was insufferable, or he didn't know it because he had the IQ of a potato.

"No," Lyndy said, refocusing on the coffee. "You startled me. I've been sneaking around in here trying not to wake you."

Cade moved in close and stretched an arm in her direction. "May I?" he asked reaching for the freshly brewed pot.

"Mmm-hmm." She moved away and finished making Gus's bottle.

He poured two mugs and offered one to her.

"Thanks." She carried it to the table along with Gus's

bottle, then helped her son manage his breakfast. "How did you sleep?"

Cade leaned against the counter and crossed his long legs at the ankles. "I don't sleep."

"No?" She waited for more on the subject, but it didn't come, so she switched gears. "What were you doing outside?" she asked, still puzzling over the fact he didn't sleep. Was that by choice? Part of the job? Personally, she'd give anything for an uninterrupted eight hours.

"I patrolled the property. Evaluated the perimeter. Checked your barn and outbuildings."

Her stomach tightened with unbidden memories of the previous night and the life-changing knowledge of exactly who Cade had been looking for. "Find anything I should worry about?"

"Just a whole lot of quiet. It's a large property. Probably best if you stick close to the house. Stay in the yard. We need to establish a tight perimeter. Eight acres is too much to monitor with any real success." He ran a huge hand over his cropped hair.

Lyndy blew across the surface of her steaming coffee, enjoying the heady scent and the current view. If she had to be trapped inside with anyone, Cade certainly wasn't the worst she could do.

He dropped his hand away from his hair and jerked to attention, suddenly focused in the direction of her front door. "Wait here." He pushed away from the counter, revealing a holstered gun in the waistband of his jeans as he passed her.

Lyndy felt her eyes go wide. "What's happening?"

Cade was already at the front window. "Someone's here."

Lyndy forced herself upright, freeing Gus from his

highchair and gripping him to her chest. A moment later, she heard tires crunching over her gravel drive. "Who is it?"

"Black SUV. Government plates." He relaxed visibly. "Feds."

"Feds?" she parroted, her voice hitching unnaturally. "Federal agents?"

He nodded. "It's protocol for the FBI to get involved when words like 'serial killer' start being thrown around."

Lyndy swallowed a brick of nausea and joined him at the door.

The world glistened outside beneath a layer of shimmering frost.

Detective Owens strode up the walk with a man in a black suit on his heels. They climbed the front porch steps in tandem, breaths coming in little white puffs. Cade opened the front door.

"Morning, Ms. Wells, Gus." Detective Owens smiled at her, then at her baby boy. "And this must be Cade Lance. It's nice to finally meet you."

Cade offered the detective his hand. "You, as well."

Lyndy cuddled Gus tighter, warming him against the chilly morning air. "Come in." She stepped back to make room for the men to pass, certain that whatever measure of peace she'd found over her first cup of coffee was soundly behind her. "How do you know each other?"

"I have a lot of family in law enforcement throughout the state," Cade said, closing the door behind her guests.

The suit offered Cade a hand before shaking hers, as well. "I'm Agent Maxwell. Sorry to show up so early and unannounced. We felt that time was of the essence. You understand."

She nodded woodenly, though she didn't understand

any of it. The previous night had been a blur, and by the light of day, the memories felt more like something she'd seen in a movie than something she'd truly experienced. If it wasn't for the scrapes and bruises on her body and the men before her, she'd question if any of it was real.

The living room felt infinitely smaller with three tightly wound men gathered inside. Agent Maxwell and Detective Owens took seats on opposite ends of her couch. Cade chose the love seat beside it, and after a moment of indecision, Lyndy took Gus with her to the armchair between the two. The apex, it seemed, of a brooding triangle.

Detective Owens cleared his throat and offered Lyndy an encouraging smile. "How are you feeling this morning?"

"I'm okay," she said, repositioning Gus in her arms. "I think we're going to be just fine." That was the prayer anyway, and she had Cade now. Presumably her attacker would move on, and there was still a significant possibility that he wasn't the serial killer they suspected he might be. What were they going on, really? Didn't every abduction happen like hers? A woman alone at dusk. A man creeping in the shadows? She shivered as a memory of her escape thrust itself forward.

"Have you thought of anything more you can tell us?" Detective Owens asked. "Anything at all. Even something that seems insignificant to you might be the exact detail the FBI needs to decide where to go next."

"No." She shook her head. Lyndy had replayed the attack a thousand times, but nothing ever changed. "Nothing new."

Cade leaned forward, drawing Lyndy's attention and

fixing his gaze on Agent Maxwell. "What can you tell us about her attacker?"

The agent studied Cade for a long moment before shifting his gaze to Lyndy. "We believe you were targeted by a man we're calling the Kentucky Tom Cat because he likes to play cat and mouse with his victims. So far, more than a dozen women in surrounding counties have reported experiences exactly like yours. He hides in the shadows near their cars or outside their front doors and waits for them to come near. He dresses in dark coveralls. Only whispers. Always wears gloves. He's very methodical in the care he takes to repeat his crimes and hide his identity."

The moments of her near abduction returned with a vivid and visceral crash. She touched the heated skin of her throat, reminding herself the assailant's arm was no longer there. It was just a memory. She could breathe. She was safe.

She felt Cade's gaze on her cheek but couldn't bring herself to look at him.

"You say he repeats the crimes?" Cade asked. "What are the details?"

"Truthfully," Detective Owens answered, "the crimes have escalated."

Agent Maxwell shot the detective a warning look. Clearly this was his information to divulge. "Two of the early victims were abducted, beaten, raped and eventually released, though none could describe their attacker and there was no DNA evidence left behind. The four most recent victims were killed," he said flatly. "Our profiler believes the Tom Cat was probably practicing early on, deciding how he wanted the scenarios to play out."

"What kind of man are we looking for?" Cade asked. "What's the physical profile?"

"White," the agent said, "in his thirties, white collar, acceptably attractive and comfortable enough interacting with people that he wouldn't stand out as dangerous." He turned his eyes to Lyndy. "We believe you probably know him. He's been in your life somehow before this and taken his time to learn your routines and patterns."

Lyndy's chest tightened, and she struggled to take a full breath. "What about the other women? You said they're from other counties, but I never leave town. Did he know all of us?"

"We believe so, yes. He likely has a job that allows or requires him to travel regularly, at least within the tri-county area."

"And he's killed four women?" she asked, feeling the coffee churn in her empty stomach.

"Four that we're aware of. There could be more, but because the deaths were in different counties, and there were a number of months between the discovery of each body, it took some time to put the crimes together, then a little longer to find and interview victims of the earlier crimes we now believe he was responsible for."

A renegade tear trailed over Lyndy's cheek, hot and unbidden. She swiped it away, desperate to appear much stronger than she was for the sake of her company. Three men who'd probably never known the bone-deep, blood-freezing terror of being overpowered the way she had been.

"Ms. Wells?" the agent asked. "If you'd like to stop…"

"No. I want to get through this. It's just that I can still feel his hands on me." She swallowed another massive lump of fear and grimaced at the ache.

To her surprise, Cade covered her small hand with his and gave her fingers a squeeze. She turned to find determination in his fierce blue eyes.

Her jaw dropped, and he released her, as if the comforting gesture and encouraging words were nothing remarkable. As if he, one of three virtual strangers in the room, hadn't noticed she was on the verge of a freak-out, then delivered the perfect antidote.

Lyndy kissed Gus's soft hair to re-center herself, then asked the question that had kept her up all night. "Why is he doing this?"

The agent pursed his lips and folded his hands on his lap before answering. "It could be a number of things. Perhaps the result of severe neglect or abuse as a child. Maybe he's off his meds or desperately in need of them. We won't know for sure until we can talk to him. Maybe not even then. First, we have to figure out who he is. We're reviewing footage from the news coverage at your crime scene. The segment drew a crowd. If the Tom Cat enjoys the spotlight, he might be on the tape, eating up the hoopla. We're also paying close attention to all the anonymous tips that come in. Sometimes guys like this will try to get involved in their own investigations, become informants, insert themselves however they can. Some want to be caught. Others want to up the stakes. We suspect the Tom Cat enjoys the hunt as much as the attack. Maybe more. He seems to put extreme thought into choosing his victims and acting on the plans."

Cade rubbed a hand over his lips, apparently processing the horror only a little better than she was. "One more question," he said. "I'm still unclear why you think Ms. Wells's attacker is the same man you're describing? Is it just because he was near her car after dark?"

"I'm afraid not," Agent Maxwell said solemnly. He opened a black leather portfolio and retrieved a stack of glossy eight-by-ten photos. He began to place them in rows across the coffee table.

Cade swore under his breath, and Detective Owens looked away.

Lyndy's lungs, eyes and nose burned as she watched photo after photo appear in the surreal lineup of the Tom Cat's victims. More than sixteen in all, each one abducted, *four killed*.

And every victim looked exactly like Lyndy.

Chapter Three

It was hours after the detective and agent left before Cade dared approach Lyndy's bedroom door. She'd taken Gus and gone straight into her room before the federal agent's SUV had made it out of the driveway. Cade had spent the meantime replacing all the old locks on her farmhouse doors and windows. He'd passed by her closed bedroom door a few times, as well, unsure if he should check on her or leave her alone. It was always quiet. Maybe she'd fallen asleep with her baby? Maybe she was on a private phone call, or was crying. How could he know? Was it his job to know? Possibly, but it was definitely not his job to intrude on her personal space. She'd clearly shut the door for privacy. In all his previous jobs, the client had gone on with his or her life while Cade simply tagged along, keeping an eye out, blending into the background while abusive exes or second-rate stalkers were located and arrested in a timely manner. He'd never been assigned to someone whose life had been essentially and indefinitely put on hold by anything so serious. The situation had him on edge. He couldn't imagine what someone half his size with none of his training and an infant to protect might be feeling.

When she hadn't made a reappearance by lunch, Cade

made a new plan. He prepared a stack of sandwiches from the meats and cheeses in her fridge and poured two glasses of ice water, then rapped gently on her door. "Hello?"

He waited through the squeaky sound of bedsprings and the featherlight pats of Lyndy's feet over wooden floorboards. He prepared himself for the worst. For a woman with frayed nerves. A woman in tears. A combination of the two?

Lyndy opened the door looking like his favorite daydream. She'd added waves to her short blond hair and traded the T-shirt and jeans for a creamy V-neck sweater and brown leggings that highlighted her curves and drew his attention inappropriately. She'd paired the flirty little ensemble with tan-and-white cowgirl boots.

"Hey," she said, her big blue eyes wide and alert. "I've been thinking, and I want to help find this guy, who I'm going to call Tom, because I refuse to call any adult person *the Tom Cat*."

Cade forced his eyes away from her clingy cashmere top only to find his gaze stuck to the iridescent coating of gloss on her perfect rosebud mouth. "Okay."

"Great." She slipped past him and headed for the kitchen with a swing in her hips. "What did you do while you were in the Marines?"

He did his best to keep his eyes off her backside as she moved to the table and helped herself to half a sandwich. "What do you mean?"

She took a bite and chewed thoughtfully. "This is delicious. Thank you. I meant, what was your job? Were you a mechanic? A medic? A sharpshooter?"

"No." But he was one hell of a shot. "I was in Intelligence."

Her eyes lit. "So you're observant."

' *Painfully so*, he thought, shifting uncomfortably in his jeans. "Why?"

Lyndy gave her sandwich a rest and bit into the thick of her bottom lip. "I thought we could take Gus into town and visit the places I go most frequently, aside from the office. I called off work for the rest of the week. I don't want to get into all this with my coworkers just yet."

"You want me to take you into town so you can show me around?" he asked, unsure of her angle.

"Yeah." A slight look of guilt crossed her pretty face. "I pulled up the social media profiles of the four fatal Tom Cat victims while I was in my room."

Cade groaned.

Lyndy pressed on. "I want to know how Tom found me and how he found them. There has to be a common denominator. Sure, we look alike, but what put us in his path? Did he just drive around looking for short blondes with bobbed hair, blue eyes and freckles?" She huffed. "I can't figure it out, but I was never in Intelligence." Her eyes flashed. "Maybe you'll notice something I haven't."

Cade crossed his arms and stared. He didn't like the idea of leaving the house with her, not when the man who attacked her was still out there. And he hated the idea of her getting any more involved in this mess than she already was. "I think we should let the feds and Owens handle the investigation. They'll do their jobs and I'll do mine. You'll be easier to defend at a secure location. If you think of anything new you want to tell them, you can give them a call."

Her brows furrowed. "Well, I can't stay in here until they find him. It's already been a year since his first murder and there were plenty of victims before those, plus I hate being idle." Lyndy pursed her lips. "I'm scared, and I have to do something."

"Why don't I help you put up the Christmas tree? Maybe hang some stockings?" He tipped his head in the direction of a stack of plastic storage bins lined against the living room wall. She'd clearly been planning to decorate soon. Why not today? "I'll make hot chocolate."

She crossed her arms, unmoved and mimicking his stance. "I want to help catch this guy before he strikes again. What if he's planning his next attack now? What if I'm not so lucky the next time? What if he hurts Gus? Or another woman? The more input I can give the police, the faster this lunatic can be caught, and the sooner I can sleep again. Preferably before Christmas."

Cade moved his hands to his hips. He couldn't hold her captive or tell her what to do, but he could stick close, and he could keep her safe. "All right," he conceded, "but you have to stay in my sights at all times, preferably within reach, and if I say it's time to go, we need to leave immediately."

She nodded. "Agreed," she said. "And I think we should pretend to be a couple." She raised a palm. "Hear me out."

Cade worked to control his stunned expression. He'd endured some wild requests from clients before, but those usually involved him staying out of the way, not faking a romantic relationship. And from an ethical and professional standpoint, given the physical effect this woman was having on him from the start, he should definitely say no.

"Sometimes having a boyfriend is the only thing that gets creeps to leave women alone," Lyndy said, sounding as if she'd had some solid personal experience on the subject.

He ground his teeth at the thought of someone not accepting her rejection immediately and with an apology.

"According to the other victims' social media statuses," she continued, "they were all single. Maybe if I have a significant other, it will diminish his interest in me while we look for where he and I might have initially crossed paths. I'm not suggesting anything inappropriate," she said, clearly on a roll. "You don't have to kiss me or anything. Just some hand-holding or close walking while we're in public. I wasn't asking you to…" She motioned between them until her cheeks went red. "Never mind. Forget I suggested it."

Cade laughed, then frowned. Pretending to be her boyfriend, for her safety's sake, sounded like just enough fun to cause him trouble later. Though he wasn't ready to think too long or hard about how much or what kind of trouble. What worried him more was the fact he couldn't say no to her. *He didn't want to.* If walking through town made her feel like she was helping save other women, if it made her happy, then they were going to town. "How long have we been dating?"

Lyndy rocked onto her toes and beamed; a flush of gratitude and appreciation colored her cheeks and flooded her eyes. "Not long," she said. "The relationship's still new, so we're gooey on each other. That'll keep me close to you, and explain why we don't know everything about one another in case anyone asks questions. I'll get Gus." She hurried away, the soft material of her leggings caressing the curve of her backside.

Cade let his head fall back and his lids go shut. He swallowed an internal groan. If she kept looking at him like that, he wouldn't be able to concentrate long enough to spot a charging rhino before it hit her, and that was the absolute scariest thought he'd had since leaving Afghanistan.

LYNDY KEPT HER eyes on the scenery as they rode into downtown Piedmont. Her nerves were shot. Her bravado had failed, and she was certain that going home might actually be the smartest thing she could do. Instead, she'd soon be strolling around town with Gus and a man wearing a cowboy hat and blue jeans that made her think anything was possible. Plus a few other things she hadn't thought about in a year. She blamed the lapse of judgment on discovering her favorite clothes fitted again and the unfounded confidence that came with wearing them.

Beyond the glass, her town had openly welcomed the holiday season. Shops had dragged faux snowmen and artificial decorated trees outside their doors. Oversize wreaths hung from lampposts and familiar Christmas tunes piped through hidden speakers on the more highly trafficked streets. "Here." She pointed to a small lot between brick office buildings. "We can park for free as long as we don't stay more than two hours."

Cade maneuvered his mammoth truck into a tiny space and cut the engine. "Are you sure you feel up to this?"

"No," she answered honestly, "but I'm sure the potential payoff is worth a walk through town on a beautiful day. Don't you agree?" She unfastened her seat belt and pulled her purse onto her lap.

Cade watched her with knowing eyes, and she forced herself not to squirm. He probably saw everything she didn't say. He probably knew she was a coward playing at brave. That she'd spent an hour checking the prices on monthlong cruises to Alaska and bus fare to Timbuktu before deciding to suck it up and become part of the solution.

She worked her dry mouth open and pulled in a steadying breath. "We'll be quick. Then we can go home and look over the other women's online profiles and photos again. See if anything matches." Lyndy glanced at Gus in his car seat on the rear bench, then back at Cade. "Let me know if you notice any man watching me."

Cade made a sour face and turned away. "With you wearing that outfit, I'm going to need to make a list," he mumbled, climbing out the driver's side door.

Lyndy smiled. It really was a great outfit.

She joined Cade on the sidewalk and tucked Gus into the sling she used to keep him on her hip when he was alert and eager to explore. The sling had been made for her and fitted nicely over the white waist-length ski jacket she'd paired with her ensemble. "So, this is our big town," she told Cade with a grin. "It's no Lexington, but it's got everything a person could want."

Cade moved in close to her side and slid his palm against hers. "Agreed." He twined their fingers and gave hers a squeeze. "Are we still doing this?"

Lyndy opened her mouth, then shut it. The unexpected pulse of electricity beating through their joined hands and in her chest was a whole lot to process. "Um." She cleared her throat. "We don't have to."

"Does it make you feel safer?" he asked.

"Yes," she answered, more breathlessly than intended and curled her fingers over his.

An hour later they'd visited a dozen places she loved to go. She'd never realized how many locations she stopped on a regular basis. Bank, post office, general shopping, ice cream…the list went on. And they hadn't even gotten to the gym.

They headed up the street to Lyndy's favorite café and climbed the steps to the door. "Have you seen anything interesting yet?" she asked. "Anything unusual?"

"I saw you dig a pacifier from the bottom of your purse and clean it with your mouth before giving it to your kid," he said. "That was weird."

"It was dirty." She rubbed goose bumps off the back of her neck while Cade opened the door for her, then she moved swiftly inside. For the first time all day, she felt strangely exposed. Lyndy gave the street outside a cursory glance. Nothing seemed out of place to her. No creepy figures glaring back. Maybe she was just running out of steam.

"You okay?" Cade asked, setting his palm against her back.

"Yeah." She gave him a small smile. "I'm definitely disappointed nothing stood out during our walk, but uneventful seems pretty good, too."

He nodded but cast his gaze in the direction she'd just looked. Had he sensed something too, or was he that in tune with her somehow? "Where do we go from here?" he asked.

"I'm not sure." She stroked Gus's cheek and led Cade to a corner table. "According to their social media accounts, the other victims worked in offices just like mine."

"What do you do in your office?" he asked.

"Interviews, mostly. I work at a local temping agency, placing folks into roles where companies have needs. We work with businesses in Piedmont and throughout northern Kentucky. Sometimes as far as Cincinnati, Ohio, but none in any of the towns where Tom's other victims were found. I checked."

He smiled. "Of course you did."

LYNDY IGNORED THE note of pride in his tone and the corresponding bolt of warmth in her core. "As far as I can tell, none of the other women had babies. Do you think Tom found me at my ob-gyn or Lamaze classes? Do you think he has my home address?" She ran a nervous hand through her hair and looked outside once more.

Cade captured her hand in his and tugged gently until she looked his way. "Hey." He stroked his broad thumb across the back of her fingers. "I've got you," he said slow and smooth. The sexy tenor of his voice mixed with the scent of his cologne and curled her toes inside her boots.

Another wave of eerie goose bumps hit, and she turned her face back to the window.

"What is it?" Cade asked, stepping forward and staring through the glass at her side. "Do you see something?"

"No. I just have this icky feeling."

The waitress appeared. "What can I get started for you guys?"

Lyndy's stomach coiled, and the fine hairs on her arms rose to attention beneath her coat and sweater. "A latte for me, please," she told the young girl with a brown corkscrew ponytail and white apron. She touched Cade's arm, reluctantly dragging his gaze from the window. "I should change Gus. I'll be right back."

Cade looked over her shoulder toward the bathroom hallway. "All right."

The waitress waited, impatiently. "For you, sir?"

Lyndy hustled to the ladies' room without waiting to hear his order. She needed to put some distance between herself and the picture window overlooking Main Street, then hopefully shake off the heebie-jeebies crawling all over her skin. When she got back to Cade, she was going to suggest they take their orders *to go*.

CADE ORDERED A house coffee and took the corner seat where he could easily watch the street, the café patrons and the hallway where Lyndy and her son had run off. Until a minute ago, the day had been peaceful, and he'd enjoyed the walk around a relatively quiet town. Being with Lyndy and her son felt incredibly normal and inexplicably calming. It was a welcome change after the last few years spent on edge. Cade had even dared to hope the FBI agent was wrong, and Lyndy's experience wasn't part of this chain of escalating attacks, but the way she'd looked outside before taking off said otherwise. Cade had learned long ago to trust his gut. Now he was going to trust hers.

The familiar bong of a special news bulletin brought his attention to the television hanging behind the register. A woman with a mic and pantsuit centered the screen outside a park. A thick line of text below her read, *Kentucky Tom Cat Killer comes a little too close for comfort*.

Cade focused on the gathered crowd. What if Lyndy's attacker was on-screen right now? The camera maintained a tight focus on the reporter, blurring onlookers' faces. Still, there were other things worth noting. A large red pickup truck in the background, for example, and a man dressed in all camouflage on the periphery.

Cade scanned the café and then the street. No activity in the bathroom hallway. No one in full camouflage.

No red pickups outside. Though there was a man in a plain black ball cap across the street about a block away, and there had been one just like that on television until the news clip ended. The cap had belonged to one of the many blurred faces.

Cade stood for a better look at the man outside, but distance and a shadow cast from a nearby building made it nearly impossible to discern anything specific about him. He leaned against a telephone pole with his back to the street, but he'd looked over his shoulder several times since Cade had begun to watch. A coincidence? Something more sinister? Maybe he was just a man waiting for his friends or a spouse. The ball cap was nothing special, after all. Lots of people owned plain black caps, though he was the only one in the immediate area.

The bathroom door opened, and Lyndy strode out. Her smile was bright and wide as she kissed her baby's little fingers. "Sorry that took so long. This little guy thought it was playtime." Her smile fell. "What's wrong?"

Cade glanced back across the street, but the man was gone. "I'm not sure," he said. Cade rubbed his chin as an interesting idea formed. "Agent Maxwell said Tom might be watching the crime scenes, and I can't help wondering if he's also watching you."

Lyndy stilled. "I wondered that, too." She wound her arm around his and moved in close. Her soft, honey-scented skin was a distraction Cade couldn't afford, but that was a whole other problem.

"There was someone up the block a minute ago," he said. "He seemed to be looking this way, but I took my eyes off of him, and now he's gone." He checked every face on the street for one that was staring back, checked every head for the simple black cap, but found none.

"Do you think he's gone?" she asked. "Or just moved out of sight?" Lyndy slid her hand down his forearm and twined her shaking fingers with his.

"I don't know," Cade admitted. *But there was one way to tell.*

He dipped his head slightly and turned to face Lyndy, forming a small cocoon between them where the conversation would be for their ears only. "I'd like to test a theory," he began carefully. "It could help us know if someone's still watching."

Lyndy glanced outside, then back to Cade. "Okay."

He ran his hands along her arms to her elbows. "Are you comfortable with me kissing your cheek?"

She nodded, a sudden storm brewing in her eyes.

"At this angle it will look like something more from outside. Ready?"

Lyndy wet her lips. "Yes."

"First, laugh," he whispered. "Pretend I've said something that makes you really happy."

Lyndy's worried expression softened into a warm smile and a bubble of tinkling laughter slipped out.

The sound burrowed deep into Cade's core, and he slid his palm against her soft cheek. He tucked a swath of short hair gently behind her ear, and Lyndy's expression changed again.

She covered his hand with hers and pressed his palm more firmly to her cheek before rising onto her toes and angling her beautiful face up to his.

Her glossy lips parted, and her eyelids drifted shut.

Cade fought the urge to take her mouth and taste those sweet lips as her breath danced over his skin.

She curved her small hand around the nape of his

neck and pulled him in closer. "How's this instead?" she whispered.

BOOM! The sudden sound of an explosion tore them apart.

The formerly crystal clear café window was now nothing more than a million tiny shards of glass. A gust of icy wind swirled through the café and down Cade's spine.

Undeniably, the Kentucky Tom Cat Killer was still hunting his mouse.

Chapter Four

Cade took the turn away from town at a crawl, half his attention on Lyndy and half on the road ahead. "You okay?" he asked, for at least the dozenth time since witnessing the café window shatter beside him.

If Cade had to guess, he'd say the culprit used a glass punch to destroy the window. He'd seen the tool used before with similar results, though never on such a large pane. It was generally used by emergency personnel to save pets or children locked in cars on hot days or free the passengers of vehicles that had become submerged, but could be effective under any circumstance. Not to mention easy to acquire and operate. Also, small and easily concealed.

Cade's grip tightened on the wheel as the reality hit home once more. The Kentucky Tom Cat Killer was still watching Lyndy. Cade couldn't help wondering what else the psychopath had in his arsenal. Or what he would do to Lyndy if Cade failed.

Lyndy dragged her attention away from the collection of lawmen shrinking behind them in the distance, uselessly littering the sidewalk drenched in broken glass. Their diminishing silhouettes reflected in the rearview mirror and the ones on the sides. "I'm still okay," she said, her eyes clear and voice steady, before turning back to her window.

She'd been equally calm as she'd given her statement to the police and listened to the statements of others standing nearby. Nearly two dozen people had heard the window break. No one had seen who'd caused it.

And Cade hadn't seen the man in the black ball cap again.

He gave Lyndy another look. She seemed fine, sounded fine, looked fantastic, but how could she be any of those things? A serial killer had recently tried and failed to abduct her and her infant son. Now the lunatic was stalking her. He didn't need an eyewitness to confirm that truth. They'd agreed to test the theory, and they'd gotten their answer loud and clear when she'd risen on her toes to kiss him. The window hadn't exploded on its own. The Tom Cat had been watching, and he'd done what it took to stop the kiss.

But why had Lyndy been about to kiss him on the lips when Cade had just explained that a kiss on her cheek would do the trick? He slid his eyes in her direction once more. Did she want to kiss him? The possibility was nearly as jarring as the effort's aftermath. He shook the thought away. They'd just met. She was in danger. People did crazy things under difficult circumstances. He cleared his throat and refocused his thoughts on something sensible. "You don't have to put up a brave front," he said. "The situation you're in would wreck anyone."

"I'm not wrecked," she said defiantly, "and I do have to put up a front. If not for Gus, then for effect." She turned to him suddenly, imploring him with those wide blue eyes. "I'm terrified. My insides are in knots and my hands are trembling, but I can't let whoever is doing this know he's getting exactly what he wants. He doesn't deserve that. And to be honest, if I let myself start crying now, I probably won't stop, so it's better that I just schedule my complete emotional breakdown for another time, I think."

Cade felt the corners of his mouth edge up, impressed with her humor and fortitude despite it all. Though he knew the words she'd spoken in jest were likely true. He'd thought a number of similar things in bad situations. There was a time to fight and a time to let go. Clearly it was still time to fight.

"Do you think he did it to stop the kiss or to let me know he's still here?" Lyndy asked, pulling Cade's attention once more. "Is it a game to him? Or was it a power move?"

"Maybe both," Cade answered honestly. "I've never studied serial killers, but this feels more serious than a game to me." In truth, whatever this was felt more like a hunt.

Lyndy wet her pink lips and exhaled long and slow. "Great."

Cade signaled his next turn, then cast a careful look at the petite blonde beside him. "I might've made it worse by showing up. Not that you had a choice. You obviously need the protection, but I'm willing to bet the nut doesn't appreciate the competition."

She turned to him at the word *competition*, eyes wide in understanding. "I'll be harder to take now. We've inadvertently upped the stakes."

Cade turned his attention back to the road. "I will protect you," he vowed. "You and Gus. You can count on that. It's what I'm trained for."

"Protected a lot of helpless victims?" she asked, self-deprecation thick in her tone.

"Yes." *Entire towns full*, he thought sadly. "But you aren't helpless. You've already fought and won against this guy once. Don't forget that. You're the victor here. He's the loser."

Her crystal eyes brimmed with unshed tears as she shifted on the seat, angling her body toward him. Her sweet honey scent wafted through the warming cab. "It was still a good idea to try to draw him out," she said. "Even if the authorities don't catch him today, at least we've confirmed he's still here. The feds won't leave now, and the story will be all over the news. Everyone will know about him, and that'll make them safer. Plus, he'll be forced to move carefully. All good things."

That was all true, but he hadn't expected her concern about the town to warm him to her further. He cleared his throat and attempted to get mentally back on course. "The police presence definitely drew a big crowd. Lots of faces to compare with those in the news footage shot outside the park following your attack. I'm sure it won't be long before officials have the Tom Cat in their crosshairs."

Lyndy settled back in her seat once more, a grin on her pretty lips. "Then we really did do a good thing. I heard the detective say they were opening a tip line, too."

"Tip lines can be complicated," Cade said, taking the final turn onto Lyndy's road. "Those numbers generally bring out half the nutjobs and attention seekers in the county."

"Isn't that what Tom is?" she asked. "A nutjob and attention seeker? Maybe he'll call in."

Cade cocked an eyebrow. "Why does this awful conversation seem to make you happy?"

"Because I'm doing something, even if it's only brain-storming. I can't sit idle and be a duck."

"A duck?"

She rolled her eyes and turned away once more. "A sitting duck."

"Right." Cade shook his head, strangely proud of her go-getter attitude. Guarding this blond beauty and her infant son would be more complicated than he'd originally bargained.

But Cade was up for the challenge.

LYNDY SETTLED GUS into his crib for a nap, then went to hunt down some sweet tea. The drink jazzed a lot of folks up, too much sugar and caffeine, but the combination was balm to her jagged nerves. Her mother and grandmother had poured sweet tea for every occasion, whether they'd needed to talk, laugh or cry. These days, the mere scent of it tossed her into fits of nostalgia, but for a long time after each of their deaths, the scent had pushed her to tears. At the moment, she needed a tall, cold glass to re-mind her she would get through this, the way she'd gotten through their losses, Sam's and everything else life had unfairly thrown at her.

She sighed at the blessed sight of a nearly full pitcher in her refrigerator, then poured two Mason jars full when she caught sight of Cade, making his way across the property outside the kitchen window. His steady gaze jumped to meet hers in the window above the sink and his scowl seemed to fade.

"Sweet tea?" she asked, projecting her voice and lift-ing a jar into Cade's view.

He cleared the back porch steps with an effortless leap, then crossed into the kitchen a moment later. "I love sweet tea." He set his hat on the counter and accepted the jar. His lips curved into a smile as he sipped. "That's good."

"Thanks. It's my grandmama's recipe. According to her this tea could fix anything that ails ya." Lyndy returned his smile. "I'm not sure how well it'll work on fending off serial killers, but I'm willing to give it a try." She raised the jar to her lips, a fresh ribbon of fear tightening around her heart.

Cade moved into the space beside her, leaning against the sink and sipping his tea. "You've got a nice place here."

"Thanks." She breathed in the calm radiating from him and prayed the tea would do its work.

"I'm truly sorry you lost your fiancé like that. I'm sorry Gus lost his daddy."

Lyndy's heart wrenched at the kindness spoken toward her son, and at the reminder that her boy, like her, would grow up without a father. It wasn't what she'd want for anyone, certainly not for her own child, but here she was. Her father had left by choice. Gus's had been taken. A vicious cycle of loss.

"They never got to meet," she said, her grandmama's tea making the story a little easier to tell. "I couldn't eat or sleep for days after Sam died. I was sick all the time, and I'd assumed it was shock. It was morning sickness, but I didn't know. I was too mired in grief to realize he'd left me with a new life."

Cade watched her. "Sam never knew?"

"No." She turned the cold jar in her hands, letting cool drops of condensation roll over her fingers.

"How long has he been gone?"

"A year." She pulled in a long breath, then released

it slowly, the way she'd learned at her support group for victims of sudden loss. "Somedays the memories feel more like bits from movies I've almost forgotten than reality." She puffed out her cheeks and let her eyes fall shut. Just like the memories of her attack. Her brain's way of dealing with the trauma. "Sorry." She shot him an impish smile. "Talk about oversharing."

"It's not," Cade assured. "I want to know, and what you're describing is typical in the aftermath of trauma. My time spent overseas feels like that to me sometimes. I know I was there. Know I saw and experienced certain things, but my mind puts a filter on them for distance. It cushions the impact, and I don't always mind. There was a time when those cushions kept me moving forward."

Lyndy finished her tea and set the jar aside, enjoying the companionable silence that followed. "We might be kindred spirits, Cade Lance."

"We might," he agreed.

Lyndy felt the brush of his arm against hers as they stood side by side in her kitchen. The musky scent of him warmed her, and she leaned closer, hungry for more of whatever it was about him that made her feel so safe. So strong. And so insanely feminine. She did her best to remember their relationship was professional. That she'd hired him to protect her and her son. And that it would be reckless and stupid to read into anything he said or did as attraction to her. Still, she enjoyed the strange stirring his nearness created in her. And she didn't mind the distraction.

Cade turned toward her, eyebrows drawn, as if he'd somehow read her mind. "Lyndy?"

She bit into her bottom lip, reminding herself that she needed Cade for protection, and that she wasn't in the market for a man. For the next eighteen years or so Gus would come before everything else, her hormones included. "Yes?"

Curiosity danced in his narrowed eyes. "In the café today…what were you planning on doing before the glass broke?"

She stared dumbly back, unable to admit she'd planned to kiss him. That she'd been caught in the moment, trapped in his spell, and it had felt like the exact right thing to do.

Until it hadn't.

Cade's lips parted, and his gaze fell to her mouth.

She imagined the taste of him. The warmth and pressure of his tongue on hers. The delicious scrape of his unshaven cheek against her skin.

Gus's angry cry ricocheted through her home and heart, throwing ice onto her fire and embarrassing her to the core. She jumped away, unable to look at Cade as she dashed down the hall toward Gus's room.

She had no idea what was wrong with her, but one thing was for sure.

If she kept behaving like that, the Tom Cat wouldn't have a chance to kill her. She'd already be dead of humiliation.

Chapter Five

Cade spent the rest of the afternoon alone. Lyndy had only returned once from the bedroom. She made a bottle with Gus on one hip, poured another jar of iced tea, then vanished back down the hall, leaving Cade to himself. He hadn't minded the silence at first. He'd been wholly thankful, in fact, for the break that allowed him to collect his wits and breathe again without her presence skewing his thoughts.

He'd expected a logical explanation for her behavior at the café. Perhaps it was an off-the-cuff improvisation. Something she'd thought would be more effective in drawing Tom out than a peck on the cheek. Cade had been certain that Lyndy would answer with her usual directness and the same matter-of-fact attitude he'd come to appreciate. But instead, it had looked as if she wanted to kiss him again! Could that be right?

Either way, it left a more dangerous and pressing question unanswered. What would Cade have done if Gus hadn't broken the spell? The *correct* answer was that he would have pulled back and stopped her. He should have been prepared to explain politely that their relationship was professional. But before her son had uttered a peep, Cade had already imagined the weight of her against him as he curled her in his arms. He'd anticipated the press of her lips on his and the soft skim of her fingers against his chest.

UNABLE TO MAKE sense of the emotional collision, he'd decided to double down on the job at hand. First by walking a sensible perimeter around Lyndy's farmhouse and evaluating various access points. Then by checking his messages and the local news sites for updates on law enforcement's progress on the case. He started with a cup of coffee and his laptop, intending to search the headlines for details on the Kentucky Tom Cat. Instead, he found himself typing Lyndy's fiancé's name into the search engine.

The story of his tragic death had dominated headlines for days, but Cade was oddly curious about who Sam had been in life. He quickly learned that Sam had held down a sensible office job and volunteered at the county animal shelter. He'd played baseball on a community league and judged the annual children's fishing tournament. Sam's life had been wholesome to the extreme, and comparatively, Cade's life was a hot, sometimes dangerous, mess.

He clicked the link below a photo of Sam and Lyndy in the next set of search results and landed on her neglected social media page. The only update she'd made in weeks was to showcase Gus's smile. He frowned at a photo of Sam. The man's appearance was average in every possible way, from his nondescript khakis to his bland, neutral-colored polos. He'd worn white sneakers and the same haircut Cade had stopped accepting in middle school. Furthermore, Sam was painfully clean-shaven in every photo on her page, and had an air of purity and innocence Cade couldn't fully understand. No wonder Lyndy had loved him. Sam appeared to be everything Cade's father had never been and everything Cade wasn't. Everything a son needed.

He shut the laptop and went to refill his mug. Sam had been Mr. Perfect, but if Lyndy was ever in the market for a man with limited money, a jacked-up biological family and a questionable past, Cade was the guy for her. He'd gone to the military instead of college. His brothers-in-arms were his family. He'd die of boredom behind any desk, and he sure as hell didn't own a pair of khakis. Though he did have a few black Fortress Defense polos, if she was into that.

He laughed at the ridiculousness of his thoughts as he rifled through her kitchen in search of a nine-by-thirteen pan and a few chicken breasts. He needed to get his head on straight. Sure, Lyndy was beautiful, kind and fierce, but that didn't mean he had to start wondering if he was good enough for her. He was there as her bodyguard.

He set the oven to preheat, then grabbed his phone. He needed to let his team know how the job was going and see if they had any advice for securing the vast perimeter.

His ears pricked at the sound of running water as he dialed. Bath time for baby? Or shower time for mama? Cade swallowed a groan, then stepped onto the frigid rear deck to wait for his call to connect.

If Lyndy was getting into the shower, he'd need plenty of fresh air to combat that image.

LYNDY ADJUSTED THE bathwater for Gus, losing herself in mommy mode, thankful for Gus's perfect, or possibly terrible, timing. Either way, she'd needed the reminder that her desires came second now. Gus would always be first. Bathed and changed, he now sat contentedly in his playpen while she opted to follow his lead with the cleanup. She tossed the soft sweater and leggings, gathered her barrel curls into a ponytail, then adjusted the water to her preference. Maybe a hot shower would keep her from trying to attack her protective detail for a third time today. She blushed, recalling the absurdity of her behavior. Clearly, it had been too long since anyone had looked at her the way Cade did. *Then again*, she thought, *no one has ever looked at me the way he does.* And looking at him did pretty thrilling things to her, too.

Twenty minutes later, she dried and dressed in her favorite jeans and a faded blue T-shirt, and then added fuzzy socks. She returned to Gus feeling more like herself than she had in a year, maybe longer. "What do you think?" she asked her baby. "Snack time?"

Gus opened his mouth in a broad toothless grin that melted her heart, and she scooped him against her. "I love you," she sighed, cradling his warmth to her chest and treasuring the feel of him in her arms. "You will always be my number one guy. Even when you're big enough to carry me instead." Assuming she survived the looming serial killer and lived to see Gus grow up at all.

The ugly thought ruined her moment and sent a round of chills skittering down her spine. Her gaze snapped to the windows, laden with shadow, then to the closed bedroom door. Much as she'd tried to avoid Cade after her infinitely lame attempt to kiss him, again, she suddenly needed to see him more than she needed to protect her pride.

She hurried down the hall toward the sound of his strong and steady voice, thankful not to be alone. She owed Detective Owens and his wife a casserole and all her gratitude for sending Cade her way. She couldn't imagine what the nights would be like without him here to protect her. Heck, without him, she wouldn't even know she was still a target. And that would've only ended one way. She cringed at the thought.

"You'd like her," he said to whoever was on the other end of the call. "She's brave. She's got that mama-bear vibe."

Lyndy paused. Was he talking about her? The mama bear reference was true enough, but how had he gotten the impression she was brave? She'd practically spent every moment since her near abduction fighting tears.

"Nah, I've got this," he went on, "but I could use some input on the perimeter situation and feedback on the pics and files I sent to your Fortress email account. Property details and county auditor information on the surrounding lands."

Lyndy stopped at the end of the hall, unsure how to announce her arrival and admiring the contours of his muscular back beneath the pale gray shirt.

He raked a hand over the top of his short hair, and her gaze lifted to his curled biceps. "Nah. I'm good. She's not what I expected. That's all."

She could only imagine what that meant. His tone implied the situation wasn't anything good, and she instantly regretted thinking the electricity she felt was mutual.

Gus cooed and gurgled, changing her train of thought from one of self-pity to panic.

Cade spun in their direction before Lyndy took a single step back.

"Add stealthy to that list I was giving you," Cade said, eyes wide and cheeks slightly flushed. "I'm going to have to call you back. Let me know what you think of those files."

"Sorry," she muttered, lifting her free hand hip-high in an embarrassed wave. "I suppose being caught eavesdropping is only slightly less embarrassing than getting into your personal space the way I did earlier."

"Don't worry about it," he said, a strained expression on his brow. "Either thing." He tucked the phone into his back pocket, and Lyndy tried not to envy the device. "I'm glad to see you again. I was beginning to wonder if you'd make a reappearance or secretly order your dinner for delivery to the bedroom window."

"Can I do that?" she asked, tossing a contemplative look over one shoulder.

Cade laughed. "No. Not tonight anyway. Weatherman's predicting rain, and the temperatures are dropping. I went out to check the property. The air's bitter cold." He cast a glance at her stove, then pushed his hands into the front pockets of his jeans. "You've had a big day, so I thought I'd make dinner. We can stay in, take it easy, maybe watch a movie or play cards."

"Well, it's all the same because my bedroom window is ancient and makes a terrible sound when it opens. You would've known what I was up to." She followed his gaze to the baking dish and chicken breasts on her counter. "You're cooking?"

He shrugged. "I'd planned to lure you out of your room with food if you didn't come back on your own."

She laughed and Gus kicked in her arms, reminding her she'd had more than one reason to leave the bedroom. "I got the creeps in there alone, so I had to come out. Plus, this guy wants a bottle." She kissed Gus's head and stroked his back as she made her way to the kitchen table, then strapped Gus into his seat.

Cade slid the baking dish into her preheated oven and set the timer. "I hope you like chicken parmigiana."

Lyndy shook her head, impressed but not surprised. "Everyone loves chicken parmigiana. I can't believe you cook, too. It doesn't seem fair."

Cade's mouth tipped into a lazy half smile. "What do you mean by *too*? What else do I do?"

She smiled as she tightened the lid on Gus's finished bottle. "You protect damsels and babies in distress for starters."

"True."

"How'd you learn to cook?" Lyndy returned to Gus with the bottle, more eager than she should be for Cade's answer.

"Necessity," he said. "There wasn't always enough money or food to go around when I was young, so I learned to make the ingredients we had last as long as possible for my siblings and me. I had to get creative with the cheap stuff, but I made it into a game, and I wasn't terrible at it. I know because even my older brother, Sawyer, ate without complaints. I still play around with recipes sometimes, but tonight, I went traditional."

Lyndy took in the touching story, the way he stepped in and met a need then and now without being asked, and she warmed impossibly further toward him. Cade Lance was definitely more than a handsome face.

An hour later, Lyndy finished the last bite of the best meal she'd eaten in ages. Her stomach was full and her brain was halfway to a carb coma from the double helpings of angel-hair pasta and parmesan-topped chicken. "That was amazing."

Cade carried their plates to the sink and rinsed them. "Thank you." He loaded the dishwasher and wiped down his work space.

"You don't have to do that," she said, pushing onto her feet to help. "You cooked. You don't have to clean, too." Though she appreciated his willingness. Sam had never done either. His view of the world was a little more black-and-white; or maybe pink-and-blue was the better analogy. She hadn't noticed until they'd bought the farm and moved in together, but Sam had a definite idea about what his roles would be in their relationship and none of those included anything that looked remotely like house-work or shopping. And he'd once chastised her for mow-ing the lawn, even though it was her day off and she'd meant to surprise him.

Cade slung a dish towel over one shoulder and leaned his backside against the counter, successfully blocking her access to the sink. "I made the mess. I clean it up."

She frowned. "That's not how division of labor works."

"Why don't you choose the movie. Maybe Gus can help."

Lyndy narrowed her eyes. "Fine."

"So you'll accept his help?" Cade asked.

Lyndy fought the urge to smile or stick out her tongue.

Cade turned back to the sink with a grin. "No chick flicks."

"Sorry. Gus likes chick flicks." Lyndy collected her baby from the swing, where she'd placed him after his bottle. Gus had enjoyed the soothing motion, music and lights while the grown-ups enjoyed dinner.

To Lyndy's surprise, the conversation had been nearly as good as the food. Cade had been candid and charming. Sharing more than she'd expected and listening intently as she shared in return. They'd talked at length about their jobs, hometowns and futures. She suspected that most of what he'd asked had been by design, intended to unearth details about her life that would be useful to the case at hand. Not really a casual dinner conversation at all. But she didn't mind. Cade had made her feel at ease when she needed it most. And he'd been forthright about his goals and future. Cade wanted to see Fortress Defense grow. He was enthusiastic and single-minded in the endeavor. Everything else would come in second for a long while, and she understood that kind of dedication. It was how she felt about raising Gus to be a good and honorable man. For her, everything and everyone else needed to get in line. Her goal probably seemed small and silly to Cade, a man who'd seen the world and started a thriving business with friends, but to Lyndy, her one goal was everything. And his goal only reminded her that Cade wasn't in the market for a relationship, and he didn't have time for a family. Not that he wanted one. He'd made that crystal clear the night they'd met. He was afraid he might discover he was like his father. He didn't want to make some poor woman a guinea pig, and she didn't want to be one. Though, from what she'd seen so far, she couldn't imagine he had a selfish or sinister side.

He passed her on his way to the couch, powering on the television while she played with Gus on the floor. A strange tension seemed to roll off him, and she knew instinctively where his thoughts had gone. "Lyndy?"

She pinched her eyes shut, knowing she'd be unable to look his way if he asked once more about her intentions toward him at the café, then again in her kitchen.

"We should probably still talk about…"

The phone cut him short.

He shifted on the cushion with a sigh, retrieving the phone from his pocket. "Cade Lance."

Lyndy dared a look in his direction, gauging the content of the call and wondering how to apologize for her earlier behavior without embarrassing herself again.

Cade's expression grew more grim with each passing second. "All right," he said finally, his voice thick and low. "I'll let her know."

Lyndy felt her bones go soft and her stomach coil. "Something happened," she guessed. "Something bad."

Cade worked his jaw a moment, processing or perhaps choosing his words.

"Say it," she demanded. "Tell me."

"There's been another attack."

Chapter Six

Cade carried the bulbous little car seat to his truck with Gus tucked inside. Lyndy had made the task look easier than it was. The contraption was heavy and awkward, and Cade was certain he'd knock it into something and somehow hurt the baby, or at the least make him cry. He would consider either a complete fail, and he never failed.

Lyndy opened the passenger-side door with trembling hands. "Thanks for carrying him."

"It's no problem." And he was secretly thankful for the carrier. He wasn't sure how he would've responded if she'd handed him the baby directly. He'd made it twenty-seven years without holding an infant, and tonight wasn't the night he wanted to learn a new skill.

"Here," Lyndy said, motioning to the open rear door of his extended cab. "The car seat will snap into place on the base."

Cade moved closer. He'd seen her remove the seat when they'd returned from town, but he hadn't paid any attention to how she'd set the thing up on the way there. He rested the little pod on the base, feigning confidence. Nothing happened. He wiggled and shimmied the seat until it slid in his grip, causing Gus to throw his hands wide and wrinkle his pink face. The prelude to a scream. Cade cursed inwardly. "It doesn't fit."

"It fits. You have to turn it around. Gus needs to face backward for a year."

"Why?"

Lyndy stepped against him, guiding his hand to turn the carrier until an audible click sounded and the car seat locked securely into the base. "Because it's the law. There. He's ready."

Cade dropped his hands away, determined to ignore the undeniable heat passing between them, despite the predicted drizzle of icy rain. He supposed part of the problem was a natural physical attraction. To be expected between two young, single people. The rest was likely a result of heightened emotions and increased adrenaline. Not to mention the internal, unspoken need for an outlet. It was the reason there were baby booms about a year after any major tragedy. People turned to one another for comfort. And at the moment, Cade needed to turn away from the woman standing too closely beside him and find another outlet. "Ready?"

The drive to the hospital was long and laced with tension. He'd planned to address the issue of their attraction casually after dinner. Make sure they were on the same page about personal boundaries and professionalism, but the call had put a stop to that, and he couldn't bring himself to mention it now. Not when they had no idea what they would find at the hospital. He doubted the Tom Cat's newest victim would be unconscious and hospitalized if her condition wasn't serious. And he suspected seeing her would be more difficult for Lyndy than she realized.

"You don't have to see her," he said, hoping to ease Lyndy's burden. "The detective said she's unconscious and pretty beat up. Maybe you can just speak with Detective Owens instead."

"I'd like to meet her," Lyndy said. "I feel like I should. It's the least I can do, considering my escape is likely the reason he acted out again so soon. From what I read online, his attacks were usually months in between. I want to let her know I'm here for her, and she's not alone."

Cade parked in the hospital's visitor lot and went around to help Lyndy with Gus. The temperature had dropped since they'd left her home a short while ago, and the rain had turned to snow in the air. Slush on the ground.

She removed Gus from the harness, leaving his seat behind. "Hey, little man," she cooed, cradling him to her chest and swaying gently to an unheard song. "Do you mind handing me that sling?"

Cade passed her the length of material spread across her seat. He'd seen her use it to carry Gus before.

"Thanks." She turned the baby in his direction. "Hold him while I put it on?"

He stepped back. "What?"

"I need to arrange the material. It's easier if I'm not holding him."

Cade stared. Arms glued to his sides. "Maybe I can help you with the material."

Lyndy stepped forward, and Cade stepped back. She cocked her head and narrowed her eyes. "Are you afraid of my baby?"

"No."

"Then take him."

Cade shook his head. "He doesn't know me. I don't want to scare him. Or drop him. Maybe just put him in his seat while you fix the sling."

Determination furrowed her brow, and she turned the baby expertly, arranging him along the length of one forearm. "Bend your arm like mine."

She gripped Cade's wrist and wrenched his arm into position when he didn't comply. "I'm going to move him into your arm, and you're not going to drop him, because that's ridiculous. When was the last time you dropped anything you were holding?"

Cade wanted to say he dropped things every day, all the time, only a few minutes ago, but it wasn't true, and it was too late. She set the baby in his grip, wedged between his arm and chest. The little blue pacifier bobbed in his mouth.

"Hey," Cade said in greeting.

Gus locked eyes with him and cooed. Lyndy had secured his hat beneath his chin, framing his pudgy face. His mouth opened slightly, lips parting in a wide toothless smile. The pacifier tilted away, and Gus chomped down, setting it back into motion.

"Come on," Lyndy said, already headed for the hospital, her smug expression giving a little kick to his chest.

Cade easily matched his pace to hers, feeling nonsensically proud of the fact Gus hadn't screamed when she'd handed him off. "I thought you wanted to put him in the sling."

"I will, but you're doing such a nice job, and he's happy, so why interrupt?" She grinned mischievously. "Besides, I saw the mild panic on your face when you carried his car seat to the truck."

He smiled back. "Mean."

She bumped playfully against him as they walked. "You're right. Sorry. I can take him whenever you're ready."

Cade glanced at Gus, whose narrow eyebrows moved

high on his forehead as he gaped at the brightly lit building ahead and babbled delightedly about the view. White
lights had been strung through barren trees and along
the rooflines. Holiday well-wishes were painted on the
broad atrium windows and doors. "Maybe once we're
inside," he said.

Lyndy's pleasant expression fell as they reached the
sidewalk outside the Emergency Room, reminding Cade
of the gravity of the visit.

"You should know that seeing this victim might cause
a resurgence of the emotions you experienced after your
attack," he warned. "Sometimes a simple sound or scent
can set it all off again. Seeing her is almost certain to."

"I'm fine," she said. "Do you want me to take Gus
now? I think you've proved my point."

"What? That I could carry him across a parking lot
without dropping him? Give me a little more time. I'm
kind of a klutz."

Lyndy stopped to give Cade a long, slow review. "I
doubt that, and no. The point was that I trust you, and
so does Gus."

Gus cooed, as if on cue, and something in Cade's tight
chest unfurled.

The glass hospital doors parted, and Lyndy reached
for her baby. She tucked him fluidly into the ring of fabric around her body and smiled. "Nice work, Lance."

He snorted at the official-sounding clip to her words,
thoroughly enjoying the praise. "Thanks."

A moment later, the pungent slap of hospital scents
knocked the smile off his lips. The hallmark odors of
bleach, stale coffee and bandages met them at the threshold and stripped every nice feeling away. Cade had visited too many brothers in direct care units and military

treatment facilities that smelled just like this one, and those friends hadn't come home. He fought against the visceral gut punch, instantly thankful Lyndy had taken her son back.

She stopped at a cart selling flowers and balloons near the elevators and removed Gus's hat. "Carnations or daisies?" she asked Cade, sincerely, as if he knew what either looked like. Sunflowers or roses, sure, but carnations and daisies?

"The yellow ones."

She bought a small bouquet, then motioned him down the hallway. "They brought me in this way the other night. I'm guessing the paramedics would've done the same with the new victim. Hospital staff won't be permitted to tell us where we can find her. HIPAA," she added in explanation. "But we should at least be able to find a cop who can point us to Detective Owens."

Cade squared his shoulders and matched her determined pace.

Detective Owens soon appeared outside a line of pulled curtains. Lyndy moved confidently in his direction, passing a nurse in the busy space without a glance. The man in scrubs took notice but didn't stop her from breaching the restricted area where Owens spoke with a uniformed officer. She slowed when the lawmen looked up.

The officer's face was pale and drawn. His expression said more than he probably ever would about what he'd seen tonight.

"Oh no," Lyndy whispered, casting a pleading look onto Cade. "Do you think she…didn't make it?"

"I don't know," Cade muttered, knowing firsthand

there were worse things for the officer to have seen than death. "I guess we'll find out."

LYNDY WATCHED THE men's expressions as Cade extended a hand to each. "Detective. Officer. Thanks for the call."

Owens bobbed his head, his attention fixed on Lyndy and Gus. "How are you and the little guy holding up?"

"Okay." She kissed her baby's head and said yet another prayer of gratitude for that truth. "Gus is doing better than me, but that'll always be my preference."

"Ain't that the truth," the older man said. "I've got three of my own and seven grandkids now. How about this one?" He smiled at Cade. "How's he working out for you?"

Lyndy felt the heat spreading over her chest, neck and cheeks, as if the three men before her might be able to read her mind, and all the utterly inappropriate things she'd thought about Cade Lance in the last hour alone. "Good," she said, hoping the flush of color to her skin might be misconstrued as anxiety over the situation instead of what it really was. Lust. "How's the woman? Is she still here in the ER or has she been given a room?"

"She's still here," Owens said. "She's stabilized, so she'll be admitted soon. Her family's on their way from out of town. She's a few years younger than you, though another dead ringer. A senior at the local college."

Cade cleared his throat and widened his stance. "What can you tell us about the attack?"

Owens frowned, his remorseful gaze moving to Lyndy briefly before meeting Cade's eyes once more. "She was grabbed from behind. Her mouth covered. The man was taller and stronger. He pulled her against him and whispered Lyndy's name into her ear."

Lyndy's heart froze. "What?" Her lungs burned from the gust of air that whooshed out of her, and her ears began to ring.

The detective shifted uncomfortably. "She told responding officers that he repeated those two words throughout the attack. Your first name and your last. Calm and collected, in slow, level whispers while she screamed for help. No chance of identifying him by voice, and she didn't see his face."

"How's that possible?" Cade asked, while Lyndy willed herself to breathe so she wouldn't faint with Gus in her arms.

The officer's stricken expression darkened and his chin tipped in defiance. "He attacked from behind. It was dark, and after the first blow her vision blurred. Add fear and panic to the mix, and she could barely recall what she'd been doing before he grabbed her. He hit and kicked her to within an inch of her life, then left her under a streetlamp where we'd find her in time. He called it in himself to be sure."

"That's not like him," Cade said, echoing Lyndy's thoughts. Tom had killed his last few victims, and he'd meticulously covered his trails in every case.

The officer dipped his chin in a nearly imperceptible nod. "We think he wanted to send a message."

"To whom?" Lyndy whispered, afraid she already knew.

Owens and the officer exchanged a look, but neither answered.

The tremor that had begun in Lyndy's hands spread through her body. A woman had been beaten, nearly to death, while a monster repeated her name. This was Lyndy's fault. Someone had been punished because Lyndy had gotten away. She forced her sticky, swollen tongue to work and willed herself to be brave. "What's her name?" she whispered, realizing only then that she didn't know.

"Carmen," Detective Owens said. "Carmen Dietz."

"When can I see her?"

The officer's gaze jumped to the curtain at his side. "You should probably give it a few hours or wait until morning. She's not awake, and she'll look better once some of the swelling goes down."

"I don't care how she looks," Lyndy said. "She's here because of me." She turned her attention to Owens. "Do you think there's any chance I met this guy through my work? We don't do job placements in the towns where other attacks have occurred, but I meet a lot of people. I could get you a list of men I've spoken with, interviewed and placed in jobs this year. I'll need to talk to my manager to get a full account, but if I met the lunatic through my work, there will be records."

"We're already looking into that," Detective Owens said, "but it's unlikely you met him through your place of business. The feds' profile suggests he's already gainfully employed, likely in some capacity that allows him to travel."

"But you're still looking at my work ties."

He shrugged. "I'm a strong believer in due diligence. Feds have been wrong before."

Satisfied, Lyndy turned to the curtain where the officer's traitorous glance had darted. Her insides churned. She reminded herself to breathe as her sweaty fingers slid over the waxy paper around her bouquet. "I want to leave these on her nightstand for Carmen."

Cade turned with her, strong and confident at her side. She wasn't alone, and neither was Carmen. Lyndy would be there for her now, and they would get through this together.

She reached for the thin cotton wall, then stepped inside the drawn curtain.

The monster's work came gruesomely into view.

A gasp of air escaped her as she instinctively angled her baby away from the hospital bed. Carmen's grossly swollen and misshapen face barely seemed human. Her eyes were nearly invisible beneath the newly stitched and deeply purple skin. Thick layers of gauze wrapped her head and each arm had been encased in a heavy pink cast. Her lips were split, and IV lines connected her to a mass of machines. The rest of her body was hidden beneath white hospital blankets, but Lyndy could easily imagine what her abdomen and torso looked like. If he'd done all this to her face, a face that had once looked like Lyndy's, the rest would be just as bad. Or worse.

A cascade of hot tears rolled over Lyndy's cheeks, and her breaths grew shuddered. This could have been her.

It could have been Gus.

A pair of strong arms wound around her, turning and pulling her and her baby away from the scene before them. She didn't need to look to know it was Cade, the man who'd become her personal fortress of strength and comfort. She curled her fingers into the fabric of his shirt, crushing the flowers between them.

A small complaint rose from Gus.

"I've got you," Cade whispered, tightening his protective arms and holding her as she cried. He'd been right about the emotions, she realized. A freight train of terror and desperation hit her hard and fast enough to buckle her knees, and all she could do was let it out as quietly as possible for Gus's sake, while Cade supported her through it.

Shockingly, when the tears had dried, Gus was snoring, his head resting peacefully against Cade's chest.

Lyndy wiped her eyes, then slid her fingers between her son and their protector, shifting him back against her alone. "Sorry," she whispered.

"Do you want to sit?" Cade asked, releasing her in the direction of a small wooden armchair.

She didn't have the strength to pretend otherwise, so she lowered herself onto the seat at Carmen's bedside and snuggled Gus against her.

Cade poured a glass of water from the plastic pitcher on the nightstand, then passed it her way. He took the crushed flowers and set them beside the returned pitcher. Lyndy sipped the water to steady her nerves.

The curtain opened and Detective Owens slipped inside. "Well, Carmen's attack has been leaked."

"What?" Lyndy set her cup aside, swapping it for the offered digital tablet in the detective's hand.

"We were first on the scene after his call, and we intentionally kept it under wraps. The paramedics and hospital staff were instructed to do the same. No need to give this guy what he wants."

Lyndy turned her attention to the tablet. A local news article centered the screen. Coverage of a young woman's attack and speculation surrounding the Kentucky Tom Cat Killer.

"He probably alerted the media himself," she said, skimming the article for some detail about Carmen that would provide a connection between them beyond appearance.

Cade moved in close. "The hat," he said, pointing to the screen. "I saw a man in a plain black ball cap like that outside the café a few minutes before the window broke."

Breath caught in Lyndy's throat. "Is it him?" Was it so simple? Tom was so obsessed with the spectacles he caused that he'd accidentally gotten himself on camera?

Detective Owens took the tablet from Lyndy's trembling hand and inspected the image. He nodded several times without speaking, then dug a cell phone from his pocket. "I saw a ball cap like that in the crowd after Lyndy's attack. Let's see if we've interviewed anyone wearing one." Owens pressed the phone to his ear and sidestepped an elderly volunteer carrying a vase of flowers into Carmen's makeshift room. "Excuse me."

The volunteer smiled sweetly at Cade, then Lyndy. Her gaze lingered on Gus's sleeping face a moment, the longing nearly written on her forehead. "Seems like mine were that small yesterday," she whispered, an air of sadness in the words. "They're all grown now, and my grandbabies live too far away to visit, but it's nice I can see so many young families like yours while I'm here. Keep him close," she said. "He'll be ready to leave long before you're ready to let him go."

Fresh emotion clogged Lyndy's throat. She knew the woman was right because she never wanted to let Gus go.

"I'll just leave these here for Ms. Wells and get out of your way." She set the simple glass vase with baby's breath and roses on the stand beside the water pitcher and the smashed bouquet, then turned to leave.

"Who?" Lyndy asked as Cade lifted a hand to stop the older woman.

"Did you say the flowers are for Ms. Wells?" Cade asked, his body rigid and voice tight.

She glanced back at the vase, wrinkles racing across her brow. "Well, yes. Lyndy Wells. Is that not Ms. Wells?" She looked at Carmen for the first time and winced.

"I'm Ms. Wells," Lyndy whispered, thankful to be sitting so she wouldn't collapse. "Who are the flowers from?"

"Owens!" Cade bellowed, already striding toward the nightstand. His skin went pale, then flashed red as he retrieved and read the card.

The flower lady jumped and clutched her necklace as Detective Owens and the officer burst into view, both scowling. Each with a hand on the butt of his sidearm.

Cade pressed the card into Owens's hand, then moved into the old woman's space. "Who bought these flowers?"

"A man in the hallway," she said. "From the flower cart."

"Is he still here?"

"I don't know." Her shoulders climbed to her ears, and her eyes went round with fear.

"What did he look like?" Cade demanded.

"I—I—don't know," she blundered. "He wore brown coveralls, I think. We barely spoke."

Cade burst into a jog with the uniformed officer behind him.

Detective Owens moved to Lyndy's side and handed her the small white card.

A beautiful sacrifice has been made in your name.

Chapter Seven

Cade's military-issue boots gripped the tiled floor as he ran through the crowded emergency room, dodging chairs and people. He scanned the alarmed faces, searching for a man in coveralls as he raced toward the main hallway.

The uniformed officer kept pace behind him, barking orders and acronyms into a walkie-talkie that emitted intermittent responses and white noise. Backup was on the way, but it would be too late. The Tom Cat had made his move. Shown his superiority. And likely made his escape, all before Cade had known he was there.

They skidded to a stop at the first intersection of hallways.

Cade pointed to a kiosk several yards away. "The flowers came from that cart."

The officer jogged away, calling out to the attendant at the register while dozens of people moved in swift determined strides around them. Doctors. Nurses. Hospital staff and visitors. None of them realizing there was a serial killer in their midst.

Cade bolted back into a run, moving first to the automatic doors for a look at the illuminated lot outside, then at the more dimly lit streets and the low roof above the hospital's main entryway. Nothing but snow and silent cars in the lot. No one on the nearby streets; given the hour and temperature, that was no surprise.

He passed back through the doors at a slower, more methodical pace, willing himself to sense the fiend if he was still near. He retraced his steps through the waiting room and walked the hall, cursing and gripping the back of his neck. *Think*, he told himself, falling back on his military intelligence training. What would someone like Tom Cat do next? The nut had made his point. Had his fun. Now what? Cade had assumed he'd run, but that wasn't right. The Tom Cat was the one calling in news of his escapades. He enjoyed the chaos and fear he'd caused.

Cade turned in a small circle, muscles tightening with instinct. The Tom Cat craved the rush. The adrenaline. He was upping his own game now. And Cade was willing to bet the son of a gun was still here. Watching. Basking in the horror and feeling superior while Cade and the cops chased their tails.

Fear and rage welled in Cade's core as he lengthened his strides, searching every man carefully for signs of that telltale black ball cap. He'd evaluated dozens of people, checked coatracks and men's rooms before another, more nauseating realization hit.

One thing the monster wanted more than acknowledgement without consequences was Lyndy. Cade was charged with protecting her, and he'd left her behind.

His heart in his throat, Cade sprinted back toward the emergency room, praying he hadn't done exactly what the psychopath had wanted.

The halls seemed to lengthen beneath his feet as the realization he might have already failed her twisted knives into his gut. He cut through the waiting room

with less grace than before, clipping chairs and wing-
ing a nurse who wasn't watching where he was going.

"Lyndy!" he called, unable to wait before yanking
back the curtain where he'd left her. "Lyndy!"

His pounding heart seized as the view before him took
hold. The space was empty, save for a crumpled, unmade
bed, a rumpled bouquet of yellow flowers and the water
pitcher on the nightstand.

His ears rang and the world tilted. How could it be?
How long had he been gone? Where was Detective
Owens?

"Cade?" Lyndy's voice turned him on his heels. She
rubbed Gus's back in the sling and looked expectantly
at him with those big, trusting eyes.

He inhaled deeply for the first time in too long and
his head went light.

A small smile formed slowly on her perfect mouth as
she headed for the nightstand. "They moved Carmen to a
room. I forgot her flowers. I guess you didn't find him."

"No." Cade rubbed a heavy hand across his mouth and
bit back a fervent round of relieved cursing. He thought
he'd lost her, and the pain had been profound. For one
moment he'd felt...vulnerable, and the notion left him
speechless. Statistically speaking, the Tom Cat was probably some middle-aged nobody stuck in a dead-end job
with no friends, money or personality. Cade was a trained
marine and hired protector. Tom's havoc shouldn't have
been able to reach him emotionally. Not like that. And
it had. The reason for it stood before him, gently strok-
ing her son's fuzzy brown hair and clutching a mashed
bouquet of flowers.

"You look spent," she said, trading the flowers for
the pitcher and filling a cup. "Maybe water will help."

Maybe whiskey will help, he thought, shaking himself off. He took the cup and guzzled it, then reached for Lyndy, determined to keep her close from now on.

He opened the curtain and ushered her toward Detective Owens as he traded words with a pair of uniformed officers.

"Owens ordered an escort," she said. "The officers will follow us home and sit outside the house tonight."

"A protective detail." Cade wholeheartedly approved. Three men guarding Lyndy and Gus were better than one. If the Tom Cat managed to get near her again, all three men had been trained to use a sidearm and hit a moving target if necessary. Two could even make an arrest if the shots didn't kill him.

"Don't take this the wrong way," she whispered, "but you look like I feel, and that's not great."

Before he'd thought better of it, Cade stopped moving and wrapped his arms around her, careful not to disturb Gus.

Lyndy tensed for a moment before melting against him. "I'm okay," she whispered, the words coming thick and tight.

The speaker on the nearby officers' walkie-talkies engaged and a male voice rattled through. "I've got something. Elevators. North hall."

Owens met Cade's gaze above Lyndy's head as the uniforms broke away. He appraised him with sharp eyes and a hefty amount of scrutiny. The embrace was unprofessional. It crossed lines, and Owens would likely never recommend Fortress to anyone again, but Cade couldn't will his arms to release her. Instead, he lowered his mouth to her cheek and whispered. "We've got to go."

She turned stoically away, her arms immediately

wrapping the sleeping baby in her sling, her absence leaving Cade's chest hollow and cold.

He stuck to her side as they moved with purpose toward the north hall, following Owens and the uniforms. Cade's senses were on high alert, his every nerve on edge, muscles tensed. Hyperaware of everyone and everything, especially the woman and child beside him.

Soon, the officer who'd gone to speak with the worker at the flower stand came into view outside a bank of elevators. He raised one hand to gain the group's attention. In the other hand was a pair of brown coveralls.

LYNDY LOWERED GUS into his crib with shaking hands. She'd held it together through his bath and bottle, thankful he'd slept through the horrors of the hospital the way only an infant could. He'd likely wake her before she found two moments of sleep for herself, but that was the life of a single mother. She slid the small dial on the baby monitor until the indicator light came to life, then she crept from his room, companion speaker in hand.

She paused outside the door to gather her wits before facing Cade, and attempted to model herself after his strong example, outwardly anyway. Gus deserved at least that much from her, and at the moment, she preferred feigning strength to admitting she was seconds away from booking two one-way tickets to Peru.

"You okay?" Cade asked, drawing her eyes open. He'd asked her the same question countless times since they'd met. A good indicator that she didn't look okay. In other words, she'd have to try harder if she wanted to convince either of them that she was fine.

"I'm doing super," she answered with a wry smile. "You?"

"Oh, you know," he said, matching her overly casual tone. "Not bad. Thinking about some sweet tea."

Her smile widened. "Oh yeah?"

Cade stepped aside and stretched one arm toward the kitchen. "After you."

She peeled herself off the wall and forced a little swing into her hips. If she was going to pretend everything was fine, she might as well go all out. "Any news from Owens or the federal agents?"

"Only that the coveralls recovered from the elevator have been delivered to the lab. Techs will process it for fibers, hairs, residue, anything that might hint at who was wearing them and where they've been outside the hospital. It was a cocky move on the Tom Cat's part, but I suspect he'll only get worse." He retrieved the tea from the refrigerator and filled two mason jars already waiting on the counter.

She accepted the offered jar. "I'm hoping cocky also means easier to catch."

The air in the room seemed to thicken and Cade's jaw locked.

"Or does bolder mean more dangerous?" she guessed, wincing at the image of Carmen that flashed through her mind.

Cade's eyes were dark as he leveled her with his trademark stare. "Not more dangerous to you. And not to Gus."

"But to other women," Lyndy said, setting the tea aside in favor of wrapping her shaky arms around her middle.

He moved in on her then, eyes locked on hers. The confident swagger in his gait fully derailed her train of thought. "The police and FBI are handling that. You want to tell me how you're really doing? If we're going to be spending so much time together and not sleeping, I think we should at least be honest with each another. Don't you?"

"I'm fine," she said, willing the words to be true.

And if being honest meant having the talk he'd suggested earlier about her attempt to kiss him twice, then no, she didn't think that was best. *Unless he felt the same way*, she thought, far too hopefully.

"Not likely," he answered.

For a moment she wondered if he'd heard her thoughts. Relief flooded her when she realized he'd been talking about her personal assessment of her condition. Which was a definite lie.

Cade raised the jar to his lips, one broad palm curled around the cup as he took a long, deep drink.

She tried not to laugh as she became both thankful and disappointed that she wasn't his cup of tea. *Literally and figuratively.* If he wanted her the way she wanted him, they'd be goners. Too distracted, naked and defenseless to see Tom coming.

"Let me know when you're ready to talk," Cade said, returning the drained and sweating jar to the countertop.

She mentally reworked her earlier evaluation as she watched him head for her living room with his signature self-assurance. Cade was probably never defenseless. Naked, distracted or otherwise.

He caught her eye from his position on her sofa and watched her silently, with knowing eyes. She was far from fine, and they had a lot to talk about, beginning with her stalker, what he'd done tonight and what could possibly be yet to come.

She moved slowly in his direction, fighting against the rush of awful memories all trying to pull her under.

"Tom came to the hospital," she said, kicking off the miserable conversation and sinking onto the sofa beside him. "Do you think he was there to see Carmen, or was he trying to lure me out?" And was it possible he'd followed her home?

She checked for the cruiser outside her front window. The officers were still there, but that didn't mean Tom wasn't. She'd learned tonight that he could be anywhere at any time.

"I don't know," Cade answered her nearly forgotten question. "Owens is reviewing hospital security footage with the feds now, hoping to get a look at someone the right size for the coveralls coming or going. Local uniforms are canvassing the building and nearby businesses. I still can't believe he was in the building and we missed him. He never should've been able to get that close."

"I hate knowing Carmen was hurt because of me, and that Gus might be." Her gut clenched, and a wave of heat crawled up her neck, pooling bile in her mouth. The thought of her baby in the hands of the deranged psychopath who'd beaten Carmen beyond recognition made her stomach churn and her face go numb. She set the tea onto her coffee table, then tipped over, resting her hot cheek against the cool cushion, certain she'd be sick.

The couch shifted beneath her, and Cade walked away. He returned a moment later with a glass of ice water and a wet dishrag. He set the water on the floor where she could reach it, then spread the cool wet cloth over her forehead. "Breathe."

She pulled in a fresh breath and felt her lungs expand. She blew the air out and repeated the process slowly and intentionally until the room stopped spinning and the black dots in her peripheral vision faded away. Then, as if nearly puking in Cade's presence wasn't bad enough, a round of tears began to leak from the corners of her eyes. So much for feigning brave.

Cade presented a handkerchief.

She mopped the renegade drops from her cheeks with a self-deprecating groan. "Thanks. You carry a handkerchief?"

"Yeah." He lowered himself to the floor beside her water. "My granddad gave them to all his grandsons. As far as I know, we all still carry them."

"That's nice," she said. "I've always wanted a big family, but it was just Mama, Grandmama and me."

He scanned her, searching for what, she wasn't sure.

Changing the subject seemed like a good idea. "I'm sorry you were dragged into this," she said, adjusting the cool cloth and feeling slightly less ill. "Talk about drawing the short straw. Your company was probably founded to protect normal people from everyday problems. Frenemies and exes. Maybe a stalker or a disgruntled former employee. Somehow you got stuck between me and a serial killer." A wave of guilt brought the nausea back around. "I'm a disaster magnet."

He snorted. "You think I feel unlucky?"

She raised her brows in challenge. "Aren't you? You're here with me. Is there anyone I haven't put in danger? Gus. You. Every blond-haired, blue-eyed twentysomething female in three counties."

Cade shook his head. "You haven't put me in danger, and I will protect you and Gus. That's a promise."

"Some serial killers are never caught," she said, allowing the panic to swell. "What then?" Even if there wasn't a time limit for his protection, she couldn't go to work while being stalked like this, and if she couldn't work, then her bank account would eventually run dry and her ability to pay him would vanish.

"I won't leave you," he said. "Not until your peace and safety are restored."

Lyndy closed her eyes to stop them from rolling. He probably believed it, but everyone she cared about left eventually.

She swiveled upright on autopilot, caught off guard by the unprompted thought. She didn't care about Cade. Not like that. She was attracted to him, sure, but she'd just met him, and attraction was different than caring. She blamed the intensity of their circumstances for her confusion. She was probably experiencing the opposite version of the Nightingale syndrome, except instead of saving her from a deadly injury or illness, Cade was protecting her from a human killer, and she was getting everything all mixed up in her head.

"I never leave a job unfinished or a client unsatisfied," he continued, tossing her thoughts back to the gutter. A place they'd frequented since his arrival and despite the atrocities around them. Or maybe because of them. Who wouldn't need a distraction at a time like this?

She swallowed at his unfortunate choice of words and tried to pay attention.

"You're stuck looking at my face everywhere you go until the Tom Cat is caught or you send me away."

"I wouldn't send you away," she said softly, and her insides pinched. Maybe it was his promise to leave her satisfied or the look in his eyes as he refocused on her mouth, but she was sure he meant it. And she didn't want Cade to leave. She liked having him around. He was kind and thoughtful and brave. He let her do what she wanted, then backed her up while she did, like a true partner.

Slowly, his gaze returned to meet hers. "Then I'll stay as long as you want me."

Lyndy let her head fall back until it rested on the cushions and the ceiling came into view. "Okay." What had happened to the sensible, levelheaded woman she used to be? Where was her small, predictable life with intense concerns about calories and daily step counts? And why had any of those things ever seemed so important?

"Do you think Tom intends to hurt more women?" she asked, recalling the awful note attached to his flowers. "He called Carmen a sacrifice in my honor."

"He hurts women because he's insane," Cade said, his voice lowering. "He doesn't do any of this because of you. You're a victim. Not a cause. Or a reason. Keep reminding yourself of that, because he's probably going to keep trying to manipulate you into thinking otherwise."

"Manipulate me?" She lifted her head and locked gazes with him once more. "Into doing what? Giving myself over to him so he'll stop hurting others?"

"Maybe, but killing you won't stop him. A man like this won't stop until he's caught."

Lyndy locked her gaze on his as a wave of resolve rushed through her. "Then let's make sure he's caught."

Chapter Eight

Lyndy woke to the rich, buttery aroma of pancakes and the thick, greasy scent of bacon.

Shafts of sunlight danced above her, angling down from the window to the carpet beyond the couch where she'd apparently fallen asleep. *When did that happen?*

She squinted and rolled onto her side, trying to get her head around the strange situation. She never slept on the couch, and who was cooking if she was still lying there?

Gus laughed, and Lyndy's heart leaped.

She swung herself into a seated position and stared wide-eyed at the scene before her, unsure if she was really awake.

Gus was strapped into his highchair and belting bold, boisterous belly laughs as Cade flipped pancakes in a skillet.

Lyndy was on her feet in the next heartbeat, recalling every event that had brought her here in vivid detail. She drifted in the direction of her son, buoyed by the sound of his laughter and so thankful to Cade for the extra rest and breakfast—not to mention the joy he was giving her baby—that she was sure to burst.

"Morning," Cade said, taking notice and looking somewhat guilty as she entered the room.

She unfastened Gus's safety strap and lifted him for a cuddle.

Cade ferried the platter of pancakes to the table and set them beside a plate piled high with bacon, then pulled out a chair. "I hope you're hungry. I'm usually flipping hotcakes for four hungry men. I think I went a little overboard on the batter."

"And the bacon," she said, snagging a piece with her free hand and taking an immediate bite. "An error in my favor." Her eyes fluttered shut in pleasure. "I haven't had bacon since Gus was born. I was hooked on it during my pregnancy and gained more than forty pounds. I'm still trying to work it off."

Cade's mischievous grin heated her cheeks. Thankfully, he shook his head and kept whatever he'd been thinking to himself.

She took a seat and arranged Gus on her lap, then showered him in kisses. "How are you, my sweet little man?" she asked, nuzzling his neck and making him coo. "Mama feels rested. I'd almost forgotten what this felt like, but I love it."

Cade set a cup of coffee in front of her, then delivered a plate and set of silverware. The syrup and butter came next. "Anything else you need?"

"Just a little company," she said, pointing to the chair across from her.

Cade obeyed, then filled a plate with food and dug in. "I wasn't sure if I was overstepping. Taking the baby from his room when he woke, feeding him, helping myself to your groceries again. No offense intended."

Lyndy rolled her eyes. "None taken. I haven't slept this long in over a year." Not since Sam had died. "And

I don't think anyone, other than my mother, has ever made me breakfast."

Cade stopped chewing and stared. "No one?"

"Nope." She forked a pair of golden pancakes from the stack and centered them on her plate.

"Sam didn't cook for you?" he asked, genuine curiosity creeping into his tone.

"Sam didn't cook," she said flatly. In hindsight, Sam hadn't done a lot of things, but the inequality in their relationship had never seemed so significant before. "He was…traditional."

Cade wrinkled his nose. "A misogynist?"

"No," she laughed. "Not like that. He was never mean about it."

Cade pursed his lips and tented his brows. "Well, I like to cook, and I love pancakes. So anytime you're in the mood, just holler."

"I will," she said, wondering if the smile on her face was permanent. She hadn't stopped grinning since the moment she'd woken. "You're going to make some woman very lucky one day. Or some man. No judgment."

Cade set his fork aside with a laugh, then lifted his coffee. "I don't think so. I'm sure no man could handle me, and fairly confident no woman would put up with me. I'm not all bacon and pancakes."

Lyndy smiled, wanting more information, but not sure it was okay to ask. "Fair enough."

"What about you?" He examined her with sharp, probing eyes. "You'd planned to get married. You had a terrible loss. Then a baby. But it's been a year. Why aren't you dating now?"

She shrugged. "I guess I was busy grieving at first. Then I was trying to figure out how to have a healthy pregnancy, then how to juggle work and a newborn. Now I hate the thought of bringing anyone into Gus's life who he might get attached to and miss, in case they leave. That just doesn't seem fair, and I know firsthand that people leave, even if they don't want to. Life happens." And death.

"Right. Can't get your heart broken again if you don't date."

"It's more than that." She shifted uncomfortably, hating the way he'd oversimplified her complicated life. "I've had enough heartbreak to go around, and I'm not interested in inviting more."

Sure, maybe the next guy would live, but what if he didn't? Was that a crazy thing to worry about? Lyndy was a worrier by nature, but she'd never worried about Sam being hit by a sleeping trucker or about herself being nearly abducted by a serial killer, and those much more far-fetched things had happened. So, anything could. She rubbed heavy palms over the chilled skin on her arms, hugging Gus closer and willing her suddenly twisting stomach to settle.

"Fair enough," Cade answered, clearly still satisfied with his black-and-white interpretation of her behavior.

"What about you?" Lyndy asked. "Why wouldn't any woman put up with you?"

He caught her eye and frowned, stretching long legs under the table and leaning back in his chair. "I told you, my old man was a son of a gun. A drinker. Jealous. Mean. And I already look like him. I'm not in any hurry to find out if I'll act like him if the situation's right."

"Fear of failure," she assessed as quickly and flippantly as he'd passed judgment on her. "Got it." She kissed Gus again and nibbled on another piece of bacon.

"No." Cade narrowed his eyes and straightened in his seat. "I just can't be sure I'd do the job justice."

"Who can?" she asked. "And how could we? I spent my entire pregnancy worried about whether or not I could be a good mother to Gus. I had no experience for this job and no partner to share the weight. But in the end, I loved him so much, even before I'd met him, that I was willing to do whatever it took, and I have. That's love. That's relationships in a nutshell. We have to be willing to give the other person all of ourselves and trust them to do the same. It's a little more one-sided for Gus and me, but it's the same concept. If I do all I can to meet his needs and fill his heart, then however much that is, it will be enough."

Cade didn't respond. His gaze moved from her face to Gus's and back.

"You say you don't think you can be a good partner," Lyndy continued, unsure why the subject mattered so much to her, or at all, but determined to say her piece. "You're already a partner. You have been for years. All that time you were in the military. Now with your teammates at Fortress. You guys rely on one another, sometimes for your lives, and you trust each other. That's all it takes. Trust. Loyalty. Dedication and perseverance."

"Is that all?" he asked, a coy smile replacing the cranky frown.

"Sure." Lyndy made a mental note that mind-bending sex probably helped, but she wasn't about to add that at the breakfast table. And to be honest, she'd never had the mind-bending sort, but she wouldn't turn away an opportunity. "We should probably talk about what's on the agenda today."

Cade nodded but averted his eyes.

For a moment, she wondered if he'd had a similar thought about the sex, but she shoved the idea quickly aside. The last thing she wanted to think about was Cade having great sex with another woman when the only sex Lyndy had wanted in a year was with him.

"What do you want to do?" he asked.

Lyndy buried her face in Gus's baby curls and inhaled deeply to ground herself back in the moment. Prepared for an argument, she suggested, "I thought we could go back into town."

Cade froze. "Why would we do that?"

"I told you last night. We have to help the police identify the Tom Cat. I think I fell asleep while I was making a list of all the places I go on a semi-regular basis, but it's a small town. I can make a new list. We've already visited my usual stops, but there are plenty of places I can be expected like clockwork, just not as often. We still haven't visited my office, and I haven't been to the gym in a year, but I was a regular before. Since we don't know how long I've been followed, it's possible I ran into the killer before I quit going. Some of the other victims were fitness enthusiasts."

"But they weren't all from the same town," he pointed out. "They wouldn't have gone to your gym."

"But," she countered, "anyone can buy a day pass. Tom could have first taken notice of them here, then stalked them in their hometowns. We should start at my gym, then move on to the library, grocery and park. I'd like to save my office for last since it seems least likely I met him there, and I'm in no hurry to explain any of this to my coworkers who surely know more than me by now, between the local news and gossip mills."

Cade worked his jaw but didn't protest.

Lyndy interpreted his silence as acceptance, then helped herself to another slice of bacon.

CADE UNDERSTOOD LYNDY'S need to do something, her desire to be useful and even her misplaced sense of responsibility for what had happened to Carmen, but he didn't like any of it. And if it had been his place to tell her as much, they'd still be at her house, where he could better protect her. As it was, he could only offer her instinct and training. There were no protective perimeter options when she was on the move.

The officers who'd kept watch through the night had pulled out just after breakfast. According to Owens, another cruiser would be back at sundown, but Cade was on his own during the day. The Tom Cat's note sent to the hospital had created an all-hands-on-deck situation for the FBI and local PD. Everyone was in agreement. He would act again. The question was only when. And Lyndy wanted to go marching around downtown.

Cade rounded the truck's hood to her side and waited as she removed Gus from his car seat and arranged him in her sling. It was strange to hear her admit she'd been afraid of being a terrible mother when she was so clearly a natural with him. She seemed more in tune with her baby than any mother he'd ever known. Maybe that was because it had just been the two of them for so long, or maybe that was just Lyndy. Maybe she was naturally in tune with everyone. She certainly saw through Cade's masks and pretenses without any trouble. He could only hope she wasn't a mind reader, or he was sure to soon be slapped.

She shut the passenger door and turned to face him, a mix of hope and trust in her eyes. "We can do this," she said. "All we need is some tiny thread to start the whole ball rolling toward finding this guy's identity. The police will get their man, and the female population of Kentucky will be safe once more."

"No problem," he deadpanned, eliciting a smile from Lyndy.

Her cheeks were rosy from the cold, and she'd tugged a knitted pink cap over her hair and ears; a giant round pom-pom sat on top.

"Love the hat," he said, giving the ball a little flick.

"Hey. I made this hat," she said. "Do you want one?"

"Please, no."

She grinned, and he took her hand, feeling much too light for the quest she was on.

"Remember the rules," he warned. "Stay in my sight at all times. And if I say we're done, we're done. You're going to have to trust my survival instincts, since apparently you don't have any."

"Funny," she said, not looking as if she thought he was funny at all. She turned her soft hand beneath his then spread her fingers so he could slide his in between.

He rolled his shoulders and resisted the urge to adjust his jeans. "Whatever you want."

"If only real boyfriends were so accommodating."

Cade flashed his wickedest smile and gave Lyndy's fingers a little squeeze. She had no idea how accommodating he could be.

She stopped at the crosswalk, a crimson blush spilling across her cheeks, and it was all he could do not to grab her and kiss her.

They crossed the street at the signal and headed toward the local gym, a wide one-story building with broad windows and tinted glass doors. He opened one to let her pass inside.

"I haven't been here since my second trimester," she said, taking a long look around the foyer. "My membership ran out the same month Gus was born, so I decided to walk at the park instead. That way I could keep him with me. Clearly not my brightest idea."

Cade frowned as Lyndy's presence turned a number of heads, mostly male. He nodded at the men who stared a moment or two longer than necessary, letting them know she was spoken for. *Exactly like a Neanderthal*, he thought, unimpressed with whatever had gotten into him. Lyndy wasn't territory to be marked, but the idea someone wanted to hurt her, maybe even one of these ogling men, made him want to tell the world that anyone who tried would have hell to pay.

"Morning people," Lyndy said with mock disgust. "Mornings are always packed. I'm sorry, but I'm wired to stay in bed as long as possible."

She was right about it being busy. There was a body on nearly every machine and a respectable mix of ages and fitness levels from what he could see. A near fifty-fifty split between genders. He turned for a better evaluation of the space across from them. Several women on cardio equipment smiled in his direction.

"Do you get stared at like this everywhere you go?" Lyndy asked.

"Usually," he admitted. "I've been told I put people on edge."

She laughed, and he smiled.

"Good morning!" a pert voice interrupted. A young brunette beamed from behind the counter. She wore a logoed shirt and nearly fizzed with a level of enthusiasm

Cade couldn't imagine. Her name tag said Becky. "Can I help you with anything?"

Lyndy released Cade's hand and stepped forward, resting her elbows on the tall counter. "Hi, yes. I was a member here about a year ago, but—" she pointed at Gus, gnawing toothlessly on a Santa-shaped teether and drooling like a faucet "—I had a baby, and it's been fun, but I'd love my old body back."

"I completely understand," Becky chirped. "And we can help. A lot has changed here. How about I show you around?"

Cade and Lyndy followed Becky through the members-only turnstile.

She led them room to room, pointing out every obvious thing imaginable.

"This is the men's locker room. This is the ladies' locker room. This is where we hold spin classes. This is the café."

Lyndy nodded along, oohing and aahing at their guide's ridiculous tour.

Cade focused on the patrons' faces as they turned to watch Becky's little parade.

"This is the sauna," Captain Obvious continued.

Lyndy looked over her shoulder, then twisted at the waist for a better view of the patrons.

Cade slid his arm around her back and tugged her against his side. "Something wrong?"

She looked around again. "I don't think so."

He followed her lead, examining everyone and everything more carefully, but finding nothing and no one of interest.

"We ask that you sign up for treadmills and elliptical machines when we're busy," Becky said, pointing to a row of clipboards hanging on the wall beside the cardio machines. It was the first piece of useful information she'd managed, if they were really thinking of joining the gym. "And try to limit yourself to thirty minutes when the wait list is more than three people long. Oh, will you excuse me for a minute?" She hurried toward the desk, where a pair of women in spandex waited.

Lyndy turned a longing look toward the ellipticals, arranged before the window overlooking the street. "I used to love these. I came at night, when I knew the place would be empty, just so I could stay on as long as I wanted. Most nights I did ninety minutes with my favorite audiobook, a view of the town and a smoothie reward."

Cade moved behind her, aligning his chest to her back, and groaned inwardly when he felt her relax against him. The curve of her boldly placed bottom tested his control. He wrapped an arm around her on instinct, splaying his fingers over the gentle curve of her hip. He lowered his lips to her cheek, letting the stubble on his chin graze her ear on the way down. He grinned as he watched her lips part in the reflection of the large window before them.

"You're playing your part in this very well," she whispered. "You seem invested."

"I am, and you make it easy," he said. Though, in truth, she was making things very hard for him, and if she moved another inch to the left, she'd know.

He scanned the street for onlookers but found none of interest. An elderly couple, a crowd of teens laughing loudly. Families. Little Leaguers. Women with strollers. A man and his dog.

A large delivery truck pulled away, and a squat yellow-and-white building came into view across the street. The sign on top proclaimed its name: Sunshine Smoothie.

The shop had floor-to-ceiling windows, a long line at the counter and café seating outside. "Is that where you went for your smoothie fix after a workout?"

"Every time."

Sunshine Smoothie would have been the perfect place to watch Lyndy on an elliptical at night, ninety contented minutes at a time, without her ever knowing.

Cade lowered his mouth to her cheek once more and pressed a testing kiss. "Let's see if he's still watching."

She shivered, then raised her arm, hooking a hand behind his head and pulling him down to her. She let her head fall back and roll to one side, exposing the creamy skin of her neck in offering.

Cade didn't need to be asked twice. He pressed his lips against the tender hollow at the base of her jaw, just below her ear, and inhaled the sweet vanilla and honey scent of her.

Lyndy gave a soft purr of pleasure.

The repetitive blasts of a car alarm sounded outside, and Cade snapped upright, instinct clutching his gut.

He grabbed her wrist and pulled her with him as he raced through the door and onto the sidewalk.

As expected, the lights on Cade's truck flashed, and the horn bellowed.

They crossed the street to find a large rock smashed against the now concave windshield, covered in a spiderweb of cracks. Below the rock, another note rippled on a half sheet of paper in the wind.

Peekaboo. I see you.

Chapter Nine

Hours later, Cade and Lyndy were still in town, a trip he hadn't wanted to make, to begin with. Now his truck was vandalized, another deranged note had been delivered and Cade was hungry. Not a winning trifecta. In fact, he'd had drill sergeants in better moods than his unapologetically nasty one. Which Lyndy had already pointed out twice.

"Try this," she said, passing a tall disposable cup covered in cartoon suns his way.

The air inside Sunshine Smoothie was fragrant with the sweet scents of blended fruit and churned by a blender that never seemed to rest. The interior was perky in the extreme, brightly colored with murals of dancing produce and the sort of music he'd expect at Disneyland. He ground his teeth in annoyance as a pair of FBI agents explained to Detective Owens that there were no witnesses, yet again.

Lyndy wiggled the smoothie. "Trust me. One sip." The cup had a clear lid and a big yellow straw. "Tasty Tropic was always my favorite. It has bananas, orange juice, coconut and pineapple."

Cade accepted the offering, reminding himself that his mood wasn't her fault. Though he had no idea why she wasn't the one ready to go door-to-door, through the whole darn town, shaking every man by his neck until one confessed.

She removed Gus from the sling and turned him to face Cade. She hooked an arm across Gus's chest and he kicked chubby, dimpled legs. He'd finished the bottle she'd brought in her bag and decided it was playtime, obviously thrilled to be rid of the stifling snowsuit. She hovered him over the tabletop, where he performed a half-bounce, half-dance routine while making a fountain of spit bubbles.

Cade fought the unbidden smile twisting his lips. He needed to hold on to his mood for when he got his hands on the nut threatening Lyndy and her child. He pushed the big yellow straw between his lips and took a gentle pull, hoping whatever was in the cup would be predictably terrible and restore his ugly mood. Cade wasn't a fruit guy. Meat, vegetables, pizza, tacos, yes. Maybe the occasional apple. But multiple fruits blended with yogurt in a cartoon-sun-covered cup where smiling suns wore dark glasses, and an obnoxious script wished him a "Happy Sunshiny Day"? *No.*

Lyndy's brows rose in anticipation as the mixture met his tongue.

Dammit.

It was good. And Cade took a longer, deeper pull, enjoying the smoothie far more than he wanted.

Detective Owens broke away from the agents and ambled in Lyndy's direction. He made a few goofy faces at Gus before turning a more serious look on Lyndy. "I'm sorry you're going through this, Ms. Wells, but I want you to know we're doing everything we can."

She smiled warmly in return. "I believe you are, and it's appreciated."

"What'd you learn?" Cade asked, his smoothie nearly gone.

Detective Owens gave a small shake of his head. "No one saw anything."

"That seems to be a real pattern in this town."

"It's a real pattern everywhere," Owens said. "Most folks have to concentrate just to keep putting one foot in front of the other. Life's busy and demanding, especially this time of year. Christmas is only three weeks away, you know. Besides that, we're preoccupied as a culture and rarely look at strangers longer than necessary. We learn in elementary school that it's rude."

"What about security feeds?"

"So far we've got plenty of footage but no decent angles. We've got the rear of your truck in one, a side shot in another where the hood is out of sight. A great view of the windshield from a rotating camera that caught before and after footage with no in between. There's a camera on the roof of this building, so we might have something there once the manager comes in." Detective Owens checked his watch. "We gave him a call about an hour ago."

Cade felt his blood pressure rise. "What's taking so long? What's more important than catching a serial killer?"

"Nothing!" a new voice called from behind the counter.

A man in a white polo shirt and khaki pants hurried in their direction. "I'm sorry to keep you waiting." He was in his late thirties, with glasses and a sling on one arm. "It's been a harried morning, and no matter how many times I work through my routines with this thing, I never seem to get any faster." He flapped his bent arm like a wing, in case someone hadn't noticed the injury.

Cade didn't like him. He didn't particularly like any man at the moment, but he was sure this one ticked him off. "What happened to your arm?"

"Torn rotator cuff," the man answered congenially. "The result of my courageous battle on the racquetball court."

Cade pushed onto his feet. "When?"

"Uhm." The man straightened, casting a worried gaze from Cade to Lyndy, then Detective Owens. "About six weeks ago now, I guess. Why?"

Cade looked to the cashier, watching raptly from behind the register. "That sound right to you?"

She looked at her manager, then nodded quickly. "I guess so."

Cade returned to his drink. If that guy had been in a sling for six weeks, he wasn't the man who'd attacked Lyndy at the park a few days ago.

"I'm Terri Fray," the man said, extending his good hand to Detective Owens first, then Lyndy. He put the hand in his pocket instead of offering it to Cade. "I manage this store. I got your call while I was at physical therapy. I had to run home and dress for work before coming in. I showered, too—you'd thank me if you knew." He gave a little smile. No one laughed. "Anyway, I didn't know it was an emergency. I was only told there was an act of vandalism on the street, and the police wanted to speak with me at the shop."

"It was my truck," Cade said. "It's in the lot at the end of the block. They're replacing my windshield now."

"Oh." Terri frowned. "What can I do about that?"

Detective Owens stepped forward. "Nothing, but I'd like a look at your security feed. The camera on your roof points in the right direction, more or less, and we're reviewing material from every camera on this block."

Terri cringed. He tipped his head and guided Owens away from the bulk of blatantly eavesdropping customers seated quietly at nearby tables. Cade and Lyndy followed.

"It's a dummy," Terri said. "The equipment is expensive and upkeep is worse, so I just let it go a few years ago. No one steals smoothies and there are very few robberies in town, so I thought it would be okay. I left the camera up as a deterrent in case I was wrong."

Cade rubbed a palm against his forehead.

Lyndy passed Gus to him, and he accepted the child on instinct.

"Hey." Cade's protest came too late. His hands were already around Gus's middle, and pulling him to his chest. They both looked at Lyndy. "What are you doing?"

"Going to the ladies' room. We left home hours ago, and I'm on my second smoothie."

Cade gave the door at the end of the short hall a long look, then led the way with Gus. He knocked, then pressed his way inside and scanned the small area. "All clear."

Lyndy rolled her eyes. "Was there any chance the Kentucky Tom Cat Killer was hiding in the ladies' room?"

"Sounds like I'm not the only one getting cranky," he whispered to Gus on his way out.

"I can hear you," Lyndy called through the closed door behind them.

Cade grinned. "Looks like you won't be getting away with anything when you get older, little man." He tucked Gus against his hip and smiled. Cade dropped an unplanned kiss on the top of the baby's head and realized how thankful he was that he'd been the one answering Fortress Defense's phone when Detective Owens called.

LYNDY TOOK HER time in the ladies' room. She needed to pull herself together before her inner emotional breakdown began to show. She'd been calm, collected and pleasant far longer than she'd thought possible, and despite two delicious smoothies, she wanted to cry. No. She wanted to wail and kick and beat her fists against something, preferably the lunatic wreaking havoc on her life. It wasn't fair that Gus was in danger. That Carmen had been hurt. That one man was outsmarting a team of local police and trained FBI agents. The entire situation was just wrong. And she was about two heartbeats away from curling into a ball and losing it.

She splashed cool water on her overheated face and growled at the pink-cheeked reflection staring back at her. She closed her eyes against the suddenly tear-blurred vision, then pressed the heels of her hands against the lids. "Come on, Wells," she whispered. "Toughen up. All you've got to do is outlast Tom. Keep going until he gets caught."

Several minutes later, she opened the bathroom door and stepped out, half expecting Cade to be waiting on the other side. Instead, he'd moved to the window overlooking the street and seemed to be having a serious conversation with Gus.

Her baby looked incredibly tiny in his arms. Arms she knew would fight to protect him. If she and Gus had to be wrapped up in this nightmare, at least they had Cade. It was too bad he had to leave when it was over. Nonsensical or not, it would hurt to see him go.

"Hello." Terri moved carefully in her direction, his good hand up in surrender. "Sorry. I didn't want to alarm you."

She paused and worked up a smile. "Hi."

"You probably don't remember me," he said, "but I think I remember you. It's been a while, and you didn't have a baby then, but I think you used to stop in at night?"

"I did." Her smile widened. "I don't think we ever met."

"No. I rarely work the counter, but I'm good with faces. Not as much with names."

"Lyndy," she said.

"Right." He bobbed his head in agreement. "I'm sad to say I've seen you on the news. It's awful, isn't it?"

Lyndy did her best not to scream any number of sarcastic remarks. She settled on, "Yes. It is," keeping things short and sweet, but the venom in her voice said what she wouldn't. Terri was an idiot.

His smile drooped. "Well, if you or your boyfriend want another smoothie, they're on the house. I've already told the cashier to provide anything you'd like. Free of charge today."

Lyndy forced a tight smile as she stepped around him and headed for Cade.

He turned to face her and frowned as Terri scurried away. "Owens says we can go. My window's fixed, and the cops have done all they can for now."

"Thank the stars." Lyndy took Gus and kissed his ruddy cheek, more than ready to go home.

Owens lifted a finger, indicating they should wait. He had a phone pressed to his ear and a look of frustration on his face. He turned tired eyes to Cade, grunted, then disconnected the call. "We got something on a private feed. Some kid in an apartment down the street set it up to watch women coming and going from the gym." He shook his head. "That camera caught a man throwing the stone at your truck. He had his back to the camera, but he's wearing a black ball cap like the one you noted outside the café."

Cade stiffened at Lyndy's side, tension rolling off him in waves. "Anything else?"

"Afraid not."

"Approximate height, weight, build, hair color, visible tattoos?"

Owens shook his head again. "There's a good six feet of shadows along the base of the building beside that parking lot at this time of day. Shielded the guy almost completely."

"Thank you," Lyndy said, grabbing her things and shouldering the diaper bag. "Keep in touch."

"Yeah."

Cade opened the door for her, then followed her onto the sidewalk in silence.

She could sense the anger in his strides.

He beeped his door locks open as they approached his truck, and she reached for the door. "What was that guy talking to you about in the hallway back there?"

"The manager?" she asked, strapping Gus into his five-point harness with shaky hands. "Nothing much. He thought he recognized me from my many trips to the shop last year." *And the news*, she thought with a twist to her gut. "He said my boyfriend and I could have free smoothies, but I think that offer ran out once we left."

"Bummer," Cade said, closing the door behind her when she climbed in.

They rode away from town in silence, both clearly

lost in thought. Likely about the same thing. Somehow Tom was always near but unnoticed. And even when he made his presence known, he was little more than vapor. Intangible, then gone.

Desperate for a silver lining, Lyndy focused on something nice about the day. "I knew you'd like the smoothie," she said, watching Cade for his reaction. "Now you see why I went there every night."

Cade's jaw tightened as he signaled at the next intersection.

"What?"

"I think that shop is the key to this. The location is perfect for watching you at the gym. Your favorite cardio machines are lined up in front of a window. Your routine was predictable, and the smoothie shop does enough business for the guy to go unnoticed. The setup can't get much better for someone like him. And every night that you bought a smoothie, he got an up close look at his favorite fantasy in the flesh."

"I didn't buy a smoothie every night," she said, a long-faded memory pushing its way to the surface of her tired mind. "Cade. Sometimes my orders were already paid for."

He jerked his face in her direction, eyes narrowed and expression tight. "What?"

"Only once or twice," she said, hurrying to get the words out and half-afraid she'd choke on them. "Sometimes the girl behind the counter wouldn't charge me. She'd say it was on the house. My usual was already made, and someone else had it covered."

"Who?" Cade barked, slowing his truck as he stared at her.

"I don't know."

"Who was the girl behind the counter?"

"I don't know," Lyndy repeated, her shoulders creeping toward her ears. "A teen? Black curly hair. Glasses. I think. I'm not sure. It's been so long. And it wasn't a big deal."

Cade muttered a curse under his breath and wheeled the big truck into a U-turn, causing traffic to weave and horns to blow. "I'd say that's one hell of a big deal."

Chapter Ten

Cade pulled his truck onto the curb outside the Sunshine Smoothie and flung the door wide as Lyndy scrambled down from the passenger seat. He collected Gus and grabbed Lyndy by the hand, then swung the glass door open with unnecessary oomph. Adrenaline spiked and pounded in his veins as he marched through the smattering of patron-filled tables. Finally, their search for a link to the Tom Cat was getting somewhere.

"I don't see Owens," Lyndy said, stating Cade's thoughts aloud. "No officers, either. Did they leave? Did you notice their cars outside?"

"No," Cade admitted, releasing her hand as he pushed his way to the front of the line. "Maybe they're in the back or in Terri's office."

A man in hipster glasses and a bowling shirt scoffed as Cade blew past. "Excuse you!"

Cade glared in the man's direction before pressing his free palm to the counter. "Hey," he called to the teen working the register.

The girl jumped, looking inexplicably guilty and as if she might run. It was her lucky day, because whatever the girl had gotten into, Cade doubted it had anything to do with him. He just needed information. "We were just in here. Do you remember?"

"Yeah."

"We need to talk to the policemen who were with us, or your manager."

The girl shook her head. "You can't. They left. First the cops, then Mr. Fray."

Cade ground his teeth.

"It's okay," Lyndy said, tugging Cade's coat sleeve. "We'll call Detective Owens."

"Hang on," he said, shooting the hipster another look. "You ever work nights?" Cade asked the worker.

"N-no," the little blonde spluttered, her cheeks growing impossibly darker.

"How long have you worked here?"

"S-six months. Why?"

Cade knocked on the counter in frustration. That wasn't long enough, but it was a small town, and this lead was all he had. "You live around here? Maybe you know the girl who worked nights last year?"

"What's her name?"

Cade shot Lyndy a pointed look.

"She had black curly hair and glasses," Lyndy said. "I can't remember her name. We hoped you might."

The cashier's mouth opened. Then shut. A measure of relief crossed her brow, though her skin remained unnaturally pale. She was definitely guilty of something. "Maybe you mean Ramona?" she asked.

"Maybe," Cade said. "How can we get ahold of her to ask? Do you have her contact information? An address or phone number?"

"No."

Cade scowled. "You have to have access to employee contact information."

"Yeah, right." The girl laughed. "Even if I had access to that information, I'm not giving it to you."

Cade pressed his lips against a tirade. Was the world conspiring against him? What was wrong with this day? "Fine. Get me your manager's number. I'll get Ramona's information from him."

Her eyebrows rose in disbelief and defiance. "No."

The overwhelming scent of crushed fruit and yogurt wound into his nose and deepened his frown.

Lyndy inched forward. "Hi," she told the cashier, re-winding the conversations, then turning to the restless crowd behind them, all of whom had settled in to listen instead of complain, even the hipster. "I'm very sorry to have bothered y'all, but this is truly important. We need to find Ramona, so if anyone knows how we can do that, it would be greatly and sincerely appreciated."

The cashier dragged her gaze from Cade's steaming expression to Lyndy's much calmer one. "Ramona hasn't worked here in months."

"Do you know where she works now?" Lyndy asked.

"No."

Cade followed Lyndy's lead and addressed the crowd this time. "How about you guys? Any of you know where Ramona works now?"

"Is Ramona in trouble?" a middle-aged woman wondered.

"No, ma'am," Lyndy replied. "But I think she might be able to help me identify the man who attacked me."

The hipster raised a brow at Cade. "That's what all this is about? Someone attacked your girl, and you're looking for him?"

Cade dipped his chin. The statement was true enough, though Lyndy wasn't really his girl. But the act felt far more authentic than it should in a short period of time.

Satisfied, the hipster removed a cell phone from his jacket pocket and swiped the screen. "I think she lives in the off-campus housing near my sister. I can call and ask."

"Miss?" The middle-aged woman stepped out of line and skirted around the crowd, careful to give Cade a wide berth. "I saw Ramona this morning."

Cade and Lyndy moved away from the counter, and the line reformed.

"Where?" Lyndy asked kindly, a hint of desperation in her voice.

The woman swung an arm toward the big window, pointer finger outstretched. "The diner on the corner. She was waiting tables."

Cade followed her gaze to a small restaurant across the street, separated from the gym by a narrow alley partially blocked by a dumpster. "Thank you." He pulled his phone from one pocket and dialed Detective Owens. The police needed to interview Ramona. He and Lyndy could speak with her now, if they got lucky and caught her at work, but federal agents assigned to the Tom Cat case would want to add her to the possible witness list and get her interview on record. Maybe something she remembered would be the key to naming this psycho.

Lyndy looked visibly shaken as Cade dialed Detective Owens and waited for the call to connect.

He set Gus's carrier on the nearest table and faced him, angling his back to the bulk of the crowd. "You okay?"

She nodded quickly, sipping and releasing air in little

puffs. "No." Her eyes darted to the restroom sign on the wall beside them. "I just need a minute."

"I'll be right here," he assured her as the detective answered.

He relayed the new information to Owens while admiring Gus's ability to sleep ten times a day and through absolutely anything. He pinched the cell between his shoulder and ear as he turned for a look down the hallway toward the ladies' room. Instinct clawed at his chest.

"I'll call you back," he told Owens, then stuffed the phone into his back pocket.

He hefted Gus's carrier off the table and went to knock on the restroom door. "Lyndy? Everything okay?"

The door opened easily under pressure of his touch, but the room was dark and empty.

Adrenaline spiked in his veins as he turned for a look into the dining area where he'd just been. He couldn't have missed her on his way there. She hadn't returned to him, but it looked as if she hadn't arrived in the ladies room, either.

"Lyndy?" he called, pushing his voice out and willing her to respond.

He marched through the door marked Employees Only and checked the lounge, supply closets and office. "Lyndy!"

The wobble of a swinging door drew his attention as Gus began to cry. The cashier stared at him, mouth agape. "What are you doing? You're not allowed back here!"

"Lyndy's gone." The words stung on his tongue. He needed to call Owens. Needed to find her. The back door came into view as he paced. "Call the police," he demanded. "Tell them Lyndy Wells was just abducted from your shop. Do it now!"

Cade bolted through the back door and into an alleyway with cars parked along one side. His stomach rolled and his nerves screamed along with her son, wailing in his car seat. If her stalker had been in the alley with a car, she could be halfway to the county border by now. All while he'd been on the telephone!

He moved toward the main road, where he'd left his truck.

Shoppers moved jauntily in every direction, heavily laden with packages and steaming logoed cups. Their voices merry and faces bright. All while Cade's world crashed down around him.

The traffic light changed, halting the stream of cars. The digital screens on each corner seemed to be counting down to another tragedy. One Cade couldn't bear. "Lyndy!"

Gus screamed louder, and a woman with a double stroller and toddling child approached him. Her gaze rolled protectively over Gus, then up to Cade's face. "Are you okay?" She asked, glancing quickly back to the wailing child.

"I'm looking for a woman," he said quickly. "She's small and blonde. Short hair. Blue eyes. She's been taken." His eyes raked the street and crowds. "She's his mother."

A heartrending scream shook the world around them as the cars inched forward once more, signaled by the changing light.

Cade's body went rigid. The woman turned in the direction of the scream. A cocktail of dread and panic burned in his chest. He couldn't see her. Couldn't pinpoint where the sound was coming from. Across the street? Up the block?

The car seat swung and bounced in his grip as Gus freaked out.

"Help!" It was Lyndy's scream again, and Cade knew.

"She's in the alley." Between the gym and diner. He took two long strides forward, debating the best angle to dart into traffic when the weight of Gus's carrier hindered his steps.

He couldn't take a baby on a foot chase. Could he? To save his mother? To confront a killer? He swore long and loud.

He couldn't run with Gus. And he couldn't leave him.

Something dragged against his arm.

"Go." The woman said, gripping the carrier beside his hand. "Go!" Her children gathered around her, along with a growing crowd outside the Sunshine Smoothie. "I'll take him inside. Out of the cold. He'll be safe," she insisted, tugging Gus's carrier once more. "Help her." Her eyes burned with determination and fear. "Go."

Cade released the carrier.

He launched himself into the street, racing for the alley, terrified of what he'd find and horrified by what he'd done. He'd left Gus with a stranger. The act had been a bullet cutting through his chest.

"Hurry!" A girl on a cell phone waved to Cade from the mouth of the alley. "He's got her. I've called 911! Hurry!"

Cade skidded around the corner between old buildings where shadows hung thick and long, leaving only a small strip of light at the alley's center. The air was stale and wet like mud and moss and weeks of old trash. Worse than that was the dark figure ahead of him. One arm around Lyndy's middle and one hand across her mouth as he struggled to drag her backward.

Cade strode forward, fire raging in his core. "Let her go or I will shoot you," he seethed, his voice low and deadly serious. He flipped the snap on a holster nestled against his back and relieved it of its weapon.

The assailant slowed, probably weighing his options. He didn't appear armed. Was a head and shoulders taller than Lyndy, though only slightly broader. He wore black shoes, pants and a hoodie. His face was covered in a matching, thin, stretchy mask.

Cade raised his weapon without losing step. "She's not much to hide behind. I've got a clear shot of your head. And I never miss."

The man yanked Lyndy off her feet, raising her higher on his body, eliminating Cade's shot. He considered the man's legs, ankles or feet. All were solid options, though smaller and moving more rapidly than his head. A hit would take him down, but be admittedly less satisfying.

"You've got nowhere to go," Cade taunted, smug satisfaction growing in his chest.

The assailant turned his head left and right, likely looking for an escape route, but there was none that Cade could see.

He lengthened his strides, eating up the distance between them. "Release her and you can live. Test your luck. You. Will. Lose."

Lyndy closed her eyes and grabbed the arm across her middle with both her hands. She pulled her knees up in a crunch, then straightened them with a roar and a grunt. Her feet connected with her abductor's shins, and a wail of pain burst free from him.

He stumbled back, arms flung wide for balance, only to snake an arm out and catch her by her hair as she stumbled to regain her footing on the broken concrete and asphalt.

Cade struggled for a clear shot as Lyndy wailed, clutching at her head where he'd grabbed her.

She flew suddenly forward, tossed and skidding over the filthy, slush-covered ground. The scream that had erupted from her core struck instantly silent as she collided headfirst into the nearby brick wall. The impact was audible.

Chapter Eleven

Lyndy's teeth chattered despite the layers of blankets wrapped around her coat and shoulders. Misplaced, or leftover, adrenaline thrummed in her system as the EMT added two stitches to the cut on her forehead. She hadn't blacked out, thankfully. Hadn't gotten a concussion, but the pain had been excruciating as she'd hit the rough and unforgiving brick with a hellacious whack. Her vision had blurred, maybe from the impact, maybe from the tears, and she'd collapsed in silence as the pain stole her breath. But Cade had been there to pick her up.

Now her throbbing head was only one of her many parts wishing for aspirin, ice and a bed. Her neck and shoulders were whiplashed. Her back was achy and sore. Her hands and knees were scraped and bleeding, though at least the wounds had been cleaned and treated by a paramedic with an angel's soft touch.

Cade paced several feet away, clearly livid and fresh out of patience. He barked at local law enforcement officers, federal agents and a growing number of bystanders who he thought should've done more to catch Lyndy's attacker before he'd disappeared. Apparently, the back door of one building in the alley made an excellent escape hatch, and the attacker had fled after nearly knocking a woman's head off. He was long gone by the time police arrived. Cade had been forced to choose between chasing the bad guy and caring for Lyndy. He'd chosen her, and her heart had cracked irreparably open for him. A pain she would surely deal with later.

Despite Cade's frustration that citizens hadn't given chase for him, many had rushed to help provide triage and countless others had called 911 when they'd heard Lyndy scream. According to her angelic EMT, the lines had been jammed with reports of Lyndy's abduction. Thanks to local media coverage following Carmen's attack, everyone was on the alert for the Kentucky Tom Cat Killer, so they were quick to call but slow to act. Perfectly understandable to Lyndy, who wasn't convinced she'd have tried to take on a potential serial killer if the tides had been turned. Cade was, clearly, less forgiving.

She homed in on the local news crew that had set up just outside the perimeter established by the police. The crew had nearly beaten officers to the scene, and she couldn't help wondering if they knew more than she did at this point about what had happened.

"The Tom Cat Killer has escalated," the reporter in a navy suit and festive tie explained to the camera. "He's got one local woman on his mind, and he's desperate to have her. Proof? He struck again today, right here in this familiar downtown alley, an offshoot of Main Street, amidst a brood of holiday shoppers. But the people of our community responded with a resounding no!" He paused for dramatic effect, and Lyndy felt another welling of tears. She loved and appreciated Piedmont's sense of community in a crisis, but she hated being a victim.

The paramedic handed her a small plastic cup with a pair of painkillers in the bottom, then opened a bottle of water for her to wash them down. "You're going to be all right," the older woman said, her thick black hair worn in a braid that resembled a halo around her head. She smiled warmly and nodded. "This too shall pass. Remember that."

"Thank you," Lyndy whispered, taking the pills and wiping her eyes for the millionth time.

"I call them as I see them. That's all," the paramedic said, her voice thick with sincerity and concern. "You're shaken right now. You're hurting and afraid. Rightfully so. But whoever this Tom Cat is, he's just a man, and you've got a whole lot working on your side. For one, he's been called out, and everyone's watching. We're not going to let a wolf into the henhouse without a fight. And that man of yours looks more than capable of taking care of business than anyone I've seen in my life."

Lyndy glanced at Cade, who had Gus pinned to his chest, hugged tight in a sling made for her, a woman half his size. The murderous look he threw at the reporter, while wearing the baby in a too-small polka-dotted sling, did something to her insides. Despite everything else, she smiled. A moment later he headed in her direction, waving a hand absently while apparently talking to Gus.

"I want you to take this for pain," the EMT instructed. "Plenty of rest and fluids. Ice your neck and shoulders as needed." She handed Lyndy a prescription. "At least twice a day for the next few days. You'll heal faster if you aren't hurting."

Detective Owens arrived at the open ambulance doors a few steps before Cade. "How's she doing, Marla?" he asked the paramedic.

"She's going to be just fine."

Cade scoffed.

Marla smiled kindly and patted his arm. "You'll keep her safe, and Detective Owens will find that man. I have faith."

Cade slid his eyes to Lyndy. "Yes, ma'am." He helped Lyndy out of the ambulance and wrapped a protective arm across her back.

Overcome with need, she rolled against him, pressing her cheek against the warm contours of his chest and wrapping an arm over her baby in the little sling.

"I've got you," he whispered against the top of her head, pulling her into a strong and protective embrace. "I'm so sorry I let that happen."

Detective Owens cleared his throat, and Lyndy jumped. His expression was judgmental, bordering on hostile, as she stepped away from Cade. She wanted to tell Cade that what happened wasn't his fault. That no one could've seen Tom coming. The whole thing had happened so fast. He'd been waiting in the hall outside the ladies' room, wearing a ski mask and pointing at something hidden under his jacket. He'd said he had a gun. Threatened to shoot someone waiting with the crowd by the register if she didn't go quietly. And no one had paid any attention as he'd nearly pushed her across the street. It wasn't until he'd repositioned the small metal bar beneath his coat that she'd realized he didn't have a gun. And she'd screamed.

"I've got Ramona Tinner's contact information from the diner," Owens said. "I'm headed there now while the feds finish here. I'm sending a cruiser to the Wells residence, and I'll keep a unit in position full-time. I'd appreciate it if you stay in touch with them and with me."

"Yes, sir," she said, feeling inexplicably guilty as the older man walked away.

CADE FED AND played with Gus until the baby fell asleep. There was something oddly comforting about caring for him. Maybe it was the fact Cade had done such a terrible job keeping Lyndy safe today, which made seeing her baby smile all the more reassuring. Maybe it meant he wasn't a total failure at something he'd been charged with doing this week.

He'd spoken to the members of his team several times and been told at length that he'd done nothing wrong. That the timing had simply been perfect on Tom's end, but Cade couldn't relieve the nagging sensation that there was more he should've done. Instead, the serial killer had only needed Cade to let his guard down for a moment, and Cade had. He couldn't let that happen again. There was no room for error. Tom had proven that yet again, and Lyndy had paid the price.

At least his caring for Gus gave Lyndy an opportunity to shower and rest. Though he doubted she'd sleep well tonight after what she'd been through. He wouldn't blame her. Given the last week of her life. In all honesty, he wasn't sure how she'd ever sleep soundly again, even after the monster had been caught. Not until Gus was grown.

Caring for the infant all afternoon and evening had already done something to Cade that he wasn't sure he'd recover from. He'd removed the baby from the sling only to realize an invisible tether had formed between them, linking the chubby, toothless infant straight to Cade's heart. More shocking, still, was the misplaced feeling of personal responsibility sure to extend beyond Cade's limited time in the child's life. He'd already wondered multiple times if Lyndy might allow him to come back and visit once in a while. He wanted to see Gus learn to walk, ride a bike, play T-ball and Little League. He shook the irrational thoughts away as soon as they came, but they lingered on the periphery of his mind, never far and always quick to return.

Thoughts of the child's mother were the same. Would she want to see Cade again when this was over? Did he want that? If he didn't, then why couldn't he stop thinking about it?

A door creaked open at the end of the hallway, followed by a soft set of footfalls. Lyndy appeared a moment later, looking sheepish and wearing a pale pink T-shirt and white cotton shorts. Her feet were bare, her toenails red, and her hair was slightly mussed. She looked like something pulled straight from Cade's favorite fantasy. Except this woman was real, and she'd been hurt today. She'd been attacked twice this week, and there were stitches along the red and swollen skin of her hairline to prove it. Her knees and palms were scraped and raw, only just beginning to scab. And suddenly all he wanted to do was scoop her off her feet and hold her until this nightmare was over.

"Hey," he said, his voice coming lower and thicker than intended. "How are you doing?"

She crossed her arms over her chest and Cade's protective PG thoughts took a turn.

The room was a little chilly, and she obviously hadn't been sleeping in a bra.

"Couldn't rest," she said. "How's Gus?"

"Out cold," Cade said with a swell of pride, pointing to the playpen he'd converted into a makeshift crib. "I hated to put him in his room where I couldn't see him, so I thought this would work for tonight."

Her sweet mouth curled at the edge as she moved toward her son. "Thank you."

Cade forced his attention away from her lush lips, short shorts and lucky pink top. "Can I get you something?" he asked. already moving toward the counter. "Water, coffee, tea? Are you hungry?"

"Just sore," she said, touching a hand to her forehead. "The pain pills knocked out the worst of it, but my palms and knees itch where they're scraped. I couldn't get comfortable in any of my pajama pants."

His gut twisted, and the urge to hold her hit again. The image of Detective Owens's disapproving expression held him at bay. It had been a well-needed reminder that Cade's thoughts and behaviors were crossing a line where Lyndy and Gus were concerned. And it wasn't fair to them.

"On second thought, maybe I should have some water," she said, moving in his direction. She tipped her head side to side and rubbed at the bunched muscles along her shoulders. "And another pain pill. I feel like I was hit by a bus."

Cade filled a glass with ice and water, then passed it to her. "You're a warrior. That's the second time you bested him."

"Well, desperate times," she said hoarsely before sipping the water, brows furrowed. "I was in a helpless panic until you pulled a gun and started threatening him. Seeing you made me brave."

"I'm glad." Cade passed her a pill from the prescription he'd insisted they have filled on the way home, and waited while she took it with another sip from her glass. "You're supposed to take that with food. How do you feel about grilled cheese?"

"You don't have to do that," she said, gripping the back of her neck. "I can throw a slice of bread in the toaster."

"And I can make grilled cheese."

She rolled her eyes. "Then, thank you."

Cade got to work on the sandwich as Lyndy padded back in Gus's direction.

"He looks so peaceful," she said. "I'm sorry you were stuck babysitting today. Now you're making meals and administering pills. I hate that you're doing all this extra stuff and I'm doing nothing."

"I'm not stuck, and this isn't extra," he said. "I'm going to see you through this. You and Gus. Whatever you need. For as long as it takes." He just hoped he could bring himself to leave when the job ended. He might be good at grilled cheese and watching her baby, but he wasn't good for her. He didn't stick with anyone long term for a reason. His dad had been a special kind of awful, and Cade didn't want to accidentally follow in his old man's footsteps, ruining the lives of those closest to him. He might be a better man, or he might not, but he refused to test the waters on Lyndy. She deserved more and better.

The tension in Lyndy's posture had disappeared by the time her sandwich was gone, along with the lines between her brows.

"Feeling better?" he asked.

"Definitely." She carried her empty glass to the sink, then stared through the window into the darkness.

"Maybe now you'll be able to sleep."

"Maybe." She rolled her shoulders and stretched her muscles. "The pills are working. The pain's gone, but my muscles are still tight."

"May I?" he asked, moving around to stand behind her.

Her eyes met his in the reflection of the glass, reminding him of the moment they'd shared at her gym. "Yes."

He brushed the hair away from her neck with the tips of his fingers, then grazed his palms along her tender flesh. He pressed gently on her shoulders, allowing the pads of his thumbs to caress her nape and watching her expression in the glass for signs of discomfort.

Her head fell back against his chest with a soft groan. Eyes closed, lips parted as he worked the remaining tension from her muscles. Despite all she'd been through. She trusted him.

"Better?" he asked.

Her eyes drifted lazily open. "That's amazing."

He smiled at the breathless words. "Thanks."

"Is it wrong that I wouldn't mind knowing what else your hands could do for me?"

Cade barked a laugh, but his body responded instantly and powerfully to the possibilities. "Not wrong," he said, "but I have a feeling that's the pain pill talking."

She turned lithely in the small space between the sink and his body, rubbing her warm breasts against him as she stretched onto her toes and fitted her hands behind his head. "I'm feeling much better now."

"I see that," he said, setting his hands against the gentle curve of her waist and allowing himself a moment of selfish indulgence. She smiled, and he slid his hands over the curves of her hips before drawing his fingers back up, tracing the line of her spine.

She shivered, and he moaned.

Lyndy tipped her head back and locked him in her heated blue gaze. "I like the way you touch me."

"How do I touch you?" he asked taking baby steps backward, leading her toward the hall.

"Like my body is a treasure."

His smile widened. "Not your body," he whispered against the narrow curve of her ear. "You. And I think it's time I take you back to bed." He hooked one arm behind her knees before lifting her off the ground and carrying down the hall. "Don't get any ideas," he warned, speaking to Lyndy as much as himself. "I'm only going to tuck you in."

Her bottom lip jutted out in disappointment. "Will you kiss me good-night?"

"Not this time, Sleeping Beauty."

But he hoped that maybe one day he could.

Chapter Twelve

Lyndy woke rested but sore when the pain medication wore off, and the effects of her most recent attack ruined her peace. She eased upright, then shuffled to the bathroom in preparation for her day. Tantalizing aromas of bacon and eggs floated down the hall on a chorus of Gus's laughter. Lyndy smiled. Despite it all, Gus was safe and happy, and that was all that mattered.

She climbed into the shower and lingered beneath the searing spray until her skin was as red as a sunburn and the water had loosened her aching muscles. When the throbbing pain in her head demanded she get out, Lyndy toweled off and pulled a cotton t-shirt over her head. She chose a wide, stretchy headband to keep her hair away from her face. More important, away from the angry, puckered wound on her forehead. She dabbed ointment on the itchy stitches and then concealer over the unsightly bruises along her cheek and jawbone. The mascara and lip gloss were administered in sheer defiance. An attempt to feel more like herself and less like the Tom Cat's little mouse.

Finished, she hurried down the hall to see Gus and pour some coffee. She refused to think about how much she wanted to see Cade, too. "Good morning, pumpkin" she called, rounding the corner in a beeline for her baby in his highchair.

Gus cooed and babbled at the sight of her. Cade had dressed him in a black T-shirt and jeans with white socks. "What are you wearing?" she asked, kissing his chubby fingers and the bottoms of his kicking feet.

"What's wrong with what he's wearing?" Cade asked, stepping in from the living room and pocketing his phone.

"He looks like a greaser."

Cade frowned, and Lyndy noticed with a smile that Cade was essentially wearing the same outfit, though his T-shirt was a V-neck and Gus's shirt had a little pocket. "What do you mean?"

She filled a mug with coffee and suppressed a laugh. A little ball rolled against her foot, and she realized part of the kitchen floor was covered in them. "What happened in here?"

Cade scooped a red, white and blue stress ball from the floor and set it on Gus's tray. "We're training."

Gus flung his arms until the ball went over the tray's edge, then squealed and clapped his hands together.

"Gus wants to be a professional pitcher," Cade explained, "if football doesn't work out."

"Ah." Lyndy sipped her coffee and smiled. "That's quite a plan."

"Well, it's important to have dreams," Cade said, tossing and catching one of the squishy balls. "Fortress Defense swag. I found a bag of them in the truck."

"Did you go out?" Lyndy asked, feeling a shard of fear slice through her at the idea she and Gus had been alone.

"No. I was looking for a bag of surveillance equipment I normally keep on hand. I think it's at the office, so I'm going to need to make a run back home. I left in too big of a hurry when Owens called."

She bit her lip, a fresh wave of guilt riding over her. Now he was tied up indefinitely and dealing with a serial killer. She turned for the bottle of pain pills on her windowsill and cracked it open.

Cade smiled.

"What?"

He shook his head. "Nothing. Did you sleep okay?"

"Yeah." She removed a pill and used a paring knife to break it in half. A whole pill had put her to sleep so deeply last night that she didn't remember going to bed. She couldn't afford to conk out like that again until after dinner. Until then, she'd do her best to be useful if yesterday's attack had generated any leads.

Cade watched her carefully as she took half the pill and returned the rest to the bottle. She appreciated the concern in his soulful blue eyes. "How are you feeling?"

"Okay. Sore and scared. Sorry you were dragged into this, but thankful you're here."

He smiled "Yeah?"

"Yeah."

Gus pounded the highchair tray, and Lyndy gripped her forehead. "That pill has not kicked in yet."

Cade loaded Gus's tray with stress balls, then pulled out a chair at the table for Lyndy. "How about some bacon?"

Lyndy ate greedily while a torrent of questions blew around her mind. "If you hadn't been with me yesterday, I would've had Gus when Tom took me."

Cade's level expression met hers. "I know."

"You can't stay with us forever, so what are we going to do?" she asked, hating again that the first part was true.

His frown deepened. "Let's concentrate on today. For starters, I thought we could decorate your Christmas tree together after dinner. I put it up while you were asleep. Just the tree and lights. All the ornaments are still in the totes. We can string popcorn. Maybe watch that movie I've been trying to get to. Something fun for the holiday?"

She paused, a strip of bacon at her lips. "You put up my tree?"

"Is that okay?"

She pushed onto her feet and went to see for herself. Sure enough, her mother's thirty-year-old artificial tree had been assembled near the front window. Her homemade, childhood tree skirt fanned out beneath it. Rows of chasing colored lights danced and flashed erratically below a star made of cardboard and tinfoil. A star she'd made in preschool and her mother had cherished. Sam had insisted she leave it in storage and use an antique glass star of his family's, instead. "Thank you," she said, breathless with appreciation. "It's perfect."

Cade smiled. "While you're so happy with me, what do you think about a road trip this morning?"

"Back to Fortress?" she guessed, remembering his comment about needing to go home.

"If you're up to it. I'd like to pick up some supplies and possibly another team member, if that's all right with you."

Lyndy gave the tree and star another look. "I'd love to."

She bit into her third slice of bacon, contemplating her life.

"Penny for your thoughts?" Cade asked, pouring a mug of coffee and taking the seat across from her.

"I had a really normal life last week," she mused, wondering if the pain pill was kicking in. "Small, but comfortable. A little lonely, but I was happy. I'm not sure how I got from there to here. Now my face is on the morning, evening and nightly news. Some psychotic murderer is after me. I've got a bodyguard living with me and a police detail outside."

Cade frowned. "What were your days like before? What would you be doing right now if none of this had happened?"

"What do you mean?" she asked, turning intentionally away from the pile of bacon before she took another slice.

"You wouldn't be making a road trip with your bodyguard to collect weapons, surveillance materials and a second man for your protection," he said. "So what would you be doing instead?"

"Well," Lyndy began, slightly stumped. It had only been a few days, but that small, quiet life she'd just mentioned seemed so far away now. "I guess I'd be at work." She checked the clock on the wall for confirmation. "If none of this had happened, I would've gotten up at five thirty. Gotten myself ready, then Gus. I'd have grabbed a granola bar on the way out the door at seven and taken him to day care by seven thirty before racing across town to work by eight."

"Where you interview folks who need employment?" Cade asked.

"Correct."

"You like it?"

Lyndy smiled. No one had ever asked her that before. "I like the people," she said. "I like knowing I can help folks."

He shifted in his seat, stretching long legs beneath the table. "After work?"

"I pick Gus up. We walk at the park, then head home. We do our nighttime routine after dinner and he's usually asleep by nine. I read until I fall asleep, too."

"When do you go out with your friends?" Cade asked.

She shook her head, suddenly feeling a little sorry for herself. "No friends." The busyness of her life had made it seem so full. She hadn't realized how solitary she'd become. Not like now, with Cade there to talk to, share meals and laugh with even when she wanted to cry. "What about you?"

"I love what I do," Cade answered.

"Is this what you'd be doing on a normal work day?" she asked, curious now. What were his other cases like comparatively? "Making clients' breakfast and coaching infants for a career in professional baseball?"

"Wait a minute. Baseball only happens if football fails," he said with a wink that made her grin.

Lyndy waited, desperate for more information about his life and clients before her. She wanted to know this assignment was different. Not because of the circumstances, but because of her.

Cade watched Gus for a long beat before answering. "I'd be outside the home monitoring the perimeter at this time of day. Or maybe in my truck outside the client's office while they worked. I normally keep my distance. I try to blend into the background of my clients' lives so they feel safe without having to explain why I'm there to everyone they know."

"That seems…" Lyndy struggled to find the word "… sad." She offered a weak smile.

"It's not sad. It's the job."

"Okay, so when do you get to feel like you belong instead of like you shouldn't be seen?" she asked.

"Between jobs. Anytime I'm back at Fortress."

"Do you spend a lot of time with your teammates then?" she asked, trying not to sound so deeply interested.

"No." Something in his tone seemed off, as if he was noticing the same thing she was. They both had lives built wholly around something they loved. And somewhere along the line, they'd each given themselves up for the cause. Her thing was Gus. Cade's was his job. But was that enough? For now? Forever?

His brows tented. "We stay busy. There's often more jobs than we can take on. We're looking to expand, add to the team, but it takes time to vet potential employees when we're already gone more days than we're home."

Lyndy's heart broke for him. Was it possible he was surrounded by people he cared about and just as lonely as she was?

Cade cleared his throat and stood, collecting their empty plates. "I need to make some notes about your property before we go. It'll help with the supplies and planning. Feel like a quick walk?"

"Sounds good." She bundled Gus then grabbed her coat and joined Cade outside a few minutes later, where they examined the land she'd bought with Sam. Everything about it looked different now. Without him. Without the grief. With a finally healed heart, she could truthfully say this property was never what she'd wanted. And once this mess was over, she was going to sell it and move.

"I've covered most of the ground and pulled up details from your county auditor's site," Cade said, slipping into a sort of businessman mode she hadn't seen before.

"But those sites are often outdated, and they don't include the details human can provide. So, what can you tell me about your land?"

Lyndy breathed in the fresh morning air and surveyed the vast spread before her. "There's 8.9 acres. The road out front is the only way in. The property butts up against four others. One on each side and two behind. Those properties are all larger. Two have homes. Two don't. The nearest home is nearly a half mile away." *A quick walk, but too far for them to hear her scream*, she thought morbidly.

"Neighbors?" he asked.

"I've never met them. The home to the south is part of a dairy farm. The house next door belongs to an elderly couple who don't get out much."

"What about outbuildings?"

"Just the two in the backyard. The old barn is decrepit. Sam planned to restore it, but it seems like a death trap to me. The small building was going to be my henhouse." She smiled at the sweet thought. "All I've ever wanted was a nice little backyard with a grill and a swing set. Someplace I could enjoy my grandmama's sweet tea and watch my kids play. Funny how perfect that sounds when you're young and the world's still full of possibilities."

Cade looked from her face to Gus's and then back. "I think it sounds nice. So how'd you end up with all this if you only wanted a small yard and a henhouse?"

She shrugged, adjusting Gus in his sling. "I met Sam when he was in my hometown on business. We dated, then got engaged quickly. My mom had just died, and my grandmama not long before her. My dad's always been absentee, so I was alone and didn't want to be. Sam was nice, so I left everything I knew and came here to be with him. Now he's gone and I'm alone. With Gus, of course, but irony, right?"

Cade didn't answer, but his searching gaze sent chills over her skin. He turned back toward the house and set a heavy palm against the small of her back to guide her along with him.

The gentle pressure of his fingers sent shock waves through her core. She wanted to know what those fingers felt like beneath the coat. On her skin. In her hair.

Cade opened the back door for her and locked up behind them once they stepped inside.

She removed a sleeping Gus from his sling and coat, then crept down the hall to his room and nestled him in his crib. She gripped the tensing muscles along her neck as she made her way back to Cade in the kitchen. "I expected the headache," she said, absently reaching for a bottle of aspirin in the cupboard, "but I can't get over how much everything else aches. Do you think I can take these with the prescription?"

"Why not take the other half of your pill?" he asked with a gleam in his eye.

She wrinkled her nose. "The painkillers I took after Gus was born made me goofy, and I don't even remember going to bed last night. I have to wait until we're in for the night before I take a full pill again."

Cade grinned. "Define goofy."

Her cheeks heated with the humiliating memories. "I said anything I wanted, usually the minute it came to mind and completely without filter. I told the man delivering my pizza that his breath stank and a mother breastfeeding her baby on a park bench that she was a hero."

His grin widened. "So the pills are like truth serum?"

She felt her jaw drop. "Did I say something last night?"

He shrugged, a wicked expression on his handsome face. "To clarify," he said, stepping into her personal space. "You always say exactly what you mean when you take the pills?"

"Unfortunately."

He chuckled, then raised his palms and brows in question. "I can help with the muscle tension. Do you trust me?"

"Implicitly."

His mouth parted and his gaze darkened as he set his broad hands against her shoulders, pulling her closer and working his fingers carefully over the tender skin. "The tugging and tight feeling you have is probably caused by spasms. They're common after a trauma and are normally painful, but the prescription you're taking is knocking the edge off. I'm going to try to relax the muscles so they stop gripping and releasing."

Lyndy's breath caught as his hands slid down the length of her arms, then moved to the curves of her waist, his strong steady fingers massaging the muscles of her back. Her head rolled over one shoulder as his hands glided up her spine and between her shoulder blades, probing and testing, expertly releasing the painful knots of tension.

"I have another idea," he said, stepping away. "Be right back."

Lyndy couldn't imagine what he was up to, but if it was going to feel half as good as that back massage, she was all in.

Cade swaggered back a moment later, a tube of cream in his hand. "My sergeant introduced me to this after I rolled my jeep in Kabul. I still use it when I overdo my workouts. It's warm at first, but it's great for muscle pain." He lifted a hand tentatively to her shoulder. "May I?"

Lyndy bit into her bottom lip, nearly vibrating with anticipation of his touch.

He stepped close again, the scent, heat and presence of him flooding into her senses as he curled his hands over the slope of her shoulders and tugged the wide V-neck of her T-shirt off one shoulder.

She released an involuntary moan of pleasure as the cool cream hit her skin, then froze as an intrusive and fuzzy memory presented itself, effectively ruining the moment. "Did you rub my neck last night?" she asked, knowing the truth, remembering with sudden clarity how perfectly delicious his touch had felt and how badly she'd wanted more.

Cade pulled his hands away, as if he'd done something wrong. "Yes."

She covered her mouth, recalling the things she'd been thinking. The fantasies she'd been enjoying. "I was doped up on that pain pill." And she'd wanted him to touch her. She'd asked him to kiss her good-night. But he hadn't.

"I stopped the moment I realized," he said. "I put you in bed. Alone."

Lyndy added *honorable* to the growing list of reasons she was falling hard and fast for her protector. Before she could say so, the scent of the uncapped lotion in his raised hand brought a rush of other, more awful memories to the surface. "Oh my goodness."

"Nothing happened. I swear."

"No." She grabbed the tube from Cade, her hand shaking hard against his and inhaled deeply. Instantly, the dark lake at the park flashed into mind. The slip of her feet on wet grass. The pressure of an arm on her body. A hand on her mouth. "He smelled like this." She blinked against a rush of unbidden tears. "Cade. The man who grabbed me smelled exactly like this!"

Chapter Thirteen

Cade dialed Detective Owens as Lyndy moved away, her breaths coming shuddered and quick.

She collapsed onto a kitchen chair, cheeks pale as he waited for the call to connect.

"Hey. This is good," he promised, crouching before her to look into her eyes. "You've just come across the most viable clue the police have had in months. This is better than good," he amended. "It might be the break they need to finally name this lunatic."

Lyndy nodded, whether in understanding or agreement, he wasn't sure.

He stood and squeezed her shoulder gently as he listened to the infuriating rings of a call going unanswered. Pressure grew in his gut. Linking this scent to the killer was big. No one used muscle cream unless they needed it. Whoever the feds had on their suspect list could be narrowed significantly with this. "Come on, Owens. Pick up," he muttered.

The gentle pressure of Lyndy's small hand on his unfurled something in his core. She'd set her palm over his hand on her shoulder and curled her thin fingers around his for support. The simple gesture was so sweet, so innocent and so wholly welcome that his leathery heart gave a heavy thump. *She* was comforting *him*. Even in a moment when she was speechless. No one had ever done that before. Cade had always been the strong one. The provider for his siblings. A warrior for his country. The Fortress member always on assignment so the others could be with their loved ones. Nothing and no one in his life had ever been about him. All his present and past relationships had been based on what he could do for someone else.

The sound of Detective Owens's recorded voice mail message pulled Cade back to the moment. "No answer," he said, his voice unexpectedly rough. He turned the phone around and dialed again, only to receive the same result. This time he cleared his throat and left a message.

"Detective Owens," he began, unable to hide his irritation. He needed to speak to the man himself. "This is Cade Lance. Lyndy Wells has something I think you and the feds can run with on the Tom Cat case. She's identified the scent of the man who attempted to abduct her. It's a muscle cream called Hayden's Own. It's holistic, no chemicals, just oils and extracts, with a unique eucalyptus and lemongrass scent. It's hard to find, and it's not sold nationally. I'm willing to bet it was bought locally." He freed his hand from Lyndy's and paced as his temper grew. "The manager at the Sunshine Smoothie wore a sling. I'd like to verify his injury, the cause and timeline."

Lyndy's distant gaze snapped up to meet his, and she sucked in a deep, ragged breath.

"That guy told me he had a torn rotator cuff, but I'm starting to think a sling and exaggerated injury are the perfect ways to make a guilty man seem innocent." It was possible that an injured manager at the most likely location to host Lyndy's stalker wasn't the man they were looking for, but it made for some strong coincidences. Cade didn't believe in coincidences.

Lyndy pushed onto her feet, looking ill. She darted to the sink and turned on the water as Cade disconnected the call. She pulled a rag from the drawer and pumped soap from the dispenser then began to scrub her shoulder in short, frantic strokes. Removing the small amount of cream he'd applied.

Cade pocketed the phone on his way to the sink. "Lyndy." He shut the water off and pried the rag from her fisted hand, saving the red and swelling skin, which she'd rubbed to excess, from any further abuse. "Hey," he said more softly, pulling her into his embrace. "I've got you."

She pressed her forehead to his chest and curled her fingers into the fabric of his shirt. "I hate him," she whispered. "Why can't they stop him?"

"Me, too," he said, "and they will." Cade stroked her back and folded her deeper into his protective embrace. "I won't let him hurt you again." He felt the truth of the words in his marrow. No one would hurt Lyndy again, not without going through him first, and no one got through Cade.

She eased her head back and leveled him with a warm, trusting gaze. "Okay."

He smiled. "Just like that, huh?"

"Yeah." She forced a tight smile, but made no move to release him. "I didn't mean to freak out. That smell just…"

"That smell will probably always make you sick now," he said, knowing firsthand how strongly the sense of scent was tied to memories. There were a number of things he'd prefer to never smell again. Diesel exhaust in the desert. Freshly turned earth. The cloying scent of too many flowers on caskets of men too young to have gone home in them. "But it won't always be so intense or scary when the memories come. Time will make that easier." Time and knowing the son of a gun was locked up for life.

Lyndy wet her lips and slowly uncurled her fingers, releasing the material of his shirt. "Thanks for saying that. Logically, I know Gus and I are safe, and that the outside threat won't last forever, but sometimes it just feels like too much. Like this is our life now, and we'll never be safe again." She flattened her palms against the wrinkled material on his chest then slid her hands up and over his shoulders, bringing their bodies tightly together once more. "It's nice to feel anchored again."

Anchored. The word reminded him of the invisible tether he'd imagined between himself and Gus. That undeniable connection was looped tightly around Lyndy, too. He cupped her sweet face in his hands, searching for the words to thank her for reminding him he was more than a bodyguard, more than a former marine, more than a vessel moving from duty to duty. He was a man who wanted things for himself, like a home and a family. A man who wanted *her*.

Before he could verbalize his gratitude, Lyndy rose onto her toes. Without breaking eye contact, she dusted her lips gently across his in a touch so light it might've been her breath if he hadn't felt the aftershocks of it in his core. She pulled back slightly when he didn't reciprocate.

Need burned in him as he deliberated. He wasn't supposed to want her. Not in his arms, in his bed, or in his future, but right now, with her looking at him like that, it took all his remaining self-control not to take her mouth with his. She deserved more than a man who'd take advantage of her while she was in danger. And he didn't want to be a distraction from her fear or a temporary anchor in the storm.

Lyndy's cheeks reddened as he held her in place, turning scarlet with humiliation. "I'm so sorry." She slid her hands off him and lowered slowly from her toes. She pressed her lips tight and averted her gaze. "I misread the situation. I was out of line." She turned quickly away.

Cade followed, pulled by the tether. "Wait." He snaked out an arm to stop her, unsure what to say next. He couldn't explain the chaos and confusion raging in his heart and mind. There weren't words, and it wasn't right. Not now. Not until her life was her own again and she could make clear decisions, unaffected by external circumstances.

She spun on him, and he rocked back on his heels. Her chin rose in defiance. "It's fine. I'm fine. The truth is that I think you're handsome and kind, and I feel connected to you. It's peaceful and exhilarating and really very confusing. Maybe it's the extenuating circumstances. I don't think so, but I don't know. And honestly, I can't say that I care. I've wanted you since the moment I set eyes on you, and that isn't like me at all."

Cade's muscles seized as her words hit like missiles to his heart.

"It's okay that you don't want me, too," she continued. "I'll get over it, and I promise not to try that again, but please don't go. I don't think I can get through this without you."

Cade caught her chin in his hand and slid his palm

against her cheek in a desperate caress. "I'm supposed to be here as your protector," he rasped.

A peppy country tune began suddenly, and Lyndy started.

He released her, and she dashed away, leaving a chill in her absence.

"That's my cell phone. It could be Detective Owens," she said, digging into her bag for the device. "Hello?"

Cade watched, willing his heart rate to slow and wishing equally that he could thank and throttle whoever was on the other end of the line.

"Okay," Lyndy said, alarm in her voice and on her brow. "I'll be right there." She pressed the phone to her chest and stared, horrified, at Cade. "That was my office. I just got a delivery."

LYNDY STROKED GUS'S soft hair and peppered him with kisses, hating to wake him, especially for this reason. The last time they'd gone into town together, it hadn't ended well.

"Hi, sleepyhead," she whispered as his little lids dragged open, and his mouth pulled into an enormous yawn. "We're going to take a little trip." She lifted him into her arms and hugged him tight, wanting to infuse and fortify him with her love.

Cade shifted against the doorjamb, where he watched. "Anything I can do to help?"

"I've got this," she said, setting Gus on the changing table and willing the instant memory of Cade's rejection away. She'd said her piece. She'd told him she wanted him despite all sense and logic. And he'd told her he was only there as her protector. She'd done the brave thing by being honest, and he'd done the same in return.

Theirs was a working relationship.

"Did your office tell you what sort of delivery it was?" he asked.

"No." And she hadn't thought to ask. She changed Gus, then gave him a hearty snuggle before heading in Cade's direction.

He slid smoothly out of her way, careful not to touch her. "Do you normally receive deliveries at the office?"

"Sometimes," she admitted, though her company frowned on it. "I'm rarely home during the hours deliveries are made. I can't sign for anything here, and I'd hate to leave a package on the porch all day."

Lyndy made Gus a bottle, then tucked the makings of another into her bag in case they were in town longer than expected.

"Have you ordered anything recently?" Cade asked, sticking to her heels as she moved through the house.

"Not that I can recall, but I have standing orders for things I get often like diapers, formula and wipes." She paused to sigh. "Look, I'm having a bit of a day here, and whatever is waiting for me at the office is probably something awful. We both know that. So you might as well call Detective Owens back and leave another message."

Cade pursed his lips, brows furrowed.

Lyndy slid her feet into the ankle boots beside her door. She'd changed into her softest jeans and white tank top with a pale green sweater before waking Gus. The ankle boots would go well with the ensemble while keeping her feet warm in the inch or so of snow that had added up from the day's flurries. "Let's just get this over with before I lose my nerve." She turned the knob and waited, suddenly immobilized by the thought of walking out alone.

"I've got it." Cade reached for the knob, forcing her back, then motioned her onto the empty porch.

She wanted to sail dramatically down the steps and across the lawn to his waiting truck but couldn't. Instead she froze, scanning the wide-open space in search of an assailant cloaked in black and coated in muscle cream.

"Pretty day," Cade said, passing her on the porch.

Lyndy tried to appreciate the view. Endless blue skies above snow-dusted fields and distant mountains rising in the background. The scene would've been picture-perfect if her world wasn't falling apart.

The truck's locks popped up, and Cade opened her door. Her palms were clammy as she buckled Gus into the safety harness, and her knees were shaking as she climbed onto the seat.

Cade stood silently for several long beats before shutting the door behind her. He rounded the hood with a troubled expression, then folded himself behind the wheel. "I'd like to hold your hand in town," he said, casting a furtive look in her direction. "If you put Gus in the sling and I hold your hand, I'll have the both of you within arm's reach and a free hand for my sidearm if needed."

"Of course." She buckled up while he ignited the engine.

The world blew by in a blur. The commute to her office went both as fast and as slowly as she'd ever known. Her mouth was dry and pasty with anticipation by the time they reached the stout five-story building on the edge of town.

"Ready?" Cade asked, pulling the glass door open for her to pass.

Lyndy wrapped her arms around Gus, and a blast of

dry heat poured over her shoulders as she breached the threshold. She led the way to the welcome desk at the center of the first-floor lobby. A giant Christmas tree rose in the corner, covered in cheery holiday decor and sprinkled with paper tags shaped like angels. Names of local families in need were printed on one side of each angel and a massive box beside the tree held gifts already purchased by building employees for the family members. Lyndy still had to wrap her purchases before bringing them in.

The oversize welcome desk was lined in twinkle lights and silver garland. The security guard watched astutely as they approached. Anyone who entered the building needed a pass to get beyond the desk.

"Hi, James." She waved, and James stood. He was in his late fifties and often surly, but he kept people out who didn't have an appointment, and he seemed to know every employee in the building by name.

"Ms. Wells." He stood to greet her, taking pointed notice of Gus in his sling before lancing Cade with a near-threatening look. "New beau?" he asked, turning away before she answered.

Cade linked his hand with hers and gave her fingers an encouraging squeeze.

"He is," she said, hoping to sound light and carefree, though the bruising and stitches on her face would make the facade hard to pull off. "This is my boyfriend, Cade. Cade, this is James. He makes sure the entire building runs smoothly."

James gave Cade another look, cocking his head before suddenly standing straighter. "Military?"

"Yes, sir. Marines. You?"

"Air Force." James unbuttoned his shirtsleeve and

rolled one cuff above his elbow. The letters USAF were inked on his skin.

Cade released Lyndy, then extended a hand to the older man. The pair gave one strong pump of their arms. When Cade released him, he raised that hand in salute. "Thank you for your service."

James's usually stern expression eased, and for a moment, emotion clouded his eyes. He returned the salute quickly, then looked to Lyndy with an approving smile. "Nice to see you found a good one." He issued their pass and took his seat with shoulders squared.

When they'd stepped onto the elevator, Lyndy pressed the button marked five and slid her eyes in Cade's direction. "I see him every day, and he's never said more than hello to me."

Cade smiled. "He pegged me for military. Probably felt some camaraderie. It can be tough coming home after the service. Not everyone acclimates. Some never get a real footing."

"Did you?" she asked. He'd founded a successful business with his teammates, but had he really adjusted to being home? Had he even tried? From the way he'd described his life, it seemed like work was all he had, and that didn't seem like enough. Cade deserved to have more. To have whatever he wanted in life.

He stepped closer and set a hand against the small of her back. "I'm working on it."

The elevator doors parted, and the office receptionist nearly launched from her seat to greet Lyndy. "Oh my goodness! There you are!"

Cade moved away as Sylvia slung her arms around Lyndy and Gus, her silver pixie-cut hair and cat-eye glasses going slightly askew with the effort. "Oh, sweetie, look at you," she said, pulling back with a frown. Her gaze slipped over the bumps and bruises on Lyndy's face. "I am so sorry this is happening to you. None of us can believe it. You poor thing."

"I'm okay," Lyndy said, willing the words to be true.

Sylvia brushed a hand along Lyndy's arm, then squeezed her elbow. "Well, at least you aren't going through it alone." She slid her gaze in Cade's direction then back. "Hello, handsome. Am I right?" she asked, not bothering to quiet her voice. "Where on earth did you find him? Cause I'd like to stop there on my way home."

Lyndy laughed. "Sylvia, this is my boyfriend, Cade. Cade, meet Sylvia."

He stepped forward, one hand extended. "How do you do?"

Sylvia wrapped her arms around his solid core and pressed her cheek to his pecs. "Very well," she said. "Very, very well."

When Cade gave in and hugged her back, she lifted one peep-toed pump off the ground like a cartoon princess.

Lyndy laughed at Cade's shocked expression. "I believe you mentioned a delivery for me, Sylvia."

The older woman released Cade with a little goodbye pat to his abs. "I did." She hurried around her desk and grabbed a large vase of flowers positioned beside the stacks of mail and unopened boxes. "But now that I see you have this nice fella, I suppose they're from him."

Lyndy's gut clenched and her head felt light. Roses and carnations. Just like the bouquet delivered to Carmen at the hospital.

Cade's arm came protectively around her waist. "I

didn't send those." He pulled his phone from his pocket, snapped a picture, then immediately began to dial.

Lyndy pulled the envelope free of the stems. It was bulky and too heavy for the typical card insert. Her fingers trembled as she broke the seal and pushed the flap out of her way.

A name badge from the local diner fell onto the reception desk. The white plastic tag was splattered with crimson stains and engraved with the letters R-a-m-o-n-a.

The attached card was scripted in matching crimson letters.

See you soon.

Chapter Fourteen

Cade recognized the first uniform to arrive on scene. Officer Sanchez had been with Detective Owens at the hospital after Carmen's attack, and he'd located the coveralls Tom had shed. The look on Sanchez's face said he was just as unhappy as Cade, and there was a strange comfort in that. It meant that he wanted this guy caught, too.

Sanchez spoke with James at the front desk while waiting for a second officer to arrive. As usual Tom had gotten his message to Lyndy in broad daylight, and no one knew anything.

Cade listened raptly as James relayed all he could remember. A delivery man had brought the flowers in a white logoed truck from a florist he recognized. The delivery man was one he'd seen many times and knew by name. A bright side, if there was one to be found. The man left the flowers, and James had called Lyndy's office. That was that.

Officer Sanchez promised to speak with the driver and whoever took the delivery order after he'd finished speaking with Lyndy and her friend Sylvia, but that too was a bust. Sylvia knew even less than James. She'd picked up the flowers in the lobby then rode the elevator back upstairs to call Lyndy.

The front doors opened, and a second uniformed officer walked inside.

Cade tensed, irritation clawing at his already heated temper. "Where's Owens?" he asked Sanchez. "I called him twice before all this. I called a third time to let him know Lyndy had a delivery, and I called again once we knew what it was. He should be here."

Sanchez scoffed. "You're not the only problem we've got today, Lance. So chill out and let us work."

Cade's frame went rigid. "What's so important that he can't return the calls of a woman being stalked by a killer?"

Lyndy shot Cade a warning look, then moved into the officer's path. She cocked her head and bounced slightly, playing with Gus's little fingers. "What other problem do you have today?"

"Try turning on the news," Sanchez said, looking defeated. "Any channel." He shook his head as he pushed his way past them, joining the second officer at the welcome desk. The flowers, note and name tag had been bagged and labeled. The second officer was on a call.

Lyndy swiped her thumb over the screen of her cell phone, then navigated to a local news site.

Cade moved in for a look over her shoulder.

A breaking news bar scrolled along the bottom of the screen: Death on Campus.

Lyndy gasped, and Cade pulled her closer. "Oh no," she whispered, going soft and weak at his side. "The man at Sunshine Smoothie said he thought Ramona lived in off-campus housing near his sister."

Cade guided her to the nearest bench, eyes fixed on the scrolling feed. He remembered the guy's words. When he coupled that information with Ramona's bloody name tag, it wasn't hard to guess who the report was about or why.

Tom had silenced his only witness in a permanent way.

"He killed her because of me." The horror in Lyndy's eyes hit like a sledge to Cade's chest.

He lowered himself beside her and scanned the growing crowd on screen. No signs of the infamous black ball cap.

Detective Owens appeared on the live feed, moving purposefully alongside the strategically placed caution tape, backdropped by emergency lights and controlled chaos. Hordes of gaping students loomed on both sides of the flimsy barrier, staring, chatting and filming the scene with their phones.

A pair of officers and paramedics followed Owens away from the building. The officers tended to bystanders while the paramedics guided a gurney carrying a body bag to a van with the county coroner's logo.

Lyndy made a small choking sound, her expression stricken.

Cade rubbed her back. "Remember this isn't your fault."

"Isn't it?" she snapped, looking as forlorn and weary as any marine he'd ever seen.

"We talked about this," he reminded her. "This is all him. And you can't let yourself think otherwise."

She dropped her face into a waiting palm. "I can't believe this is happening."

"They're going to find him," Cade assured.

"Ramona was our only hope of finding out who paid for my smoothies last year. She was the link I needed."

"I know."

Sanchez looked up from the desk, having clearly been

eavesdropping. "Owens said the same thing. He's been trying to nail her down for a talk since you made the connection. Then he found her this morning."

"So it is her?" Cade asked, leveling Sanchez with his most no-nonsense stare.

The officer turned back briefly and dipped his chin in confirmation.

Lyndy cuddled Gus, pressing her cheek to the top of his head. She rolled her eyes up to meet Cade's. "Does this feel like another direct link to Terri at Sunshine Smoothie, or am I reading too much into it?"

"No. I'm right with you." Cade pushed onto his feet. "Are you finished with us here?" he called to Sanchez.

"Yeah, but watch yourselves," Sanchez said with a grimace. "Call me direct if you need me."

Cade hoisted Lyndy onto her feet, then patted his pocket where the officer's card was tucked away. "Will do."

He followed her into the sunlight, then slid his hand into hers. "You think you can help me find that apartment building from the news?"

She nodded. "Maybe we can catch Owens there."

LYNDY MOVED TOWARD the crime scene in long, even strides, determined to hold herself together in the face of the tragedy she'd inadvertently caused. Gus was as cooperative as ever, content to watch the flashing lights and rushing people. Unaffected by the blowing winds and falling snow.

Cade stuck close to their side, occasionally brushing a palm against her back or his arm against her arm as they moved. His cologne and very presence were both undeniable and comforting.

She kept her chin up and put one foot in front of the other, pretending she belonged there. A trick she'd picked up long ago. People in positions of authority only stopped those who looked confused or guilty. As long as she stayed in motion, appeared to be on a set trajectory, no one tried to stop her.

They passed knots and clusters of students and lookie-loos, amateur vloggers and a news crew as they dipped under the flimsy yellow caution tape, but few paid any attention as they headed up the walkway to the building where Ramona had been found.

They'd nearly breached the threshold when a female officer stepped into the foyer and started at the sight of them. "Ms. Wells. You shouldn't be here." Her tone was firm but calm. There was a gentleness in her eyes that nearly buckled Lyndy's knees. "This is a restricted area."

Lyndy opened her mouth to speak, but the words failed. Officer Lee had been on traffic duty the night Sam died. She'd arrived at the door with her hat in hand and delivered the devastating news with a directness Lyndy had never forgotten. Her tone had been kind then, too, her words straight and piercing as arrows. When she'd learned Lyndy didn't have any family, Officer Lee had shown up at the memorial service and stood at Lyndy's side until the end. It was the last time they'd spoken.

"I'm Detective Lee," the officer said, offering her hand to Cade. "I'm sorry, but it's authorized personnel only beyond this point."

"Cade Lance," he said. "Detective Owens called me in to look after Lyndy and Gus. We've got information we think he needs."

"Would you like his number?" she suggested.

Lyndy's already tense muscles bunched tighter and her

patience thinned. "No. We need to see Detective Owens. It can't wait," she added, summoning as much urgency as she could muster without losing her mind.

"I'm sorry, but no. This is an active crime scene. Interfering now could cause us to miss something. Maybe a key piece of evidence. Surely you understand and don't want that." Lee's expression went flat and stern. They wouldn't get past her without a fight. Possibly a physical one.

"Owens," Cade called, cupping his hands around his mouth. "Owens!"

Lee unleashed the handcuffs from her belt and muttered something about obstruction. She clamped a hand on his arm.

"No!" Lyndy yelped. "Please! Don't! We'll go. I swear. Please don't take him from me, too." Her mouth clamped shut at the slip of that final word, and Lee released Cade as if she'd been burnt.

Owens strode into the hallway, concern etched deeply on his brow. "Lyndy?" He opened his arms to escort Lyndy and Cade aside. "Is everything okay?"

"No." She choked out the word as tears began to fall.

Gus began to cry with her, shaken by her sobs and the tears dripping onto his cheeks.

Cade turned her toward him. "Give us a minute," he told Owens. "Don't leave."

He pulled Gus free from the sling and cradled him against his broad chest, shushing and bouncing her son until his cries morphed into a babbled tirade of complaints.

Lyndy wiped her eyes and popped a pacifier into Gus's little mouth, then kissed his head. "Thank you," she mouthed to Cade, deeply moved by his ability to save the moment. His continued willingness to go above and beyond for her and Gus.

"What can you tell us about what happened here?" Cade asked, squaring off with the detective while comforting her baby, as if it was the most natural thing in the world.

Owens looked from Cade to Lyndy, then back, curiosity pinching his brow. "You've probably heard the victim was Ramona. Beyond that, we don't know much. There were no signs of a break-in, but there was clearly a struggle to the end."

Lyndy crossed her arms, attempting to hold herself together. "Was it him again?" she asked, already knowing the answer. The Kentucky Tom Cat Killer had been there. Had murdered another woman just a few yards from where she stood. With Gus. Her throat thickened and her breaths came short and fast.

She'd brought her infant to a murder site. What was wrong with her? What kind of mother was she?

"We believe so," Owens said.

Cade scoffed. "You know this was her manager from the smoothie shop. There weren't any signs of forced entry because she knew him. And he knew how to find her from employee records. Ramona knew it was Terri buying Lyndy's smoothies last year. He knew we'd make the connection."

Owens rubbed his forehead, aging before her eyes. "I don't disagree. Problem is, without Ramona, our theory becomes circumstantial at best, and that's a stretch."

Lyndy bristled. "Have you talked to Terri? Did you get Cade's message about the muscle cream? Does Terri own or use that brand?"

"Unfortunately, we haven't been able to reach him,"

Owens admitted. "I've been here all morning, but my men are out looking. Trust that we're building a case. Collecting facts that, when combined, will hopefully tell the story of who's behind these things, explicitly and without room for reasonable doubt. We will get our man, Ms. Wells."

Lyndy leaned instinctively against Cade's side, exhausted, deflated and in need of his seemingly endless strength.

His arm wrapped instantly around her. "Why can't you reach Terri? What does that even mean?" Cade asked Owens, pulling the words straight from Lyndy's mind.

"It means he's not at home or at the local shop, and he's not answering his phone, but there are lots of reasons people can't be reached. You couldn't reach me two hours ago."

"We're here now," Cade said. "And it's a small town. How long have your men been trying to reach Terri?"

Owens lifted his palms, indicating Cade should settle down. Lyndy bit the insides of her cheeks to keep from screaming.

"You need to be patient while we try to make sense of what's happening here, but we will. That's a promise."

A dark, humorless laugh erupted from Lyndy's core. "Sense?" she snapped. "How will any part of his murderous rampage ever make sense?"

"What about Terri's friends or neighbors?" Cade asked. "Surely someone has a guess about where he could be."

"They assume he's at work," Owens said. "Terri manages four Sunshine Smoothies in Kentucky."

"Where?" Cade asked, his tone low and threatening.

Owens released a long, slow breath. "One in each of the counties where a connected fatality has occurred."

Lyndy's head lightened and her stomach jolted. "So you know it's him. You aren't looking for him so you can question him. You're trying to find him so you can arrest him. And you can't." A sheen of panic-induced sweat broke over her forehead as the terrifying reality of that settled in. "What's left to keep him in check now? If he knows he's going to be arrested? If he's backed into a corner?" She recalled the way Terri had cornered her in the hallway outside the ladies' room, offering her free smoothies and wondering how she was holding up. All while knowing he was the one responsible for her misery. While he plotted his next grab at her.

She clenched her jaw as her teeth began to chatter. "Did Sanchez tell you the flowers sent to my office with Ramona's badge were identical to the ones sent to Carmen's hospital room?" Lyndy asked. "I'm worried that could be significant."

Owens grimaced, his gaze flicking from Lyndy to Cade, then back. "Carmen was released from the hospital this morning, but we haven't been able to reach her."

Chapter Fifteen

Cade piloted his truck across county lines with a white-knuckled grip. He'd never been so eager to put distance between himself and any specific place since his return stateside. Every instinct in his body told him to keep driving. Pass Fortress Defense, leave Kentucky, leave the Midwest, leave every trace of Lyndy's former existence in their dust and hole up in a cabin off the grid somewhere. Maybe then he could keep her safe until the Kentucky Tom Cat was caught. Until then, there was no room for error, and Cade was making far too many mistakes.

Unfortunately, stealing her and Gus away to a cabin off the grid would probably sound a lot like kidnapping to Lyndy, and she had enough reasons to be wary already. He rolled his shoulders and let his head rock left then right, trying and failing to ease the painful tension gathered there.

Beside him, Lyndy slept. She'd gone silent just outside her town, then began breathing deeply as they'd made their way onto the turnpike. Gus had outlasted her for a bit, whacking at the plastic reindeer attached to his car seat and cooing out a song that only he knew. Then, slowly, the song had faded and his little snores had fallen in sync with his mother's.

Cade had turned down the radio to better hear the sweet sound.

He exited the turnpike an hour later and took the long route through his town, keeping careful watch on his rearview as he had from the start. The truck cab went dark as he eased them into the underground parking area reserved for Fortress Defense team members and guests.

Lyndy stirred as they circled the space. "Cade?"

"Yeah." He squeezed her hand on the seat between them. "We're here."

She straightened with a jolt, tired eyes on alert. "I fell asleep." She twisted for a peek at Gus, then turned back to the cavernous parking area ahead. It was about ten times the number of spots Fortress Defense needed, but it came with the building, which had been exactly what they'd needed. From the metal interior-locking doorways to the extensive camera and security system already in place, the foreclosed property had felt like a sign to him and his teammates. This was what they were meant to do.

Cade cut the engine and went around to help Lyndy out. "Welcome to Fortress," he said, hoisting Gus in his car seat and leading Lyndy to the building's foyer.

Her gaze drifted over the tile floors and freshly painted walls, then the elevator doors marked with a large Fortress Defense logo. "Wow."

His chest puffed with pride at the little word. Cade had put everything he had into this business. Heart, soul and savings. And her approval meant more than he'd expected. "Wyatt and Sawyer are meeting us inside."

"Your teammates?"

"Yeah. Starting Fortress was Wyatt's idea. He was the first of us to be discharged. He brought Sawyer on next. Then Jack and me."

"How'd you meet Sawyer?" Lyndy asked, following him onto the elevator.

He cast a sidelong look in her direction. "Sawyer's my brother."

The doors closed, and Lyndy's eyebrows rose, then a smile bloomed. "The picky eater?"

Cade warmed impossibly further to the woman beside him. She'd somehow remembered his story about making meals from scraps.

The doors parted before he could answer and a small group of faces stared back at them. Sawyer, Wyatt and their significant others.

Cade groaned at the sight of the crowd. Lyndy had had a bad enough day without having to be personable and make small talk with two extra strangers. Not that the guys would bother her. Neither of them was any more talkative than Cade, but the women... He sighed inwardly, recalling the first time he'd met each of them. Their questions had seemed endless. Intrusive. Exhausting.

Lyndy touched a self-conscious hand to her bruised face.

Cade pulled her fingers away, locking them with his own. "You don't have to worry about that here," he said quietly. "Not with them." If there was an upside to the bombardment she was about to walk into, at least these women had an idea of what Lyndy was going through. They'd both been through recent ordeals of their own.

The Fortress Defense floor plan was open at the center with offices and halls flowing out like spokes in a wheel. A seating area had been arranged several feet from the elevator. Comfortable chairs, a couch, end tables and a bar with water, snacks and coffee when someone bothered to brew it. Thankfully, someone had.

Sawyer opened his arms as he headed in Cade and Lyndy's direction, then pulled his little brother into a quick but firm embrace. "Any trouble on the trip?"

"None," Cade answered, stepping free. "You didn't tell me you were bringing the whole family."

"I didn't," Sawyer said. "It's just Emma and me. She thought she could help."

"Hi." Emma stepped forward and raised a hand hip-high in greeting. "I'm Emma. Sawyer's fiancé."

Sawyer grinned at the introduction, then wrapped an arm around her waist.

"Hi." Lyndy worked up a small smile that didn't reach her eyes. "I'm Lyndy. This is my son, Gus."

Sawyer, Emma, Wyatt and Violet chimed in with coos and welcomes to the baby.

Cade lifted Gus's seat to give him a better look at the crowd. "Lyndy Wells, Gus, this is my brother Sawyer Lance. You just met Emma Hart. And this," he pointed to the couple hanging back, "is Wyatt Stone and his wife Violet."

The group exchanged pleasantries with Lyndy, who looked borderline bewildered.

Cade narrowed his eyes on Sawyer. What had he and Wyatt been thinking, dragging their women in for this? The trip to Fortress was supposed to be for stocking up on surveillance equipment, not social hour.

Violet reached for Lyndy's arm and pulled her toward the couch while Emma descended upon her in a flurry of comforting words and offerings.

And here we go, he thought.

"Oh, honey. It's going to be just fine," Emma said.

"Have a seat," Violet instructed. "Let's get you some coffee and something sweet. Do you like hot chocolate? We brought cookies."

"How old is your baby?" Emma asked, taking Gus's seat from Cade's hand. "Look at those eyes!"

Wyatt tipped his head and moved toward the arsenal and stock room. Sawyer followed.

Cade gave Lyndy another look. She was on the couch now, her feet up and a hot cocoa in hand. Violet had Gus in her arms, and Emma was doling out tissues to blot Lyndy's tears.

He hurried after his teammates, a strange new emotion constricting his chest. Was it gratitude? To Emma and Violet for making Lyndy comfortable? To his teammates for having the forethought to bring their significant others? For the Universe for aligning these things? He entered the next room to find his brother staring.

Wyatt hefted a full pair of duffel bags from the shelf and passed them to Cade. "I packed everything you requested, using your texts as a checklist. Jack's meeting you at Lyndy's place tonight. He's got some time between gigs and gets restless."

"Right." Cade should've guessed it would be Jack to join them.

Jack Hale was the fourth partner, and like Wyatt, a close friend of Sawyer's. The three of them had become like brothers while serving as army rangers. One more thing Cade envied. Most of the folks Cade had gotten close to overseas had either opted to stay through until retirement or they'd come home early by way of a funeral. Regardless, even in the company of three former military men, Cade was the odd man out. As if Sawyer and Wyatt weren't tight enough before, they'd both recently found love and started families. The change had added a new type of camaraderie to their friendship that Cade didn't begin to understand.

Though he was beginning to envy that, too.

Cade rifled through the duffel bags, quickly assessing the contents, knowing Wyatt never did anything less than two hundred percent. "Thanks."

"So?" Sawyer widened his stance and crossed his arms. "What's up?"

Cade frowned. "What?"

"You always hold your clients' hands?"

Cade cringed internally. He'd gotten so comfortable with Lyndy he'd forgotten to drop the boyfriend facade before introducing her to the crew. Faced with the opportunity to explain himself, he didn't want to. Maybe because he shouldn't have to, but more likely because he wanted the lie to be true. It was getting harder to deny his feelings toward the beautiful, fierce and funny, nurturing and selfless woman. What had started as physical attraction had gotten out of control, and now his heart was involved.

Sawyer's eyes narrowed when Cade didn't respond. He shook his head slowly. "Told you," he said, shooting a look in his best friend's direction. "I knew something was up. Didn't I say so? I knew it on the phone the first time he called."

Wyatt grinned.

Cade shouldered the bags, unwilling to bite. "I've got to get moving if I'm going to set a surveillance perimeter outside Lyndy's place before dark. It's another hour back."

"Give me just a second," Sawyer said rubbing a hand

over his stubble-covered cheek. "What was it you told me when I fell for Emma while trying to save her sister?"

Wyatt smiled. "I know this one. I think I heard something similar when I fell for Violet."

Cade turned for the door.

Someone snapped his fingers behind him. "We were asking for trouble," Sawyer said. "That was it."

"No, it was work and romance don't mix," Wyatt said, "especially in this line of work."

"That's right. That, too," Sawyer said.

Cade marched into the next room to grab an extra charger for his phone and more batteries for the cameras.

"We were crossing lines," Sawyer continued, repeating Cade's warnings for him when he'd gone goofy-eyed for Emma while he should've been working. "We could've ruined the company's reputation." He moved into view, ticking off fingers as Cade searched for more AAA batteries.

Cade straightened. "Fine. I shouldn't have said all those things to you. And you could be right about me and Lyndy, but I don't know. For the record, we hold hands because it keeps her in arm's reach and it pisses off her stalker."

His teammates exchanged another look.

"Stop," he warned, zipping the bag over its additional contents. "What was my tell, anyway?"

Sawyer laughed. "I knew the minute you stopped calling her the asset, the client, or Ms. Wells." He made ridiculous air quotes around each of the things Cade had originally called Lyndy. "You switched to using her first name within twenty-four hours."

"Then, you started saying *we*," Wyatt added. "Day one, you were assessing the client's property. The next morning, you were accompanying Lyndy into town for something or other, and twenty-four hours later, everything was *we*. *We* just had dinner. *We* plan to visit her gym tomorrow. That's how it happens. It starts out about you, then it's all about her, and then you become a *we*."

Cade turned on his heels. That was exactly how it'd happened. "Thank you for the help prepping my supplies, and for your profoundly unwarranted assessment of my personal business."

The men followed on his heels.

Cade slowed at the sound of a familiar newscaster. The women had quieted and turned to face a television mounted on the far wall. They'd also made their way through a sizable pile of cutout cookies.

He dropped the bags near the elevator doors, then headed for his part-time bunk. "I'm going to grab a few of my personal things, and we can head out."

Lyndy nodded without taking her eyes off the screen.

Cade moved down the hall where each of the men kept a bed for late nights, an array of personal items and a few changes of clothes for times they were too tired to make the trip home between jobs. Cade needed everything he had in there and possibly a few things from his place if the assignment went on too long.

Someone pumped up the television volume and the words *Kentucky Tom Cat Killer* drifted down the hall, tightening Cade's muscles. He swiped a backpack off the closet floor and stuffed it with his things while straining to hear the reporter.

"They're interviewing a woman outside a home near here," Sawyer called.

Cade moved a little faster, eager to hear what the woman might say. "Is she a witness? Or a victim?" he hollered.

"She looks a little shell-shocked," Violet said, her voice carrying down the hall as Cade hurried back to the group.

Cade took up position on the couch at Lyndy's side and tuned in to the voice-over, regaling the world with details of the hunt for a serial killer.

Violet was right. The woman in the background seemed harried. She was willowy and had raven hair and dark eyes. And she was visibly pregnant. She gaped at the reporter and camera, then scooped a young boy off the ground and headed for the house behind her. The home was small but charming and well maintained, on a street of similar properties. "Who is she?" he asked again.

Lyndy tilted her poor battered face to look into his eyes. Her small hand slid into his. "That's Terri's wife."

Wife? Cade tried and failed to process the word. Terri, the potential serial abductor, rapist and murderer, apparently lived in a little yellow cottage with flower boxes and a tic-tac-toe board drawn in chalk on his sidewalk. He had a wife, a son and a baby on the way. Was that even possible?

Did this woman live in a secret hell? Or did Terri have two completely different lives, two masks and two personalities?

Or were they all wrong about Terri?

What if the killer was someone else entirely, and everyone was wasting precious time chasing an innocent man while a killer was still on the hunt for Lyndy?

Chapter Sixteen

Lyndy buckled into Cade's truck feeling oddly refreshed. Despite everything else, and the shocking revelation that Terri had a wife, it had been wonderful to sit and talk with the other women at Fortress Defense. Lyndy had walked into the building feeling alone and walked out feeling like part of a team. Others had been in her shoes, and they'd survived. They'd thrived. As thankful as she was for Cade's presence and protection, she doubted he'd ever felt as vulnerable and helpless as she did, and she knew he'd never experienced a mother's fear for her child. But Emma and Violet had. They, too, had been hunted and afraid, all while protecting their babies. And the fact they'd both come out happy gave Lyndy hope. Something she desperately needed.

Cade checked his rearview mirror for the millionth time, probably looking for a killer on their tail. It was hard to tell, and he hadn't said much since they'd arrived at Fortress. He'd traded some pointed looks with his brother before leaving, but none of the men had said much and the tension between them had been palpable.

Lyndy had a feeling the tension was directly related to her, but she wasn't sure how to ask.

He slowed at a traffic light, then made a right into a residential area.

"It was nice that your brother and Wyatt brought Violet and Emma," she said, hoping to break the silence and perhaps find out what had happened between the men that she hadn't seen. "They were really nice. I didn't realize how much I needed that."

His eyebrows rose in response. "I'm nice."

"Yes." She laughed. "You are. I meant it was nice to have girlfriends again for a little while. I lost touch with people after Sam died. It turns out that most of the people I knew in town were through him. Wives and girlfriends of Sam's friends. Without him, they just stopped coming around. By the time I was on my feet again after the funeral, they'd vanished completely. The women at my office are a lot older than me. Their kids are grown. Their lives are different. Spending that time with Violet and Emma made me think I could probably use some mom friends."

"Everyone needs friends," Cade said. "People you trust implicitly. Who have your back. All the time."

Lyndy pursed her lips. She'd had people. Important ones. Her mom. Her grandmama. Sam. They'd all died. And the devastation following each loss hadn't gotten easier. In fact, it was probably good that Cade had shut down her budding feelings for him because she'd have to be crazy to set herself up for another heartache of that magnitude. She turned to watch the town go by, no longer in the mood to talk.

Cade took the next left and huffed out a sigh. "I forgot about the road construction over here. This used to be my shortcut back to my place."

The passing shops and homes seemed strangely familiar, though Lyndy had never been there before. "Where are we?"

"We just entered Bolton." Cade glanced in her direction. "I need a few things from my place. I was going to put it off, but we're already this close. Do you mind?"

"Of course not," she said, oddly eager for a look at the place Cade called home.

"Great. Are we still decorating that tree tonight?" he asked with a wink.

"Sure." She sank against the seatback at the mention of decorating. Cade was trying to make the best of her awful day, but it didn't feel like Christmas to her. Not when another woman had died today and a second was missing. She trailed her fingertip across the cool glass, watching snowflakes land and melt as they rolled through a cute little town.

A cobblestone shop caught her eye and she straightened. "I know that café." She'd seen it on the news.

The truck slowed, and Cade gave the world around them a more thorough exam. "Did the newscaster say Bolton?"

"He said Jefferson County when the clip started." She peered down each street as the truck regained speed. "What if he's here? What if he's in the crowd around his house? Enjoying the chaos."

"The cops know what he looks like. They'll spot him."

Lyndy chewed her lip as a throng of walkers came into view, all moving in the same direction. The streets were crowded up ahead, narrowed by parked cars on either side, and the number of pedestrians continued to thicken.

Cade didn't respond as he fell into the line of traffic attempting to get through the congestion.

Lyndy sat taller, suddenly feeling like a live wire,

nearly certain this was the block of homes she'd seen on the news. Her attacker lived here. Carmen's attacker. Ramona's killer.

Watching that poor woman learn that her husband was being sought by the police as the main suspect in a serial killer investigation was gut wrenching. And the woman was pregnant. Visibly so, maybe near the end of her last trimester. And there was another small child with her. A boy, like Gus.

The scene had been surreal. She'd imagined Terri living alone in an apartment over his parents' garage or at a run-down hotel in the boondocks. She'd assumed he spent his free time creating and maintaining a creepy stalker wall complete with surveillance photos and planning his next abduction. Not in suburbia with a pretty young wife, child and a baby on the way.

How could he be both a normal, productive member of society and a monster?

A news van barreled past them at the next intersection, and Cade cursed.

He adjusted his grip on the wheel, then pressed on, following the van down the narrowed road. Police cruisers blocked the road ahead. An officer leaned close to a car window, pointing in their direction while another redirected traffic.

Clusters of people lingered on the corners and along the sidewalks, watching the pretty yellow cottage across the historic brick street. Neighbors loitered under pretense of collecting mail from snow-covered boxes, shoveling their drives or clearing their windshields, but were blatantly fixed on Terri's home where a police cruiser and news van shared the drive.

"It all looks so normal," Lyndy said. "Aside from the mass interest."

Cade grunted, his jaw tight. He pulled into the nearest driveway and performed a three-point turn, heading back the way they'd come and cutting down an unobstructed alley between picket-fenced backyards. "He's one of those guys who all the neighbors will say was polite and kept to himself. The guy no one suspected."

The driver's-side door opened on a parked sedan at the back of the yellow cottage, and a familiar detective climbed out.

"Look!" Lyndy pointed, her finger bobbing and heart hammering. "It's Owens! If he's here, it could mean they've got Terri in custody. Pull over." She tugged her mittens over shaky hands and hopped out the moment Cade shifted into Park.

"Detective Owens!" she called as he meandered up the red cobblestone walk. Her voice was lost in the clamorous shouts and horn honks stretching from the chaos out front.

Owens scanned the snowy yard as he moved, stopping to tug the door on a small yellow shed.

"Detective Owens!" she tried again, sliding as her feet slid on frozen stones outside the truck.

He turned on the steps, tracking the sound with his gaze, and his expression turned to shock at the sight of her. "Ms. Wells?"

Lyndy exhaled a long sigh of relief. She unfastened Gus's seat as Cade rounded the bumper and met her on the walkway.

"I've got Gus," he said, taking the car seat in one hand. He reached for Lyndy with the other.

Lyndy gripped his hand tightly as they hurried in the

detective's direction. "Did you find him?" she asked, breathless with hope.

Muffled sobs and the distant sounds of an unhappy child drifted from the little home behind him. Agent Maxwell opened the door. "Detective?"

Owens raised a palm to hold off the man. Lyndy stared, immediately reminded of the morning Owens and Maxwell had come to her house to deliver the horrific news that the man who'd attempted to nab her the night before was believed to be a serial killer.

"Who's there?" The pregnant woman from the news arrived in the open doorway at the man's side. Her eyes were red with tears, her face puffy from crying. Her gaze leaped to Lyndy's bruised and stitched face. "Oh dear." Her knees buckled, and Maxwell released the door in favor of catching the woman.

A preschool-aged boy screamed at the sight of the collapsing woman.

The sounds of heavy footfalls and a dozen voices registered in the alley behind them.

Owens waved a hand to Lyndy and Cade. "I suppose you'd better come in."

Owens shut the door behind them, and the woman stared at them through glossy eyes. The agent had sat her in a chair, the child had climbed onto her small lap. She wrapped her arms more tightly around him as her bottom lip quivered. "Did Terri do this to you?" she asked. "Did my husband hurt you?"

Lyndy touched her battered face on instinct.

The agent braced his hands on his hips. "Why are you here?"

"We were leaving Fortress Defense and got stuck in the chaos," Lyndy answered, the words rolling effortlessly off her tongue as she stared back at the petite woman before her. "I saw Detective Owens and thought it meant he'd made an arrest. Maybe he was here to let Mrs. Fray know." She pressed her lips tight to stop from saying more.

Mrs. Fray's gaze slid to Gus, snoozing comfortably beneath a quilted blanket, his small face framed by the earflaps of his favorite winter hat. "I'm so sorry," she whispered, then burst into heart-wrenching, frame-shaking sobs.

The little boy on her hip slid to the floor and clung to her leg, also crying now.

"She's been like this since we got here," the agent said, addressing Detective Owens. "We're waiting for permission to search the house or a warrant, whichever arrives first, and we still need to interview her."

Lyndy moved into the room, snagging a box of tissues from a nearby stand and delivering them to the woman's hands. "Do you want to move someplace more comfortable? Your bed or the sofa? You can put your feet up," she suggested softly.

The woman lifted her face, remorse and gratitude blending in her teary eyes. "Sofa."

Lyndy knelt to speak with the boy. "Hi." She wiped the tears from his cheeks. "Can you help me? I want to take your mama to the sofa, but I've never been here before."

He nodded, then stood. And like a little angel who loved his mama, he led the way through their kitchen and into a sweetly decorated sitting area near the front of the home.

Lyndy wrapped an arm around Mrs. Fray and helped her follow. She patted the boy's head, then crouched beside his mother. "Can I get you anything? Maybe some water or a cold rag for your neck or eyes?"

The woman choked back a heavy sob. "Why are you helping me?"

Lyndy's broken and mangled heart lodged in her throat. "I was about that pregnant not long ago." She let her gaze fall to the baby bump beneath Mrs. Fray's dress. "I remember how uncomfortable it can be. I know what it's like to be pregnant and devastated."

The woman swung her feet onto the cushion beside her and cradled her arms around her middle. "I can't believe this is happening."

"I know," Lyndy agreed. It was exactly the way she felt, and she couldn't imagine what it would feel like to be Mrs. Fray. "I'm Lyndy."

"Jane."

"Jane." Lyndy smiled. "How about your son?"

Jane worked a tissue under her eyes. "Alex."

Cade and the other men stood silently at the edge of the room.

The home was as charming inside as out. The tree dripping with twinkle lights and handmade ornaments. A handful of wrapped gifts waited on the red-and-white velvet skirt beneath.

The cottage walls were pale blue and trimmed in wide white woodwork. Doilies centered tables and decorative pillows topped seats. Dozens of family photos lined the walls.

Lyndy watched as Jane wiped her eyes, wondering what she could possibly say to comfort a pregnant woman whose husband might be the man trying to kill her.

"Did my husband do that to your face?" Jane asked, her eyes refilling with tears as she awaited the response.

"Maybe," Lyndy said, her throat suddenly parched and tight. "I bet you can help the agents figure that out."

"He rapes women?" she asked, the words little more than squeaks. "He murders them?" Jane covered her mouth, the final words barely audible.

Lyndy willed herself to be strong, even as she shivered with a terror-inducing rush of memories. "You have to help us," she whispered. "If it's not Terri, then you can help clear his name, but if it is, then you can help stop him."

"He's my husband," Jane cried. "My son's father. My baby's." She curled forward, hunching her body protectively over her bump once more. "It can't be true. This can't be real."

"Jane," Lyndy said, "It's very real, and I know you don't want to deal with any of this right now, but if you don't tell us where your husband is, the next time he gets his hands on me, my son will be left without a mother."

Chapter Seventeen

Twenty minutes later, Cade watched, impressed and mildly astounded, as Jane took her seat at the head of the dining room table. She sat poker straight, expression tight and ready to deal with the inexplicable catastrophe her life had suddenly become. The change was extreme and borderline miraculous, but Lyndy had been with her each step of the way. She'd made coffee, found Jane's phone and the sitter's number, then doled out a pair of aspirin.

Soon, the woman had rallied. In the face of near-paralyzing grief and heartache, she'd squared her shoulders, wiped her tears and asked the sitter to take Alex out for cocoas and sledding. Then she'd given Agent Maxwell her blessing to have a team search her home, and she'd gone inside to clean herself up.

Now the five of them sat at the dining room table. Three men with coffee. Two women with iced water. Cade and Lyndy on Jane's left, Detective Owens and Agent Maxwell on her right. Gus lazed in his mother's arms, enjoying a bottle.

"I've seen the news," Jane said softly. "I've heard about the man they're calling the Tom Cat, but I haven't paid much attention to the details. It seemed so completely separate from my life, like a thing that had nothing to do with me and was none of my business. I thought it didn't matter because I didn't fit the profile." She folded her hands on the table and inhaled audibly, releasing the breath through thin, tight lips. "Help me understand who you're looking for and why you think that man is my husband."

Lyndy leaned against Cade's shoulder, the warmth and weight of her steadying him.

He hoped she knew he was there for her. Whatever she needed. And he knew he had to make that clear at his next opportunity.

Across the table Maxwell rattled off an unnecessarily cold and forensic recount of the Kentucky Tom Cat Killer's crimes, dates and locations. Heinous crimes he now accused Jane's husband of committing.

She shuddered in response.

"Stop," Lyndy interrupted, reaching for the woman's trembling hand. "That's enough." She locked a heated gaze on the agent, and Cade squelched a smile. "Maybe Detective Owens can take it from here."

The agent frowned but relented, and the older detective picked up with a profile that fitted Terri to a T.

Cade's heart swelled with nonsensical pride for the woman beside him, who'd officially stolen his heart. He'd never seen kindness given with the wholehearted compassion and conviction that Lyndy showed. And her tenderness was next-level for anyone, but under such duress, it was nearly unfathomable. Wasn't it only an hour ago that Violet and Emma had comforted Lyndy? Now she was here, advocating for the woman whose husband had attacked her twice. Wouldn't any other victim want to scream at Jane for being blind or willfully ignorant? Wouldn't another person in Lyndy's place even blame

Jane for the situation. For not seeing her husband as the psychopath he was and turning him in? Cade wouldn't have blamed those women, but he admired Lyndy.

"I see," Jane said, drawing Cade's attention back to the conversation at hand. "It's true that Terri can be a little distant and demanding, but he's not capable of those things. He's too self-contained and tidy." She lifted a hand to indicate the home around them. "Terri is centered. He likes everything in its place, and he's clean to a fault. The trauma of attacking someone, of fighting a woman or hurting her would be too much. It's just not who he is."

"But he is distant and demanding," Maxwell said, repeating her words. "He's clearly hyper-organized. Controlled to a fault, wouldn't you say?" He cast an intentional gaze to the small coatrack visible near the back door. Coats were zipped neatly on hangers, all facing the same direction. Shoes and boots beneath, each lined carefully by the heels, according to style, then color, dark to light. "The pathological need to control is often associated with men who do outrageous things."

Jane sipped her water, then pressed her palms to the table and averted her eyes. "Terri has no reason to rape. He comes home frequently to me, and I'm always available." Her cheeks reddened at the disclosure. "Anyway, he's often too tired when I make the suggestion. His job takes a lot out of him."

The men across from Cade exchanged a look.

"Mrs. Fray," Detective Owens said carefully. "The calm you see could be a recuperation period of sorts, a downtime, after high intensity acts of violence elsewhere. And for the record, rape is never about sex. It's always about dominance and control."

Jane sat back in her seat, gaze distant.

Maxwell retrieved a small notebook from his jacket pocket and made a notation, then cleared his throat. "How did your husband injure his arm, Mrs. Fray?"

"Racquetball." She answered, surprise arching her brow. "How do you know about that?"

Cade frowned, no longer able to butt out. "He wears a sling that's hard to miss. When we asked him about it, he said the injury happened six weeks ago. Is that true?"

"I suppose, but I haven't seen him wear the sling in a month. He said it was too cumbersome and the doctor gave him an all clear almost right away. When did you speak to him?"

"This week," Cade said. "His doctor gave him a nearly immediate all clear on a torn rotator cuff?"

She wrinkled her red nose. "A what?"

One of Maxwell's men emerged from the nearby hallway with evidence bags and a concerned expression. He arranged the bags inside a cardboard Bankers Box on the kitchen island, then stared at Maxwell.

"Excuse me," Maxwell said, stretching onto his feet and crossing the small space into the open kitchen. "What do you have?" he asked, voice low.

Detective Owens went to join them while Cade, Lyndy and Jane listened in.

"Several small weapons," the other agent explained, using gloved hands to handle the bags and materials inside. "A number of palm-sized blades and two slings fitted with makeshift interior pockets, presumably to store and hide the blades. I've flagged a number of websites and transactions on the family laptop." He paused to glance in Jane's direction, his expression going grim. "And a false floorboard in the home office, covering what appears to be a stash of mementos."

Jane pushed onto her feet and swayed from the effort. "What does that mean? Mementos?"

Lyndy moved Gus against her chest, setting his finished bottle aside and reaching for Jane's hand. "You should sit."

"Then we're right?" Cade asked. "It's been Terri all along?"

The agent with the bags gave a tiny nod.

Maxell lifted a palm. "We'll need to send these items to the lab before we know what we have."

Cade scoffed. He checked his watch, then turned to Jane. It was well after five, and he still had to drive back to Lyndy's, meet Jack and set a surveillance perimeter. "Where is your husband now?"

"I don't know," she said, letting Lyndy help her back into her seat. "I told Agent Maxwell. Terri called this morning to say he had to take care of something. The task was unplanned. Unexpected. He apologized and said it would take two days. Alex was screaming about his breakfast, and I didn't ask anything more. I assumed it was another business trip and we'd talk later." She slid her eyes back to the agent who'd been holding the bags. "What kind of mementos?"

Lyndy gripped Cade's fingers on the table between them.

He turned his hand to lace their fingers and gave them a strong squeeze "Where's Terri staying? How can we reach him?"

"Maybe the mementos are my things," Jane said weakly, her voice shaking as badly as her hands. "Maybe he's held on to souvenirs from our past."

"And he hid them under the floor?" Maxwell asked.

Lyndy shot the agent another hard look. "Jane, please,"

she pleaded. "We need to know where Terri is. Another woman went missing this morning. She barely survived the last time he got ahold of her. I doubt she'll be so lucky again. If these men are right about Terri, and you know where he is, you can help save her life."

"If my husband is a serial killer," she said, her words broken by a swallowed sob.

"If he is," Lyndy said quietly, "where would he take her?"

"I don't know," Jane blurted, hard and loud, startling Gus. "I don't know him. I don't know anything anymore." She covered her mouth and paled. "What does this mean for my kids? Will they be like him? Are they broken?" Tears dripped from her cheeks onto her enormous belly as her body rocked with sobs.

Lyndy pressed onto her feet, looking more exhausted than Cade had ever seen her. "Someone needs to call her doctor," she said. "Jane should be monitored and probably given something to keep her calm. None of this is good for the baby."

Detective Owens returned to the table, reaching for Jane and helping her up. "Do you have someone who can stay with you through this?" he asked.

"My mother," she cried. "I want to talk to my mother."

Cade steadied Lyndy as she swayed. Everything about her expression said she would give anything to speak to her mother right now, too. "Come on," he whispered. "I think it's time we go."

They donned their coats and bundled Gus for the ride home, then moved into the inky darkness amid the falling snow. Cade's heart was full and tight. Full of love, he realized, for the woman and child in his protection.

Tight because Terri Fray had told his wife he'd be gone for two days.

Which meant Carmen Dietz had less than forty-eight hours left to live.

Chapter Eighteen

It was after midnight when Gus finally went to sleep. Lyndy nearly wept in relief. This day, like too many before it, had simply been too much for her little guy, and Lyndy completely understood. She'd cheerfully turn in for a week when it was over, if she could, but she suspected she wouldn't rest at all tonight. And she doubted Gus would make it through to dawn without waking. The negative energy and tension in the air was palpable, and everyone felt it, including her little guy.

She crept carefully from the room, tugging the door nearly closed behind her, the speaker of his baby monitor in one hand. When he needed her again, she would know and be there in a heartbeat to comfort him.

Snow fell in continuous white clumps outside the warm farmhouse, piling on windowsills and adhering to the frames. Lyndy paused to admire the way the world shined beyond her small hallway window, a landscape of snow, drifting and glittering as far as the new security lighting allowed her to see. Cade had been working on the lights for hours. His partner Jack had been at her place when they'd arrived, already outlining the work to be done. News of a coming snowstorm had cut the niceties and chitchat short and put the men to work.

So much for decorating the Christmas tree. This year they'd be battening down the hatches against a murderous psychopath on a rampage, instead.

She padded down the hallway in her fleece pajamas and fuzzy socks, ready for bed and knowing the men in charge of her protection wouldn't sleep tonight so that she could. She'd ordered pizza hours ago and eavesdropped shamelessly while Cade brought Jack up to speed on the details of her case. When they'd gone out to walk the property, she'd stayed in the front room near the window and played with Gus, her phone close at hand. Every sound in the quiet home had seemed amplified as she kept one eye on the police cruiser stationed out front and the other on her kicking baby. Thankfully, the men had returned inside an hour with a detailed plan for securing her home and a manageable perimeter around it.

Jack's sharp hazel eyes snapped up to meet hers before she reached the kitchen, an uncanny habit of his. He was seated at her small table, his laptop open before him and a swirl of steam rising from the mug near his hand. The tang of reheated pizza mixed with fresh black coffee in the air. "Everything okay?"

"Yep. You?" She poured a jar of sweet tea and leaned against the counter, examining the lean man before her. He'd arrived in a Jeep at least as old as himself, which she guessed to be midtwenties. He was unconventionally handsome, with a sandy mustache and beard, but a completely bald head. He listened more than he spoke, and from what she could tell, he didn't miss much. Which was good for her, and hopefully bad for Terri.

"Good."

She sipped the tea and contemplated her next words. She wanted to pull up a chair and ask to be caught up on whatever she'd missed while wrestling with a nearly inconsolable infant for the last two hours, but she didn't know Jack. Cade trusted him, and she trusted Cade, but in many ways, Jack was as new and uncomfortable to her as all the other things that had sprung into her life this week. Her feelings toward him were typical and expected, she presumed. Unlike her feelings for Cade, which had been confusing and powerful from moment one.

Cade had never felt strange or new. Cade felt like coming home.

"Hey." Cade appeared in the doorway, and she smiled. A strange and conflicted expression battled across his brow.

Jack looked from his partner to Lyndy, then excused himself to check on their equipment, leaving her alone with Cade in the kitchen.

"Hey," she repeated, feeling the flight of butterflies in her chest. "Everything okay?"

"No," he said. "Not really." He crossed the kitchen to her in slow, confident strides, then reached for her hands. "We need to finish the talk we were having about why you kept trying to kiss me."

Her cheeks flared and her stomach clenched. "We really don't." He'd made his stance abundantly clear. Cade was there to protect her. Nothing more. "I get it," she said. "And it's okay."

"It's not," he said. His Adam's apple bobbed and his expression darkened as his soulful blue eyes searched hers. "I love you," he said softly, giving her hands a gentle squeeze. "I didn't tell you sooner because I was worried about being unprofessional. Then I realized I was putting my reputation and the reputation of my business first. And I hurt you doing it. I was wrong to do that. I don't ever want to be the reason you're sad, and I won't put anything before you again." Sincerity dripped from the words, evident in his eyes and touch. "Lyndy, I'm truly sorry."

"You love me?" she asked, not quite sure it could be true.

"I do."

Joy burst through her in an explosion of heart-lifting fireworks and she moved onto her toes in response. "I love you, too," she said, locking her hands behind his head and drawing their bodies delightfully close.

Cade gripped her waist and lowered his mouth to hers in the sweetest kiss she'd ever known. He was warm and strong against her. His lips teasing and light. The chemistry coursing between them was electric as his mouth moved with hers. Lyndy tilted her head and parted her lips, eagerly inviting him in, and Cade slid his tongue against hers, hungrily accepting the offer. He wrapped her in his arms as he deepened the kiss and she held on more tightly to enjoy the delicious ride.

He pulled away a few moments later and caressed her cheek as he pressed his forehead to hers. "I have to set the cameras up before the storm takes over, but I think we should continue this conversation when I come back inside."

She bit her happily swollen lips and smiled. "Me, too."

Cade dressed in his coat and hat, then slipped through her French doors into the cold.

Jack returned to her table without a word.

The night seemed warmer and more full of hope than it had before, as Lyndy busied herself tidying the kitchen. She replayed the kiss on a loop in her head, eager to see the camera work finished and her hero return. Cade Lance loved her, too! She could hardly believe her good fortune in a week of pure misery, but she was immeasurably glad.

She ripped the crust off a slice of pizza before putting the box in her fridge. She'd barely finished a single slice when the delivery was still warm, and she'd been longing to get back to it. Gus had been too tired and miserable to be comforted by Cade, who'd tried to bounce and cheer him so Lyndy could eat, but sometimes, Lyndy knew, there was no substitute for Mom.

She finished the crust, then put the rest of the slice on a napkin and made her way to the table with it and her jar of tea. "How's it going?" she asked Jack, peering over his shoulder at the laptop before him. The screen was divided into numerous, somewhat alien-looking images. All grainy, and strangely lit, presumably from the cameras' night-vision modes. The scenes changed as Jack tapped a fingertip against his wireless mouse, showing a variety of points and angles around her home's exterior.

"Wow. You have been busy." She strained for a glimpse of Cade, but he was nowhere to be found. Just the darkest of nights, streaked with the endless contrast of seemingly luminous white snow. Wind beat through the little laptop speakers, sending shivers along Lyndy's spine. "Notice anything unusual out there?" she asked, nearly holding her breath for the answer.

"No." Jack clicked the mouse faster, forcing the images into a streaky black-and-white blur until Cade came suddenly into view. He crouched near the small outbuilding where she'd once dreamed of cooping chickens in the backyard.

Her lungs expanded at the sight of him, strong and

steady in her sight. He bent and stretched, working with the cables and camera despite the dropping temperatures and blustering winds. Doing all he could to protect her and her son.

She'd truly enjoyed spending time with him at his office, meeting his teammates and their significant others. The too-short experience had sparked a need in Lyndy she hadn't realized she had. And she longed for the things she'd almost forgotten. Like the joy of community and the importance of a strong social network. Of family and friends who were there for one another. Cade had a fantastic collection of people who loved him, and she hadn't had that in a very long time. She promised herself to begin building something like it for herself once Terri was caught and she and Gus were safe again. She could only hope that Cade would consider staying on to be part of it.

"You're going to be okay," Jack said, his eyes meeting hers in the reflection of his laptop screen. "We're good at what we do, and Cade's a force of nature when he's protecting something that matters. I don't know what went down between you two while I was on my last assignment, but you clearly matter to him. I'll almost feel bad for this Tom Cat if Cade gets ahold of him. He'll have that guy begging to be arrested."

Lyndy laughed at the ridiculous and unexpected imagery. "Let's hope you're right."

And like a glutton for heartache, she let herself imagine what it would be like if Jack was right. What if Cade truly cared for her the way she cared for him? What if one day she was like the ladies she'd met at Fortress? Sitting with Emma and Violet, comforting another woman facing unfathomable danger. Lyndy could be someone else's proof that things would all work out. Being a part of that and belonging to Cade the way Emma belonged to Sawyer or Violet belonged to Wyatt was a fantasy she'd fall asleep to long after Cade had gone, no doubt.

The winds beat against Jack's laptop speakers and howled around the doors and window frames. "Storm's starting to pick up," Jack said.

Lyndy turned for a look through the patio doors overlooking the rear yard. The storm was doing more than just starting to pick up. "It's a whiteout."

The lights flickered around her, dimming then flashing before blinking completely out. Lyndy clutched the countertop, terror-stricken and breathless.

Jack cursed.

"It's just the storm," she whispered, moving seamlessly into action. A summer storm had left them without lights the month Gus was born, and she'd been unprepared. This time, she wasn't. "I've got battery-powered lanterns and candles." She accessed the flashlight app on her phone a moment after Jack illuminated his, then began to unpack her tackle box of batteries and flameless candles.

"Lance, you there?" Jack asked, cell phone pressed to his ear. The beating sounds of wind through his laptop speakers had gone silent with the lost electricity, and the images on the laptop had gone black. A battery backup kept the screen on, but the cameras needed electricity to do their jobs.

"Yeah." Cade's voice boomed across the phone's speaker, and Lyndy nearly collapsed with relief.

"Power's out at the house," Jack said. "And we lost the cameras."

"Storm's here."

"What do you want to do?" Jack asked. "Press on or go to Plan B? Fortify the doors and windows for tonight? Get the cameras back online in the morning?"

Lyndy shook her hands out hard at the wrists, then got to work illuminating and placing battery-operated lanterns and candles around the room. Cade and Jack couldn't work if they couldn't see, but she could provide light. And as long as the gas furnace stayed on they'd be warm.

When the kitchen and living room flickered with the warm glow of a dozen strategically placed candles and two dozen tea lights, she breathed a little easier.

"Lyndy?" Jack called, zipping his thick black parka to his chin. "Can you watch the laptop for me? I'm meeting Cade at the outbuilding. We might be able to get the cameras up with your generator."

"The generator?" Lyndy had forgotten it existed. Sam had picked it up at an auction shortly after they'd bought the farm, but she hadn't seen it or thought about it in ages. "I'm not sure it works."

"It does," he said. "Cade's already got it running. We've just got to get its power to the cameras."

A smile curled her lips. "Perfect."

"Lock up behind me, then give me or Cade a call when the cameras come on."

Lyndy obeyed, carefully securing the door and watching as Jack moved through the storm and into the night. She took his seat in front of the laptop at her kitchen table and bobbed her knee frantically, waiting for the cameras to come back on. Time ticked by inside in gonging silence. Outside, the wind howled and the windowpanes rattled. Lyndy tried not to panic.

She chewed her lip until it ached, then nearly squealed

in relief as the laptop screen began to show signs of life. Her home remained in relative darkness, battery-operated candles aside, but the men had gotten their security perimeter back up as promised, and camera by camera, the images reappeared on-screen.

She swiped her phone to life, prepared to share the good news with her heroes when her phone began to ring instead. An incoming call from Jack's number. "Hey!" she perked. "You did it!"

She clicked the mouse, flipping through the images like she'd seen him do, and something strange caught her eye on-screen. A figure that looked like Jack lay sprawled in the snow, arms and legs splayed at awkward angles.

"Hello, Lyndy," Terri growled, his voice spilling like poison through the line. "I've got one down and one to go," he said.

"No!" she yipped. "No, please. You don't have to do this." She stared hard at the screen, willing Jack to stand up, begging Cade to find him and save him. Praying Cade would reach Terri before Terri reached her.

"You're right," he agreed too easily. "I don't have to. I don't even want to. You know what I really want."

"Me." Tears blurred her eyes. It had all been leading to this, and Terri had won.

"That's right. Why don't you join me willingly, then I won't have to put bullets in the two lawmen out front or your boyfriend out back? I have to tell you, if you make me do that, there's no promises about how your baby will fare."

Bile rose in Lyndy's throat as she imagined the amount of damage she could cause by staying. Somewhere deep inside, she'd always known it would come to this. Maybe that was why the universe had sent Cade her way. Not so he could love her, but because he would see that Gus was cared for. Somehow, after her death.

The silhouette of an outstretched arm, gun in hand, appeared on the bottom corner screen. Cade worked on the old generator a few yards away.

"Don't," she sobbed, scribbling a note for Gus and for Cade on the back of a logoed pizza napkin. "Don't hurt anyone else. I'm coming."

She donned her coat and mittens, then left the note beneath the silent baby monitor.

Please take care of my baby.

Chapter Nineteen

Lyndy told her future murderer she'd meet him at her bedroom window. With the security lighting down, the east side of her home would be virtually invisible from the street and backyard, masked further by the unforgivable snow. She squared her shoulders, then made her way down the hall, thankful that at least leaving the note meant the last thing she did would protect Gus.

Her mind raced as she crept into her room, struggling between the acceptance of what she knew was to come and the hope that she was wrong. She wanted to live. To see Gus grow up. See his first steps. Hear his first words. She wanted to hear his voice change and cheer when he walked across a stage to accept his high school diploma. She wanted to kiss his skinned knees in childhood and comfort him through his every heartbreak. More than all of that, she wanted him to know how deeply she loved him.

She could only hope Cade would tell him every day if it came to that, and that just maybe Cade would remember what she'd told him about her bedroom window. She flipped the rusty metal window lock and lifted it with a horrendous squeak. The frame rattled and groaned as she raised it above her head. The pealing shriek that accompanied was like nails on a chalkboard.

But no one came running.

Lyndy gasped as the biting cold rushed over her skin and stole her breath She racked her brain for another idea, some alternative to leaving the safety of her home. She'd hoped the window would be her salvation. She'd counted on it. If not the noise from the window, then Gus's screaming as a result. But the badgering wind had apparently masked the sounds of her window, and Gus had miraculously slept through it.

A silhouette moved into view from the shadows and Terri gave a menacing wave, pistol in hand.

Determined not to put Gus in danger to spare herself, she slung one leg over the sill, then the other. She squeezed the sill with trembling fingers, her heart thundering in anticipation. Of Gus waking. Of feet pounding down the hall to her rescue. Of Cade throwing open her door and saving her one last time. Instead, she was met with endless, deafening silence. Only her ringing ears and the howling wind remained.

Terri latched an impatient hand around her ankle and yanked, jerking her from the sill and landing her against his surprisingly solid chest. His hold was abrasive and painful despite the layers of clothing and coats between them. "Good girl," he whispered.

His hot breath seared a path across her frozen cheeks and temple. "Finally. We can be together." He eased his grip on her, looking her over, taking in every detail from head to toe. "And this time you won't fight," he said. "Understand? At least not until I tell you to."

Her stomach rolled and her cheeks flared with the

memory of Detective Owens's words. *Rape is always about dominance and control.*

"Why are you doing this?" she asked. "Why hurt all these women? Why hurt me?"

"I like it," he said simply. "The chase. The fight. The triumph. And I've been waiting a long while for you." He pushed her forward, away from her home, and she gave it one last look.

She closed her eyes against the tears.

Why hadn't Cade noticed that Jack never showed up? Why hadn't he gone looking for him? He should have found her note and alerted the officers. Why was this happening? She stumbled forward, sucking air and trying not to fall over her own feet as Terri shoved. "You didn't hurt anyone else, did you?" she asked, suddenly afraid that Cade hadn't come to her rescue because Terri had made sure he couldn't. "You promised."

"And I promise to deliver my first bullet to your son if you try to run."

She stopped, lungs burning and breath lost. "Did you kill them? The men protecting me?"

He moved to her side for a look into her face, then stroked frozen hair away from her tear-stained cheeks. "Don't worry about them. Right now, you worry about me." He scanned her features, squinting slightly, whether against the wind or something else, she couldn't be sure. "You look just like her, you know. And I hate her. So much."

Lyndy struggled to swallow the boulder of fear in her throat. "Who?"

His fingers grazed her cheek, his expression flat, lost in thought. "My mother. She was a wretched, horrible being who controlled everything. Is that what you'll do with your son, too? Control his every breath?" he snarled. "If not now, then soon. You'll decide where he goes, what he wears, how he spends his time and with whom. Shame him. Isolate him when he doesn't live up to your impossible standards. Hit him, spit on him. Hate him."

Lyndy's jaw locked against the protests piled on her tongue. She'd never do any of those things to Gus, but she was beginning to see why Terri had targeted her and the other women who looked so much like her. His mother was his abuser. The one woman he probably felt he couldn't hurt in return. So he was making up for that now. Punishing all his mother's look-alikes. Lyndy included. Especially her, she realized, the mother of a son.

Without warning, he burrowed his fingers deep into her windblown locks and knotted them against her skull. "Move."

Terri shoved her forward once more, this time releasing her and causing her to fall. She flailed for balance before landing hard in the snow. Her hands plunged into the icy mix, her knees sinking along with them. "Get up," he seethed, jerking her back to her feet and groping her breast roughly as she came against him with a stumbling thud. He lowered the offending arm to lock her in place, then groaned into her ear.

Bile rose in her throat. "Where are we going?" And why hadn't Cade realized she was missing?

"Barn," he growled, directing their path toward the decrepit old barn where Sam had planned to raise livestock.

Was that where he planned to kill her?

"Where's Carmen?" she asked, suddenly recalling that she wasn't the only woman taken by the psychopath today. Was it too late? Or did the other woman still have a chance?

"She's waiting for us. We're going to play a game."

Lyndy's gut clenched at the onslaught of gruesome possibilities and she lurched forward just in time to lose her meager dinner in the snow. She wiped her mouth as she struggled upright, certain there wouldn't be a miraculous rescue for her tonight. If she was going to survive, it would have to be on her own. She fisted her hands to fight as a second set of footprints registered in the snow.

Cade's prints? Jack's? The officers stationed outside her home?

Hope lifted her heart for one fleeting moment before a small, familiar sound nearly doubled her over once more.

The thin, muffled sound of her infant's cries. Coming from inside the closed barn doors.

CADE STILLED AS a strange noise registered on the raging wind. He turned and waited, listening intently and trying to place the sound. Had Jack been the source? If so, then what was he up to? If not, had Jack heard the brief rumbling, too?

Cade liberated the cell phone from his pocket and dialed his teammate.

A second later, another noise drew his attention in the direction of Lyndy's home. Louder and higher in pitch. The short, shrill blast of unforgiving hinges or perhaps... a window.

Cade's feet were instantly in motion, propelling him through the storm, as he pressed his cell phone to his ear. His gut twisted and sank with an inexplicable understanding. He'd just heard someone force Lyndy's bedroom window open. Somehow her home had been breached while Cade was outside setting up equipment to protect it.

If there was a measure of reassurance in the horrific situation, it was that she wasn't alone. Jack could defend and protect her and Gus until Cade arrived. As long as he realized Terri was there.

The call went to voice mail, and a fresh blade of fear sliced through Cade's chest. He cursed and redialed, willing his partner to pick up.

Was Jack fighting the intruder? Was he hiding with Lyndy? Did they know what had happened? Surely Lyndy had recognized the sound.

Cade's sliver of hope turned to panic as a dark figure appeared lying on the ground up ahead.

"Jack!" Cade fell at his friend's side, stowing his weapon and pulling off a glove to check for vitals. "Get up," he snapped, as a strong pulse beat against his fingertips.

Jack groaned and pushed onto his elbows, jerking free of Cade's touch and swaying slightly as he sat. A slew of curses flew from his lips as he rubbed his head, an angry scowl on his previously slack face.

"Come on." Cade clutched Jack's arm and pulled him to his feet. "Terri's inside."

Jack collected his phone and then broke into a run at Cade's side, strides gangly and awkward as his limbs caught up with his will.

Cade pressed his back to the wall outside Lyndy's French doors, anger and adrenaline flowing fast and free through his veins. He turned the doorknob carefully and eased the barrier open.

Jack crept inside, sidearm drawn, and moved strategically through the kitchen.

Cade headed silently down the hall toward Lyndy's room, senses on high alert and stomach rolling with the knowledge of what happened to women who spent time alone with Terri.

A sharp whistle stopped him in place. "Cade!" Jack called, his voice deep and angry, nowhere close to the volume used in pursuit. He strode into view with a scrap of paper in one hand and Lyndy's cordless landline telephone clutched in the other. He pressed the phone to his ear and passed Cade the note with a remorseful frown. "We need boots on the ground," he told whoever he'd called. "Terri's got her. She left a note. Take care of her baby."

Cade's gaze fell to the paper, quickly crushed in his closing fist. He ran for Gus's room, as Jack relayed details of the ugly truth behind him.

He crossed the silent nursery in two determined strides before his heart ripped completely in two.

The crib was empty.

LYNDY'S MUSCLES LOCKED. Her ears tuned to the sound so familiar it could've originated in her heart. "Gus!" She bolted forward, running to the barn and wrenching the door wide. Her baby lay crying, cold and alone in a trough of ancient dirt and hay. His pitiful blanket had been kicked off and his skin was red from the falling temperature. "Gus!" She swept him into her arms and worked the zipper on her coat low, tucking her precious infant inside and cradling his head against her collarbone. "I'm so sorry," she repeated in a whisper, bouncing and shushing him as her already wrecked heart wrenched further.

"A beautiful reunion," Terri said. "I thought it was smart to bring him. In case I need to motivate you once we get where we're going."

Anger boiled in Lyndy's blood as the truth of the setup

slowly connected in her mind. "The other set of footprints was yours."

Terri's mouth cocked at one side. "Now we need to get someplace warm. Otherwise your little man could develop frostbite. Start losing fingers and toes. The fingers are looking awfully red already."

Lyndy curled Gus against her more securely, willing her love and body heat to be enough to restore him. She kicked herself mentally as she realized this was her fault. She hadn't checked on Gus before leaving. She'd been too focused on Terri's threats, and his demand she meet him outside.

"Back door," Terri said. "We're almost there now."

"Where?" she whimpered, breathing warm air against her baby's frigid palms.

"To the truck, of course. I borrowed it on my way here, then followed the gravel road that links the dairy farm to your property. It worked out rather well since your second-rate bodyguards made such a small perimeter. No cameras out here. Even if they get that old generator working, we'll be long gone."

"You stole a truck?" she asked, struggling to make sense of anything beyond the fact her infant son had been taken from under her nose and was now being kidnapped along with her.

Terri sneered. "You didn't think I walked here, did you? In the storm? Surely you've realized by now that I'm a planner. The storm is a convenient assist I hadn't been expecting. Most folks will be inside and off the roads as we leave town. Fewer witnesses."

"Why are you doing this?" she cried. "What about your family? Jane is pregnant and being bombarded by the media and authorities because of you. You're ruining her life and endangering the baby she's carrying. Don't you care? And what about your son? Alex has to grow up knowing what you've done. How can you live with yourself?"

Terri's expression relaxed into the smooth veneer of a man detached. "Those people have nothing to do with this," he said coolly. "They have a nice life because of me. The right house in the right neighborhood. Fancy clothes and the best preschool. Unlike you and your baby, they're going to be just fine."

Lyndy swallowed a sob. The true answer to her question crashed over her head like a hammer. Terri was doing this because he was unhinged, deranged and evil at his core. The real question was how she could survive this time. How could she fight and run while keeping Gus safe inside her coat with no way to secure him there?

"Do you know I watched you every night at the gym?" he asked, controlling the conversation the way he controlled everything else. "I waited for you, hoping you'd come to my shop when you were done, with your ready smile and sweet, freckled face. It was my nightly treat. Just seeing you. Then you stopped coming," he snarled. "And you didn't come back. I took it personally. Then, as fate would have it, I followed Carmen and her friends to the park and saw you there. With him."

Lyndy knew Terri meant Gus. Gus was the only person she'd ever been to the park with. And there was a senseless relief in knowing she hadn't been the reason Terri went after Carmen this week. He'd already had his twisted eye on her.

"Now things are getting back on track. We're finally going to be alone, and I'm going to get to take my time

with you. If you don't cooperate, your baby will be sorry."
He smiled, and her stomach plummeted.

"Lyndy!" her name echoed in the night outside the
barn.

Terri's head jerked in the direction of the calls. "Time
to move."

"To where?" she asked, carefully angling her back
to him, putting as much space between her son and her
assailant as possible. Hoping to drag her feet until she
was rescued.

When other voices joined the party outside, Terri
jammed the barrel of his gun against her spine and
shoved. Forcing her away toward his waiting truck. The
barn's big back door swung easily open, revealing a
rusted red pickup, nearly covered in snow.

"How long have you been here?" she gasped, wondering if her temporary safety had been a ruse, one more
part of his wicked game.

He wrenched the passenger door open with a satisfied
smile. "Since your power went out, of course."

Of course. Because he was always one step ahead.

Lyndy stared into the gaping mouth of the stolen truck,
its dark interior sure to be the last she and her baby would
ever know. She'd read the reports, seen the photos. Whatever happened at their destination would be painful, gruesome and fatal.

She kissed Gus's cold head and felt the devastation
of the moment seep into her bones. He rolled his tiny
red face up to hers. Eyes wet and wide with tears. His
sweet bottom lip jutted forward. His little chest moved
in bursts, too short and quick. Breathing air too cold for
his infant lungs.

Lyndy's heart expanded with love for her son, and

her will grew strong with the knowledge she was his only hope.

She wouldn't get in that truck.

"Lyndy!" Her name was in the air again, louder now. Closer. "Tracks!" Jack called.

She jerked in the direction of the precious sound, and so did Terri.

Her heart lightened the way it had in the alley and resolve curled her arms more tightly around her terrified and whimpering son.

And Lyndy ran.

Chapter Twenty

Lyndy spun in the snow, her body launching into motion. Her legs and heart pumping wildly as she flew through the night.

She couldn't look back. Couldn't stop. Had to believe he wouldn't catch her. Had to trust he wouldn't shoot her as she fled.

Gus flailed, rightly terrified and frustrated as she struggled to keep him safe inside her coat while she ran. His little body shivered and convulsed with panic. His cries ratcheted into Hollywood-worthy screams.

And finally finding her voice, Lyndy joined him.

"Help!" The word exploded from her core in a white puff of fear and desperation. "Cade! Jack!"

Tears blurred her vision as she passed the edge of the barn, pointed in the wrong direction and moving swiftly away from her home, from the road and her protective detail.

"Help!"

Terri's footfalls reached her in seconds, coming swift and sure compared to her awkward ugly flight. His hand snaked out, catching the hood of her coat, and yanking her off her feet with one sharp pull.

In the next moment, she was airborne, her feet coming up and her body going down. Her back collided with the frozen ground in a teeth-jarring thud. Gus bounced against her chest. The air whooshed from her lungs. She wrapped her arms around him on instinct, cradling his head and body, unable to brace or protect her own. Praying fervently he wasn't injured and that this wasn't their end.

Behind her, the rear barn door slammed open and heavy footfalls pounded the earth.

"Freeze!" Jack called, skidding to a stop several yards away, then moving in slowly. "Officers are on site. And you're done."

Terri cursed as the beams of distant flashlights traced broad paths across the snow in their direction, and the deep, repetitive beating of helicopter blades broke through the blustery night. Searching, she realized, for the Kentucky Tom Cat Killer.

A deep breath of relief flooded her scrambled mind. She and Gus were going to be okay.

Terri put his hands up, then lunged for her, skidding to the ground at her side and gripping the zipper on her coat, attempting to yank it down.

"No!" she screamed and bucked against him, wrestling for control of the fabric, desperate to keep the monster from getting his hands on her baby.

The telltale click of a gun registered like a shot beside him, and he stilled.

Cade stood tall and strong, his outstretched hand only inches from her attacker. "Get your hands off her," he said, the words cold and deadly serious.

Terri released her as a pair of officers appeared behind Jack, guns drawn. The helicopter began to descend, its blinding halo of light illuminating the scene.

Lyndy scrambled backward, pushing her aching and bruised body into a seated position and regaining her hold on Gus. She could no longer feel the freezing wind or falling snow. Couldn't hear beyond the ringing in her ears and the pounding of her heart. She clutched her son instinctively, the effects of shock numbing her mind and senses.

"Terri Fray, you're under arrest!" an officer called, closing the gap between them. "Get down on the ground and put your hands behind your head."

Cade's fierce expression tightened as he lowered his weapon, relenting his position to the lawman. "Do it," he warned, "or this time I will shoot you."

Terri ignored them, staring hotly into her eyes as anguish washed over his face. He'd never touch her the way he wanted. Never hurt her or her son again. Terri had lost the game he'd worked so hard to set up.

In the next heartbeat, he reached into his coat pocket and pulled out his gun.

Her heart seized as a single shot rent the night.

BLOOD SPLATTERED OVER the snow, dousing the immediate area and sending another long scream through Lyndy's lips.

Terri's body jolted forward with the force of Cade's bullet ripping through his flesh, and Cade's lips twisted in grim satisfaction. He would've preferred administering a head shot, but he supposed that wasn't the right thing to do in front of a baby.

He landed a fist against Terri's shocked face, then smashed his boot against the psycho's bloody shoulder, burying it deep into the snow.

Jack kicked the gun away as officers approached.

"Told you," he muttered in Lyndy's direction, though Cade couldn't understand why.

He scooped Lyndy into his arms and held her tight, reassuring the three of them that the nightmare was finally over. "Sorry I'm late," he whispered as additional officers and federal agents rushed the scene. He pulled the beanie from his head and stretched it over Gus's hair, then stripped the warm down coat from his body and wrapped it around Lyndy, securing it behind Gus. "Come on," he said. "We need to get you both inside."

"You saved us," she said, emotion flowing through her words and burning hot in her eyes. *Love*, he realized, and recognized it now, because he felt it, too.

"Always," he said, planting kisses on her forehead, then Gus's.

"Paramedics are on the way," an officer called, hauling Terri to his feet and wrenching his arms behind him to administer cuffs.

Cade turned, searching until the promised ambulance trundled into view, plowing slow and steady through the snow, past the old red barn. A pang of intense hope and relief lifted his hand to flag the paramedics down. The killer was caught, but Cade wouldn't find peace until he knew Lyndy and Gus were both going to be okay.

He swept an arm under Lyndy's legs and carried her to safety.

Chapter Twenty-One

Snow drifted magically outside Lyndy's kitchen window, lending a fantastical snow globe quality to her Christmas Eve view. She had a lot to be thankful for this year. The health and safety of her son for starters. Her ability to spend Gus's first Christmas upright and no longer nauseous from the concussion she'd suffered only a few short weeks ago was high on the list, as well. She attributed it all to the unbridled love and devotion of Cade Lance. He had shot the Kentucky Tom Cat Killer after all. Though he wouldn't accept the praise. He preferred to insist it was Lyndy's quick thinking that had gotten him to her in time. They'd reluctantly agreed on a middle ground over sweet tea and snickerdoodles. They were a powerhouse partnership.

No matter how anyone spun it, her life had gone from endangered to enchanted in Cade's arms, and she never wanted anyone else as her partner.

Laughter erupted from the living room where Cade stoked a fire in the hearth and his mother, Mrs. Lance, danced with Gus in her arms. It was becoming a familiar and beloved scene at Lyndy's house, and she'd surely miss it when the holidays ended. Seeing Cade between jobs wouldn't seem like nearly enough after the way she and Gus had been spoiled these last few weeks.

Cade and his mother had taken turns holding and fussing over Gus around the clock while Lyndy had recovered slowly in bed. Paramedics had immediately diagnosed her little guy with mild frostbite and identified the early stages of hypothermia, both of which were thankfully treatable. Since then, Gus had been swaddled and cuddled enough for ten babies, and the only person more thankful than him was Lyndy.

"Penny for your thoughts?" Cade asked, sliding into place behind her and wrapping his strong arms securely around her middle. He leaned down to press a kiss to her cheek and nuzzle his fantastically grizzly beard against the sensitive skin of her neck. He'd been growing the scruff since they met, and Lyndy was a fan.

She rested her head against his chest and basked in the familiar scent of him. "I'm thinking about how spoiled and happy Gus and I are, partly because Terri was caught. But his family is broken and hurting right now for the same reason. And that makes me a little sad."

Cade's arms tightened around her, the way they always did when Terri's name came up. "Jane and the kids will be okay," he promised. "According to Detective Owens, they've moved back to Jane's hometown and are staying with her parents. She's got a strong support system there to help get her through this." He kissed her head. "And I know you've been worried about Carmen, so I got the scoop from Owens on her, too."

Lyndy craned her neck, immediately filling with hope for the other woman. "You did?"

"Yeah. Carmen's going to be okay," Cade said.

Authorities had located Carmen within hours of Terri's

arrest. She'd been terrified, bruised and dehydrated, but otherwise physically okay. Unfortunately, Lyndy had had no idea what had happened to her from there. "How is she?"

"Her mother and sister moved in with her. They're staying until she gets back on her feet."

"That's fantastic," Lyndy croaked, speaking past a growing lump in her throat. "Maybe I'll take Gus to see her tomorrow. I can bring them cookies. Enough for Carmen's mom and sister, too."

"I'm sure they'll like that," Cade said. "There's no such thing as too many friends or cookies."

"True." Lyndy's smile widened. Carmen would love Gus. Everyone did. And she couldn't wait to make the introduction.

"Is there anything I can do to help you in here?" Cade asked.

"I'm just getting paper plates and napkins," she said, feeling slightly guilty that they'd ordered delivery on Christmas Eve, forcing someone else to work so she didn't have to. "Maybe next year I'll make a ham. Gus might even have teeth to try it with by then."

"I love ham," Cade whispered, planting a heated kiss in the hollow beneath her ear. "And have I mentioned I love this dress?"

"You have." She laughed, enjoying the flirtation and feel of his hands on her waist.

It'd been a long time since she'd had enough help with Gus that she could afford the time to get fancied up. She'd forgotten how amazing it felt when she did. Her hair was curled. Makeup and nails were done, and the dress was new, a gift from Cade's mother. She tilted her head for a peek at his face beside hers. "Your mama said she'd keep Gus tonight and bring him back after breakfast tomorrow so I can sleep in. Normally, I'd say he should be here when he wakes, for Santa's sake, but I like the idea of a night alone with you too much to pass up." Besides, at five months old, Gus was more excited about the gift wrap than the gifts.

"Man, I love my mama," Cade said, resting his chin on Lyndy's shoulder. "Bless that woman."

"Indeed." Lyndy blinked against the sting of emotion that always came with Mrs. Lance's kindness. Lyndy missed her own mother so much it hurt, but having Mrs. Lance around these last couple of weeks had been just the emotional therapy she'd needed. Being a caretaker was nice, but being cared for had been balm to Lyndy's weary soul.

"Any news from the Realtor?" Cade asked, bringing her thoughts back to yet another point of pleasure.

"Not yet," she sighed, "but I suppose it is Christmas." Selling the oversize property she never really wanted and buying something she adored, preferably closer to Cade, was at the top of her holiday wish list.

He pressed a kiss against the curve of her neck and she abandoned the plates and napkins.

She spun in his arms and locked her hands around his back, arching to peer into his sincere blue eyes. "You know we were standing right here the first time you told me you loved me?"

"I love you," he whispered again, drawing her closer and holding her tight.

She slid her palms up his broad chest and drank in his sizzling stare. "And then you kissed me."

Cade's lips were on hers in an instant. A definite perk of having him near. He never seemed to tire of kissing her.

The doorbell rang, and he broke the kiss with a smile. "How do you feel about surprises? And company?"

"I like both, but I'm pretty sure everyone I know is already here, and you've given me more than I need already," she said, suddenly wondering what he was up to. "Plus, we agreed, no gifts."

He wrinkled his nose and raised his shoulders.

"I've got the door!" his mother called. "Gus and I can manage. You two keep kissing. It's Christmas!"

He kissed her nose and grinned.

Lyndy snickered, and Cade took her hand, lifting it to kiss her wrist before leading her toward the living room.

"Wait!" she called. "The plates."

"It's not a food delivery," he said. "Not exactly."

She frowned. "What's that supposed to mean, and how do you know?"

He tapped a finger to his temple as he pulled her along with him to meet the guests spilling into her home.

Jack, Wyatt and Sawyer took turns hugging Mrs. Lance and greeting Gus in his little pajamas printed to look like an elf costume. Each man's hands were heavily laden with shopping bags, all filled with wrapped packages. Emma and Violet each carried a toddler on one hip and a thermal-covered dish satchel in the opposite hand. Behind them Sylvia from the office bounced and waved, her red velvet Santa hat falling over her ears. Detective Owens and his wife brought cookies and fudge, and James saluted Cade from behind a massive poinsettia in his arms.

Tears blurred Lyndy's eyes. "What did you do?" she asked, shocked straight to her toes by the arrival of so many familiar faces in a town where she'd thought of herself as alone. Nurses from the hospital, women from the gym, Gus's day care worker and Officer Sanchez soon followed.

"I thought it would be nice to have some friends over," he said. "I was fielding so many phone calls from folks checking up on you while you were still in bed that I thought I might start asking them to drop by. Every one of them said yes."

Lyndy grinned until it hurt and pulled his lips to hers once more.

Soon, her home was full of warm conversation and laughter. Her heart was filled with unprecedented peace. Detective Owens assured her the Kentucky Tom Cat Killer would never be free again, and she believed him. There was no more room in her world for fear and sadness. Only joy and love and chocolate. She snagged a piece of fudge from Mrs. Owens's pretty tray on the kitchen counter and smiled at the beautiful scene before her. Backlit by her mother's blinking artificial tree and underscored with carols and laughter.

Cade emerged from the crowd a moment later with his mother and Gus on his tail. A throng of guests gathered to follow.

"What's up?" she asked, unable to read Cade's strange expression, a mix of mischief and hope.

He offered her a little velvet box.

She scanned the crowd, his mother's teary eyes and his teammates' knowing looks.

"Cade?" she asked, unwilling to hope for the thing she wanted so badly to be inside the box.

He took her hand in his and lowered to his knee.

A hush rolled through the crowd, but her eyes were fixed on Cade's as he opened the small ring box and revealed the perfect gift.

"Lyndy Wells," he began, his voice low and thick with emotion, "I have loved you since the day I met you. You make me want to be a better man, and you make me believe I can be. You are smart and loving and fearless, and I don't want to live another day of my life without you by my side. Be my partner in this life. Please, do me the honor of becoming my wife?"

Tears fell hot and fast as her heart overflowed. "Yes," she sobbed. "Yes!"

Cade rose and lifted her in his arms, a look of joy on his suddenly boyish face. "Yes?"

She nodded wildly, and he kissed her deep as the crowd cheered around them.

He set her onto her feet a moment later, too soon as always, and wiped her tears with his fingertips. His smile was brighter than she'd ever seen, and his chest puffed with pride. As if he'd just won a prize of unparalleled magnitude or maybe the Super Bowl all by himself.

"I didn't get you anything," she croaked, waffling between tears and laughter.

"You're wrong about that," Cade said, winding gentle arms around her waist and pressing his forehead to hers. "Baby, you just gave me everything."

* * * * *

COMING SOON!

LET'S TALK
Romance

For exclusive extracts, competitions
and special offers, find us online:

 facebook.com/millsandboon

@MillsandBoon

@MillsandBoonUK

Get in touch on 01413 063232

For all the latest titles coming soon, visit
millsandboon.co.uk/nextmonth

MILLS & BOON

THE HEART OF ROMANCE

A ROMANCE FOR EVERY KIND OF READER

MODERN

Prepare to be swept off your feet by sophisticated, sexy and seductive heroes, in some of the world's most glamourous and romantic locations, where power and passion collide.
8 stories per month.

HISTORICAL

Escape with historical heroes from time gone by. Whether your passion is for wicked Regency Rakes, muscled Vikings or rugged Highlanders, awaken the romance of the past.
6 stories per month.

MEDICAL

Set your pulse racing with dedicated, delectable doctors in the high-pressure world of medicine, where emotions run high and passion, comfort and love are the best medicine.
6 stories per month.

True Love

Celebrate true love with tender stories of heartfelt romance, from the rush of falling in love to the joy a new baby can bring, and a focus on the emotional heart of a relationship.
8 stories per month.

Desire

Indulge in secrets and scandal, intense drama and plenty of sizzl hot action with powerful and passionate heroes who have it all: wealth, status, good looks...everything but the right woman.
6 stories per month.

HEROES

Experience all the excitement of a gripping thriller, with an inter romance at its heart. Resourceful, true-to-life women and strong fearless men face danger and desire - a killer combination!
8 stories per month.

DARE

Sensual love stories featuring smart, sassy heroines you'd want as best friend, and compelling intense heroes who are worthy of the
4 stories per month.

To see which titles are coming soon, please visit

millsandboon.co.uk/nextmonth

JOIN US ON SOCIAL MEDIA!

Stay up to date with our latest releases, author news and gossip, special offers and discounts, and all the behind-the-scenes action from Mills & Boon...

 millsandboon

 millsandboonuk

 millsandboon

It might just be true love...

MILLS & BOON
True Love
Romance from the Heart

Celebrate true love with tender stories of
heartfelt romance, from the rush of falling
in love to the joy a new baby can bring,
and a focus on the emotional
heart of a relationship.

MILLS & BOON
MEDICAL
Pulse-Racing Passion

Set your pulse racing with dedicated, delectable doctors in the high-pressure world of medicine, where emotions run high and passion, comfort and love are the best medicine.